1597, London. When Beatrice's husband returns from exploring the New World, he comes home with unexpected company: a mysterious woman, and an enormous painted globe.

As Hugh refuses to explain who their female guest is, Beatrice's foreboding grows. The unwieldy globe now strikes her as sinister – a reminder of the world of secrets pervading her household.

Then one night, the great, hulking globe begins to turn of its own accord. Terrifying new illustrations appear on its face – and when untimely deaths ensue, Beatrice is convinced that the drawings are connected.

Desperate to prove that she is not paranoid, Beatrice risks everything to uncover the truth. What sinister force is behind these killings? What really happened on Hugh's excursion to the Americas? Who is the strange woman who won't leave her house? And on this otherworldly map of murders, who will be painted as the final victim?

The
DARKENING GLOBE

Naomi Kelsey

Harper
North

HarperNorth
Windmill Green
24 Mount Street
Manchester M2 3NX

A division of
HarperCollins*Publishers*
1 London Bridge Street
London SE1 9GF

www.harpercollins.co.uk

HarperCollins*Publishers*
Macken House, 39/40 Mayor Street Upper
Dublin 1, D01 C9W8, Ireland

First published by HarperNorth in 2025

1 3 5 7 9 10 8 6 4 2

A catalogue record for this book is
available from the British Library

HB ISBN: 978-0-00-853480-6
TPB ISBN: 978-0-00-875992-6

Printed and bound in the UK using 100%
renewable electricity at CPI Group (UK) Ltd

This novel is a work of fiction. Some of the names,
characters and incidents portrayed in it are the
work of the author's imagination.

FSC
www.fsc.org

MIX
Paper | Supporting
responsible forestry
FSC™ C007454

This book contains FSC™ certified paper and other controlled
sources to ensure responsible forest management.

For more information visit: www.harpercollins.co.uk/green

Copy to follow ...

'Remember thee!
Ay, thou poor ghost, while memory holds a seat
In this distracted globe.'

William Shakespeare, 'Hamlet'

Prologue

Moonlight seeps through the workshop window, seawater-grey. Along with the candles either side of his work, there is enough light for the craftsman to do what he must, what he has been asked – no, coerced – to do in secret, when his master is long abed. But it is a stark light, unwavering and cold, the kind of light that makes him feel he is being watched. And it is far from ideal: he distracts himself with the thought that the colours are warped, dulled. Verdigris becomes the hue of old bruises, saffron the shade of autumn leaves mulched underfoot, so the voice that is always lurking inside his head constantly chides *not good enough, not good enough*.

Though this piece is not about artistry so much as impact. It has been commissioned not to impress, to thrill, to astonish with its beauty and intricacy; no, it has been commissioned to harm.

And he has agreed to make it. He is as guilty as his customer.

'Is it done?'

The words hit him like scalding oil, and he recoils, jolting his brush, his inks. He just manages to wrench the pot of cochineal (scabbing wounds) away from the gores, but the black (gangrenous flesh) slops as he shoves it, spattering the work surface. He curses under his breath, swiping it with his sleeve, but the damage is done: iron gall stains, and he will have to sand it away and oil the wood before his master sees, for not only would he be scolded for clumsiness and waste, but his night time exploits would be exposed, and he dare not contemplate that disaster.

'Well?'

The word is a tap of tongue and foot, impatient, imperious, and ever so slightly amused: his customer is toying with him. Were it anyone else, he would be angry at the humiliation. But the customer frightens him, and he knows he must not let his anger show.

'Not – not yet,' he stammers, fumbling for cloth and sandpaper. 'I need more time. Perhaps a week –'

'You do not have a week.' The customer steps forward; rich black velvet gleams like eyes in the shadows. 'Not only is the ship expected, but I have learned the others are to be presented at court in four days' time.'

He knows this: his master has bellowed it at them every day for the past month. How is it that his customer has only just discovered this? Or is this announcement yet another way of toying with him? They have all been working on this commission for far longer than a month, of course, over a year – and he has been working on this secret commission for as long as his master has been bellowing, in snatches of stolen time, pilfering an hour there, light-fingering a midnight here. Always alone, always in half-light, always twitching at every noise and shifting shadow.

'Four?' he echoes numbly. 'I cannot – I thought perhaps this one could be set aside from those to be presented …' So they do not risk his master discovering what he has done – discovering it in front of the queen, her courtiers, men who hold the keys to the Tower and all the sharp metal instruments within. The craftsmen cannot cart them all to Whitehall, and he had hoped, prayed this one might be overlooked in favour of those to be gifted to the queen, to earls.

'Have I not already warned you? The consequences of failing to meet the terms of our bargain would be … painful.'

He swallows. 'I understand.'

'What a relief.' The customer is dry, mocking as only the rich can mock the poor. 'Still, let me inspect your progress.'

There is no *letting* about it; he has no power here. Even the skill he has with pen and ink is not his own: it is bartered and bought, hired and sold, like everything else in London, and he almost never sees a profit, let alone a reward.

The customer steps forward and the air in the workshop shifts. Overhead, the drying gores beat almost silently, like the wings of hunting owls. The craftsman smells parchment, the vinegary tang of ink – and then the customer's own scent writhes through the familiar ones: frankincense and cardamom, the sharp kiss of foreignness, of far-off lands he will only ever paint with as much knowledge as he might paint Eden.

The customer peers over his shoulder; it is all he can do not to flinch away, to prevent his homespun workman's smock from brushing that thrice-clipped velvet, his callused, stained hands from touching that perfumed skin. What is he afraid of? That richness will scald him, that leprous sores will devour his flesh at a single touch? No. He is afraid that cruelty will stain him, irrevocable as iron-gall ink. That it will first hurt him, and then, worst of all, corrupt him, until he is as ruthless and manipulative as the customer.

'Hmm,' the customer says, and for a moment the fear of disapproval is as cold as ice. 'I like the bear. That expression of abject fear – yes. Just right.'

He never knows how to respond to compliments, but all the more so now, when he is certain there is something he cannot hear in those words, something coiled, crouching, waiting for the perfect opportunity to lash out. 'I am glad it meets with your approval.'

'The mermaid though,' the customer sighs. 'I told you. Dark, not fair. In fact – not dark, but dull. Workaday brown.'

Every other mermaid he has painted on the drying gores, the ones his master knows about, is golden-haired; it looks far better against the blue-green of the sea. But he knows better than to argue, even as he winces at the wasted paint: every grain of saffron is ruinously expensive. 'I will paint her again.'

'Good,' the customer says. 'For this will only work if you paint to my exact specifications.'

He does not want to ask: fear twists like a turning claw in his belly, raking entrails out. But he cannot stop himself. 'Forgive me, but … what is it you mean, precisely, by *work*?'

The customer smiles, and it is the curve of the claw already in his gut, gleaming even as he bleeds. 'I mean, precisely, to gain my revenge.'

'But …' He swallows. 'What we do, is it … godly?'

He knows what he has mixed into his inks, what papers were used to shape each hemisphere. He knows the answer already: he is not looking for the truth, but the kindest of lies.

But his customer is not kind. The moonlight shivers: tomorrow's rain stalks across the sky in wolf-grey clouds. The customer's smile widens, and the craftsman has never felt so cold.

1

Beatrice thrashed awake, fingers scrabbling at the blankets, the pillows, hauling in air, sweet, blessed air –

Lavender-scented air.

She froze. It couldn't be. She'd banned lavender from her chambers, was even slowly crowding it out of the gardens with silver artemisia and dense-leaved box. Only rosemary in her rushes, she'd ordered, and sachets of rose petals or sandalwood to keep her gowns and linen fresh. No lavender.

And yet. Was it just the tendrils of her dream, writhing about her still? Because in that dream there was always lavender – and with lavender came the struggle to breathe, her muscles howling what her lungs could not, because his hands were so strong, unnaturally strong. For a moment she was there again, with the blood on his hands – on hers, no longer able to tell whose nails were torn ragged, whose skin scraped and slit.

No. The smell was real.

Rage was far cooler than fear. A steady seethe, confident of erupting imminently, and then all havoc could ensue.

Beatrice lifted the pillows one by one and sniffed, slowly, carefully. Pillows that in her dream had muffled any screams, so that all she could hear was a desperate, animal keening – and then that faint whisper: *'Beatrice.'*

But there was no lavender on the pillows – they smelled only of rosemary and her own panicked sweat. Yet the scent was somewhere here, worming its way into her nostrils, grey and sickly. She yanked the bed-hangings wide. And there it was. Rising out of the blue-glazed vase on the mantelpiece, like a plague of bruise-coloured insects, clustered and cloying, and reeking.

Her eyes watered. Lavender, feathers and sweat. The smell of death. 'Maria!'

Sudden pain stabbed her and Beatrice gasped, dropping the pillow. The third finger on her left hand throbbed: she'd gripped the pillow so tightly one of the feathers had pierced the linen, her clutching hands driving the tip underneath her fingernail.

She had to stop this. Her aversion to lavender was already shameful enough, without adding feathers to the list of items to ban from her chambers. No doubt the servants already gossiped about her silliness behind closed doors. *One step away from Bedlam. If Master Hugh were here year-round, he'd have had her locked up long ago.*

But Hugh wouldn't do that to her. Surely.

The door opened and Maria backed in, turning round to reveal a tray bearing beef pottage and a fresh manchet roll. The butter dish was askew, Beatrice noted, and Maria's black corkscrew curls were escaping her lace cap: she must have started running at the fear only she would have been able to detect beneath Beatrice's imperious summons. Maria had known Beatrice all her life: she'd been maid to Beatrice's mother, and when Jane died, she'd become a far better replacement than the woman Beatrice's father had chosen for her stepmother.

'What on earth's the matter?'

'The vase,' Beatrice said, gesturing weakly. 'Someone's put lavender in it.' And then, embarrassed at her own feebleness, she adopted an imperious tone. 'I trust there is an explanation?'

No doubt the wives of Sir Walter Raleigh and Sir George Clifford never cared about being embarrassed before their servants. Of course, those women were nobly born.

Maria glanced over at the mantelpiece and swallowed. A retort, Beatrice suspected – *I'm no gardener, madam.* 'It's been ten years, madam. Perhaps it's time …'

'It's unacceptable,' Beatrice stated flatly. 'Who's been into my chamber this morning? Hannah? Alice?'

'They must have forgotten,' Maria said, diplomatically avoiding naming the housemaids. 'I imagine it was intended as a kindness. To make the house pretty for Sir Hugh's return.'

Beatrice kept her face still. No twitching eyebrow, no flaring nostril. Nothing to show Maria how those words made her feel. 'You know this was no kindness. Not to me.'

Maria's lips tightened, as they had when Beatrice was a child, silencing the scolding she'd probably deserved. 'I know that. And you know that. But to let other people know, to make them remember, we'd have to tell them why. Since that would be impossible, sometimes you may need swift recourse to your pomanders, or a scented handkerchief in every pocket. Or would you have Master Ridley dismiss a perfectly good servant for not understanding something she was never told?'

Beatrice could already imagine Ridley's expression. How gently pitying his dark eyes would be. How his mouth would quirk in a way that was somehow both deferent and yet faintly teasing. And how she would be reminded of the terrible mistake she'd made.

'No,' she sighed, hoping it came across as impatient and losing interest rather than flustered and still edged with fear. 'Just … just put it in Ursula's room.'

'Very good, madam.' Maria set down the tray beside Beatrice's bed. 'What gown shall I lay out?'

'Oh – the russet velvet will do.'

'Not the blue sarcanet, madam?'

Her finest gown? Beatrice paused, her roll half-spread with butter. 'Has – has word come?'

'The rumour came at dawn. Spotted off Gravesend. Sir Hugh's nearly home.'

Beatrice finished buttering her roll, calculating; like anyone who not only lived by the river but made their living from the ships that sailed up and down it, she knew the tides as well as her prayers. 'The blue sarcanet then. And my pearls.'

As Maria disappeared into the garderobe, Beatrice set her roll down and flattened her palms against the blankets. It wasn't enough to still their trembling.

Hugh was coming home. Any wife ought to have been overjoyed: expeditions to the New World were hazardous, often fatally. She was supposed to be delighted, eager, excited.

Not frightened.

Every year she grew used to being in command. Hugh sailed away in spring, taking his nephew William with him, leaving Beatrice in Chelsea with Walter (despite their son's pleas) and Ursula. Hugh would captain the *Silver Swan* on her voyages to the New World, trading, discovering, occasionally doing battle with Spaniards, and Beatrice would resume control of the spice and silks trade she'd inherited from her father. She was sole custodian of the accounts ledgers, the one who decided which merchants to sell to and for how much, whether to purchase more saffron or indigo, whether to send her faithful captains to seek out a new silk merchant in Venice or maintain their relationship with the usual one despite the flaws in the last shipment's weave. She decided whether she wanted a peaceful evening, or the company of her half-sister, along with Florence's five daughters, not to mention her rather buffoonish husband Robert. There was no one else wanting to be consulted about her plans, whether for dinner, or the layout of the orchard, or a new tapestry, or replacing the lintels and gables and whatever else was demanding her attention and coin.

Until late autumn. When Hugh returned.

Now, as she descended the stairs, pulling on her riding gloves, Beatrice couldn't help noticing all the things she would no longer hold sovereign sway over. That painting of the Dorset coast, where Hugh's family hailed from: she'd decided it would look far better in the gallery, where the sunlight could make the waves glow sapphire, rather than here on the oak panels lining the stairwell – and then the portrait of her father could be moved somewhere she didn't have to see it every day. Somewhere she didn't have to be reminded of him.

Beatrice looked away from her father's dark sneer, and caught sight of the carved swan finials on the banister: they'd been damaged by Walter jumping the last five stairs and stumbling at the bottom. And there was another choice: did she want to replace them with identical swans, or something with a less breakable neck and either no wings, or at least ones folded close to its body? For the next few months, she would have to discuss, debate, evaluate every decision, rather than simply making one, acting, and moving on to the next problem.

It wasn't that she didn't love her husband, or long for his company when he was away. It was more that she forgot, in the long months and seasons of his absence, how to be his wife. How to be obedient.

And sometimes, when he was away, she failed him.

'Walter!' she called. 'Ursula! Hurry up!'

Clatter and chatter above: her children were bickering and barging their way down the stairs. They overtook her in the hallway, Ursula's cloak still flapping loose, Walter patting every bust and carving with his hat as if crowning each one the king of beasts, and both charged out into the October sunshine. Beatrice followed them, distractedly answering questions about which would be fastest, unicorns or centaurs, and whether King Arthur was braver than Achilles, all the while thinking about the stable roof that needed fixing, the rose bushes that had to be cut back now the first frost had come, the fountain whose stone rim was cracked: all issues she'd planned to resolve today. But instead, they would be sailing downriver to greet her husband, Sir Hugh Radclyffe, and she would have to begin lying to him.

'The oarsmen are ready, madam.'

Ridley.

Tall, soberly dressed, with the ever-present roll of small tools tucked into his doublet in readiness, Ridley bowed a greeting and fell into step just behind Beatrice as they crossed the gardens. She felt the skin on the nape of her neck prickle.

Any other woman would have sacked him immediately. But here was her steward, the man she'd trusted for almost a decade since he came glowing with recommendation from Robert, her brother-in-law, as the best groom he'd ever met, and thoroughly deserving of promotion. And now still in Beatrice's employ. Even though he'd kissed her in the stables only three days ago.

She'd been ignoring it. Easy enough to do, here in Chelsea where her world was bracketed by beeches and yews, with the river a silver veil between them and Battersea, the willow-shaded eyot mid-stream allowing the horizon to feel closer, cosier. Fifty years ago they'd called Chelsea the Village of Palaces: Thomas More, the old king's chancellor before he'd fallen foul of Anne Boleyn, had started the fashion for retreating upriver, and the gardens of Beaufort Place had teemed with tame rabbits, foxes, weasels, and ferrets, whose cacophony must have seemed fairly harmonious against the cries of the heretics More had apparently flogged among the mulberry trees. Inspired by his fonder memories of More, King Henry had built a manor on Cheyne Walk, and the two queens who'd outlived him had both dwelled there, as had Queen Elizabeth – though she'd never been back since Thomas Seymour attempted to seduce her while her stepmother, his wife, Katherine Parr, looked helplessly on. The Dukes of Norfolk had plotted treason, one after the other, in their mansion, until they were all escorted downriver to the Tower; the Earl of Shrewsbury and his countess had groused in theirs about the cost of imprisoning the Scottish queen. Chelsea was an escape from the city of London and the queen's court at Whitehall, somewhere the rich came to hide, to rest, to misbehave unseen, and only the dark-winged cormorants and sinewy herons soaring over the garden walls could see what the wealthy inhabitants were really up to.

But now Hugh was coming home.

She'd reached the wharf: Walter and Ursula were already scampering down the steps, eager to board the waiting barge. Beatrice hauled in a breath. The Thames was no longer a veil, a fourth wall to her gardens. It was a leash, tethering her to the world, and it was pulling her back to truths she could no longer avoid.

'Is all well, madam?'

No, Beatrice wanted to say, no it isn't. But she'd spent a decade hiding secrets, and she knew exactly how to straighten her shoulders, tilt her chin, and set her gaze. And so she dismissed Ridley's query with a mere raised eyebrow, and stepped on board her barge as if she had never, not once in her life, doubted herself.

*   *   *

Walter was dashing from port to starboard, his long-since tumbled hat safe on Beatrice's lap as she watched from her cushions beneath the canopy. 'Sea monster off the port bow! Man the cannon!'

'Aye aye, captain!' Ursula called, trotting after her older brother obediently, both of them wielding the spyglasses Hugh had given them after he returned from that failed attempt to find a north-east passage. Ursula's had now transformed into a cannon, while Walter's veered from east to west with gleeful abandon.

'Watch out for the white bear! There, on the ice floe!'

At Beatrice's shoulder, Ridley chuckled. 'Probably the first time a white bear's been sighted in the Palace of Whitehall. Might Queen Elizabeth be flattered or enraged by the comparison?'

'To the bear – or the ice floe?'

Their eyes met as they shared a wry smile. As always, Beatrice was first to look away.

'Beatrice –'

'Did you order quinces, as I asked? They are Sir Hugh's favourite.'

She didn't look at him, but she sensed Ridley's eyes linger on her neck, on the pearls Hugh had acquired from a captured Spanish galleon.

'Of course, my lady.'

'And no fish, at least for the first fortnight. He'll be thoroughly sick of it by now. Rabbit, capon, venison – make sure we are well-supplied with those.'

Ridley shifted his body slightly. Straightening up, turning forwards, no longer curving towards her. 'I have already made the arrangements, my lady.'

'Good.'

This was better. Curter, brusquer – she'd never known how to strike the balance between authority and kindness, firmness and civility, but if Ridley thought her abrasive today, what harm could that do? Certainly less than if he thought she might want more from him than any mistress needed from her steward. A well-stocked cellar, a reliably-run malthouse, and a good eye for horses. Not a gentle touch after months of loneliness.

They were passing the riverside mansions now – Bedford, Somerset, Arundel, Essex and Durham, the former bishop's palace, where two of old King Henry's wives had lived, where poor Lady Jane Grey was married, where Queen Elizabeth herself had dwelled for a time – and where Sir Walter Raleigh now lived, provided, of course, he was neither on an expedition himself, nor imprisoned in the Tower for offending his royal mistress. These houses, and Sir Walter's in particular, were, Beatrice suspected, the real reason why Hugh insisted on sailing home in the barge – on keeping the barge at all, in fact, despite its hungry gnaw on their accounts ledgers. So that Hugh could glide past the vast white stone houses, their private landing stages, their elaborate, beautifully-tended gardens stretching down to the river bank, all in the hope that the Countess of Essex, or the Earl of Arundel might be strolling past their mulberry trees and say to their equally noble companions, 'Oh, there goes Sir Hugh Radclyffe, the gallant explorer. We must invite him to supper so he can regale us with tales of his valiant exploits!'

To date, however, Lady Essex had been content to listen to her own husband's stories of the Azores, or to be invited to dine at Lady Raleigh's table – and expense – a mere stroll away. They kept their own barges too, these great families in their great mansions, and Beatrice remembered several balmy summer evenings when Hugh had suggested the two of them dine on the barge: she'd been blissfully content, his arm around her shoulders, sipping rich malmsey as a lutenist plucked a gentle madrigal and the reflected torches glimmered gold in the deep blue current. And then they'd heard the laughter. The Essex circle had been out on their barges too, the earl and his friends daring one another to leap between the boats. As their barge neared the revels, Essex had shouted, 'A new target, Raleigh – much too far for your game leg, I'll wager!'

Hugh had risen, striding to the railings. 'Do I hear talk of boarding? You know how I treat pirates, Raleigh!'

'Prepare to be attacked!' Raleigh had retorted, springing onto his railings and launching himself across the water. His earrings had glinted as he soared, lit pipe in one hand, goblet in the other, an arc of wine flying behind him like crimson sparks from a firework. He'd barely made it: he'd clattered against their railings, nearly landing face first in a blazing torch. Hugh had helped him scramble over the side, both men laughing.

'Might I avail myself of a drop of sack?' Raleigh had asked. 'I seem to have spilt my drink.' His pipe had also gone out, and he relit it on the torch that had almost set his beard alight, before clapping Hugh on the shoulder and saying, 'Fancy joining my buccaneer crew, Radclyffe?'

Before Beatrice could protest, Hugh had bounded onto the railing and leapt across to Raleigh's barge. She'd spent the rest of the evening nursing her cup of malmsey and trying not to shiver: without Hugh's body beside hers the evening no longer seemed so balmy. At one point, the lutenist had started to play a song about a jilted lover, and she'd contemplated first pushing him into the Thames – and then whether such an act might secure her own invitation onto the other barges, or simply ensure that she'd remain alone. And alone she often was: in Hugh's absence, Beatrice had never attempted to extend an invitation to these noble wives, certain they would continue to show no interest in the merchant's daughter who occasionally lurked in the background of their revels. Rather than expose herself to confirmation of her own ignominy, Beatrice reverted to spending her evenings with Florence, with Maria, or in solitude she told herself was her choice.

They were approaching Tower Bridge: she could hear the water-wheels churning away under the southern arches and the calls and chatter of the throngs trying to cross the bridge, or merely live on it. Walter had darted to the bow and was pointing up at the bridge, at the heads rotting on pikes.

'Look, Ursula –'

'Walter,' Beatrice called, 'no. A gentleman does not seek to frighten his sister.'

'I'm not frightened!' Ursula insisted. 'What is it?'

Walter met his mother's eye and changed his mind. 'Mermaids!' he crowed. 'Swimming between the stanchions!'

'I see them!' Ursula cried in delight. 'They have golden hair, just like mine!'

Just like Hugh's. And despite everything, Beatrice was suddenly filled with a desperate yearning to see her husband again. To run her fingers through that grey-shot gold as his lips met hers. She just hoped Ridley wasn't standing nearby when Hugh kissed her for the first time in eight months.

Their barge couldn't go through Tower Bridge: it wouldn't be long until the tide changed, and in any case, only the foolhardiest wherry-men ever shot the bridge. Everyone knew the rapids, formed by the stanchions and worsened by the waterwheels, were treacherous, and whilst many young men, Hugh included in his heyday, had taken an inebriated wager to dare it, not all of them had lived to tell the tale. As the barge tied up at the wharf, Beatrice wondered how long she could keep Walter from trying it. He was only nine: at present he'd be more likely to terrify Ursula with tales of drowned men's bodies lurking in the stanchions' shadows – which was also something she'd prefer to avoid as long as possible.

Ridley had organised horses to take them to the docks: it wasn't far, but the crowds trying to get on or off Tower Bridge were always daunt-ing, and it would be far too easy to lose Ursula or Walter in the crush, or for one of them to be trampled, or robbed. In any case, Hugh would want horses. The ones Ridley had hired were suitably impressive: glossy coats, new shoes ringing on the cobbles, not bridling or whinnying once as they rode through the throng and down to the docks. Ursula rode pillion with Ridley so the little girl could gaze to her heart's content at the goose drovers, the boys hawking hot pies, the girls sell-ing oysters and whelks, the great pale walls of the Tower. Even Walter couldn't feign nonchalance, and the merchant's daughter in Beatrice was oddly proud: London was fascinating, rich and poor alike, and her children should be fascinated. This city was their heritage, after all – and so was its river.

The docks were heaving: when had they ever not been? Even a frozen Thames hadn't stopped trade. A steady tide of sailors, carpenters, coopers and merchants flowed along the docks, ferrying cargo to or from moored vessels. As children, Beatrice and Florence had played a game, trying to guess what cargo each ship was carrying – furs and seal oil and wax from Russia, silk and spices from Syria, glass from Venice – until their father had ruined the game by pointing out that you could accurately pinpoint these things merely by looking at the names of the vessel and her captain, and knowing what kind of crates would be required for different kinds of cargo. So Beatrice wouldn't mention that the number of wine casks coming off the ship newly-arrived from France was fewer than her captain would have hoped, nor that she knew the wool being carted onto the vessel bound for Flanders was far from the finest her brother-in-law had ever sold. She had no intention of ruining Walter and Ursula's fun as her father would have done.

'Children,' she said, 'what do you think Papa's ship might bring back today?'

'A dolphin!' Ursula declared. 'A tame pink one.'

'Sea coal with gold hidden inside!'

'Not tobacco again,' Ursula said, frowning suddenly. 'Papa's breath smells funny afterwards. But I liked the potatoes he brought last time, especially the orange ones.'

'The yellow were better.'

'No, orange!'

'Yellow!'

'Look' Ridley interrupted. 'The *Silver Swan* is sailing into view.'

And there she was. Beyond the merchant vessels unloading silk and wool, Hugh's ship was approaching, not delayed by unpredictable tides or the overcrowding of the river. Every time, Beatrice felt as if she'd been struggling through a forest made of houses and wherries and cutters and fishing boats, and now the masts with their canvas leaves parted, opening up to reveal clear air and light. The *Silver Swan* towered over the tiny boats towing her up the Thames, her white sails curving proudly, serene as a mother ushering her cygnets back to their nest. She couldn't pick Hugh out from the men on board lining the deck yet, but she knew where he'd be: still striding the quarterdeck, reminding sailors to check the knots, coil ropes out of the way to make unloading easier, holystone that stain again. They might be moments away from shore, and the responsibility of actually sailing the ship given over to the pilot boats, but a captain's tasks were never done, even when the men were all on land and the cargo delivered to warehouses. Much like a mother running a household.

Beatrice tried to suppress the thought. But being in command was a hard habit to shake off, and she'd never mastered Florence's ability to make her husband believe he was in control while herself never truly relinquishing the reins. Perhaps Hugh would be tired and content to let her continue running things for a while. Just because he never had been before didn't mean this time would have to be the same.

Ridley was watching her again. He'd have to stop that now Hugh was back. They would all have to change – and at the same time not let Hugh realise that anything had been altered by his return other than the joy of his family.

'They're tying up!' Walter announced. 'I could go and help them, Mama, I can do clove hitches and bowlines and reef knots and –'

'So can all the dockhands,' Ursula pointed out. 'They don't need silly boys to help –'

Walter lunged for her hair and she yelped as he seized a blonde curl.

'Enough!' Beatrice snapped. 'Do not shame your father by brawling in the streets like common peasants!' She yanked Walter's reins, pulling his pony close to her mare, and Ridley nudged his horse into a sidestep, moving Ursula and her hair out of reach. Though not before those nearest had seen: a boy selling chestnuts sniggered, a blue-robed apprentice gave them all a disdainful look, while a woman of Beatrice's age, whose rich wool cloak and gown revealed her as a merchant's wife, paused her debate about ship berths to give Beatrice a sympathetic smile. Once, Beatrice would have returned it. But Hugh hated for her to fraternise with mere merchants' wives now – and hated it even more when she reminded him that her mother had been a merchant's wife, or that her sister now was too.

'There's Papa!' Walter cried, knots and squabbles entirely forgotten as the gangplank was lowered and the crowd cheered.

Londoners cheered any returning ship, Beatrice knew, sometimes sardonically, if the helmsman had bumped their prow against the wharf, and usually only for a moment, briefly acknowledging the ship's safe return. A superstition – another superstition. As if failure to cheer meant someone would tumble overboard to be crushed between keel and wharf, or a sudden leak would spring open in the hold, ruining the cargo and scuttling the ship, drowning all hands within spitting distance of home. But even Beatrice, who'd seen hundreds of returning ships cheered as a child, and dozens as a wife, thought the cheers might be a bit louder, a bit longer than usual. They knew where the *Silver Swan* had been; they knew how much coin lay behind such ventures. Anyone wiser than a gosling would have the sense to cheer money. And fame too? Never enough for Hugh, but perhaps this voyage might prove the one, depending on what he'd brought back from Virginia.

And there he was, no longer imagined, no longer a memory, but suddenly above them. Hugh paused at the top of the gangplank, lifting a hand to acknowledge the crowds, the silver embroidery on his doublet sparkling in the autumn sunlight. He always wore his finest clothes to disembark: polished black leather boots, a suit of green velvet and a tall hat adorned with a matching green velvet band, studded with pearls and finished with a spray of curling white feathers. Just at his shoulder stood his nephew William, a slighter, less gleaming version of Hugh, like a gilt imitation of a golden statue. The master of the *Silver Swan* descended the gangplank, smiling broadly, and Beatrice knew she was smiling too, helplessly proud and relieved and swelling with the knowledge that he was *hers*, just as she had twelve years ago when he'd asked her to marry him.

'Papa!' two voices squealed in unison, and Hugh spread his arms wide to catch Walter and Ursula as they half-scrambled, half-tumbled into his embrace. Beatrice couldn't see his face for the tumult of blonde and brown curls, of dislodged hats and tangled green and blue arms. She needed to see his face. Needed to know what the voyage had truly been – what it had done to him this time. What that might mean for her. For them all.

He was extricating himself from his children now, Ursula still clinging like a limpet to his leg as he straightened up to see Beatrice still seated on her mare. 'Well, wife? Have the privations of my voyage made me repulsive to you?'

He always asked this question, and they both knew the answer. Even if his teeth were blackened and his face scarred, even if, God forbid, he came back with fewer limbs or eyes or ears than he started out with, he would never be repulsive, not to her. Even after that terrible expedition north, even when frostbite had blistered his hands and cheeks, he had still been her beautiful Hugh. But there was an agony of fear beneath the bravado of his question, anxiety tautened and twisted by months of absence and not knowing, and it had become their own superstition now. If Hugh didn't ask it, if Beatrice didn't answer in the same way she always did, then something would be broken beyond repair.

'Hideous,' she said, holding out her hands for his shoulders (still broad, muscles not wasted by shipboard provisions) as he set his hands (ten fingers still) to her waist, and she slid from her horse and into her husband's arms.

Oh, she had dreamt of this kiss. That one, foolish twilight in the stables with Ridley was nothing, nothing to her husband's lips on hers. She'd forgive him anything as long as he came back to her and kissed her, not caring who saw – or perhaps caring that everyone saw and carried tales to every tavern of the great Sir Hugh Radclyffe's bravery being all for the sake of his beloved wife, that he might return to her side.

He broke the kiss long after propriety dictated, and long before she was ready – but with that familiar promise in his eyes of more later.

'Did you see sharks, Papa? Or whales?'

'Or mermaids?'

Hugh ruffled Walter's hair. 'Nothing like that. We only went as far as Gravesend – we've just been eating cockles and drawing pictures in the sand for eight months.'

'Papa!'

Hugh grinned, chucking him under the chin. 'I'll tell you all about my adventures later. There's someone I'd like you to meet.'

He turned, extending his arm in both welcome and command. Beatrice arranged her face into warm politeness, ready to greet an exceptionally brave sailor, a talented navigator.

But it was none of those.

A woman was descending the gangplank, stepping hesitantly, as if she didn't trust the gangplank not to tip her in, or herself not to slip and fall. Her skin was the deep brown of polished mahogany, seeming even darker against the rich scarlet of her gown – an expensive gown, Beatrice noted, as costly as some of her own, if not her finest. But the woman did not move as such a gown should have inspired her to move, gliding imperiously; instead, she turned almost sideways to edge through the crowd, shoulders tense and hunched as if she didn't want to be touched by anyone. Yet when she reached Hugh and his hand took hers, even his tanned skin looking drab beside her brown shine, she didn't flinch.

As if she was used to his touch.

'This is Catalina,' Hugh said. 'She'll be staying with us now.'

Catalina – just Catalina. No family name, not Catalina Moore, or Catalina of Seville, or Catalina the seamstress – nothing to reveal who she was or where she'd come from, or why, in God's name, Beatrice's husband had brought her back from an eight month sea voyage to stay with them!

And what did 'stay' even mean, Beatrice wondered as they rode back to the barge, trying not to glower at the sight of Catalina riding pillion with Hugh. They'd only brought one additional horse, assuming William would, as always, deal with unloading the cargo, and when Ridley had offered to ask the nearest inn for another, Catalina had looked to Hugh in mute horror, and Hugh had said, 'Catalina has never ridden a horse before. She'll ride with me,' and the woman's dark brown eyes had briefly closed in what might have been relief, or gratitude, or perhaps even more fear. Certainly she was now clinging to Hugh as if he were the only spar in a tumultuous sea, her forehead pressed against his back, bowed as if in prayer. Was she Christian? Some of the Moors in London still practised their own faith, albeit discreetly; until his death Maria's grandfather had prayed to his deity of choice at first light before ambling along to church, mainly, Maria had said, because he liked chattering to his neighbours afterwards. Would Hugh really have brought a heathen into their household? Though why would her faith make a difference? Presumably she wasn't here for spiritual guidance.

But why was she here? Was she to be a servant? Her gown was expensive, but her hair was simply dressed, bound back with a red ribbon: clearly she had no maid of her own. Or at least no maid on board: was Catalina a rich woman in her own land? Or was she to be Beatrice's maid? Maria would hardly be best pleased at being supplanted, pointing out she was only ten years older than Beatrice and insisting her hands were still supple enough for aglets and buttons – though she'd be even more disgruntled if she were expected to dress Catalina as well as Beatrice. Even if it were only temporary.

Just how long would this stay be? The longest they'd ever had anyone stay was after Cecily was born, since Robert had been delayed on a business voyage to Flanders. At first Beatrice had rather enjoyed adorning her new niece with lace bonnets and mixing honey into almond caudles for her recovering half-sister – but after six weeks of Florence retying the bonnet ribbons and suggesting more saffron in her drink, Beatrice had had quite as much of Florence as she was willing to endure. Even if Catalina proved to be quieter and less prone to complaint or judgement, six weeks of anyone in your own house was quite a cross to bear. Even William, who'd lived with them since his mother, Hugh's sister, died ten years ago, and who spent much of his time onshore in taverns, or hunting, or generally not indoors if he could avoid it, sometimes irritated Beatrice merely by his presence. Though where else would Catalina have to go afterwards? William's occasional alternative sleeping arrangements were hardly suitable for a woman. Where was her family? Where had she come from, and why on earth was she riding to Beatrice's barge with her arms wrapped around Beatrice's husband's waist?

Ursula was saying something about the flower sellers, and Beatrice couldn't remember what her initial question had been: with Ursula, there was no guarantee her current words were linked to her first words by any logic discernible to other people.

'… and the yellow ones are the same colour as the potatoes Papa brought back before, but do you think rabbits would eat both if you put them out by the archer statue?'

'Don't feed the rabbits,' Beatrice said. 'Scraps are for the pigs, not wild animals.'

'But rabbits are much prettier than pigs.'

If they fed creatures according to how pretty they were, Catalina's plate would be piled high for the duration of her stay. Those curling lashes and full lips; her soft brown breasts. She was younger than Beatrice, perhaps closer to twenty than thirty. Not a line around her mouth or eyes, not a crease in her forehead –

'Help them!'

'They're drowning!'

Beatrice jolted alert at the voices from the bridge overhead, immediately twisting to check: Walter, still on his pony, Ursula's reins still in Ridley's firm grip. But Hugh was leaping from his horse and running towards the river, leaving Catalina to fling herself flat along the horse's back, clutching at the reins.

'Hugh, no!'

Beatrice sprang down from her own horse and ran after her husband. He was heading for the bank, elbowing his way through a gathering crowd, and she struggled after him, pushing at fustian elbows and baskets of eggs and wool until she could see what was happening.

The tide had turned. White water churned between the stanchions, flinging salt spray like grapeshot as the rapids grew steeper and more treacherous with every haul of the tide. And just below the third stanchion, a wherry had capsized: its stern was being sucked back into the waves forming at the bottom of the rapid, as if a great white cat were toying with a wooden bird, letting it escape only to swat it back underwater.

'Here! Reach up!'

The wherryman, still somehow clutching an oar, had been washed out of the rapid. Hugh dropped to his belly, heedless of the mud staining his doublet, and stretched out.

'Grab my legs!' he ordered, inching further out even as two men crouched to hold him. He reached for the floundering wherryman, whose eyes were wide and wild with cold and terror. 'Give me the oar!'

The wherryman lifted the oar – and immediately sank beneath the water. But Hugh was hauling, and so were more men now, and the wherryman's head emerged, then his shoulders, his torso, and others grabbed handfuls of his clothes, heaving him onto the bank.

'Thank God,' Beatrice murmured, as much for Hugh, now kneeling next to the spluttering wherryman and clapping him on the shoulder.

'No harm done, eh?'

The wherryman shook his head, coughing. 'The boy – where's the boy?'

Beatrice knew what Hugh was going to do before he turned and she started forwards. 'Hugh, no!'

But he was already kicking off his boots, tossing his hat and doublet aside, and just as she reached for his arm, he dived into the river.

'Papa!'

Ursula's cry yanked at Beatrice. Torn between racing to comfort her daughter and desperation to know Hugh was safe, Beatrice hovered helplessly on the bank, unable to move, staring at the rushing waters for Hugh's head to emerge.

There! He was swimming against the current – and thank heaven he could swim, unlike most sailors. But even strong swimmers had been drowned in the Thames, and Beatrice tried to crush the thought.

A thin wail came from the rapids, and Beatrice caught a glimpse of a dark head next to the recirculating boat. As the rapid hauled at the wherry, the head disappeared. The boy, who couldn't be more than twelve, was clinging to the inside of the capsized boat, managing to breathe within the curved hull – but being pulled back and back into the wave. Each time the boat was dragged in, the prow reared up and then crashed down as the vessel was spat back out again. Christ's wounds, it was a miracle the boy's skull hadn't been split by the falling boat.

And now Hugh was swimming for it.

He had the oar. She hadn't seen him grab it – but it was the other oar, bobbing in an eddy below the stanchion.

'Grab this, lad! I'll do the rest!'

Tears stung her eyes and she wanted to howl at him to stop being so damned noble, stop trying to be Walter bloody Raleigh! Whoever this boy was, she couldn't lose Hugh for a stranger who was already half-drowned – Ursula and Walter couldn't lose the father they'd only just got back. Being a mother made you the most selfish and selfless creature imaginable when it came to your children, and she would not, could not see them hurt.

'Come on! Henry, come on!'

The cry came from the bank, from a drenched man crouched on the wharf. The boy's father, Beatrice assumed, and she wanted to scream, 'He's your son! You should be the one risking your life for him!'

As if the boy had heard his father, he reached out for the oar Hugh was extending, one hand still clinging to the upturned boat. He was so close, so close. But the circulating water was about to jerk him back in and the boat under, and how many more times could he survive that? Despite her terrified rage and resentment, Beatrice found her nails in her mouth and her lips bitten, and she whispered, 'Please, please.'

The boy stretched. Hugh stretched. And the boy's hand closed around the oar just as the boat was yanked back into the wave. Hugh dragged the boy towards him, grabbing his shoulders and pulling him close against his chest.

'Here – catch!'

Ridley had found a rope: one end wrapped around his waist, he hurled the other end to Hugh, who caught it and began to kick. Beatrice ran to Ridley, desperate to help, but two burly men pushed past her.

'We'll get them in, lovey.'

And they did. Miraculously, blessedly, the three men pulled Hugh and the boy to safety. At the bank, Hugh insisted – damn him! – on the boy going first, boosting the child up into his sobbing father's arms before finally letting Ridley and the other men pull him back ashore.

'You're a hero, sir!'

'Bravest thing I've ever seen!'

Hugh shook his wet hair out of his eyes. 'Nonsense. Any man would have done the same to save a child.'

'Not any man,' Ridley said, proffering Hugh's boots. 'There's not many as brave and selfless as you, my lord.'

As Hugh bent to pull his boots on, Ridley's eyes met Beatrice's, and she had to look away.

Hugh reached for his doublet and grinned at Beatrice. 'Well, wife? No words to greet your heroic husband?'

'You could have drowned,' she managed, throat tight with tears. 'I – we – almost lost you.'

'You can't get rid of me that easily,' he laughed. 'Besides, how could I leave the lad? He's the same age as …'

He didn't finish. Even Hugh's jokes faltered at the prospect of imagining their boy in the water. And Walter was even younger than this child, just nine, nine too-short years, too few years yet.

As if her gaze could protect her son, Beatrice looked back to the horses. Where she saw Catalina standing, one arm around each of Beatrice's children, holding them close to her. Comforting them, as Beatrice should have been.

For the first time, Catalina's eyes met Beatrice's, and she couldn't tell if the foreign woman's gaze were judgement, or accusation – or jealousy.

2

The candles cast a copper glow over the remains of Hugh's homecoming feast: capon bones scattered with uneaten barberries; a crumbled piecrust spilling red meat and dark juices like a caved-in skull; shreds of rabbit surrounded by congealing brown smears of mutton broth, one of the currants the rabbit had been stuffed with winking like a black eye. Flagons of malmsey and burgundy had been refilled several times, mostly due to Hugh's younger brother Nicholas, who always overindulged when away from the Heralds' College and the austere judgement of the ageing King of Arms Nicholas hoped to replace one day. Florence's husband Robert hadn't been far outdone by Nicholas: he drank much more at Beatrice and Hugh's table than at his own, complimenting their fine selection of wine far too effusively, gushing about the notes of blackberry and oak, 'And someone else's coin?' Florence had once offered, with that silky purr that concealed her sharpest claws – and the wink that inevitably made everyone forgive her.

'We were remarkably lucky with the weather,' William was telling Nicholas at the far end of the table. 'Clear skies all the way from the Canaries to the Caribbean – astronavigation has never been so easy. Even you could have managed it!'

Nicholas flushed, mumbling something incoherent and Beatrice thought, not for the first time, how anyone seeing the three Radclyffe men for the first time would have taken Hugh and William for brothers. With their golden hair and golden earrings, their broad shoulders and broad grins, they looked like buccaneers, whereas Nicholas's skin was pale from a life spent indoors, his shoulders growing ever more hunched from sitting at a desk, his white hands soft and unscarred. Perhaps the contrast was another reason why he drank so much wine.

'You're being modest,' Hugh said lightly, his arched eyebrow warning William to stop goading his uncle. 'Besides, have you forgotten the storms and riptides off Roanoke? They were far from easy to navigate.'

'I wouldn't know,' William said dryly. 'You wrenched compass and charts out of my hands.'

Robert ventured the beginnings of a laugh before wincing: Florence's too-placid face revealed she'd kicked him under the table. Robert cleared his throat, eyes fidgeting at the recognition that everyone knew his aborted laugh hadn't been a cough. 'But, ah, surely Sir Hugh is the more experienced navigator?'

'And will remain thus for eternity,' William retorted, 'if he keeps snatching my instruments away.'

'They're the ship's instruments,' Hugh pointed out, 'and the ship is mine, along with the responsibility for all who sail in her.'

'I could have plotted the same course you did –'

'And if you hadn't?' Hugh's voice was gentle, but his eyes were flinty. 'I've never lost more than five men on any voyage. That's far better than any other living captain, and I intend to keep it that way. If that means your pride is dented from time to time, so be it.'

He lifted his glass to his lips, but didn't drink straight away, and Beatrice knew he was seeing the failed attempt to find the Northeast passage in the flickering shadows on his malmsey, and the five men who hadn't returned from that bitterly cold disaster four years ago.

William's scowl vanished as soon as it had appeared, and he turned to Robert. 'Wait until you see the fruit we brought back from the Azores. Peaches the size of –' He waggled his eyebrows and glanced to the end of the table where Beatrice and Catalina were sitting.

Beatrice narrowed her eyes at him, itching to upbraid him. There came a point when men ought to outgrow boyish lasciviousness, when it became sinister rather than an eagerness to taste the untasted – but there also came a point when men were too old for their uncle's wife to scold them.

William didn't even notice her glare, just carried on comparing the food grown in the Azores to the fruit grown in Beatrice's garden with a jovial tone that was meant to make his rudeness endearing. After the fourth reference to 'luscious globes', Beatrice stopped listening.

Beside her, Catalina remained silent – as she had done throughout the evening. Did she even speak English? Did she understand what William was alluding to? Or was she, like every woman Beatrice knew, so used to hearing their bodies described by men who wanted them to hear, that she'd perfected the art of arranging her face into calm poise?

Catalina was wearing another fine gown. Ivory satin this time, a colour that made Beatrice look like spilled milk, but which made Catalina gleam, like mahogany inlaid with pearl. Her hair was still bound back with a ribbon: Maria said she'd refused to let her dress it, and Beatrice thought again of how reluctant Catalina had been to allow anyone on the docks to touch her.

Anyone except Hugh, of course. And Beatrice's children.

Florence ran her spoon around her bowl of strawberries preserved in sugar and red wine. 'Tell me, Beatrice,' she said softly, so the men couldn't hear, 'what fruits did Hugh bring back for you this time?'

Beatrice poked at her own bowl: a tiny bit of ginger and cinnamon-spiced syrup lingered at the bottom. There was always a tightrope to walk in any conversation about Hugh's voyages with Florence: no matter how much Florence cooed over gleaming porcelain and insisted she was eager to try the blueberries from the Azores shrubs now attempting to flourish in the gardens, Beatrice couldn't help feeling guilty at the jealousy she was certain she was provoking. Beatrice couldn't show Florence the spoils of Hugh's voyages for long without feeling sorry for her, not to mention guilt-ridden, knowing her richer situation was because she was older, because her mother had brought a far greater dowry than Florence's, including this house. When their father died, Beatrice had inherited almost everything, and she'd never stopped feeling undeserving of her good fortune.

Especially after what Beatrice had had to endure to get it.

'A coral necklace,' Beatrice said at last, 'and a pair of silver-backed mirrors.'

'They make those in Virginia, do they? Should I advise Robert to trade there instead of with the Low Countries?'

Beatrice bit the insides of her cheeks to stop herself rising to Florence's bait. Of course the gifts Hugh brought weren't necessarily produced in the New World: it was the worst-kept secret in Christendom that Queen Elizabeth's gallant explorers regularly plundered the Spanish ships they encountered on their voyages. Privateers, they called themselves, though pirates would have been more fitting. 'I believe he acquired them near Dominica.'

She saw Florence's lips purse at the euphemism. 'Imagine how I'd feel,' she'd said to Beatrice once, 'if a Spanish Hugh boarded the one ship Robert owns. We'd be destitute. How can you stomach him leaving other women beggared?' To which Beatrice had no answer, save that you didn't argue with the queen's commands. No matter how much it weighed on your conscience.

'And what of the other gift?' Florence leaned closer, her voice a soft breath in Beatrice's ear. 'Has he said what it is *for* yet?'

Catalina didn't move. Either she hadn't heard, or understood – or she wanted to pretend she hadn't.

'I'm yet to discover that,' Beatrice said quietly.

'But are you expected to keep it? Feed and clothe and care for it?'

As for the first, Catalina had barely eaten: perhaps English food wasn't to her taste. As for the second, she seemed to be clothing herself, or someone else was clothing her perfectly adequately. And the third?

'You know as well as I do, Florence – sometimes it's best to feign pleasure at a gift from one's husband. I know you've sold cushions you hated and accidentally lost earrings on many occasions.'

'Indeed,' Florence purred, 'but this gift is rather harder to lose than an earring. One cannot sell such trinkets in England. But perhaps it will prove breakable before long.' She licked her spoon slowly. 'Or maybe you will.'

'Florence, neither of us is made of glass –'

'Reputations are made of something far more delicate,' Florence countered. 'Do you want everyone to lose all respect for you?'

Beatrice opened her mouth to – what? Snap at her sister, scold her, or maybe just scratch her as she had so long ago? But before she could decide, Catalina flowed to her feet, no less graceful for her suddenness.

She understands, Beatrice thought, sick with shame at how she had let her sister make her talk about Catalina, with the woman by their side.

'I must sleep,' Catalina said, and though her words were accented and quiet, they were unmistakably English, and Beatrice felt another roil of shame.

'Of course – can you find your bedchamber, or shall I send for Maria, or Ridley?'

'I do not need anyone,' Catalina said coolly, and she left the chamber.

Beatrice stared after her, wishing desperately that she was mistaken, that she hadn't seen what she thought she had.

But as she turned back to the table, Florence's green eyes met hers, sharp and gleeful with new gossip.

Florence had seen it too. That slow walk, leaning back slightly, a barely-discernible list from side to side, and a hand drifting towards the belly before Catalina remembered to drop it to her side: if you had walked that way yourself, you would recognise it at once. Beatrice had three times, Florence five, and their silent certainty seethed between them like a lit fuse no one else could see.

Catalina was carrying a child.

Hugh was kissing her neck, murmuring softly. 'From Gravesend, around the coast of France ... Spain ... Portugal.' He traced his route lower, around one breast. 'And south to the Canaries, to buy wine and water ...' He kissed a line from her nipple to her hipbone.

Ordinarily, Beatrice enjoyed this game, revelled in it. Even after the horrific expedition north, Hugh had sought refuge in her, obliterating his memories of the Røst islands and Tartary in the soft, yielding warmth of Beatrice's body. Since then, he'd only journeyed to the New World, and she knew exactly which of her body parts were the Azores and the Virginian coast; long afterwards could feel the echoes of the latitude lines he'd traced between her breasts, between her hips, and the longitude line he'd kissed from her mouth to her hungrily, eagerly parting legs: it was a memory she prayed to dream of instead of the lavender-scented room.

But tonight, she couldn't give herself over to Hugh's touch. Even as he moved slowly down her body, murmuring, 'It took us a long time to make safe port at Dominica,' she couldn't help wondering, *is that where you found her?* As his thumb brushed against her thighs and he whispered 'Strong winds kept us off course. We had to circle around, waiting and waiting,' she thought *and where was her child conceived?*

Florence had been all too eager to share her suspicions. 'I heard of a negro woman taken aboard Francis Drake's ship a few years back, off the coast of Guatemala. Maria, she was called, like your Moorish maid. Some say he took her from the Spanish by force, outraged at their treatment of her. Others say he was given her as a peace offering to stop him boarding their ship. And he and his men continued to treat her as the Spaniards had.'

Hugh wouldn't, Beatrice thought. How could he do that to a woman – any woman – and then be so tender with *her*?

But he wasn't always tender. He was a sea captain; he'd been in the army. The man who compared the freckles on her shoulder to the constellations he'd seen halfway across the Atlantic was not the same man who'd fought in Ireland alongside Raleigh.

'Perhaps you're right,' Florence had sighed at Beatrice's objection. 'You do hear stories of women eager to leave those primitive islands – begging to come aboard as cooks or laundresses. As if they didn't know what their real tasks on board would be.'

What woman would willingly do that? Even Beatrice, a captain's wife, an heiress, a rich white-skinned woman, would balk at the prospect of embarking on a months-long voyage surrounded by men who hadn't seen women since England. Men who were often employed *because* they were violent. A woman like Catalina, with no family connections anyone would know or care about, with her exotic looks and no father or brother in sight to frighten off unwanted attention – why would she beg to come aboard a ship?

'Once we'd landed,' Hugh continued, 'we stayed for a while to acquire delicious things, like salt, livestock, and fruit.' His tongue flicked against her, and Beatrice couldn't help gasping, couldn't help her body wanting Hugh even as her mind raced.

'It gets worse,' Florence had hissed. 'After two months crossing the Pacific, Drake found an island, and left Maria there.'

'Alone?' Beatrice had asked, horrified.

'Some say he was kind enough to leave her two African men for company,' Florence shrugged. 'Either way, she wouldn't have been alone for long in any case. If she survived the birth, of course.'

Even Florence had looked grim at that, however much she enjoyed gossiping. They were both mothers: they knew the mortal danger every woman faced when she gave birth. And if she'd been lucky enough to survive the birth, it was hard enough recovering and looking after a new-born even in a comfortable Chelsea house with family and servants and nursemaids to care for you and the baby. As for giving birth alone on a remote island … the prospect was horrifying.

'At least Hugh wasn't that cruel,' Beatrice had defended her husband. 'He brought her somewhere safe.'

'Oh, Beatrice,' Florence had groaned in exasperation, 'you don't really think he brought her here out of kindness, do you?'

'We left Dominica reluctantly,' Hugh sighed, and was that part of the game, or had he noticed she was distracted? 'We headed north, up the coast of Virginia.'

'I must say,' Florence had mused, 'you're taking this rather calmly. I'd have clawed Robert's eyes out by now.'

'And then on the return voyage, we stopped at my favourite place for fresh water and fruit. Berries this exact shade of red.'

Why couldn't she just enjoy this? Hugh, here, safe, worshipping her body with hands, lips, tongue. And she was: her back arched and she clutched at his golden head, delighting in his sojourn in the Azores too. But all the while, Florence's words ran down the inside of her skull like a cat's sheathed claws, soft and dangerous.

'There aren't many women who'd show such magnanimity.'

'And at long last,' Hugh grinned, 'we returned home to London.' He kissed her lips at the same time as he slid inside her, and now she could bury her face in the hollow she loved, between his neck and shoulder, and he couldn't see the suspicion in her eyes.

Or the guilt. Because if she had been betrayed, didn't she deserve it?

But one kiss, and not even a kiss, the briefest brush of lips, never, ever to be repeated – that wasn't the same as this.

'He's the father of her child,' Florence purred. 'That's why she's staying with you. Maybe she'll never leave, and you can raise a parcel of brown babies in your lovely house, all with a lovely smile on your face as your lovely husband *fucks* his lovely mistress.'

It couldn't be true. Hugh was hers, and she was his, and in desperate defiance, Beatrice wrapped her arms and legs tight around her husband and clung to him as he gasped and shuddered. Even after he'd collapsed against the pillows, she curled her body around his, draping one leg across his hips, one arm across his chest, kissing his cheek, claiming and reclaiming him.

'God above, I missed you,' Hugh sighed, flinging one arm behind his head and the other around her waist. 'Remind me, why did I become a sailor again?'

'Exactly that,' she said. 'To remind you how much you love me.'

'My clever wife,' he smiled, eyes closed. 'That's the only possible explanation for depriving myself of you for almost a year. So I get a wonderful welcome home.'

'Always,' she said, propping herself up to kiss his still-smiling mouth. Then, before she could help herself, 'Hugh, I wondered …'

'Mmm?'

Are you the father of Catalina's child? Did he even know she was pregnant? But what other explanation could there be?

'Just … how long is Catalina going to stay?'

Did his jaw tighten? *Open your eyes*, she implored silently. *Let me see if you're telling the truth.*

'As long as she needs to.'

'Needs to? You mean, until she finds somewhere else, or until she finds work, or …'

'Beatrice.' He opened his eyes and met hers. 'Catalina stays until it is safe for her to leave.'

'Safe?' She was parroting him, she sounded like a fool. 'Hugh, tell me the truth. Do you mean until she's recovered from childbed?'

She forced herself to hold his gaze, unblinking, as if that could stop the tears burning to fall. She wouldn't cry, she wouldn't be a weeping, wailing, *weak* wife.

Hugh sighed. 'No, that's not what I mean. It's part of it, but …' Abruptly, he sat up, dislodging her, and she fell back against their rumpled sheets. Running his hands through his dishevelled hair, he said, 'Look, Beatrice, it isn't what you think. The baby – is not mine. Couldn't possibly be mine.'

Florence's voice, needling in her ear: 'That's what all unfaithful husbands say …'

'There were reasons,' Hugh began, then stopped, shaking his head. 'I couldn't just leave her. I've abandoned many people in my time, and I cannot, will not leave another one behind, not while there's breath in my body. You have to understand that.'

But you leave me behind, she thought. *Every year, you sail away to discover the world, when without you my tiny world is fractured, and wounded, and gaping.*

'Tell me the reasons,' she said instead. 'Please.'

He was silent. At last he said, 'Cannot it be enough that you understand they were important, and I could not disregard them? She is here, in my house, and she stays in my house.'

Your house, that I run for more time than you ever spend in it. My mother's house, that you leave over and over again, and yet return to without the slightest doubt of your mastery.

'As what?' Beatrice asked. 'My maid? My seamstress?'

'Your companion,' he said. 'I believe some women deem it a symbol of fashion to have a dark-skinned companion. You could even have your portrait painted together.'

A painting of his wife and his mistress (for what else could Catalina possibly be?), hanging above her fireplace for the rest of their lives?

How could he be so cruel? Tears stung again, and one traitor drop fell. She dashed it away before he could see.

'Hugh, this isn't …' She floundered for words. Fair? Right? Perhaps it was, after what she'd done: not just Ridley, but the other sin, years before. Hadn't she always known she deserved punishment? Now here it was, at her husband's hand.

'It isn't many things,' he said, and the bleakness in his voice startled her. Hugh was never despondent. Even when he swung into a fit of rage, within moments he always had a jest, a smile – he always had hope. 'But it is what we must bear, and I never did shy away from my share of burdens.'

What did he mean? Was he talking about the northern voyage again – or was it something else?

But then he swung around to face her, and there was Hugh again, grinning and saying, 'Enough of this. I've got some good news to cheer you up. Tomorrow, we're invited to court.'

3

Beatrice ran a hand over the linenfold pattern carved into her clothing chest: neat, predictable, it was far preferable to the confusion she knew awaited her. Gritting her teeth, she heaved it open, and the floral scents of orris root and violets wafted up, failing to calm her.

Usually when she opened this chest, she selected gowns and kirtles because they were near the top. But today, she and Maria would have to delve deeper, dislodging muslin sweet bags that hadn't been disturbed in months, unwrapping her clothes from their linen shrouds, resurrecting decisions and worries she'd thought buried for good. Because now she had to choose a gown to wear to Queen Elizabeth's court.

She hadn't believed him at first. Women – wives – in general were scarcely ever invited to court: Queen Elizabeth liked to have all her men to herself. As for Beatrice Radclyffe, formerly Beatrice Gardiner, merchant's daughter, she'd only once been invited to Whitehall, and it wasn't an experience she was eager to repeat.

And Hugh had given her less than a day's notice. Oh, he'd been on a ship, of course, and perhaps he hadn't known himself until yesterday – though he would certainly have known prior to coming to her bed. But it was so like a man to drop such news on a woman, not knowing what problems might arise.

She hadn't been to court for nine years, not since the Armada celebrations. She'd been heavily pregnant with Walter then, and the let-out gown had been taken in again before Ursula, and let out again as Ursula grew, then in and out once more, and neat as Maria's needlework was, and however lovely she'd thought the green silk at first, Beatrice couldn't wear a nine-year-old gown with unpicked seams to Queen

Elizabeth's palace. She'd worn the blue sarcanet yesterday, and if anyone had been in the gardens or summerhouses of the riverside mansions, its peacock hue might have caught the eye of the Countesses of Essex, or Arundel, or Salisbury, and she couldn't have them whispering that Lady Radclyffe only had one good gown. One whisper led to another, and Beatrice had more reason than most women not to wish to be the subject of court ladies' gossip.

'This one?' Maria suggested, holding up a peony pink damask embroidered with clusters of flowers. A girl's dress, a young wife's dress. Not that of a woman of thirty-four with two children.

Beatrice shook her head. 'Something more sophisticated. But not matronly.'

What she wanted to wear was Catalina's red velvet: it would make Beatrice's pale skin look snowy rather than sickly, and her brown hair against the crimson would glow chestnut instead of hanging drably. But Catalina hadn't yet emerged from her bedchamber today – exhausted or nauseous, Beatrice supposed, and even if Catalina were neither, how could Beatrice ask a stranger for what might be one of only two gowns?

Where had they come from? Were there seamstresses in the Azores skilled enough to make such clothing? Had they been plundered from a Spanish galleon? Or had they always been Catalina's? In which case, where did her wealth come from – and why hadn't it led her into a secure marriage instead of leaving her pregnant on an English vessel?

'Plum velvet?'

Beatrice shook her head again. 'It looks like curtains. No doubt I'll be stood against them all night anyway – I'd rather not disappear more than I have to.'

'Green damask?'

She'd worn green last time. This was ivy rather than olive, true, and embossed with intricate vines. It had always made her feel elegant: did she really want to taint that sensation by having the Essex circle sneer at her?

'With your ivory kirtle and sleeves, perhaps? And that enamel and pearl girdle?'

Beatrice bit her lip. 'And jewels. Both far more than I normally wear, and few enough not to be gaudy.'

Maria nodded, eyes warm with sympathy. 'I know just the ones.'

She let Maria tug and drape and pin. Cloth had turned Beatrice from a merchant's daughter into a knight's wife; could it even turn her into a courtier? Her father had thought it would, but Arthur Gardiner had lived in a world where ledgers and coins were alchemists' potions, transmuting dust to gold. He'd never understood that there was a limit to how much money could change people. Especially in the eyes of those who had always had it.

Maria ushered her onto the stool before the mirror to dress her hair.

'Can you arrange the pins so as to hide …' Beatrice gestured at the grey hairs speckling the brown.

'Of course.'

No need to ask: Maria would have done it anyway. But Catalina had no grey hairs. Even after a sea voyage with salt-roughened winds whipping at her, that black hair had glowed like ink.

'Have you seen to Catalina today, Maria? Is she well?'

'She didn't eat her breakfast,' Maria said, coiling and plaiting. 'Fast asleep. Then at noon she ate some bread and looked as if I'd just given her caterpillars.'

'Did she … say anything?' About her child? About Hugh?

'She asked if there were many people like me – like her in London.' Maria placed pearl-topped pins carefully to anchor her handiwork. 'I said a few, but that the barmaid at the Lion and those midwife sisters weren't the sort you invited to the house.'

And Catalina was? How was Beatrice supposed to judge?

'And then she said, "Where did your people come from?"' Maria turned away to fetch Beatrice's pots of face paint; as she turned back, Beatrice glimpsed a pulled face disappearing. 'So I told her there were plenty of people born in Lambeth, and she had only to cross the river to find them.'

'Was she angry? Or amused?' Beatrice couldn't imagine.

'Confused, I think,' Maria said, dipping her fingers in lily-root paste and daubing it on Beatrice's cheeks. 'She said "Are we near Lambeth?"

So I felt sorry for her and told her my grandfather had been a doctor in Granada. And then she asked if he was still alive and if she could see him, so of course I told her his grave's in Lambeth but that's probably not much use to her, and people often feel a bit funny after long voyages, but would she like me to ask you to send for Doctor Chamberlain instead?'

'And did she?'

Maria brushed ground safflowers across Beatrice's cheeks and lips. 'We need some more of this, it's all dried up. I'll tell Ridley to order some. No, she didn't. Just turned away and lay down to sleep again.'

Maybe she should send for him anyway – it would be helpful to know how far along Catalina was. At least four months, perhaps five, if Beatrice was any judge.

'Did that man find you?'

Beatrice frowned. 'What man?'

Maria dabbed at the crease her frown had caused. 'He came by while Miss Ursula was having her dancing lesson, so I told him you were busy. But he wouldn't give me his message. Said it was only to be put into your hands.'

'How odd. And it was for me, not Hugh?'

'I told him Sir Hugh was in the library, but he insisted only you would do. I offered him honey cakes while he waited, but that wasn't to his liking either.'

'A man of poor taste then – perhaps I ought to be glad he didn't come back.'

'Never trust anyone who refuses cake,' Maria said with mock solemnity. But she frowned as she brushed dark powder along Beatrice's eyebrows. 'Mind, I didn't think him trustworthy before then.'

A fleck of powder caught in Beatrice's eyelashes, and she had to blink it away rather than search Maria's face for meaning. 'How so?'

'His clothes, for one. A black hat pulled low, a black cloak pulled high. And …' Maria hesitated. 'Sometimes you just know, madam. The kind of men who are dangerous to women. And he was definitely the sort I'd cross a dark street to avoid. Women learn to recognise them young.'

But that wasn't always true, Beatrice thought. Sometimes dangerous men were handsome and kind and generous. Sometimes they made you love them before they hurt you, and then you loved them so much your own tears salted your wounds.

They took the barge to Whitehall. Bells echoed coldly across the water from dozens of different churches, tolling the hour, none of their seven strikes exactly in time with the others, like unseen voices all clamouring to be heard. The dark had settled in over an hour ago, and the river rippled black between the shadowed banks. Beatrice pulled her cloak tighter, wondering if Hugh would insist on using the barge all winter. Perhaps the Thames would freeze again, removing the option entirely.

Whitehall was unmistakable: nowhere else were the torches so numerous, making their approaching barge lights seem like interlopers. Laughter and music carried across the water, and even though no one would be looking and the canopy all-but concealed her, Beatrice felt as if the laughter was already directed at her.

Another barge was tying up as they reached the wharf; Beatrice recognised the coat of arms with dismay. She'd hoped to be in a crowd before having to meet the Essex circle. She wanted to linger on her cushions awhile, let them all get into the palace before she disembarked – but Hugh was already ashore, holding out his arm for her, and she had no choice but to take it.

There was the Earl himself, resplendent in black and gold, his perfectly oiled beard gleaming, his teeth flashing white as he shared a jest, his wife Frances, her gold and black garb the inverse of the earl's, her dark hair dressed in a complicated style that Beatrice envied. The Earl of Northumberland, clothes dishevelled as only those ennobled for centuries could get away with, his missing eyebrows proof that another alchemical experiment had gone awry. His wife Dorothy, Essex's sister, kept a steady hand on her husband's arm, as if she knew from experience he was inclined to wander astray, distracted by passing dragonflies or a fallen acorn. Lord Mountjoy, Hugh's erstwhile comrade in Ireland, lit cigar in one hand, his other reaching out to help ashore the woman Beatrice had most wished to avoid: Essex's older sister, Lady Penelope Rich.

'Shall we go in?' Beatrice murmured to Hugh, trying to hide her urgency.

Too late. Mountjoy had seen them.

'Radclyffe! How's the scurvy?'

'Mountjoy! They let you out of the Irish bogs for one evening?'

And they were clapping shoulders, sharing old jokes no one else understood, grinning at the earls, their noise barging and jostling and blaring as men so often did, trampling any women's voices in their wake.

'Lady Radclyffe, is it not?'

Beatrice winced. Of course Penelope would pretend to have forgotten her: too clever to truly forget anyone, it was one of the many blades in Penelope's arsenal, all chosen and wielded to cut you down one sliver at a time.

'Lady Rich,' Beatrice said with a forced smile. 'How pleasant to see you again.'

'It has been a while, has it not?' Penelope smiled. 'Of course, the queen is most particular about which ladies she wishes to spend time with. Alas, we cannot all be equally favoured.'

'All the more reason to appreciate tonight's invitation.'

'I suppose it would be.' Penelope's eyes glided up and down Beatrice's body. 'What a wonderfully … *rustic* gown.' She smoothed her own silver skirts; hundreds of seed pearls glimmered on her bodice and kirtle and Beatrice felt exactly as Penelope wanted her to feel: as if the moon had deigned to acknowledge a nettle.

'Pen! The queen wants us!'

Penelope gave Beatrice another smile. 'Do enjoy this special occasion, Mistress Radclyffe.'

They were all leaving, Hugh in their midst, and Beatrice could only drift in their wake, unsure whether falling behind would be the best or worst outcome.

She'd always thought herself inured to female spite. Growing up with Florence's mother, she'd had no choice but to harden herself against it. As for her half-sister, Florence was eight years younger than Beatrice, and she wasn't their father's heir: it was much easier to put up with sniping from someone smaller than you, especially when Florence would immediately follow any catty remarks with flurries of tears and embraces and promises that she would make it up to Beatrice. When they were children, Florence's apologies had taken the form of daisy chains; now they were offers to show Beatrice a more flattering hairstyle, or introduce her to the loveliest seamstress. Penelope's spite, on the other hand, had no more cause than a wolf hunting lambs: she could, and so she would. As for an apology afterwards, there wouldn't be enough flesh left on the bone to beg forgiveness from. And her words and smiles were so pretty and sculpted that when you repeated them in appeal for sympathy, she appeared entirely blameless, and you a churlish fool.

Last time Beatrice had come to court, she hadn't known to watch out for anyone. Hugh had told her other captains' wives would be there – Drake's, Raleigh's, Hawkins's – so she had expected to be among equals. Of course there would be countesses and suchlike, but she wouldn't be outranked by everyone. Naively, she'd even hoped to make a friend, something she knew she had no aptitude for.

As the queen had gathered her triumphant captains around her, Beatrice had joined a group of ladies eating lemon possets, and smiled along with the conversation, hoping for an opening so she could join in. Then a red-haired beauty had turned to her with a smile and asked, 'Is it Mistress Radclyffe?'

'Yes,' she'd said hopefully, willing to accept any title in exchange for friendship. 'My husband is Sir –'

'Fetch my fan for me, would you? I left it just by the sundial.'

Beatrice had stared. 'I could ask a page –'

'Oh, don't be silly!' the woman had laughed. 'You're new here, so let me explain this time. I've fetched fans and gloves and cloaks for the queen, and I'm an earl's daughter – some say I'm King Henry's great-granddaughter, but don't tell Queen Elizabeth I said that! Surely you wouldn't mind fetching a fan for me?'

'Her husband fires a cannon once and she thinks that makes her the equal of a Devereux,' sighed another woman – Dorothy, Beatrice later realised. 'Honestly, someone ought to tell these sailors' wives to remember their place. Bess, they'll listen to you – why, you're practically one of them!'

A slender, fair-haired woman looked sidelong through her lashes at Dorothy, as if she didn't deem her worth turning her head for. 'If she was invited, Dorothy, her place is here. And I wish someone had told me I was a sailor's wife – I'm sure my family would have mentioned it.'

'Dorothy's over-eager,' Penelope had said. 'One secret kiss and she thinks a couple long-wed. But of course, Bess would never marry without royal permission, no matter how handsome the sailor! Have you been wed long, Mistress Radclyffe, or are the church bells still echoing?'

Beatrice had glanced down at her protruding belly: surely it was obvious she wasn't a new bride? 'Eighteen months, madam.'

'Oh, do forgive me!' Penelope had laughed lightly. 'I just wasn't sure – one never knows if sailors have the same standards we do, and you seem rather older than we are.'

'That's just because she's aged since you asked her to fetch your fan, Pen,' Dorothy drawled. 'We all have.'

Penelope, who Beatrice later discovered was a year older than her, turned a beaming smile on Beatrice. 'Would you mind, Mistress Radclyffe? It's not far.'

There had been no fan by the sundial, and after she'd waddled around the gardens for a while, Beatrice could no longer deny that it had simply been a ruse to get rid of her.

Tonight, she almost wished Penelope had given her another spurious errand: shivering in a rose bower whose roses had long-wilted would be preferable to the glacial cruelty of courtiers.

But they were inside now. Ahead, heralds were announcing the Earl and Countess of Essex, the Earl and Countess of Northumberland, and any moment now she and Hugh would be summoned forth. Already, Beatrice could see how many mistakes she'd made – ruffs had changed shape, were more lace than linen, more like silvery cobwebs than intricate pleats; sleeve ribbons were wider, designed to be noticed, not tiny enough to hide; the sleeves themselves were narrower, and –

'Sir Hugh Radclyffe and his wife!'

She gripped Hugh's arm tightly as he strode forward, barely aware of where she was putting her feet, only how disastrous a stumble would be. And now he was sweeping a low bow and she had to let go of him and sink into a curtsey without wobbling, or getting stuck at the bottom, or letting her shoulders curl.

'You may rise.'

'Your Majesty,' Hugh murmured as he obeyed, and Beatrice echoed him, mouth dry, suddenly desperate to cough.

Queen Elizabeth, a woman for whom new worlds were named, whose power spanned more of the globe each day, up close was starting to resemble a map of the world herself. Her wide skirts patterned with jewels and crimson and gold embroidery, like cartouches and islands; the gemstones on her fingers and at her throat as round and gleaming as compasses; the sparkling points of her ruff as delicate and intricate as a celestial astrolabe. And her white face, caked in heavy powder that must have cracked every time she spoke or smiled or scowled, was criss-crossed with latitude, longitude and journey lines. The most powerful woman in the world had grown old – and yet she was still hungry for more.

'Well, Sir Hugh? What have you brought back for me this time?' The queen arched a pencilled eyebrow, and the tiny puff of white powder was like that of a fuse being lit. 'More potatoes, or something more scintillating?'

For a moment, Beatrice had the wild thought that Hugh was about to say 'My mistress, Catalina, and our unborn bastard, Your Grace!' Whose face would be most worth memorising: the queen's, or Penelope Rich's?

'I must defend the humble potato,' Hugh said. 'After months of shipboard rations, there is nothing finer – baked, roasted, mashed ...'

'A cook as well as an explorer now? Perhaps I should send you to my kitchens rather than back to Virginia. Or perhaps your wife will tie you to hers, like a turnspit dog.'

Beatrice blushed at the image, dropping her gaze even further and fixing her eyes on the queen's skirts, where hundreds of scarlet and gold parrots cavorted through elaborate vines.

Hugh laughed. 'If Your Grace would rather I burn your dinner every day instead of expanding your kingdom, I would serve at your pleasure.'

'I take little pleasure in burnt vegetables,' the queen said dryly, and this time both eyebrows sent up warning signals of disapproval. 'What say you, Lady Radclyffe? Would you prefer Sir Hugh stay at home with you rather than serving me?'

Beatrice tried to hide her shock and horror: last time the queen hadn't spoken to her at all, as if she were Hugh's belt buckle rather than his wife. However demeaning, being ignored had its merits. 'I am glad to have him home, Your Grace, but only because it means he has served you well.'

The queen snorted. 'In other words, Radclyffe, she rather likes it when you're away.' She leaned closer to Beatrice; the queen's dark eyes gleamed with cold cunning, and the embroidered parrots' jet bead eyes mirrored their cruel glint. 'I know only too well how beneficial it can be to dispatch men far and wide. Stops them nagging – or trying to steal our power.'

Her cheeks were burning; she didn't dare look at Hugh in case he saw how close the queen's words were to the mark. Would he be furious? Hurt? Disgusted? Whatever was provoked, the queen had wanted to provoke it: her conspiratorial words were no overture of friendship, but a bored attempt to stir up trouble. And there'd be no alleviating that boredom: Beatrice couldn't think of a witty reply, or even a dull one.

'Sir Walter Raleigh!' the herald announced.

The queen's eyes lit up. 'My Water! Flow this way!' She flapped a hand at Hugh and Beatrice in uninterested dismissal; even if Beatrice had fallen over in her curtsey this time, the queen wouldn't have noticed. As Hugh led her away, all eyes were on Raleigh.

A lesser man might have swaggered, but Raleigh merely sauntered, as calm as if strolling the decks of his ship, knowing all was as it should be. Dressed in scarlet-shot black velvet, a matching scarlet feather in his hat and a gold earring winking at everyone as he passed, Raleigh looked every inch the buccaneer. He swept a bow before the queen and the two began conversing in low voices, the throaty royal laugh and Raleigh's baritone chuckle all Beatrice could hear.

'She's an astute woman, our queen,' Hugh said quietly as they found a spot near a window.

Beatrice swallowed. 'From what I gather, she wouldn't have sat the throne for forty years if she wasn't.'

'And all without a husband to help her.' Hugh took two glasses of claret from a passing page. 'Or get in her way.'

'Hugh, I –'

'Where are my dashing explorers?' the queen called out. 'Come, gentlemen, come!' She clapped her hands imperiously and the parrots flared like phoenixes as she led the way to a collection of large objects draped in black velvet. Hugh gave Beatrice an unreadable stare, then marched off to join Raleigh, Essex, Northumberland, and several others Beatrice didn't recognise. The rest of the court gathered round, blocking her view; it was almost a relief. Beatrice let them wash past her, drifting towards the back of the hall.

A man was speaking; she didn't know who. 'Allow me to present the master craftsman, Emery Molyneux!'

Applause: Beatrice tapped her right hand softly against the hand holding her glass – she couldn't do anything other than join in, but neither could she be the clumsy bumpkin who spilled wine on Whitehall's marble floor.

'These globes are remarkable,' the man was saying, 'truly the first of their kind. Master Molyneux will tell us more.'

Globes? Of course, Beatrice thought, vaguely disappointed. She'd seen globes before; surely everyone had. Perhaps these ones played a tune as they span – Ursula would like that.

'These are larger instruments than any crafted to date,' an older man, presumably Molyneux, was saying: between sharp-pointed lace ruffs and blooming silk sleeves, she caught a glimpse of a long grey beard and blue velvet cap. 'Most globes cannot be used aboard ship – they are unable to withstand the salt and damp, and so are ruined before their captains sail past the Isle of Wight. But I have discovered a unique way of treating the globe itself, and its frame, to allow it to withstand nearly all inclement weather.'

Movement caught Beatrice's eye, and she turned to see a thin blonde woman had entered the hall: Bess Throckmorton, Raleigh's wife. The woman she'd seen goaded by Penelope last time she was at court, about the sailor she would later marry in secret. As Beatrice watched, Bess shook her head at the herald, one long white finger to her lips. It wasn't merely a wish to avoid interrupting the presentation at the other end of the hall: Beatrice knew Raleigh's wife had been to court no more than she had in the last decade. Her offence wasn't being a merchant's daughter – the Throckmortons were an ancient family – but having married the queen's favourite without permission: an unforgivable crime.

'... as you can see, this red line demarcates the route taken by our late hero, Sir Francis Drake, when he circumnavigated the globe. And this blue one here ...'

'So now they are selling the world as well as sailing it.' Bess appeared at Beatrice's side. As she sipped her wine, Beatrice saw her bones move beneath the skin: Bess had lost weight since she'd last seen her. She'd heard both Raleigh and his wife had been imprisoned in the Tower after their elopement, and their infant son had died of plague in a hot London summer before they were released. Their misfortunes had evidently taken a harsher toll on Bess than on her husband. 'Twenty pounds each, I heard, and of course best displayed in pairs – one terrestrial and one celestial.'

'One doesn't have to buy all that is sold,' Beatrice said, silently cursing herself for sounding like Arthur Gardiner's daughter.

'True. But if Northumberland wants one – and if it glitters, or moves, or boasts of strange knowledge, Northumberland will buy it – Essex will have to buy one too, and Walter cannot be outdone by his arch-rival.'

And Hugh couldn't be outdone by Raleigh. Beatrice thought of her carefully balanced accounts books, the money she'd set aside for winter repairs to the stonework and for her Walter's new Latin tutor. Ursula had just started to make progress with her dancing lessons. Twenty pounds was more than four times what most Londoners made in a year; even though their coffers were far from bare, Beatrice hated the thought of her coin hoard dwindling. Savings were what kept you safe; frittering coin away only ended in Newgate.

'As for where we'll put the thing,' Bess sighed, 'I only hope it goes on his next ship.'

'The garden, perhaps,' Beatrice said. 'We'll see how weatherproof it really is after the first snowfall.'

Bess chuckled. She sipped her wine again, then said quietly, 'Once again, I find myself watching from afar as my husband launches into the world without me. I know it is a hard thing for Walter to leave us – however exciting his adventures, there is no small risk and hardship involved. But I think few understand how hard it is to be the one left behind.'

'The court is hardly my world,' Beatrice confessed. 'I am not certain I truly wish to be a part of it.'

'Likewise,' Bess said. 'Your world, I imagine, is much like mine. A house, a garden. Children playing, outgrowing their clothes, requiring food and lessons and comfort. A familiar world, a joyful world, but a small one. Our horizons are tapestries or garden walls. But our husbands' worlds … I cannot even begin to imagine their vastness, their beauty. All that perilous, intoxicating mystery.' She eyed the back of her husband's head with such naked longing Beatrice felt like putting an arm around her. 'It must be wonderful, mustn't it? Otherwise, why would he choose it over me every time?'

A mist had risen while Molyneux presented the supposedly splendid globes that Beatrice had only glimpsed. It lay across the Thames like a shroud, grey tendrils snaking between the waiting barges and creeping towards Whitehall's knot gardens. The grass was already damp underfoot, and now the air clung damply too: it would be a cold voyage back to Chelsea.

Beatrice stamped her feet, wrapping her arms tight around herself. She glanced back at the light spilling out of Whitehall: Hugh had been just behind her when Essex had called out to him, and of course Hugh had gone scurrying to the call. How much longer could he be?

Beatrice turned back to watch the mist. There was something almost mesmerising about its slow, undulating movements, like watching the river breathe, or seeing time itself creep inexorably onwards, passing her by. As everything else did. How was it, she wondered, that origins were so much more forgivable in a man than in a woman? Hugh Radclyffe was the son of a country squire, just like Walter Raleigh; Francis Drake had been a farmer's son. Yet they were favoured by the greatest in the land, had been rewarded with knighthoods – whereas Beatrice Gardiner, wealthier than all their fathers put together, was not now, nor would ever be, welcome at court.

'Lady Radclyffe?'

She turned to see a man dressed in black, cloak pulled high against the cold. 'Yes?'

'I bring a message for you,' he said, stepping closer.

Something in his voice, his bearing, the stale beer and meat odours on his grey breath, made her step back, bridling, looking about her for Hugh, for help. But there was no one nearby. Maria's words echoed in her mind. *Sometimes you just know, madam. The kind of men who are dangerous to women.*

'Then deliver it at once,' she snapped, praying for her voice to be imperious, not shrill and wavering.

'As you wish,' he said, mockery twisting his words.

The torchlight was behind him: she couldn't see his face, only black cloth and what might have been either beard of scarf. She wanted to be able to avoid him in future, yet she didn't want to see the scorn, or the threat in his eyes. He drew something out of his cloak, and she flinched. But it wasn't a blade, only a piece of paper: foolish woman to think otherwise.

'Of course, once you've read it,' the man said, 'you can't unread it.'

She glanced up in surprise and bewilderment. But he was already gone, swallowed up by mist and shadow.

The paper was sealed: she moved closer to the nearest torch to see it more clearly. But the seal was plain, revealing nothing about the sender. Telling herself it was foolish to be afraid, Beatrice broke the seal and unfolded the letter.

Written in block capitals, with a quill pressing so hard the paper was creased and almost ripped by the force, were two blunt sentences that turned Beatrice's blood to ice.

YOUR SECRETS ARE KNOWN.

YOU DESERVE ALL THAT IS COMING.

4

She cannot breathe. She's choking, and it smells like lavender and sweat and feathers, and she knows death is imminent. But dear God, she had not thought it would hurt this much.

And then the voice comes, so faint she does not know if it is spoken by the living or the dead.

'Beatrice.'

It's so dark. The candles have gone out. There is only blackness and pain, and the press of a pillow against flesh. She tastes blood, and knows she doesn't have long left.

'Beatrice!'

Her eyes flew open. Hands were gripping her tightly and she almost screamed.

But it was Hugh, wrapping his arms around her and whispering, 'Only a dream, sweet Bea. Only a dream.' He kissed her hair, stroked her back, and she tried to relax her clenched limbs, her taut jaw.

She'd never had the dream with Hugh at her side. Until now she'd thought his homecoming kept her safe. But after Ridley, after that note and all that it threatened to reveal … She had never been safe at all.

Your secrets are known, it had said. Not discovered, but *known*. Perhaps known all along. And whoever knew them had chosen now as their time to strike. What did they want from her? What would they take from her?

As for what she deserved, Beatrice didn't dare contemplate it. Nor did she have time to ruminate, because Ursula burst into the room, a flurry of golden curls and bare feet.

'Mama, mama, come and see!'

Ursula's squeal pulled her away from her bed and to the window overlooking the front courtyard. A cart had pulled up, laden with a great crate, and Beatrice knew instantly what it was.

'Is it a pet lion?' Ursula asked, scrambling onto the window seat. 'Or a bear?'

'Nonsense,' Beatrice said, fighting the urge to glance back at her stretching husband. 'Papa wouldn't bring anything so dangerous home with him.'

Later, she would remember this conversation with her daughter, and she would think that a wild beast, snarling and clawing and savaging everything in sight, would have been far less dangerous than what Hugh had actually brought into their house. But by then it would be far too late.

'Well? Isn't it splendid?'

The globe sat in the centre of the gallery, its six-legged frame making it look like a pale-bellied, mutilated spider. Hugh had placed it on the Turkey carpet in the alcove in front of the largest window, exactly where Walter sometimes lay on his stomach to play knights with his carved horses, where Ursula demonstrated what she'd learned with her dancing master, where the cabinet of curiosities held a mixture of genuine rarities and children's treasure: fossilised crabs and silver Roman siliquas, blue eggshells and jet figurines, deer antlers and Murano glass beads. No one would be looking at that jetsam now.

Beatrice could still smell the sawdust from the crate the globe had arrived in, and below that the scent of new parchment seeping insistently into the room, as if disdainful of the dust and weight of the old leather-bound tomes on the bookshelf. She'd always thought the smell of parchment comforting. Letters meant affection, meant that someone had noticed you, remembered you, thought enough of you to put quill to parchment and choose words that you needed, longed to hear. But after the note she'd received at Whitehall, the smell was no longer comforting. As for the sight of the globe … in truth there was something intrusive, almost obnoxious about its presence in the house.

'It's a marvel,' she said. 'Though I hadn't expected one to arrive so soon.'

She'd hoped, in fact, to persuade Hugh not to buy one, or at least to commission a smaller version that would actually fit in his cabin aboard the *Silver Swan*, rather than getting in the way. Not for one to arrive the day after the things had been presented at court.

Hugh grinned proudly. 'I ordered it as soon as I heard Molyneux was making them, before I set off back in January. Never hurts to plan ahead, after all!'

'Then it's already paid for?'

'Oh, I've taken care of all that.'

Which was not a response that either answered her question or stopped her worrying.

'Now,' Hugh was saying to Walter and Ursula, 'who can find the Azores first?'

'Me!'

'No, me!'

They scampered towards it, Beatrice trailing after them with a 'Careful!' she wasn't sure she wanted them to heed. If they broke it, the globe might leave their home temporarily, but no doubt Hugh's pride and rivalry with Raleigh would compel him to buy another. Which would mean forty pounds wasted on spinning hunks of wood, paper and sand.

'See how intricate the markings are?' Hugh said. 'The most comprehensive map of the globe ever drawn. Molyneux sailed with Drake and Cavendish, you know.'

'There's Drake's name!' Walter pointed out. 'Where's yours, Papa?'

Hugh laughed. 'When I circumnavigate the world, we can draw it on.'

'There's no one's name up here,' Ursula said, peering at the northern hemisphere. 'Just islands and white bears and a funny thing with long teeth.'

'Tusks,' Hugh said. 'That's a walrus, and very delicious they are too. Though damned dangerous to hunt, especially the females.'

'Can I draw your voyage up here, Papa?' Ursula asked.

Hugh's face stiffened. Beatrice could see him struggling to hide his emotions from their daughter, to maintain his cheerful façade. 'That wasn't my favourite voyage, little bear cub. When we draw my route on here, it must be for something truly special. Now, have you found the Azores yet?'

Beatrice watched them search the globe, picking out details in its markings. Veined with rivers, barbed with mountains, a rash of continents spread across the globe's skin. Cartouches and creatures pockmarked every gore: mermaids and serpents in the water, lions and strange birds on land. The mermaids aside, presumably, these things were all part of Hugh's world. Whereas Beatrice had been born in this very house. Her horizon was the Thames, her skies grey and narrow. Hugh's were vast, and she knew she could never stand with him beneath them.

It would have been wholly out of character for Hugh not to share his new treasure. He shared everything he could, after all – asking his orphaned nephew to live with them, sail with him, teaching William navigation along the way, paying for Nicholas's scholarly career, inviting Robert and Florence for dinner and theatre excursions whenever he could. It was, Beatrice reminded herself, one of the reasons she loved him. How could anyone resist her husband's generosity, unless she were wholly ungenerous herself?

And yet, as the family gathered around the globe before dinner that evening, Beatrice couldn't help feeling irritated. At least when Hugh had bought a pet monkey it had done something, even if that something had involved gnawing the curtain tassels to shreds and throwing chicken bones at Robert's head. They still saw the monkey occasionally: domesticity hadn't suited her, and instead she roamed the house and gardens as she pleased, loping into the kitchens to pilfer food and terrify the servants every week or so, before scampering off to pick the mulberries before they were ripe, or torment the hounds dozing by the fire in the hall. At least the monkey had entertained them. This globe just … lurked. There was no other word for it. It lurked, squat and bulbous. Now as she stared at it, the wooden frame looked less like a spider and more like six arms cradling the globe, hostile as elbows shielding a pregnant belly.

'Remarkable,' Robert was saying, 'quite remarkable.' It was his third choice of adjective that evening, splendid and extraordinary having been repeated already.

'Sometimes,' Florence murmured, 'I contemplate replacing my husband with a parrot. I am not sure I would even notice the exchange.'

Beatrice felt Florence's eyes seeking hers, ready to share a wry wink. But she wasn't in the mood for gently mocking her sister's husband.

'The typical wooden sphere moulds were too small for this model,' Hugh told his audience. 'Two copper hemispheres had to be used instead. Then the paper caps were sewn together. The human eye cannot perceive the joins – only a fingertip can detect it, so fine is their crafts-manship.'

'Impressive,' Robert said, 'hugely impressive.'

William was poring over the map. 'This includes Novaya Zemlya – Barentz only returned late last year. It's much more up to date than the little thing we had on the *Swan* for that voyage.'

'Raleigh's discoveries in Guiana are included too,' Hugh said proudly, ignoring William's allusion to their failed quest. 'And off the coast of China – see that long island? The first time Corea has featured on a map.'

'I hear they've bought two for Oxford's libraries,' Nicholas piped up. 'Perhaps my college will follow suit.'

'Perhaps, dear brother, you could pay for it,' Florence muttered, mimicking Nicholas's fluttering, halting speech so quietly only Beatrice could hear.

'Be kind, sister,' Beatrice chided her.

Florence tilted her head so that her lace ruff hid the mischievous face she was pulling from everyone else. For a moment Beatrice felt a flicker of fond exasperation, and it was just the two of them sharing a moment of mirth that the rest of the world couldn't see. But laughing at the world had always been Florence's talent, never Beatrice's.

'And here you can see dozens of new place names added,' Hugh continued. 'Celebe, Borneo, Batachina –'

The door suddenly opened, and they all turned in surprise.

There stood Catalina in her scarlet gown. Shadows clustered under her eyes, but there was no other sign of the exhaustion and sickness that had confined her to her chamber for two days. If those were the real reasons, Beatrice thought, immediately chastening herself for such a Lady Penelope-esque judgement.

'Hugh's lovely guest!' William said loudly, as if volume could drown awkwardness. An odd way to address her, Beatrice thought: hadn't William been aboard the same ship as Catalina for as long as Hugh? 'You are looking well, Mistress Catalina.'

Catalina's dark eyes flicked to him, then away: a disdainful gesture.

'You know my brother Nicholas, and my brother-in-law, Robert Bristow,' Hugh said, choosing politeness as his method of quashing awkwardness. 'And you met my wife's half-sister, Florence, of course.'

She'd met them all. Hugh's introductions were wholly unnecessary and he knew it. No doubt he was embarrassed, Beatrice thought bitterly. The longer Catalina remained in their household, the more shameful it would be, for Hugh and for Beatrice.

'Hugh has been showing us his new globe,' Beatrice said. 'Would you like to see it?'

Catalina stepped forward, that backwards lean still present: Beatrice hadn't been mistaken. She halted a foot away from the globe, eyeing it with a strange expression. It might have been wistful longing, though for a moment Beatrice could have sworn it was distaste, even fear.

Florence took a step closer to Beatrice, as if flanking her defensively, and Beatrice felt instinctively grateful for her sister's loyalty. But somehow targeting Catalina left a sour taste in her mouth.

'Perhaps you could show us where you are from,' Florence said. 'I'm sure we'd all love to hear.'

Catalina's head whipped around, snake-fast. 'Why?' she said softly, and was her accent Spanish, or Portuguese, or from some newly-discovered country Beatrice couldn't even locate on Hugh's globe? 'So you can send me back?'

Did she want that? Or just want Beatrice and Florence to admit they hoped to get rid of her?

'Here,' said Hugh, 'why don't I show you where we are?' He moved forwards to stand beside Catalina, his legs touching her scarlet skirts as he guided her eyes to the illustration of England on his globe. Beatrice swallowed, trying to disguise it by taking a gulp of wine. Wasn't it bad enough that Catalina was carrying Hugh's bastard and staying in his wife's home, without him flaunting their liaison before her?

'Quite shameless,' Florence murmured, her tone almost marvelling. Her fingertips brushed Beatrice's waist, a gesture of sisterly solidarity. 'Poor Bea.'

But there was nothing brazen about Catalina now. She wasn't leaning closer to Hugh, but flinching back from the globe, retreating as if she shared Beatrice's discomfort at its presence.

'I had not realised,' Catalina said, sounding daunted, 'how vast the world truly is. How far I am …'

She was closer to Beatrice now than to Hugh, and as her scarlet skirts rustled against Beatrice's dark blue, she turned, and their eyes met.

Beatrice had to say it. Even if the words tasted like bile. She had to save face – and she had to be kind. She cleared her throat. 'This is your home, Catalina. For as long as you need or wish it.'

Catalina's lips parted – but whatever she was about to say was lost as a knock at the door was followed by Ridley entering to announce that dinner was ready.

As they all filed out, Beatrice fell to the back of the group: not her place, but she couldn't help wanting to see if Hugh and Catalina touched one another again. But it was William walking at her side, holding out an arm to usher a seemingly unenthusiastic Catalina through the door ahead of him; once again Beatrice saw how the woman flinched away from the touch of anyone who wasn't Hugh.

As Florence and Robert stepped through the door, it was Beatrice's turn to ensure she walked past Ridley without any such overt avoidance as Catalina's, or any semblance of awkwardness. Just as she drew level with him, still trying to decide where best to look, there was a sudden whirring noise behind her, like a blast of wind. Ridley's eyes flew up; Beatrice spun around.

The globe had turned on its axis. As they stared, it slowed before settling back into stillness. Beatrice had the strange sensation of being challenged, as if the thing had just performed a complicated sequence of dance steps, and was now waiting to see what she could do.

'The wind,' Ridley said, his usual calm ruffled.

'But the windows are all shut.'

'A draught from the corridor then. Or everyone's footsteps reverberating at once – or perhaps its axis is off balance.'

'That must be it,' Beatrice said, hoping she sounded convincing; she couldn't say anything to Ridley now without scrutinising her own voice for suspicious undertones and secret notes, intentional or not. But guilt wasn't the only reason she hurried away from the gallery.

5

'Beatrice!'

She almost dropped her quill at Hugh's shout: a spot of ink now marred her neat columns of figures, and she sighed in disappointment and apprehension. This wasn't a ship; it was a family home. There was no need to shout when a quiet word with a servant, or simply looking would ascertain her location, which was with a writing desk on her lap in their bedchamber. For the light, she'd told herself as she set up her accounts ledger. Not because the chamber she normally preferred was occupied by that giant globe.

'Beatrice!'

He sounded angry, and she gritted her teeth. What did he have to be angry about? Of the two of them, surely she had the greater grievance?

Hugh stormed in, flinging the door open so violently it bounced against the wall, rattling the nearest paintings. Glowering, he gestured curtly for her to join him. 'Come and explain this.'

'Hugh, can it not wait? Why the urgency? I'm occupied with –'

'With our accounts?' His frown darkened as he recognised the ledger. 'Why are you doing those? I'm back now – I can take charge of our finances again. Now come with me.'

What was the good of protesting that she enjoyed them? That completing their accounts gave her a satisfaction and pride that embroidering gloves and playing the virginals never could. That handing her ledgers over to Hugh felt like she was putting a blindfold on and trusting him to lead her to the destination she hoped he'd chosen.

'Of course, husband.' She closed the book, tidied the writing desk, and rose.

'Come on!'

I am not a hound to be called to heel, she wanted to snap – but eleven years of marriage had taught her that not all battles were worth fighting.

He led her down the stairs, along the corridor; she knew already where he was taking her and tried to quash the urge to turn and run. Besides, he'd taken hold of her hand, his grip so strong one of her rings was crushed against her knuckle: she couldn't have fled.

'Hugh, you're hurting me!'

He looked at her in surprise. 'How am I hurting you? In here.'

Did he really have no awareness of his own strength? Or no aware-ness of her body's weakness? Her slipper caught on the Turkey carpet and she stumbled as they approached the globe. She almost had to clutch at the wooden frame for support with her free hand, and horror made her veer away, so she collapsed against Hugh.

Why was she being such a fool? She was no squeamish girl – spiders and worms had never frightened her; owl shrieks and whistling winds didn't make her start and flee from ghosts in the night. It was only a globe, for heaven's sake, just wood and paper.

And yet.

'Did the children do this?'

'Do what?'

He gestured curtly, so stiff with rage she wondered if he was restrain-ing himself from thrusting her forward to see what he was pointing at.

Beatrice swallowed. She hadn't been this close to the globe before. Close to, the colours were far richer, the details more intricate than she'd realised. Why, you could see the fur on that poor bear caught in the cockatrice's scaled tail, even the beast's scales and claws.

But Hugh wasn't pointing at the bear. He indicated a figure near England, drawn just below the Isle of Wight. A woman's back and shoulders emerging from blue waters, her black hair curling over brown skin.

'The mermaid?'

'She hasn't got a tail,' Hugh said tersely, sounding like Walter correcting their faulty knowledge of whatever that month's current obsession was. 'Besides, she wasn't in the original plans.'

'The artist probably changed his mind – sketches and final paintings are never identical.'

Hugh shook his head. 'I swear, she's been added. And how could the artist have known about –'

Catalina. Beatrice stared at Hugh, then the painting in horror, where a line of red could be glimpsed above the water, like the slipped neckline of a crimson gown. Catalina, half-naked, displayed in the globe commissioned by Hugh, displayed in their house. As if it wasn't insulting enough already.

But hadn't Catalina herself backed away from the globe yesterday? She'd claimed to be overwhelmed by its vastness, but was that the real reason?

'The children were talking about drawing on the globe yesterday,' Hugh said. 'You encouraged them.'

'*We* encouraged them,' she corrected him, though she was fairly certain Hugh had been the source of all enthusiasm. 'In any case, have you seen your children's drawings? I'm afraid eight months haven't wrought miracles with their artistic talents. If Walter had drawn this, there'd be blood everywhere and she'd be covered in giant claws and breathing fire like that cockatrice. As for Ursula, when she draws people, their heads are enormous, their hands look like bunches of sausages, and their hair is usually purple!'

'I'll take your word for it,' Hugh said grimly. 'Of course, your penmanship skills are quite extensive, aren't they?'

She stared at him, silenced by outrage.

'Is this because I wouldn't tell you everything about her? For God's sake, Beatrice, can't you just trust me? Or if that's too onerous and outlandish for you, can you at least afford poor Catalina some privacy?'

'Privacy! She has her own bedchamber in my house. My mother's bedroom. I haven't questioned you about her since that first night – and God knows, Hugh, most wives in my position would have demanded answers from you every hour of every day!'

'She needs protection, Beatrice! Would you have me throw her out onto the streets? Would you have me be responsible for the fate that would expose her to? If she were lucky she'd end up in a Southwark brothel with half her teeth missing!'

'There are worlds between falling into harlotry and becoming the honoured companion of the woman whose husband's bastard you're carrying!'

Her accusation hung between them, rank and unignorable, like the odour of rushes left too long and now mouldering. Too late to call the words back.

Hugh stared at her, hurt and disappointment raw in his grey eyes. 'I promised you this wasn't what you think. It's nice to know how little worth you afford my vows.'

'What else am I supposed to think?' Beatrice pointed out, struggling to mask her resentful tone. 'You won't tell me the truth.'

'Believe me, you should be grateful for that,' he said grimly. 'I asked you to trust me, Beatrice. Is that so difficult?'

'I might ask you the same thing,' she retorted, 'since you were so swift to accuse me of vandalising your precious new toy.'

'It's hardly a *toy* –'

'No, of course,' she snapped. 'I know exactly what it is. Instead of comparing codpieces with Raleigh and Essex, you're now trying to outdo one another with your splendid navigational instruments. Why don't you just see who can piss the furthest off our barge and be done with it?'

Hugh's lips thinned. 'I expect better from you, Beatrice. I'd hoped you were above such vulgarity. Perhaps you spent too much of your childhood among the fishwives on the docks.'

How dared he fling that in her face – when he lived in the house her merchant forebears had built? Beatrice almost spat her riposte. 'This from a man who spends more time with foul-mouthed sailors than with his own family?'

'You think I want to be away from you for so long? I do it because I must!'

'No – you do it because you want to be a hero! You want to be as revered as Drake, as admired as Raleigh.'

'I want,' Hugh said coldly, 'to have a wife who respects, trusts and loves me. Is that too much to ask?'

Beatrice flung up her hands, half-despairing, half-reaching for him, as if a touch could pull them back to peace. 'Of course I love you, Hugh – you're being ridiculous!'

'There,' he said, nodding bitterly. 'Only one of the three.'

He turned and stalked away. She knew better than to ask where he was going. But for the first time in their married life, she didn't know him well enough to guess.

The chamber was silent. The air still seemed to shudder with the tremors from their argument, and even her frayed breath felt like shouting in a cathedral.

Behind her, the globe lurked. Squat and bulbous as a toad: she felt stained by its presence, as if slime and venom had leaked onto her hands and skirt.

It had to be a trick of the light. But if she hadn't known any better, she would have sworn it was rocking slightly from side to side. As if it were holding in a mocking laugh.

Outside All Saints, the wind had picked up, rattling the autumn leaves covering the graves in the churchyard and bullying the last red scraps from the trees. Beatrice already felt battered after the minister's admonitory sermon, warning wives to submit to their husbands' authority lest they be punished – particularly if they were tempted to keep secrets. But how could she tell Hugh the truth after so long?

She'd burned the note before Hugh had even joined her on the barge at Whitehall, thrusting it into the nearest brazier. But its words were still branded on her mind.

Your secrets are known. You deserve all that is coming.

Another blast of wind yanked at her cloak, pulling down the hood she'd just raised. They had planned to spend the afternoon on the barge; it would be a chilly sailing if this kept up. She'd speak to Ridley about ensuring there was plenty of spiced cider and mulled wine aboard; perhaps it was time to start heating bricks before bed again.

Hugh and William were striding ahead of her towards the waiting horses, Nicholas trying to keep pace. How long were those two going to stay? There'd been talk of William finally arranging lodgings of his own closer to the heart of the city before they'd last sailed, but she'd been so distracted by Catalina's unwanted presence she'd barely noticed that this seemed to have fallen by the wayside; meanwhile Nicholas seemed in no hurry to return to Heralds' College. Lingering by the lychgate were Florence and Robert, and experience had taught Beatrice her sister wouldn't be about to invite her and Hugh to dine at their home; no doubt they wanted the barge sailing to extend until dinnertime. When was the last time they'd spent an evening in the same house as their five daughters, never mind actually in the same room?

'Madam?'

Beatrice turned to see Maria hovering behind her, shifting from foot to foot in the cold. 'What is it?'

'It's …' Maria hesitated, glancing over her shoulder. 'It might be nothing. But …'

'Is something wrong?'

Maria swallowed. Her brown skin was glistening; was she feverish?

'Are you quite well, Maria?' Beatrice put out a hand to Maria's forehead; even through her kid gloves, she could tell Maria wasn't hot, but clammy.

'It's the messenger, madam.' Maria glanced over her shoulder again, and it was Beatrice's turn to shiver.

'Come.' Beatrice tucked Maria's arm in hers and set off towards the lychgate. 'Did he come back? Is there another note?'

Maria shook her head. 'He was here.'

'I thought you didn't see his face – was he wearing his hat in church?'

Maria halted suddenly. 'I can't – might we speak of this later, madam?'

They'd reached the lychgate and Beatrice's waiting family. Beatrice squeezed Maria's hand, grateful for her discretion, even when she was clearly in a state of anxiety. 'Of course. Before dinner?'

Maria bit her lip and nodded. Her tooth came away tipped in red: she'd gnawed her lip bloody.

Beatrice knew why she had cause for fear. But Maria had always been a figure of calmness, steady and staunch as an oak tree, for as long as Beatrice could remember. And after her first encounter with the messenger, Maria had been sanguine, if a little unsettled. So why had this encounter made her shiver uncontrollably?

She'd been right to order spiced wine: a bitter wind snaked down the Thames, forcing the torch flames to stagger. The river itself seemed to breathe a chill into the air, all those unseen depths murmuring darkly as their barge cut through the inked surface. Beatrice was glad she'd donned her lambswool-lined boots; the elegant silver slippers she'd worn all summer would need to be put away until next year, or at least saved for indoor gatherings. Thank goodness she'd made sure there were plenty of blankets around: Beatrice burrowed her toes into sheepskin, bringing her wine close to her face so the steam cupped her cheeks. Beside her, Florence was swaddled in so many layers she reminded Beatrice of the baby she'd once been, right down to the little hand fighting its way free, although this time Florence was gripping a glass of wine rather than the nearest lock of hair.

At the prow, Hugh stood talking with his brother, their silhouettes almost evenly broad for once: Nicholas's shoulders had none of Hugh's strength, but he was bundled up in a marten cloak, whereas Hugh wore only a lightweight cape of embroidered velvet.

'You'd have thought he'd feel the cold,' Florence said enviously, 'after months of warmer lands.'

'He never does,' Beatrice said. 'Even the Azores must be cold at night. And wind and water are always cold, so after all these years he's used to it.'

'Perhaps.' Florence sipped her wine thoughtfully. 'Of course, after that voyage north, I imagine even a frozen Thames might feel balmy to Hugh. Even the thought of what they endured makes me shiver.'

As Florence gave a dramatic illustration of her horror, Beatrice turned away. If Florence knew the truth of what had happened on that failed expedition to the Russias, she wouldn't be behaving like a performer in a masque.

'I thought we might see Catalina tonight,' Florence continued with a sigh. 'I so want to hear her tales of wherever it is she hails from.'

'She's not a dancing bear,' Beatrice retorted. 'You can't demand she perform for your entertainment.'

Florence's eyebrows arched in amusement. 'Hark at you defending the harlot.'

'We don't know that she is a harlot,' Beatrice objected, wondering herself why she was speaking up for the woman carrying her husband's child. Perhaps it was simply the atavistic urge to disagree with Florence at every opportunity.

Florence sniffed. 'Unless a husband strolls off the next ship from the Azores, the woman's a whore. Has Hugh no idea of the shame he's brought on your house by instilling his mistress under your roof?'

'Clearly my house isn't so shamed that you'll refuse our hospitality. Don't forget, Florence, my husband is a knight, and yours a merchant.'

Beatrice regretted the words immediately. Florence turned to her, eyes glittering in the torchlight – tears or rage?

'Merchant or knight, he has hurt you, Bea! I thought you'd be grateful that I'm taking your side!' She wrenched the furs off her lap and gathered up her skirts. 'I didn't think you'd repay my loyalty by reminding me of the differences in our stations.'

Beatrice had always tried to avoid reminding Florence that it was Beatrice's mother's inheritance that had enriched their father, whereas all Florence's mother had brought to her marriage was a pretty face and empty promises to bear a son. A promise Florence, with her five daughters, had also failed to fulfil – and what was there to be gained from such cruelty? She opened her mouth, and the apology she couldn't find words for emerged as white mist. Florence was already stalking away, rigid with hurt, forced to halt at the railing and talk to the husband she'd found tedious and disappointing almost since their wedding day.

Beatrice leaned back against the cushions, gazing up at the stars beyond the gold-tasselled canopy. So often she'd eyed Florence's marriage with pity, secretly congratulating herself on winning a handsome, successful husband whom she actually loved. But Catalina's arrival – and that stupid moment with Ridley – had forced Beatrice to confront her own satisfaction. She'd had a husband who was away for months every year, and who, when he was actually in

London, exasperated her as often as he delighted her – and that was in a year when he hadn't brought a strange pregnant woman into their home. Was her marriage truly any better than Florence's? Or was it Hugh's lengthy absence that allowed them the delusion that they were happy?

A thud startled her out of her reverie: with a tangle of long limbs, a precariously sloshing glass, and a groaning laugh, William joined her below the canopy.

'Forgive me, aunt, but delightful as these cushions all are, I swear my knees will creak louder than the Tower cannon when I try to stand up again.'

'Nonsense,' she reproached him. 'You're fourteen years younger than I am – if your knees creak like cannon fire, mine must sound like the Day of Judgement.'

Another man might have flattered her, called her a beauty as ageless as she was peerless. But William wanted to win the debate. 'Ah, but your knees haven't been exposed to howling gales or Arctic winters. You haven't braced against a tipping deck, or clung to a rigging the wind and waves are determined to rip out of your hands.'

And you, she thought, haven't carried three children for nine months apiece. But to most men, pregnancy was hidden beneath velvet skirts, of no interest to them unless their own sons were growing, and besides, what could women possibly have to complain about, since babies were born every day? Perhaps she ought to lash a cannonball to William's midriff and make him lug it around all day and all night, and then see what state his knees were in.

'No indeed,' she said calmly. 'Your bravery never ceases to astonish me.'

'If mine astonishes you, what of Hugh's?' William reached past her for the decanter of spiced wine, refilling his glass.

Beatrice held hers out pointedly: was it not enough that their relatives ate and drank endlessly at her and Hugh's expense without them being rude about it? 'Hugh rarely tells me of the dangers he encounters. I hear about beaches as white as shark teeth and trees with strange shaped leaves, not deadly peril.'

William laughed. 'Typical Hugh. He never shows anyone his own fear. The ship could be a breath away from capsizing, waves battering her like siege towers, and Hugh will be the only one aboard not crying out to mother or God. I swear, I've only once seen his face go white, and that was …'

He fell silent, and Beatrice knew exactly what he was remembering. 'Novaya Zemlya,' she said quietly.

William glanced up at her, then back at the depths of his wine. 'Aye.' He tossed his wine back, and the unsinkable grin swam out of it. 'I tell you, Hugh's the sort of captain I aim to be.'

'You're ready to leave the *Silver Swan?*' She made her voice sound enthusiastic, silencing the other question: *And how precisely do you intend to pay for this ship of your own?*

'Soon,' he said eagerly. 'I've been navigating Hugh's voyages for five years, and I reckon I've learned near all he has to teach me. A helm and deck of my own, that's what I want.'

'A noble goal,' she said, trying not to sound as sardonic as she wished. 'And where will you sail?'

'Anywhere no one has gone before!' He refilled his glass again. 'Hugh's globe is a wonder, but it has gaps – so many gaps! And I have so much desire to fill them.'

'Gaps Drake and Frobisher and Hawkins failed to complete?' And Radclyffe, of course, but she wouldn't insult Hugh before his excitable, ambitious nephew: for all his praise of Hugh, she knew William's hero worship was the sort that seeks to topple statues, not polish them.

'I'm an exceptional navigator,' William said, without a hint of modesty. 'I doubt there's a man alive who knows more about the stars than I do.'

Beatrice lifted an eyebrow. 'A certain Doctor Dee might contest that assertion. Or across the channel, Tycho Brahe, or Nils Hemmingsen.'

'Old men in dusty robes with ink-stained noses?' William shook his head. 'They don't know the stars the way a sailor does. Charts with black dots and scrawled letters are no substitute for standing on a ship's deck in the middle of the ocean, blackness above you and all around, looking to the stars for the right path, trusting them to help you make a choice that will keep a hundred men alive. Until you've seen the waves glitter silver with constellations and looked up through vast nothingness to those pinpricks of light, you know nothing of the stars.'

Beatrice couldn't help following his gaze and looking up. Beyond the tassels, there were the stars, cold and remote as the queen's diamonds. If she squinted, she could pick out patterns – but they were childish things, scarcely more meaningful than when Walter and Ursula lay on their backs and pointed out cats and deer and jousting knights in the clouds. Hugh had told her the names of some constellations years ago, lifting her hand in his so their entwined fingers traced the stars in Andromeda, Cassiopeia, Orion. But she could no more have navigated her way by those names than she could by the myths they recalled. They were stories, romanticised and glittering with ancient distance. They had no practical meaning in the life of Beatrice Radclyffe.

'Perhaps we know nothing of the stars,' Beatrice said softly. 'But there's nothing so humbling as looking at those stars and realising you know nothing of the world at all. That the world could not be less interested in your ignominious ignorance.'

'Perhaps that's how a woman might perceive them,' William said with kind condescension; she wanted to pitch him overboard. 'But I don't look at the stars and think myself ignominious. I see them and I aspire to command them. One day, every celestial globe ever crafted will display my maps of the heavens, and they will never be surpassed.'

But never was a long time, and perhaps the first man to reach the mouth of the Thames had imagined his journey would never be bettered. And perhaps his wife had been toiling at home, children clustered around her ankles, throat hoarse from scolding and cook-smoke, thinking that unless the river mouth was a-glitter with coins, she'd get far more use out of a husband at home to mend the blocked chimney.

'Well,' Beatrice said dryly, 'I shall advise Nicholas's college to clear a vast space in their library for all your marvellous globes.'

'Why would I keep them in a library?' William shook his head. 'For schoolboys' noses to drip on, and dull old men to croak over? No, my globes will be for sailors. For men of action, not those who sit back, content to let us face all the danger.'

'Have you told Hugh that?' Beatrice asked, anxious: might Hugh listen to William where he would not heed his wife? The chance to get that hulking globe out of her house was too enticing.

'Not yet,' William said. 'But when I do, shall I ensure Uncle Nicholas is within earshot?'

'If you don't fear a scholar's wrath – isn't the pen mightier than the sword?'

'Not when wielded by weak monkish men like Nicholas.' William laughed, too gleefully for Beatrice to feel comfortable joining in. 'Though I could probably fight him off with a quill without resorting to my sword.'

Beatrice eyed her husband's nephew, searching for the slightest hint of self-awareness, of self-deprecation, and finding nothing. 'Be careful, William,' she said gently. 'You will not be young forever.'

'Of course not,' he retorted. 'But I need just the one chance. I won't waste my youth.'

They were all hungry by the time the barge returned, the cold winds making them even more eager for the promised venison pie, all imagining breaking into the golden lid, crumbling whatever elaborate images of ships or compasses had been carefully embossed on the pastry, seeking the rich meat and dark juices beneath. Beatrice was shivering, cold inside as well as out, the spiced wine having long cooled, while Nicholas and Robert's voices echoed too far and too long over the water, both men having endeavoured to stave off the cold by drinking endlessly. Even Hugh was blowing on his fingers and pulling his cloak around both shoulders rather than letting it drape rakishly over one.

'Why have we stopped?'

Beatrice started at Florence's tetchy demand. They'd paused barely three yards from the wharf: she could see the copper glow from her dining room, smell the pie they were all aching for. 'Is all well? Are the ropes tangled?'

Hugh strode to the railing, peering at the oarsmen. 'What's amiss?'

One of them looked up at him hesitantly. 'There's – there's something in the water, sir.'

'What?' Hugh leaned over, peering. But the torchlight flinched with every ripple of the Thames, as if trying to evade the shadows. 'Where?'

'There, sir.' Ridley was on the wharf, crouching down, his frown stiffening into concern. 'Get the oars up – get them away from her!'

'Sweet Jesus,' Florence breathed, clutching at Beatrice's arm.

'Is that a woman?' Robert blurted out. 'What's the silly jade doing in the water at this hour?'

'Shut up, Robert,' Florence hissed.

'Hugh!' Beatrice gasped, suddenly shrill. 'For God's sake, get her out!'

For she could see her now, face down in the water, dark curls bleeding into the blackened water, her brown shoulders burnished bronze in the torchlight, her red dress swelling around her like a vast, bloated mouth.

Just as she had appeared on the globe. Not swimming, not caught in the act of seduction, not standing in the water at all – but face down, drowned.

Hugh leapt off the barge, crashing through the shallows, swearing at the reeds tangling around his boots. He waded to the woman and grabbed her, hauling her over. 'Ridley, take her shoulders!'

Together, Hugh and Ridley dragged the body onto the bank, even their strength buckling under the weight of soaked skirts.

'Is she breathing?' Beatrice called, already knowing it was hopeless.

Hugh was crouched low, tipping the woman on to her side, thumping between her shoulder blades, then rolling her back and thrusting his clasped hands against her chest. Over Hugh's shoulder, Ridley met Beatrice's eyes and he shook his head. And then it seemed somehow far worse to see two men hunkered low beside a half-naked woman, as if it wasn't terrible enough that Catalina was dead but she must also lose her dignity, her privacy along with her life.

'Cover her up,' Beatrice ordered. 'For pity's sake, cover her.'

Ridley untied his cloak. He was about to drape it over the body when Hugh pushed the tangled black hair back from the woman's face – and Beatrice stared in horror.

It wasn't Catalina lying murdered on the riverbank with a necklace of purple bruises around her throat.

It was Maria.

6

Water slopped over the basin's edges, rippling coldly against the silver as Beatrice set it gingerly down on the table. She folded and refolded the linen in her hands, trying to get the corners perfectly aligned, to smooth away the creases her grip sent spidering through the white cloth. She'd always told herself rage was easier to manage than either grief or fear, but after the Justice of the Peace's visit, she was starting to doubt her own resolution.

He'd taken an hour to arrive, which might have been forgivable if he'd been attending some other murdered woman's body. But the gravy stain on his doublet hadn't yet congealed, and there were still pastry flakes in his beard, and Beatrice could have stabbed him there and then for deciding his dinner was more important than Maria, than the justice he'd been appointed to uphold. Yet that flash of anger was as nothing to the rage she felt by the time he'd left.

'You found her dressed like this?' he'd asked, eyeing Maria's half-exposed breasts rather too long for Beatrice's liking, and at Hugh's confirmation, he'd sighed. 'That makes the matter clearer at least. Did she have a particular lover, or was she … less discerning about the company she kept?'

'I beg your pardon?' Beatrice had hissed. 'Maria was an honourable woman.' And even if she hadn't been, why should that have made a difference? If one of the Winchester geese in the Southwark brothels was found murdered, it was still murder, just as it would have been if a duchess was killed.

The justice had smiled condescendingly. 'I know you will not wish to speak ill of the dead. But we must look at the evidence. The marks on her neck, her shoulders – these speak of passion gone awry. I hate to be so crude before a woman, but there we have it. An amorous encounter, a little too much enthusiasm, and her panic-stricken lover flees into the night. A name would be most hopeful …'

'This is nonsense!' Beatrice had cried. 'She's been slain, not seduced!'

Hugh had given a slight cough. 'There are some men and women who enjoy such roughness.'

She'd rounded on him, eyes blazing. 'You cannot possibly agree with this! You know Maria –'

'My darling, I wish I did.' He spread his hands placatingly, as if approaching a bridling horse. 'But I'm away for so much of the year, and in any case, I have little to do with the female servants in our house.'

'Hugh, listen!' She'd swallowed, ready to tell him about the note. 'She was afraid. There was a man dressed all in black –'

'There!' the justice had sighed. 'Clearly a blackguard if he'd frightened her before. Don't suppose you know his name?'

'I didn't even see his face – he wore a hat and scarf.'

'Pity.' The justice had donned his own hat. 'Well, if you do recall anything further, let me know. But in my experience a man who kills his lover is unlikely to pose much danger to the rest of society – unless of course he has many lovers!' And he'd chuckled as he sauntered to the door, clearly already thinking about the pudding he'd order in the nearest tavern.

Hugh hadn't seemed to grasp her fury. 'It's a terrible loss, my darling, but we cannot bring her back. We can only give her a decent burial.'

'Or bring her killer to justice!' she'd retorted. But he'd already drifted away towards the gallery, no doubt to caress his beloved globe by the firelight.

Beatrice dropped her linen in the water and steeled herself. The least she could do was ready Maria for burial. Florence had gone home, white-faced and shuddering, and Beatrice had sent the servants away: this was her task. After all, if she'd listened to Maria after church – was it only that morning? – perhaps Maria would still be alive.

Why had she been so afraid? Why hadn't Beatrice asked more questions instead of hurrying to her waiting family?

Her hands were trembling again. Hauling in a breath, Beatrice raised her eyes to the body.

The torchlight should have made Maria's skin look warm, like burnished copper. But all it could do was cast a yellow veil over dulled dead flesh, making Maria look gangrenous, not glowing. As for the bruises around her neck, their purple blotches looked like plague sores. How could anyone look at that brutality and imagine a lover had inflicted them? Or was she being hopelessly naïve? As Hugh had said, some people liked roughness – and Beatrice, who had only once left London in her entire life, knew nothing of what tastes were considered natural in Spain, or the Azores, or Novaya Zemlya – or even Exeter. Perhaps Hugh liked such things. When he bit her lip in the middle of a kiss, when he clutched her hips as he thrust into her, was that in fact not pleasure in itself, but merely the prelude to what he wanted to do? What he perhaps had done with Catalina?

Catalina, who also owned a bright red dress, who also had black curling hair and dark skin.

Beatrice shook her head. *Maria.* She owed it to Maria to think of her now. Gently, she began to wash her maid's body, starting with Maria's right hand. A hand that could turn dry, grey-flecked brown hair into an elaborate, gleaming coiffure, more intricate and beautiful than the carved wooden panels Beatrice had seen at Whitehall. A hand that could soothe a feverish child, untangle delicate silver necklaces in moments, paint a sleep-deprived face so your complexion looked smooth, dewy, invigorated.

But all of those things were about Beatrice, not Maria. What had Maria done when she wasn't waiting on Beatrice, when she had a moment to herself? She'd had family in Lambeth at one time, though her father and grandfather were both dead. Was her mother still alive? Ought Beatrice to send word?

She should have already known. Should have realised Maria was a woman, not merely a maid. A woman who could love, and laugh. Who could be afraid, and vulnerable, and alone, and hurt – and murdered.

'May I help you?'

Beatrice started, almost spilling the water again as she whirled around.

Catalina stood before her, in ivory, not red, thank goodness, her hands loosely folded in front of her belly. The door was already closed behind her: how had she entered so silently?

'Did you not hear?' Beatrice snapped. 'I sent everyone away.'

'You did.' Catalina inclined her head, infuriatingly calm. 'Even so, I would like to offer my help.'

'Why?'

Catalina took a step forward. 'We women often insist on pushing others away so we can grieve alone. As if there's dignity, or safety in that. But in my experience … it helps to have someone else nearby.'

She could have asked *what experience? Who did you lose?* But she couldn't bring herself to care.

'Besides,' Catalina continued, 'she was kind to me, though I could have been kinder to her. And few people have treated me kindly since I set foot on your husband's ship.'

Few. Which surely meant someone else had been kind to her. And if that person were Hugh … Beatrice couldn't bear to hear it, not now.

'Very well. Help then.'

Catalina dipped a hand into a pocket. 'I'll comb out her hair, if you agree. Your English combs are not kind to hair such as hers. As mine.' She drew out a comb and a glass bottle. 'I always use almond oil.'

'She liked almonds,' Beatrice said, surprised and relieved to have remembered. 'Sugared ones, or mixed into little cakes, especially when raspberries were in season.'

Catalina smiled and moved to the table. Gently she lifted Maria's head and spread out her hair in a black fan. 'I knew a little girl once who liked such treats. An almond mixture and raspberries in golden pastry, dusted with sugar. I never saw such sticky fingers – or had such cause to regret not wiping them before she touched her hair. Such tangles! Such screams!'

'Maria ought to have been there – she could have unravelled the tangles without provoking so much as a yelp, let alone a scream.'

'A talented woman.'

'Yes.' Beatrice looked away from Catalina's hands, now working oil through Maria's hair. What was she doing, sharing intimacies of any kind with her husband's mistress? Why was Catalina coaxing them out of her? Gritting her teeth, she returned to washing Maria's body, cleaning the river mud and shreds of weed from her arms and shoulders.

'Tell me,' Catalina said quietly as they worked, 'does this happen often here? To women?'

Beatrice shook her head. 'Certainly not. Although …' She remembered the Justice of the Peace, how indifferent he had seemed. 'Some women are perhaps more vulnerable to it. The Justice of the Peace assumed, because her gown was pulled down, that Maria was a … a …'

'A whore?' Catalina picked up her comb as if it were a dagger and the air the Justice's throat. 'I see. And do English men often make such assumptions about women like Maria? About women like me?'

I made such an assumption about you, Beatrice thought, unable to halt the blush creeping up her neck. How could she be so angry about the Justice assuming Maria was a whore, when she herself had made the same assumption about Catalina? Though not all assumptions were wrong. And Catalina was pregnant, and brought into Beatrice's house by her own husband under a cloud of secrecy. It wasn't the same.

Beatrice concentrated on a stubborn green stain beneath Maria's collarbone. There was a strange mark below the bruise just next to it: two sharp lines of blood, too straight for fingernails to have left them, and a cluster of scores and arcs inside the lines, almost like the corner of a drawing. 'There are some men who assume such things about all women.'

'There are some such women too.'

If it had been meant to hurt, it did: Beatrice lifted her head in guilty anger, ready to lash out. But Catalina wasn't looking at her, only calmly, gently working the comb through Maria's curls.

'Perhaps ignorance is to blame,' Beatrice said tautly. 'Which is only a sin if you deliberately choose to remain ignorant.'

'Not everyone knows themselves to be ignorant.' She might have been talking about almond oil and comb teeth again for all the blandness in her voice.

'Clearly you aren't among the ignorant – you speak English remark-ably well.'

Catalina burst out laughing. 'Almost as if I'd been born in England, you mean? Or married to an Englishman?'

Beatrice lifted her head in stubborn defiance. 'Well? Were you? Are you?'

Catalina lifted a tangle, slowly teasing strands out of knots. 'Would it make a difference? Would you no longer wish to be rid of me, if you knew I had as much right to be here as anyone?'

Was that affirmation or denial – or just evasion and provocation?

'You are a guest in my house, Catalina. The least you could do is tell me the truth.'

'A guest, is it?' Catalina kissed her teeth disdainfully. 'I wonder what the difference is in this house, between a guest and a prisoner.'

'How dare you?' Beatrice hissed. 'After the hospitality we've offered –'

Catalina gave a quiet laugh. 'Perhaps, Lady Radclyffe, it is you who chooses to be ignorant. Either that, or you're too much of a fool to know your own ignorance.'

Beatrice bridled – then caught herself. She couldn't fight with this woman beside Maria's corpse – as the mistress of the house she shouldn't lower herself to fight with anyone. Instead, she gripped her emotions as tight as the leashes of baying hounds, and said coldly, 'Do you know, when I saw her in the water in that red dress, I thought it was you.'

Catalina finally met her eyes. 'Do you wish it had been?'

'Given a choice between you, an interloper, and my loyal maid, a woman I've known all my life? Yes!'

'What refreshing honesty.' Catalina tilted her head. 'Has it occurred to you that whoever killed Maria might have shared your wish?'

Beatrice stared. 'You mean – they mistook Maria for you?'

Catalina shrugged. 'To many English folk, I imagine Maria and I look as alike as two cows in a field – if you troubled to pay attention, the differences would be plain enough, not least the twenty years or so between us. But why trouble at all over a blackamoor woman?'

Beatrice wanted to retort, to distance herself from the sort of people tarred by Catalina's brush. But hadn't she just confessed to confusing the two women? Even if Maria had been face down and the night dark, that was no excuse: she should have known her own maid. And if she didn't wish to blame ignorance, she could only blame her own spite: she'd wanted Catalina dead.

Beatrice swallowed. 'Who would wish to kill you?'

Catalina held her gaze with uncomfortable candour. 'Among others … you, I imagine. Though I suspect you wouldn't sully your own hands.'

Beatrice felt a sudden sharp pain: uncurling her fists, she saw her fingernails had carved lurid crescents in her palms. For a moment she saw torn skin, scored white and tattered red, blood beading around broken fingernails. Then she yanked herself back to the stillroom, to the broken body before her. Drawing herself up, she said, 'If neither common courtesy nor basic gratitude can induce you to speak to me with respect, you will at least have a care for the dead. Do not disrupt Maria's peace.'

Catalina took up the comb again. 'Of course. But she's got more hope of peace than any of us still living.' She pulled a shred of weed out of Maria's hair. 'A murderer came into your grounds, Lady Radclyffe, and killed someone close to you, who looked like me. We have as much chance of peace as Spaniards do when your husband ambushes their settlements.'

'What?'

Catalina shook her head. 'You've made it clear you don't like listening to me. Ask your husband. Ask his nephew. Ask what they really do on their voyages, and whether they truly believe they deserve to be welcomed back as heroes.'

The house was quiet when Beatrice left the stillroom: she'd heard midnight tolled not long since. Catalina had made her excuses about an hour ago: less out of awkwardness and more, Beatrice suspected, because she was at the stage of pregnancy where her hips and back would complain vociferously if she stood for too long, to say nothing of her need to find a chamber pot. Beatrice had remained, sewing Maria's shroud closed, moonlight and candlelight not enough to prevent her eyes aching as she forced herself to keep the stitches small and even: Maria wouldn't have tolerated careless sewing in her own work, so Beatrice's stitches had to be neat enough for Maria's standards.

The torches had all been extinguished: Ridley would have known she'd be irritated if he'd left them burning just so she didn't have to go to bed in the dark. A candle was quite enough.

Or perhaps Hugh had ordered them to be put out. She'd almost forgotten that someone else could give orders in this house – that his orders would, in fact, take precedence over hers. Somehow that made the idea of Hugh having gone to bed while Beatrice had been laying out Maria's body utterly infuriating.

Her footsteps tutted against the oak floorboards, as if echoing her irritation. Somewhere in the gardens an owl called out, and Beatrice flinched; the candle wavered, sending spiked shadow and copper flailing against the tapestries. Supposed to keep the corridors warm, now the embroidered faces twisted and leered, the darkness contorting pale limbs, transforming vines into serpents, white horses into skeletal monsters.

And then she heard it.

A soft whirring, like breathing, like purring. As if something had awoken – or had been awake all this time.

It was coming from the gallery.

The door was ajar: a silver splinter of moonlight jutted into the corridor. Why had it been left open? Had a draught dislodged it – did the catch need repairing? She'd have to speak to Ridley in the morning, Beatrice told herself, trying to ground herself in the mundane, the essential.

But then the noise came again. And it changed. The smoothness ceased and became a rattling, like knucklebones someone refused to throw, only shaking and shaking until their opponents' very teeth felt loosened and jarred.

At the door, Beatrice hesitated. Surely the rattling was a prelude to silence: it would stop soon. But it was getting louder, more frantic – frenzied, even.

Don't be foolish, she told herself. Even Ursula wouldn't be so silly.

And yet her breath juddered as she stepped into the gallery.

The globe was turning. Spinning, faster and faster, as if thrust onwards by invisible hands. A sharp wind, Beatrice thought – although all the windows were closed. Had someone pushed it?

'Hello?' she called, hating her own hesitancy, her voice's thinness. 'Walter, are you out of bed?'

No one answered. The globe spun on, its rattling now a staccato cackling. Beatrice's skirts rasped on the carpet as she hurried across the room. As she reached out, she swallowed a searing wave of revulsion, as if she were about to touch a corpse writhing with maggots. Hesitantly, she pressed her palm to the globe's surface, forcing it to a halt.

She felt heat. Not mere parchment, but heat. As if the blue rivers and black meridians and scarlet voyage routes were veins, pulsing, throbbing. Warning.

Instantly, she snatched her hand away, glancing at her palm, almost expecting to see it bloodstained or scalded. But it was unmarked. Of course her skin was unmarked – it was just a globe made of parchment and wood and ink, nothing more. She gave the instrument a scathing look, the sort she delivered to incompetent tradesmen – and then froze.

She'd almost forgotten the image. The picture Hugh hadn't commissioned, the one he'd accused first the children and then Beatrice of scrawling onto his precious globe. The picture of a brown-skinned, black-haired woman in the water.

Beatrice peered closer. She'd thought the woman was a mermaid, rising seductively from the water – but in this light, from this angle, the woman could just as easily be lying face down. Be drowning – or already dead.

And then she saw something that nearly made her drop the candle in horror.

On the woman's neck, exposed by artfully draped curls, was a mark, so tiny you'd never see it unless your face were almost touching the globe. Crimson lines and curves, a mark like the corner of a painting, and exactly like the bloodied mark etched into Maria's neck.

7

Beatrice and Ridley took the horse ferry from Westminster. They had ridden in near-silence from Chelsea: Ridley always took his cue from Beatrice, judging when to speak and when to stay quiet by her speech or silence. Even if she hadn't been exhausted from laying out Maria's body, and more unsettled than she'd ever admit aloud by the globe spinning in the moonlight so that she'd barely slept, their journey to Lambeth deserved a solemn hush, not idle chatter. Not that the rest of London seemed to notice: the wherries flitted across the river, busy as bluebottles, while the ferryman regaled several other passengers with a ribald story about an occasion when the Earl of Essex had crossed the river with a lady not his wife. Beatrice tried not to listen, or to imagine how eager Hugh would have been to hear any talk of courtiers. Instead she watched the grey water unfurl past the sides of the ferry, tattering like old cobwebs, and pressed her cheek against her mare's neck, feeling the heat flowing beneath her chestnut coat, the veins throbbing as her mare snorted and shied, disturbed by the ferry's motion.

She'd been leaning against her mare's neck in the stables that evening when Ridley had entered. Less than a fortnight ago, and yet it seemed like a lifetime. Or was that merely wishful thinking, a futile hope to distance herself from her mistakes?

He hadn't seen her at first: instead he'd gone straight to the grey palfrey who'd had colic two nights before, and murmured softly to her, running his hands over her flanks and belly, and Beatrice had noticed for the first time how broad his hands were, how strong. She'd always thought of Ridley as slight, but in the soft orange fragment of sunset that set the stables aglow, she'd realised that was false: his sober black clothes, his quiet manner all made him take up less space than the other men she knew. Than Hugh.

'With a touch like yours, I think you could tame the horses of the apocalypse,' Beatrice had said. 'War and Famine would stagger around uselessly while you charmed their mounts away.'

Ridley had whirled, his cheeks reddening almost as bright as the sky. 'Forgive me, madam, I didn't realise you were here.'

She'd shrugged. 'I am often here. I feel less lonely.'

He'd nodded sympathetically. 'It's been a long time. You must miss Master Radclyffe.'

And then she'd said it. The foolish, shameful, sluttish thing.

'Sometimes I am lonely even when he is here.'

She could hear Ridley now on the other side of her mare, talking softly to his horse, and she couldn't help leaning closer against her mare, pressing into the warmth, trying to make out what Ridley was whispering. She could remember the sudden warmth of him too. How his touch had felt – so different from the memory of Hugh, whose caresses flooded her senses, overwhelming her. How she was certain Ridley had moved first – and yet he'd been the one to jerk backwards, saying 'This isn't right'. As if she'd been the one to kiss him, immediately making Beatrice uncertain that Ridley had been the one reaching out to touch her hand, then her cheek, then her lips. Or perhaps she'd needed to tell herself that story.

'Rope ho!'

The ferryman's cry jolted her back: back to the grey waters and the smells of herring and cockles – and the miserable reality of the reason for their journey.

Ridley coaxed the horses down the ramp and onto the wharf; after he'd produced an apple apiece from his cloak pockets, the horses consented to be mounted and ridden through Lambeth. The air was rough with peat smoke, belching darkly from narrow chimneys; Beatrice, who managed her accounts ledgers so firmly that she always had funds to burn sea coal instead, felt a cough rising, and tried to swallow it back, feeling it would seem insulting to the Lambeth natives.

The streets weren't cobbled here, and the squelch of hooves through mud and ordure made Beatrice's stomach turn: it sounded too like the noise Maria's body had made when Hugh pulled her out of the river as the silt spat her ankles out.

'It's this one,' Ridley said, and she wondered if Ridley knew where everyone's family lived – not just Maria's, but the cooks and the maltsters and the stable boys. How he had known it was important to know these things, to ask people about their families, as if such strangers mattered to him purely because they were loved by those he looked after. How he had known to know, and Beatrice had not.

They had halted in front of an apothecary's shop. An iron mortar and pestle grunted as it swung above the blue sign, sounding, to Beatrice, as if it disapproved of their arrival. If she had been alone, she would have ducked into the bakery next door, or the chandler two doors down, and no doubt frittered all her coins away while plucking up the courage to enter the apothecary's.

'Here,' Ridley said, hailing two boys playing knucklebones atop a battered barrel. 'A penny each for minding our horses, and two more if they're still here when we come out again.'

The boys grinned, leaping up with chests puffed and hands outstretched for the pennies. As Beatrice dismounted, they were already glowering menacingly at anyone who dared look at the horses, let alone walk past them.

'Are you ready?' Ridley asked.

Beatrice grimaced. 'Of course not. That's hardly important.'

'It matters to me,' he said softly. 'You have the right to grieve as –'

'So do they,' Beatrice sighed. 'And the right to blame us. But most of all they have the right to know.'

She strode past Ridley, performing a decisiveness she couldn't feel. He followed her inside. Instantly, they were dizzied by a cacophony of fragrances – ambergris, cedarwood, frankincense, cardamom, jasmine, all clinging to her skin like soft hands, stroking, silken, snaking up her arms to her throat, her eyes, all insisting she pay them attention, let them sing and soothe and seduce.

'May I help you?'

She struggled to focus her gaze on the man at the counter, to look beyond the array of spices and soaps, pomander beads and pills. His blue velvet robe couldn't hide his thinness, for all the breadth of the shoulders it hung from. His hands were a blur as he chopped nutmeg fine, his blade flashing like a sharp tongue. As soon as her eyes met his, she almost regretted it: surrounded by curving wrinkles, they were Maria's eyes, the deep brown of carved walnut, clever, gentle, yet faintly amused eyes. Though of course Maria's eyes had been far from amused the last time she and Beatrice had spoken.

'This is Lady Radclyffe,' Ridley said. 'I'm her steward. We've come with news of Maria. You are her brother Solomon?'

'Aye.' Maria's brother frowned. 'News she couldn't bring herself?'

Ridley glanced at the door. 'Might we speak privately?'

'Why?'

'Is there someone else who might mind the shop?'

'Hardly – my wife's got three children to look after, and they don't make their own dinner. Out with it – I've a business to run.'

'Maria is dead,' Beatrice blurted out, immediately wishing her words back. But his tone, his dry bluntness had been so like his sister's that she couldn't bear to let him object any longer.

Solomon swayed. His knife slipped and clattered to the floor; he made no move to retrieve it. 'What? How?'

'She was murdered,' Ridley said. 'Strangled. I'm sorry.'

'Why?' Solomon snapped, suddenly brittle. 'Was it your fault?'

'She was in my employ,' Beatrice said, half-grateful for his aggression: it steadied her somehow. Tears and frailty were terrifying; anger and blame were what she deserved. 'That makes her my responsibility. So I am determined to bring whoever killed her to justice.'

'Justice,' Solomon snorted. 'You mean you'll find the nearest foreigner and have him strung up, I suppose? That's what happens in London – find a boorish Dutchman, or a slow-witted Russian, or a devious Italian, and it's as if their chests were made for pinning crimes on.'

'There's no reason to suspect a man of any particular nationality,' Ridley said. 'Unless you know of anyone Maria might have had cause to fear?'

Solomon eyed them darkly, accusingly. 'Not a particular man, no. But last time I spoke to her, she said she feared the *Silver Swan*'s return.'

Beatrice stared, aghast. 'Did she say why?'

Solomon shrugged, his gaze dropping as he remembered his final conversation with his sister. 'She wouldn't say – we were all having dinner and the little ones were chattering and climbing on her lap. All she said was that the longer the *Silver Swan* was away, the safer she'd feel.'

It made no sense. What reason could Maria have to fear Hugh's return? Had her murderer been one of Hugh's sailors?

Behind them the bell jangled as a customer stepped inside: a red-faced woman already laden with parcels, whose frown deepened when she saw she'd have to wait.

Beatrice turned back to Solomon. 'We will, of course, bear all funeral expenses. Will Thursday morning be convenient? At All Saints in Chelsea.'

Solomon gave a shrug again, his face slack with disbelief, as if he couldn't understand how they were discussing his sister's burial.

'And please accept this,' Beatrice added, drawing a leather purse out from her cloak. 'Maria's wages, and some more by way of – of –' She'd been going to say *compensation*, but the word died on her lips. Would *apology* be more apt? Or far worse?

'Charity?' Solomon's head snapped up; he eyed the purse as if it contained horse droppings. 'I don't need your charity.'

'Then call it payment,' Beatrice said. Even if the man were grieving, pandering to any man's pride grated: he had children to feed and clothe, didn't he? Practicality had to mean more than pride – or perhaps fathers could think otherwise while mothers scrimped and saved. 'I like to make my own pomander beads, and I am short of ingredients. I need labdanum, civet oil, and … ah …'

'Cloves?' Solomon moved briskly, efficiently, as if eager to lose himself in work. 'Ambergris?'

'Yes, please.'

'And for scent? Do you favour juniper, cypress, lavender –'

'Not lavender.' The refusal snapped like bone. She swallowed. 'Cypress. Thank you.'

Solomon wrapped her ingredients in waxed paper and then in muslin before exchanging her package for the purse with a curt nod, his shoulders straightening with dignity. 'Thank you for your custom, madam.'

He was already looking past Beatrice, towards his next customer. She understood: he wanted to be alone so he could grieve, and the sooner they all left, the better. She and Ridley moved towards the door.

'Wait.'

Beatrice turned to see Solomon leaning over the counter towards them and the exhausted woman looking ready to weep with weary frustration.

'Before Maria left …' Solomon hesitated. 'It may be nothing. But she was asking about the workshop by the river. If it was the only one of its kind. I said as far as I knew, but London's a big place, and the world even bigger, so I could be wrong.'

'What kind of workshop?'

'Instruments of various sorts – I couldn't tell you what half of them are. But last week there was a big crowd watching the owner's latest creations get loaded onto a barge for Whitehall – the master was to present them to Queen Elizabeth herself.'

Beatrice's throat was hoarse. 'What were they?'

She knew before he said it.

'Globes. Enormous, elaborate globes.'

'Why would Maria have been interested in the globes?' Ridley hadn't folded his arms; he would never have been so disrespectful. But his frown made it clear he thought they ought to be returning home and he to his myriad duties.

Beatrice stared at the workshop. At least five times the size of Solomon's shop, it gleamed brighter than anything else she'd seen in Lambeth: its wrought iron sign in the shape of a compass, its white-washed walls, clearly washed again in the wake of the geese and pigs driven through that morning, its broad glass windows. Few buildings in Lambeth, or anywhere south of the river contained nearly as much glass – evidently the work done inside required light and paid well enough that the proprietor had been willing to go to great expense to get it. And yet Beatrice didn't step close enough to look. Hugh's globe had come from there. The globe whose very memory made her skin seethe as if slicked in toad venom.

'She shouldn't have been,' Beatrice said. 'She never has been before. But of course she was never murdered before either.'

'You think there was a connection?'

'I don't know. But ...' Beatrice hesitated: how to explain without sounding mad? 'There was a picture on the globe. A dark-skinned woman in the water.'

'You think Maria saw it? After it arrived in the house, or before? And – what, believed it to be a threat?' Ridley shook his head. 'Why would a master craftsman threaten your maid? Or anyone?'

Beatrice squared her shoulders. 'We owe it to Maria to find out, don't we?'

'Beatrice – you're not the watch. You're not the Justice of the Peace!'

'Well, it's been made abundantly clear how little the Justice cares about finding Maria's murderer.' Without waiting for a response, she strode inside.

A bell jangled as they entered, but she saw it sway rather than heard it: the air was full of sawing wood, roaring fires, hammers driving pivot pins through brass and wood. Sawdust drifted like yellow ash, instantly rasping against her throat and nostrils. All around the workshop were men toiling at different stations: some shaping frames for small globes, or pouring sand into the bottom hemispheres; others were mixing flour paste before daubing it onto layers of paper spread over hollow copper moulds, arranging printed gores over dried globes, or varnishing completed models. Drying gores hung from ropes, rustling and arching with every hammer blow and footstep, like the wings of birds caught in lime. There was noise, but little chatter: was it forbidden, or were the craftsmen all too absorbed in their work to fritter time away?

'Yes?'

The speaker's voice was soft – and yet impatient: it was the kind of softness that could erupt into shouting at any moment, and be all the more terrifying for the contrast. His black velvet doublet and long grey beard were both constellated with sawdust; his fingertips and forehead were both smudged with ink. Beatrice doubted he'd noticed either the ink or the sawdust. He was evidently the kind of craftsman for whom the craft always came first, and the irksome duties of being a man – eating, sleeping, bathing – would inevitably be a distant second. As for anyone who impeded his craft or failed to understand its supremacy, no doubt they would immediately be on the receiving end of his wrath.

'Are you the proprietor here?' Beatrice asked.

The man exhaled sharply through his nostrils in irritation. 'Emery Molyneux, madam. I must tell you, I do not ordinarily accept customers off the street.'

Small wonder in Lambeth: other than the Archbishop of Canterbury, who occasionally dwelled in the Bishop's palace, few would be able to afford the instruments Molyneux made – or have much call for them. Astrolabes and compasses were hardly essential for most households.

'My husband is a loyal customer of yours,' Beatrice said, though she had no idea whether Hugh was: she only noted the high price of his instruments in the accounts ledgers, not their provenance. 'The explorer, Sir Hugh Radclyffe.'

Molyneux instantly shifted, straightening his back, smoothing his gown: now she wasn't merely a woman looking at shiny baubles. 'Of course. Even so, please ask Sir Hugh to write –'

'I'm not here to buy,' Beatrice cut him off. 'I wish to ask you some questions. A week ago, a woman came here. A Moorish woman named Maria, about ten years older than myself. She would have been wearing –' She hesitated: if their positions had been reversed, Maria would have been able to reel off every item Beatrice had been wearing, from linen or silk stockings to a cartwheel or pleated ruff. 'Perhaps a red gown or a black one. With a grey cloak. Did she speak with you, or one of your employees?'

Beatrice glanced around the workshop as she spoke: nearly all the eyes were either on her, or flicking swiftly back and forth between her and their work. Curiosity? Or could one of them know something?

Molyneux didn't answer her directly. Instead, he turned to the workshop and barked, 'Who spoke with a Moorish woman when they were supposed to be working?'

The men all shifted uncomfortably, trying to survey everyone else without appearing to take their eyes away from their work; evidently Molyneux was a hard master to please. Eventually one stood up, jaw working as he gnawed his cheeks nervously. He was young, thatch-haired, and either taller than he was used to, or awkward with nervousness; as he rose, the papers he'd been poring over cascaded to the floor and he scrabbled to gather them, cheeks growing pinker by the moment.

Molyneux glared balefully at the youth as he scurried forwards; as soon as he reached them, Molyneux turned his scowl on the rest of the workshop. Immediately, the noise of work doubled, the men all concentrating with ostentatious effort.

'This is Simon,' Molyneux said with distaste. 'Who will be working late today to make up for the time missed, first when he spoke with this woman, and secondly when he confessed today.'

Beatrice watched Simon swallow and twist his fingers together: the same signs Walter gave of being on the verge of tears he was convinced he was too old to shed. She wanted to upbraid Molyneux for what seemed needless cruelty – but she suspected that would only lead to further punishment once she'd left. And besides, she wanted to know why Maria had come here.

'Tell me,' she said, 'what did Maria want to discuss?'

'The pictures,' Simon said, then glanced at Molyneux. 'That is, the cartouches on the globes. She wanted to know who painted them, so I told her I did, and then she asked whether I drew from my own imagination, or if people sat for me.'

Molyneux snorted. 'People who look like sea serpents and mermaids? Foolish baggage!'

'That foolish baggage, as you call her,' Ridley said coldly, 'has been murdered. I suggest you speak of her with respect.'

Molyneux bristled. 'And you think her murderer – what? Worked here? Or – ha! – was *Simon*? He can barely talk to a woman without stuttering and stammering – if he so much as touched one he'd fall over!'

'That will do,' Beatrice snapped. 'Unless you wish me to advise my husband and his friends, including Sir Walter Raleigh and the Earl of Northumberland, to take their custom elsewhere, I suggest you remain silent, Master Molyneux.' A bluff, of course: she doubted she could influence Hugh to change his astrolabe supplier, and Raleigh and Northumberland probably wouldn't even remember her name. But it worked: Molyneux snarled and subsided. Simon, meanwhile, had ducked his head so low even Beatrice, almost a foot shorter than him, could only see the tousled crown of his head.

'I told her I work from books mostly,' Simon mumbled. 'Or daydreams. And then she asked which pictures on the new globes came from daydreams.'

'Was one of them a woman in the water?'

Simon frowned, glancing up through his thatch of hair. 'The mermaid, you mean? The one with the mirror?'

'No – the woman facing away. With black hair and brown skin.'

Simon lifted his head higher, confusion and curiosity tangling on his pink face. 'That wasn't part of the original design. But that's not what she wanted to ask me about. She wanted to know about the winged cockatrice capturing the bear.'

Beatrice stared, bewilderment pulling her in opposite directions. If the woman in the water wasn't part of the original design, why on earth was there one on Hugh's globe? Had Hugh been right when he railed about someone vandalising it? She opened her mouth to speak.

But Molyneux interrupted before she could utter a word. 'Cockatrice? It was meant to be a dragon, idiot boy! If I wanted you to design a globe, I'd ask you to design a globe. Is that what I asked you to do?'

'No, sir,' Simon mumbled, staring at his feet again.

'Then why did you?'

Simon hesitated.

'Tell me,' Molyneux said dangerously, 'or I will dock the entire cost of every one of these globes from your wages.'

'Please sir, please don't!' Tears really were trembling on Simon's lashes now, all attempts at manliness dissolving. 'My mother's not well – I have to pay for her medicine –'

'And I have a business to run, not a charity. Out with it!'

Simon bit his lip. 'I changed it because a – because someone paid me to.'

'Who?' Beatrice pressed, feeling suddenly certain.

'He didn't tell me his name,' Simon said awkwardly. 'But he was dressed all in black, with a scarf over his face.'

'A likely story,' Molyneux grunted. 'Blame it on a stranger.'

'There is one thing,' Simon said hesitantly. 'When he was getting the coins out of his purse, I noticed his ring. It was a gold signet ring – I could draw it for you?'

'Please do,' Beatrice said, her haste to speak before Molyneux and her rising suspicion making her voice hoarse.

Simon scuttled back to his workbench and sketched swiftly, his movements suddenly assured – and then, as he ceased drawing and had to cross the room again, all his ungainly awkwardness returned. He held out the drawing hopefully, putting Beatrice in mind of a too-often kicked puppy bringing you a rabbit, desperate for you to be pleased. She gave him a grateful smile as she took the paper from him.

It was a rectangular signet ring. Within its four sharp edges were three circles above a broad stripe: three torteaux above a fess. Slowly, Beatrice laid her hand over the design, covering up all but one corner, so that only a pattern of straight lines and curves could be seen.

She couldn't be certain, she had to tell herself that. And yet she had never been more certain of anything. It was the same pattern as the bloodstained bruise on Maria's neck.

8

After the smoke and sawdust of Lambeth, the Royal Exchange seemed almost offensively garish, with its marble columns and lofty galleries, its quadrangles and spiral staircases. Venetian glass gleamed: colourful beads and elaborate ewers and goblets catching the low sunlight and juggling rainbows almost as bright as the customers' robes and gowns. Blue and yellow songbirds chattered, twitched, fluttered in golden cages; thousands of buttons rattled just as fast and giddily as women ran their fingers over embroidered ones, corded, gilded, chased, domed, jewelled ones, some tempted, some overwhelmed, some feigning disdain in pursuit of a better bargain. It was glamourous and dizzying, ostentatious with pretensions of elegance and sophistication, brandishing luxuries as if the Royal Exchange could bestow, if not royalty, then at least a royal lifestyle on its customers. Florence had always adored the place, clamouring to visit from the age of five, eager to touch and possess and claim, and she still loved nothing better. Beatrice, on the other hand, hated it. The Exchange was too busy, too frenzied. If she wanted to buy something, she wanted quiet and space in which to inspect and inquire before committing to a purchase. In the chaos of the Exchange, you'd more often than not come away with ells of taffeta whose weave was flawed, or your Venetian chandelier would transpire to be from the Leith workshops instead, and its craftsmanship nowhere near as skilled as an authentic specimen would have been, and the price should have warranted. Nevertheless, she found herself wandering past rose water and orange water, lace ruffs and lacier cuffs with her sister. Sometimes Beatrice thought that although she had inherited almost all their father's worldly goods, Florence had always got her own way in every other respect. Or perhaps Beatrice's guilt at being sole heiress meant she agreed to meet her sister in one of her least favourite places in London.

'I heard the most delicious rumour from a friend yestereve,' Florence was saying as Beatrice trailed after her from stall to stall. 'Remember the campaign in the Azores this summer?'

'Indeed – I was worried it would delay Hugh's return.' Beatrice almost bumped into her sister as Florence stopped at the haberdasher's. 'Essex and Raleigh returned in ignominious circumstances, having failed to capture the Spanish treasure fleet. Or any significant territory.'

Florence pulled a disappointed face. 'Of course – you probably know more about it than me. Your husband is so close with those two, I imagine you've heard the tale from the horse's mouth.'

'If you'd ever met the pair, you'd imagine differently. They don't tell tales of their own failures.'

'Well, that's the point!' Florence was suddenly gleeful again at the opportunity to reveal a scandal. 'Apparently this was no failure. The rumour is that one of them did capture a Spanish treasure ship after all – and rather than give the loot to Queen Elizabeth, they've claimed the vessel sank and kept the hoard for themselves.'

Beatrice smiled wryly, remembering Florence's eager expression from when she'd promised an eight-year-old girl sugared almonds, a new puppy, a fan of her very own. 'I'd give those rumours as much credence as the tales of El Dorado, or millers' daughters spinning flax into gold. People always leap to believe in gold, especially the hidden kind.'

'Some of us could do with discovering hidden gold.'

Beatrice frowned at her half-sister's grim voice. 'Florence –'

'Have you found a new maid yet?' Florence interrupted, her tone no longer bitter, but light as she idly twirled ribbons in three different shades of blue. 'Such an inconvenience for you.'

'You call her murder an inconvenience?'

Florence shrugged. 'It can be both tragic and tiresome. When my mother died I obviously cried, but I was also disappointed that I'd never learn her trick for braid stitch.'

Beatrice winced at her sister's candid pragmatism. 'Maria only died two days ago, Florence.'

'Oh, true.' Florence glanced back at her. 'Mind, I could have guessed you hadn't replaced her. No wonder you've chosen that hat today. Have you considered wearing perukes instead? Now that you're going grey …'

'No,' Beatrice said through gritted teeth. 'I haven't.'

'It would save so much time – you could have one hairstyle for best, one for windy weather with tighter pins and curls –'

'Are you going to buy that ribbon?'

Florence pursed her lips and turned away. 'No.'

Beatrice frowned, striding to catch up with her sister as Florence moved on to an array of pomander beads and began sniffing. 'Are you sure? You haven't bought anything today.'

'Nothing's been good enough,' Florence said curtly, discarding a nutmeg-scented pomander as if it had suddenly sprouted mould.

'That doesn't usually stop you.'

Florence glanced up at the galleries – or at one particular gallery. The one where drapers and cloth merchants met to negotiate and barter and forge alliances. 'If you must know, Robert asked me not to buy anything today.'

Beatrice laughed in surprise. 'Robert gave you an instruction and you're genuinely following it? Not cajoling and coaxing until you've tricked him into believing that he's actually asked you to do the opposite?'

'One of our ships hasn't returned.'

Beatrice drew in a sharp breath. They were merchants' daughters. They knew those words were among the worst merchants could hear. Such a sentence could mean nothing – or everything. A fortune sunk to the seabed, saltwater ruining every hope you'd held dear, crabs scuttling over crates that would never be opened, eels laying their eggs in the shadow of a broken mast.

'Could it have blown off course? It's November now – the winds and mists will doubtless be worsening.'

'It's been a week since we expected her.' Florence shook her head grimly. 'Even in poor weather, it shouldn't take more than four days to return from Flanders.'

'They could be becalmed, or storms might have driven them back to port –'

'Other ships have made port in that time.' Florence's chin trembled as she dragged in a would-be steadying breath. 'Either the captain's turned pirate, or he's drowned, and all our cloth along with him. And not just wool. We'd bought silk and damask this time – even gold and silver thread.'

'Oh, Florence.' Beatrice reached for her sister, but Florence flung up her hands, fingers flared wide in warning.

'Don't coddle me, Beatrice. Not when your ships never fail to come back safe. What is it now, seven years since you lost one?'

Eight – but Beatrice knew better than to correct her. Besides, she had two ships for trade, the *Kestrel* for cloth and the *Starling* for spices, not to mention the *Silver Swan*, whereas Florence and Robert had only the *Mariana*. 'Can Hugh and I help?'

Florence laughed bitterly. 'Oh yes! You can scatter some of your golden luck over us!' She glared at Beatrice, her green eyes aching with longing, her jaw clenched taut against weeping. 'Why is it that everything you touch turns to gold and everything Robert and I turn our hands to crumbles to dust?'

'That isn't true –'

'Isn't it?' Florence shook her head. 'You lead a charmed life, Beatrice. You always have.'

Had Florence forgotten Maria's murder? Or Catalina's arrival in Beatrice's house, almost certainly with Hugh's child in her belly? Or, before that, the simple fact that Florence had borne five healthy children and never even come close to burying one, whereas Beatrice had lost four, three before she'd even told another soul she was expecting a child. Only Maria knew about those three, for Hugh had been at sea each time, and so it had been Maria's arms around Beatrice as she wept, Maria who nursed Beatrice back to health and the capacity to at least feign happiness. And now that Maria was gone, no one knew, and Beatrice's never-born babies had become yet another secret tightening around her body, like a corset wrought of bloodstained bone.

But Florence didn't know about Beatrice's own woes. No matter how old they grew, there was still a part of Beatrice that insisted on protecting Florence and driving back anything that might harm her. Like the worst aspects of their father.

Beatrice shook herself. There were enough shadows hanging over her without letting the spectre of Arthur Gardiner seep close.

'We could give Robert a loan,' Beatrice said gently. 'I'd like to help.'

Florence glanced up at the gallery again. 'I suspect it might already be too late for that.'

Beatrice followed her sister's gaze. In the shadow of a marble pillar stood Robert, staring blindly over the Exchange. As they watched, Robert slowly removed his hat and began smoothing the pheasant feathers with a ritualistic care that seemed achingly bleak. As if all that were left to him were the thin brown feathers of a long-dead bird, and he didn't know what else to do but try to keep up appearances.

She rode back to Chelsea with Ridley, who had apparently had a successful, if not wholly pleasant afternoon remonstrating with their sea coal supplier, who had been attempting to raise his prices extortionately. Rather than sharing his satisfaction, Beatrice wondered if Florence and Robert could afford sea coal, or if they were already burning wood instead. For Florence to cease buying trinkets and fripperies, their situation had to be precarious – perhaps far more than she'd let on. Could Beatrice help them somehow, without letting Florence realise they were being helped? Perhaps she could speak to her agent, Holbrook, to see if a loan could masquerade as a trade deal?

The setting sun had been near-blinding them for much of the ride, copper spears jabbing at them from between buildings and then scything off the river in sharp swipes. Now it finally slipped below the horizon, leaving the riverside path shrouded in shadow, though a red-blotched sky meant their horses could still see to place their hooves. And yet the cold, and the quiet seeping in its wake, were insipid, and faintly unsettling. When Beatrice glanced at the water, each red-stained ripple, each shifting shadow seemed like another body tossed away by its murderer.

'I've been thinking,' Ridley said, his sudden words making her start. 'Perhaps we ought to place a guard around the grounds, especially after dark.'

'A guard?'

'Yes.' Ridley watched her as he spoke. 'If someone entered the grounds to attack Maria, what's to stop them – or someone else with equally damaging aims – entering again?'

'You think he might return?'

'I don't know what to think.' Ridley sighed deeply in frustration. 'The business with the globe, this mysterious man in black ... The question is whether Maria was his sole target.'

Beatrice bit her lip. It hadn't occurred to her that Maria might have been the murderer's first, rather than only victim. Surely it was monstrous enough to kill one person, let alone several? And whilst she'd considered the possibility that Catalina might have been the intended victim, she hadn't imagined that the killer might return, having realised his mistake. Or that he might have had other targets ... If they hadn't been out in the barge that night, who else might have been attacked?

They were approaching the house now, and the relief she ought to have felt was nowhere to be found. She should have seen the windows glowing yellow with candlelight and thought of her children playing, bounding up to greet her with a smile and two gabbled, clashing accounts of their day; should have seen Hugh's silhouette against the gallery window and looked forward to his embrace. But instead she saw the hunchback curve of the globe outlined in black against the glass, and the candlelight no longer seemed welcoming and cosy, but a sign of ignorance. If you had candles lit at night, you could not see outside. You could not see who, or what was watching you – or whether it had already come inside.

'I would keep you safe, my lady,' Ridley said softly.

She couldn't bear the tenderness in his voice. Tersely, she snapped, 'Don't forget, Ridley, my husband is home now. My safety should fall to him, not you.'

She was glad it was dark; she could pretend she hadn't seen that wounded look hollow out Ridley's face. And she could hide the doubt on her own. Hugh was a knight, not a steward: she ought to have felt far safer with her husband than with Ridley.

But Hugh had brought Catalina into the house. He had brought the globe. And he and Beatrice both had engendered something far worse inside: distrust.

Black branches creaked overhead like the masts of shipwrecks washed up in the churchyard. It was mid-November and there wasn't a leaf left to soften the sounds, so twigs tapped against branches, against the church walls, an incessant percussion behind the thuds of soil onto oak. Watching the earth fall from the gravediggers' shovels, Beatrice couldn't help thinking of the noises as whispers: rumour-laden voices tutting disapproval, breathing sordid details. What was being whispered about Maria's death? Beer-sodden leers about the state of her clothes in the taverns; meanwhile, at the wells where women gathered to pull water, the anxious warnings would be thin grey threads hissed from the corners of mouths reluctant to accuse too loudly. Women needed to know who to watch out for – that there was someone nearby to watch out for – but anyone who pointed a finger or dwelled too long on one particular theory might well find themselves being silenced; if they were lucky their imposed silence might not be eternal.

Was Beatrice risking too much by refusing to let Maria's death go unsolved? Or would failing to search for the truth be more of a risk?

Beside her, William shifted uncomfortably: the habitual rolling sway of a sailor didn't marry well with the sodden ground. Even though the overnight rain had abated to a thin drizzle, their clothes were all pocked brown with mud and Beatrice could feel the chill seeping up through her boots. Impossible to tell, either, who was weeping, and who was merely wet: most of those on her side of the grave had been cajoled or browbeaten by Hugh into attending, especially after Florence had pleaded a clutch of aguish daughters, Florence, a motherless daughter herself, who had learned too young that both doctors and older sisters often lied when they insisted illnesses were mild, was always fretful and anxious when her daughters were sick – but Beatrice couldn't help worrying that the real reason was Florence's distress over their lost ship. She doubted William was feeling particularly sentimental, or Nicholas, who was absent-mindedly humming the tune of the last hymn sung in Maria's funeral service. If she'd let Ursula and Walter attend, perhaps they would have cried, though she wasn't certain either of them really understood that Maria having gone away was not the same as Hugh going away, and that she wouldn't be returning with pockets full of exotic trinkets when the season changed. As for Catalina, the silver glisten on her face couldn't be for Maria; it might be fear, if she still wondered whether Maria's murderer had been seeking her, and only the dark night and the man's ignorance had saved Catalina and her unborn baby.

She glanced up at Hugh, on her other side, between Beatrice and Catalina. His beard glistened, his browned cheekbones too, but not his eyes. She'd only once seen Hugh cry. Not that she'd seen any other man cry, apart from Nicholas when they'd presented him with a New Year's gift of a particularly rare edition of something or other by Copernicus, and that had probably been as much to do with the malmsey he'd imbibed as with the astrological tome.

On the other side of the grave though, those faces were undoubtedly wet with tears. Solomon gripped his hat in both hands, his eyes clinging on to the last glimpse of Maria's coffin as the shovelled earth fell. At his side, a slight woman with dark freckles clung to his arm; Beatrice recognised the pale smears on her shoulder as the milk and drool stains of a squalling, teething baby. She must have been ten years younger than her husband: had it taken Solomon a long time to be able to support a family? Why hadn't Maria ever mentioned it, if so – had she doubted Beatrice would care enough to help? The idea rankled, and Beatrice looked away from Maria's kin in shame.

She had to do something. But her actions, when weighed, seemed wholly inadequate: she'd paid for Maria's burial, asked an apprentice craftsman some questions, and contemplated putting some guards at her gate. All told, a pitiful response.

The coffin was invisible now; the gravediggers continued silently. Solomon's wife murmured something, rubbing uncomfortably at her chest, and they turned away: their small children would be waiting in Lambeth. Perhaps she should have paid for Maria to be buried nearer to her brother, rather than in a grave close to Beatrice's parents' vault.

Hugh cleared his throat. 'A touching service, all told. I'll give our thanks to the sexton.'

William and Nicholas took his words as their cue to start ambling towards the lych-gate. Catalina didn't move, but stood quietly, massaging slow circles across her stomach: either summoning the effort to move, or waiting for Hugh to escort her back to the carriage. Irritated, Beatrice jerked her gaze away – and her scowl landed on Solomon. Immediately, she tried to rearrange her expression into something more appropriate, but his narrowed eyes told her she'd been too slow.

'My thanks,' he said stiffly, 'for your munificence.'

The word sounded like an insult. And well it might. She didn't deserve thanks for scattering coins and pretending it made up for abandoning Maria to be murdered.

'It was the least I could do.'

Solomon opened his mouth as if to acknowledge her words – but he couldn't bring himself to do it, and his lips twisted in a bitter snort. 'Please – don't imagine I expected anything more.'

Beatrice blinked in surprise at the spite in his voice, even as she scolded herself for having the gall to be surprised. 'I didn't – that is, please believe me when I say that I wish I could have done more. For Maria – for you too.'

Solomon shifted slightly, as if to block Beatrice's view of his wife, who was now in quiet conversation with Catalina as the two of them walked towards the lych-gate. 'On today of all days, Lady Radclyffe, perhaps you could do me the courtesy of honesty.'

'I am speaking honestly –'

'You had your entire life to help her. She entered your mother's service when she was just a girl of ten, and it was she who offered you a teething ring and rocked you to sleep, she who did the same for your sister, for your children – and how did you repay her? By taking her for granted.' Solomon shook his head angrily. 'Oh, you'll protest that you paid her well, and I'm sure you paid her as much as your friends in their riverside mansions pay their women to do everything they cannot raise a finger to do themselves. But what you don't understand – what someone like you can never understand – is that she gave her life to you. And all you gave her in return was metal. A purse of coins, heavy enough to make you imagine yourself a great benefactress, but still meagre enough to keep Maria firmly in her place.'

'What would you have me do? Perhaps –' She was about to promise his children employment when they were grown, before realising how horribly inept that would be.

'Rest assured, I'm not asking for a fleet of horses, or great boons for my children.' Solomon eyed her coldly, and she realised he knew what she'd been about to offer and was duly disdainful. 'Merely that you treat her as a woman with a life as meaningful as your own. You took her for granted, Lady Radclyffe. And someone took my sister's life when she should have been under your protection.'

'And I am sorrier than I can say for it! I loved Maria –'

'Did you? You seem to have replaced her swiftly enough.' He cut a scathing glance towards Catalina, and Beatrice followed his gaze. From behind, where they could see neither her face, nor the swell of her belly, could Maria's killer have mistaken Catalina for Solomon's sister? They were a similar height, their skin the same walnut hue, their hair a mass of tight black curls. A man who didn't know how Maria tilted her head to listen, the ditties she hummed as she walked, the way she'd roll her shoulders at the end of the day – perhaps he could have made a mistake. Or perhaps there had been no error at all, and Beatrice didn't know which was more sinister.

'No one could replace Maria.'

'You think I don't know that?' Solomon shook his head scornfully. 'One blackamoor woman looks just as fashionable as another in the shadow of a rich woman's portrait – or is this new arrival more valued than the latest ruffs and sleeves?'

'It isn't like that –'

'You were Maria's life.' Solomon stated it flatly, wearily, as if he were exhausted by grief and by Beatrice's inadequacy. 'Do you have any idea what she gave up for you?'

Her own life. Maria had never married, never shown any inclination to marry: her deepest love had apparently been for Beatrice's mother, but was that opinion based entirely on an ignorant assumption?

Abashed, Beatrice said, 'I should have protected her better.'

Solomon's nostrils flared in exasperation. 'Did it ever occur to you that she was the one protecting you?'

Beatrice stared. 'From what?'

He eyed her curiously, suspiciously, as if she were a horse rumoured to be rabid. 'Maria used to tell me. Because she couldn't tell you.' He grimaced, rubbing the worn wool of his cloak, suddenly remembering the difference in their stations. 'How she defended you to the servants – the other servants. When they'd call you mad.'

Beatrice opened her mouth – but no denial emerged, no protestation. Her lips, her jaw, felt loose, unable to grasp hold of any words, like water flailing past reeds, pebbles, fish. That word, that single slice of a syllable, had released a gout of memory and fear, as if a reef had split her keel, and now she was being flooded, unable to stop the breach.

Solomon's wife was calling him; he was bowing and turning, and she tried to mumble some polite farewell, some final commiseration, but it was impossible.

How long had that rumour been circling? She'd tried so hard, fought so long, to keep that secret. But had it been discovered?

Your secrets are known. You deserve all that is coming.

Above her head, the branches clicked together, sly and insistent as gossips' tuts. The gravediggers' backs were broad, deliberately turned towards her: how much had they heard? How much had they already known?

This place, Chelsea, was her home. It had always been her home. How could she bear it if her home was no longer safe?

*   *   *

Ordinarily, making pomander beads in the gallery was one of Beatrice's favourite ways of stilling her mind. She'd arrange all her ingredients on an elegantly carved walnut table and settle herself on the rushes, her skirts stirring the rosemary sprigs so their scent twined softly around the pomander ingredients, soft as cats coiling around your ankles. The curtains would be open and daylight fresh and clean as linen would drape the gallery in airy brightness. Years ago, Florence had often sat beside her, embroidering handkerchiefs so skilfully it was as though she were painting with threads, briefly pausing her gossip to concentrate on her chain stitches and couching stitches. These days, sometimes Walter would come to sit beside her and recite the Latin he'd learned that morning, so that she rolled labdanum with cinnamon, ambergris and cloves in time with his declined verbs. Or Ursula would stagger over beneath the lute that was only a foot shorter than she was, and start playing a tune that was usually, after a few stutters, recognisable as a madrigal, and Beatrice would hum to guide her daughter as she tapped out drops of civet oil. But tonight, after the ordeal of Maria's funeral, the uncomfortable truths of Solomon's words, her thoughts would not be stilled. Her children were long abed, and behind her were not windows letting the light stream through, but velvet hauled shut against dark skies, and the bulbous swell of Hugh's globe, swollen even more grotesquely by flame and shadow.

She shouldn't have started this now. She should have waited until the morning, until daylight. But if she stopped now, the mixture would harden and be ruined, and even though Solomon's prices had been significantly cheaper than her usual supplier's, Beatrice was far too thrifty to waste damask water or ambergris, and it would feel like yet another bumbling ingratitude towards Maria's family. So here she was, kneeling before the fire with the globe lurking at her back.

She'd inspected it after what Molyneux's apprentice had said, forcing herself to touch the varnished surface and spin the globe until she saw the bear and the cockatrice. As she'd peered closer, she'd felt as if she were approaching a sleeping beast, could practically smell the bloody meat on the bear's jaws, feel her flesh recoil from the cockatrice's clawed feet. Simon's handiwork was exceptional, there was no doubting it: you could make out tiny scales on the cockatrice's hind legs, and the feathers on its head, the yellow and black wasp-like stripes on its body, the intricate swirls on its blue-white wings. But what on earth had Maria seen that had sent her in pursuit of the craftsman's workshop? Why would a cockatrice wrapping a bear in its tail have so frightened her?

Was this why Maria had died? The man in black, who'd bribed Simon to change a dragon to a cockatrice: was he the same man Maria had met? Was he the same man who had given Beatrice the note on Whitehall's wharf?

Your secrets are known. You deserve all that is coming.

Was Maria's death not just a despicable act of violence, but an attack on Beatrice too? And if so, then what else could possibly be coming?

She placed a waxen ball in a silver spoon. Her hand trembled as she held it over the fire, and she gripped her wrist with the other hand, trying to steady it as the mixture dissolved.

Someone had followed her to Whitehall. Someone had entered her home and murdered her maid. They knew where she went and where she lived. Had they followed her to Lambeth, to the churchyard, to the Royal Exchange too, all without her knowledge?

Still shaking, she released her wrist and picked up the vial of sweet water. As she tapped out five drops, each one echoed like a footstep.

Was someone trying to frighten her? Or was there more? Were they planning to blackmail her? But the note had said nothing about wanting money in return for silence. Only that she deserved all that was coming. And she had no way of knowing when, or what, or who they would strike next.

Behind her there came a sudden noise, like stones hurled against glass. She whirled around – and cried out in pain: she'd spilled the pomander bead mixture and the hot dark liquid had scalded her wrist. Clutching her arm, Beatrice stared in horror.

The globe was turning again.

There were no hands to push it. No open windows to let the wind sneak in to stir it. She'd felt no draught from the chimney. And yet it was turning, faster and faster, and she could only stare, panting raggedly with the pain from her wrist as the globe spun and the images blurred.

Latitude lines tangled with borders, longitude lines toppled into one another. Sea monsters swallowed mermaids and giant birds chased ships into whirlpools. And then it all became a morass of blue and red and black, like a face seething with scabs and plague sores, and she could no longer tell what she saw.

'Beatrice? I heard you cry out –' Hugh swore as he saw the spilled mixture, her gripped wrist, and he strode across the gallery, kneeling before her and gathering her into his arms. 'Let me see.'

'The globe,' she whispered hoarsely. 'The globe –'

But it had slowed to a gentle purr, and now it languidly, almost mockingly, drifted to a halt.

'It startled you?' Hugh frowned. 'One of the cats must have got in – I'll have words with the kitchen staff. I'm not having claws ruin my globe. Come – that wrist needs a salve.'

She let him lift her to her feet. How simple it would be if she could just give Hugh the weight of her secrets as easily as she gave him her body.

Just before they moved, she took one last look at the globe.

Perhaps it was a trick of the firelight. But the globe suddenly seemed less toadlike, and more akin to a tattooed face, tilted and strained to catch her attention. It had come to rest with the cockatrice facing her. As if it were saying *Look again. Look harder.*

As if it were warning her.

9

There was something wrong with the globe. There had to be: it was the only rational explanation. The distribution of weight inside it perhaps: if too much sand were slumped to one side, maybe that might cause it to spin unprompted. Or it could have been set into its frame at an odd angle – if it were listing to one side, or the meridian rings had been attached incorrectly, that could have left it lopsided and rotating erratically. Or could something unseen have set it off? A dropped weight on the floor above, or something hitting the ceiling of the room below? Though unless the kitchen staff had taken up tennis, Beatrice couldn't imagine what objects would ever come into contact with the ceiling. And in any case, surely she'd have heard the impact before the globe started spinning.

Of course it looked innocuous enough by daylight, gleaming placidly in the lemon-pale sun, round and still as an overfed, spiteful cat, smugly scheming when to strike next. Beatrice eyed it balefully from her seat at the far end of the gallery, where she'd arranged her embroidery silks before admitting that her wrist was far too sore for sewing. Instead, while Catalina mended a cloak beside her, humming softly, Beatrice stared at the globe, pretending to be watching her children at their French lesson. Snatches of recited poetry from Walter and descriptions of the gardens from Ursula floated back along the gallery to Beatrice: ordinarily their piping voices and the tutor's gentle corrections were soothing sounds. But today, each time Ursula dropped her chalk on her slate, or Walter, reminded for the twentieth time, let the front legs of his chair fall back to the floor, even when the fire crackled or a log shifted, Beatrice twitched, convinced the rattle or rustle or thud was the prelude to the globe spinning again.

She tugged at her sleeve in discomfort and irritation: even without lace cuffs attached, her sleeves kept brushing against the bandage on her wrist, tugging the honey and thyme poultice askew. Which was not only painful, but each time made her open her mouth to call for Maria to help adjust the dressing. And then came grief, followed by anger, and confusion and fear were never far behind.

Perhaps she was going mad. That would have been Florence's helpful suggestion, if she'd dared voice her concern to her sister. And no doubt any physician would have shared that opinion; he'd have given her a quietly pitying look and then asked Hugh to step aside so they could murmur together about wandering wombs and phases of the moon, a conversation that would only ever arrive at one destination: Bedlam.

Her mother had died in Bedlam. She'd been certain it wasn't something anyone knew about, save Hugh: Maria had known, true, but now only Hugh was privy to Beatrice's secret. When he'd returned from that disastrous northern expedition, he'd found Beatrice weeping and barely able to leave her bedchamber. She'd begged him not to send her away, and he, bewildered, had asked why he would. Then she'd told him of the child who hadn't lived, the child who hadn't even quickened when he sailed north, so that the first Hugh learned of her existence was when Beatrice told him she no longer existed at all.

'But why on earth would that mean I'd send you away?' he'd asked, exhaustion and grief new and old greying his face. And so Beatrice had told him about Jane.

They'd always said she'd died in childbirth: it wasn't far off the truth after all. Beatrice had been five when her mother had given birth to a fourth stillborn sibling and, almost thirty years later, she could still hear her mother's shrieks. Shrill, haunted, echoing: they had barely stopped from dusk until dawn, and even opium hadn't quieted Jane for long. Finally, Arthur Gardiner had agreed to send his wife to the asylum. 'For a rest,' he'd told Beatrice. 'She'll be back soon.'

Had she believed him even then? Perhaps he had meant to bring Jane home again. But three weeks later, just two months after she'd lost her baby, word came that Jane was dead. Puerperal fever, she'd heard her father say. But Beatrice knew it was grief. Grief at the baby – and at being sent away by the man who was supposed to love and protect her. Jane had not wanted to live. Not even for her daughter's sake. And barely six months later, Arthur had married Florence's mother.

When she'd told Hugh all this, he hadn't left the room in disgust as she'd feared, nor sent for the physician to condemn Beatrice to her mother's fate. Instead, he'd crawled into bed beside her and pulled her close. 'I could never send you away,' he'd whispered. 'I need you – now more than ever.' Then he'd told her what had happened among the ice floes, and by the end of his tale, they had both wept their eyes sore and were clinging to one another, so tight the tendons in Beatrice's wrists ached for two days afterwards. Neither of them had spoken of those things again, as if to say the words would summon up the ghosts and the grief all over again. Instead, they would say 'In the north', or 'Before Florence was born', and trail off, letting silence speak of what they could not. It was an unspoken pact, that Hugh would not speak of Bedlam or the lost baby, and Beatrice would not speak of what he had lost in that bleak whiteness. But now? If she were to tell Hugh about her fears, would he break that pact?

'Does it hurt?'

Beatrice twitched. 'What?'

Catalina had finished her mending and was watching Beatrice thoughtfully, almost sympathetically. 'You keep rubbing at it – that will not help the healing.'

'Oh, indeed?' Beatrice snapped. 'You astonish me.' She let go of her wrist as if that might somehow disprove Catalina's point, but that release dislodged the bandage further, and she snatched at it before the poultice could slip out.

'Here. Let me.' Catalina took hold of Beatrice's hand and began rewrapping her wrist before Beatrice could shake her off. She sniffed as she worked. 'Thyme and rose oil, I think? If the rose is irritating you, perhaps you might try lavender oil instead.'

'No.' Beatrice bit off the word so sharply Catalina's eyebrows rose.

'Some find it calming.'

Was that mockery in her voice? Or even a rebuke? How dare she?

'I despise lavender.'

Catalina shrugged, bending again to her task. 'We all have our preferences. Myself, I find mint leaves more soothing for burns than honey and thyme. Less messy too.'

'You should be careful,' Beatrice said, pain and fear and resentment making her spiteful. 'In England, women who pronounce too boldly on herbs often find themselves on the wrong end of a witchcraft charge.'

Catalina finished tying the bandage and met Beatrice's eyes. 'Oh, worry not,' she said coolly. 'I have learned a great deal about what the English are like.'

Again that note: was Catalina laughing at her or upbraiding her? The gall of the woman – wasn't carrying Hugh's bastard in Beatrice's home insult enough?

Before Beatrice could retort, Ursula crashed against her legs.

'Mama, I learned twenty new words today! *Les feuilles, les arbres, les nenuphares –*'

Walter broke in. 'And I can recite nearly twenty stanzas of "*Le chanson de Roland*"! Can I show you?'

'Later, perhaps, my darling.' Beatrice kissed Ursula's forehead and patted Walter's arm. 'I'm not sure we have time for twenty stanzas before luncheon.'

'Can we go in the garden until then?' Ursula begged, her blonde head whipping up immediately. 'I can tell you all the other new words I've learned. *Les poiriers et les pommiers et la lavande.*'

'Not that,' Catalina said. 'Your mother dislikes *la lavande.*'

Beatrice shot her a suspicious glance. So the woman spoke French as well as knowing herblore? Or perhaps it was merely an intelligent guess – *lavande* was far more likely to mean lavender than anything else. Although Beatrice couldn't help thinking it would be more in keeping with what little she knew of Catalina that the woman would also turn out to speak Italian and Greek and be able to recite the entirety of '*Le chanson de Roland*', rather than merely make sensible deductions.

Hiding her irritation, Beatrice smiled at her daughter. 'Of course – though not for long. Just until luncheon.'

'Can you and Catalina come too?'

Beatrice kept her smile plastered in place. That her children had so easily come to accept Catalina's presence in their home was one thing. But to actually like her? To want her company – perhaps even preferring it to Beatrice's?

'If Catalina wishes. She might be tired.'

'Fresh air is the best cure for that,' Catalina said, cupping her belly supportively as she rose. Beatrice tried to judge the size of the swell – five months, perhaps? But Catalina had already let go to hold out a hand to Ursula, and she was holding her mended cloak in such a way as to shield her belly now, probably deliberately.

'Come on, Mama!' Walter was off, charging down the gallery. Immediately, Ursula set off in pursuit, dragging Catalina behind her. Beatrice rose, tucking her untouched embroidery back into the basket.

Then everything happened at once.

She'd barely glanced away for a moment – and perhaps it was her eyes, swinging back to the three figures, that played a trick on her. Or perhaps she really did see the globe move – and not merely move, but *lunge*, its giant belly seeming to rise from those crabbed wooden legs, hurling itself out of the alcove and into Walter's path.

Impossible, Beatrice thought, but got no further. Walter stumbled against Catalina, and Catalina let go of Ursula's hand to cup her belly protectively. Ursula stumbled, and tripped, and fell.

Beatrice knew before it happened. She was a mother: for every one of her children's falls, in the moments between slip and impact she'd seen every risk – the corners of desks, the glass ornaments, the waiting steps. Almost always their fragile heads, palms, ankles would just miss. Now, Beatrice saw her daughter's skirts swing a beat behind her, saw the closeness of the hearth, the height of the fire – and she saw there was nothing she could do. And then Ursula began to scream.

Flames leapt up Ursula's skirts, pouncing from ankle to knee. Shrieking, Ursula flailed with her hands, trying to scrabble backwards, as if she could get away from her own legs. Her every scream was a blade scything Beatrice's flesh.

'Mama, help me!'

Beatrice was already running. She yanked the cloak out of Catalina's hands and flung it over her daughter's skirts. Dropping to the floor, she beat at the wool with her hands, then her body, covering Ursula as she rolled her over and over, until at last the flames were out and she could gather Ursula close. Her daughter's eyes were closed, her breathing shallow, and her drying tears mingled with Beatrice's falling tears on both their cheeks.

'Get a physician!' Beatrice choked out, burying her face in Ursula's curls, desperate to smell anything but her daughter's seared flesh.

Walter dashed away immediately, calling, 'Papa! Ridley! William!'

As his shouts grew further away, Beatrice looked up, searching for the globe – just to be certain. But between her and the alcove, on the other side of a circle of charred rushes, stood Catalina, her face horror-stricken.

'I swear, I did not push her,' Catalina whispered. 'Your son – I am certain he was just playing, he couldn't possibly have meant to …'

Beatrice shook her head, unable to speak. It hadn't been Catalina's fault. It hadn't been Walter's either.

It had been the globe.

10

Lavender crept through the bedchamber, insinuating itself into Beatrice's nostrils, hair, skin, everywhere. Dried sprigs, the grey-purple of corpses' skin, hung from Ursula's bedframe; in the shuttered dark of the sickroom they looked like hanged women swaying from silk nooses, their skirts rustling with unheard confessions. Beatrice rubbed her temples, exhausted and nauseous; she felt as if the lavender had writhed inside her skull and was seeping between bone and flesh, tainting her blood, and worst of all, raising the ghost of that memory, the one she kept locked away, except in her dreams.

But it didn't matter how much she despised lavender. How haunted, how watched it made her feel. The only thing that mattered now was Ursula.

Her daughter lay still, looking tiny in the vast bed. Ridley had made a wooden frame to keep the blankets off Ursula's legs so that the weight and chafing wouldn't irritate her burned skin, but grateful as Beatrice was, the contraption made it seem as though Ursula were half-in, half-out of her own coffin. And it only kept the front of her legs from further pain: the worst burns were on Ursula's shins and knees, but her calves had also been horribly injured, and all they could think to do there was pile wads of fine linen thick enough so the feathers in the mattress couldn't pierce the sheet and suddenly jab Ursula's poor blistered flesh. Even though they'd given her tinctures of opium, Beatrice saw every flicker of Ursula's eyelids, every parting and closing of her lips as a silenced scream.

She couldn't bear this. Seeing her child hurt in any way – a grazed knee, a bitten tongue, a stomach-ache – made some creature inside

Beatrice rise up, roaring protection, ready to desolate the entire world if it would take her daughter's pain away. But such hurt as this?

The burns had been awful to behold. Beatrice's scalded wrist was nothing, nothing to the damage done to Ursula's delicate skin. Even the memory of Ursula's seared legs, the scarlet and black, the blood and pus, made Beatrice want to scream. She'd cried out when she'd been burned by the pomander bead mixture, but she would gladly have poured the boiling potion over her entire body, have drunk a gallon of the stuff, if it would have meant Ursula hadn't been hurt.

So the smell of lavender was nothing, really. Compared to Ursula's suffering, it was nothing, and if the scent of lavender was calming for her daughter, if lavender oil mixed with thyme and honey soothed her burned body, then so be it. It was a tiny sacrifice for Beatrice to make – and besides, how could she possibly have explained? No one knew why she despised lavender so much; they just obeyed her orders to keep it out of her chambers. A whim, a rich lady's caprice: ludicrous, but decent wages meant the household accepted it without question. But if Beatrice had refused her daughter anything that might help her now, she knew what they'd all have thought: that she was selfish, cruel. Even mad.

Beatrice had begun to wonder if they'd be right.

'You should sleep.'

Her back clicked as she looked up, sending a sharp jolt of pain up and down her spine. Hugh had entered without her noticing; from his appearance, he needed to follow his own advice. His doublet was half-laced, his beard unoiled and mussed, as if he'd rested his chin on it too wearily, too often, while his eyes were bruised with exhaustion.

'I cannot leave her.'

'Beatrice ...' Hugh stared at her across Ursula's bed, their silent, unconscious child a barrier between them. 'There are others who can sit with her. The nurse. Catalina.'

Beatrice gritted her teeth. For Catalina to perform this duty, this *mother's* duty, would add insult to injury: hadn't she already usurped Beatrice's position enough? Didn't Hugh realise how offensive his suggestion was?

'And if Ursula wakes to find I am not here?'

'Then you'll be only a corridor away. Beatrice, you'll be no help to anyone if you're exhausted.'

As if she needed reminding of her uselessness. She hadn't been able to protect Ursula, she hadn't been able to save Maria, or bring her killer to justice, and clearly she wasn't beautiful, young, or fertile enough to keep Hugh satisfied. And, now Hugh was home, he'd assumed control of all those tasks that gave her days purpose. If she wasn't keeping vigil at Ursula's bedside, what would she be doing? Embroidering gloves, making pomander beads, telling the gardeners to prune here and rake there. No one would notice if these tasks went undone; no one had ever asked for them to be done in the first place.

'Just a few hours. Let someone else watch over her.'

He sounded impatient, and Beatrice bridled. 'Such as her father, perhaps? How much time have you spent with her since she was hurt?'

Hugh paled, his tanned face stiffening. Again his hand went to his beard, yanking, rubbing the bristles askew. 'Not enough,' he said hollowly. 'I can't stand seeing her like this. Besides, what comfort would I be if she woke?'

'You're her father – of course you'd comfort her.'

'I'd try,' he said. 'But all the while she'd be crying for you.' He gazed at Ursula, at the blonde curls she'd inherited from him. 'After all, I'm almost a stranger to her.'

'That's not true. At the docks, she was so excited to see you –'

'An exciting stranger who brings gifts – there are pedlars who mean as much to her as I do.' Hugh shook his head bitterly. 'And in truth, she is almost a stranger to me. Every time I return, she looks different, she speaks differently. It's as if my ship is a fairy barrow, and every time I step ashore, it's into a changed world with half-familiar faces and rules I've half-forgotten. You all change and grow, and what do I do? Bring back strange vegetables.'

She stared at him in bewildered recognition. That note in his voice: sharpened, resigned, sad – it was envy. The same envy she felt when he sailed away, the disappearing ship reminding her once again that her horizons were garden walls, her skies grey and narrow. While his were vast, and she could not share them.

'But at least you can come back,' she offered hesitantly, unwilling to reveal the true depths of her jealousy. 'Yes, you leave, but you also return. You are part of our world, and part of a world that you help to discover more of every year.'

'Perhaps,' he sighed. 'Yet sometimes I wonder ...' He trailed off, staring at Ursula, at the contraption shielding her legs, then suddenly met Beatrice's eyes. 'Am I being punished?'

'What?' *By me?* Did he take her anger over Catalina as some sort of unwarranted spite? Or was he bemoaning the fact that children grew, deeming it a personal attack? 'Punished how – for what?'

'For that voyage north.'

Even in the sickroom, with its banked fire and closed windows, the words chilled Beatrice. 'How can that voyage have anything to do with our daughter's injuries? It was four years ago.'

'I remember it like yesterday. And I won't be the only one who can't forget. His family. William. God.'

Two of the three she could allow. But William had no regrets more troubling than shooting a stag in the shoulder rather than the heart, and more for frustrated marksmanship than any compassion for the creature.

'But you told me it wasn't your fault,' Beatrice pointed out. 'You had no choice. Why would God punish you for something that wasn't your fault?'

'Everything that happens on board a ship is the captain's responsibility.' Hugh learned against one of the bedposts, pressing his forehead hard against the carved oak, as if he might break open his skull and expel the memories. 'All of it, every mistake, every injury, every death – they happened under my command and I should have prevented it.'

'You can't control the weather, Hugh. You couldn't control –'

'But I can control how my men have been trained to respond to it. How I respond. And I let my crew down on that voyage. Especially him.'

'Even so ...' She was torn between genuine sympathy for Hugh's guilt and weary frustration. She'd barely slept, her daughter had been horrifically injured, and now was the moment her husband chose to unburden himself and dredge up old guilt? 'Hugh, that voyage cannot have had any bearing on what happened to Ursula. They were running, and she slipped and fell. It was an accident, nothing more sinister.'

Except it hadn't been so simple. She could declare so aloud if only because the alternative, the truth, would see her sent to Bedlam. But she could swear it had been the globe that caused Ursula's burns.

'An accident that happened in my house, to my daughter,' Hugh said bleakly. 'Just days after my servant was murdered in my gardens.'

Beatrice swallowed. 'They are all mine too. If you blame yourself … do you also blame me?'

It was painful enough to blame herself, and God knew Beatrice wished she had done something, anything to save Ursula and Maria. But for Hugh to blame her? That would make her guilt real, and deserving of punishment.

You deserve all that is coming. Whoever had written that, were they right?

Hugh hadn't spoken. Had it been longer than a breath, or was it just her fear dragging the silence taut?

Slowly, he lifted his head to face her. 'None of this happened while I was away, Beatrice. Maybe they would all have been safer if I hadn't returned.'

It was what Maria had said to Solomon. That the longer the *Silver Swan* stayed away, the longer they would be safe. Had there been some truth in her suspicions?

Beatrice didn't know what to say. 'Hugh …'

'Get some sleep, Beatrice.' He gave her a wan smile as he moved to the side of the bed and took her hands to pull her up. 'I may not have been there to protect our daughter from the flames, but I can certainly protect her from any intruding cats or mice. Even the blasted monkey, should she deign to reappear.'

She let him kiss her goodnight. Ordinarily, Hugh's readiness to laugh, to turn from rage to smiles swifter than any tide was one of the things she loved best about him: no storm could last around Hugh, certainly not long enough to sink him, or anyone else. But now, his willingness to usher her away from this conversation, to ignore any other questions he or she might have ... it left Beatrice feeling alone. Because she couldn't stop wondering.

She kissed Ursula goodnight and stepped out into the corridor, where the torches flickered in their sconces, their flames rising and falling like fingers counting off questions.

What if this were all about punishment? The man she believed had killed Maria had given Beatrice a note stating that she deserved to suffer. The same man had bribed Simon to paint their globe differently. And now the sabotaged globe had not only foretold Maria's death, but also seemed to push Ursula into the fire – to say nothing of the times when Beatrice had seen it turning of its own accord.

But how could the globe be causing any of this? It was wood and brass, paper and ink. It had no power, no control, no influence.

Yet if it wasn't the globe orchestrating Beatrice's punishments, a person had to be responsible. And she didn't know which explanation was more terrifying.

'Mama?'

She gasped and whirled round, clutching a fist to her suddenly jolting stomach. For a moment she'd been certain Ursula had risen – or, worse, that the other daughter had. But it was Walter, a thin white figure in his nightshirt, sidling out of his bedchamber.

'Walter, sweetheart, you should be asleep.'

He shook his head, scuffing his bare toes on the tiles. 'I can't sleep. I keep remembering ...'

'I know,' she said gently, drawing her son close. 'So do I.'

He so rarely wanted her to hold him now. She could feel his bones through the linen, the jutting wings of his shoulder blades, the fragile ladder of his ribs. He'd been so round as a baby, all fat pink cheeks and bracelets of flesh around his wrists; now, at nine, he was no longer her chubby little infant, nor was he yet the broad, muscular man he would become. And yet, every time she held him, she held every version of her son, every boy he had ever been and ever would be, and the desire to protect and preserve each one was visceral, almost painful.

'Shall I sing you to sleep, Walter?'

He nodded, his forehead butting her chest, lamblike and needing. She kissed the top of his head and wrapped an arm around his shoulders as she guided him back into bed.

'Mama ...'

She paused, the blankets half-tucked around him. 'Yes, sweeting?'

'Was it my fault? What happened to Ursula?'

Like father, like son: even though Walter's guilt was less frustrating, less egotistic than Hugh's, Beatrice couldn't suppress the thought that if anyone else demanded she hear their confession before she had a chance to sleep, she'd scream. 'No, Walter,' she said firmly. 'It was an accident, and no one's fault at all.'

'But I tripped. She wouldn't have fallen if I hadn't tripped.'

'You didn't mean to. No one blames you.'

'But ...' He gnawed at his lip: he'd already drawn blood in several spots, and scarlet peppered his lower lip. 'I didn't say anything.'

'You couldn't have. It all happened so fast, there was no time.'

'No.' He shook his head, tears of frustration and guilt trembling on his lashes. 'I mean I didn't tell her about the picture.'

Beatrice strode down the corridor, brandishing a torch snatched from its bracket as if she were leading an army into battle – but she'd never felt less bold.

'The picture,' Walter had whispered, his dark eyes hollow with fear. 'Every time I walked past the globe, that was the picture I saw. Even if no one had moved it, or even if I'd turned it round to show the other half, when I turned round, that picture was always at the front. As if it were warning me.'

For Beatrice to feel warned, to feel guilty for ignoring the warnings or misunderstanding their significance – that was unsettling enough. But if her son was being frightened by the globe, if the globe had somehow both caused and foretold her daughter's injuries ... that spoke of a vile malevolence that was unforgivable. Beatrice was no innocent. But her children were, and she would defend them until her dying breath.

There was the gallery door. Closed. Beatrice's steps slowed. Carefully, cautiously, she stepped closer to the door and pressed her ear against the wood.

Nothing. Silence. She swallowed a sigh of relief and reached for the door handle.

Then she heard it. A stirring, like the breathing of someone unseen as they rose. Then the noise altered. As if the person were no longer merely breathing, but murmuring, whispering, hissing. A warning – or a threat?

Steeling herself, Beatrice thrust the door open.

The gallery was dark. Shadow upon shadow swarmed in the curtains' velvet folds, clustering beneath chairs, twisting their carved backs into gargoyle hunches. The tapestries were stained black; here a silver thread ringed a narrow eye, there an outflung white arm reached out through the darkness. In the curiosity cabinet, spiked shells gleamed like bared teeth, and the coiled salamander skeleton seemed to hang like a noose in her torch's glow. Meanwhile, in its alcove, the globe was stirring.

It wasn't spinning. Instead, it was shifting, drifting almost to the left, one tiny increment at a time, its brass meridian ring winking as her torchlight fell on it. Like a vast head, tilting and beckoning her over.

She'd thought she'd chosen to come here, to confront the images on the globe. But now, Beatrice had the disconcerting sensation of having been summoned.

She stepped closer, her skirts chiding against the rushes as if to stay her steps: *go no closer*. She ignored the voice in her mind: she had to see. She wouldn't be caught unawares again.

The varnished surface gleamed in the torchlight: not so much a head as one eye, rolling in its wooden socket, bloodshot with red and blue veins. Ignoring the revulsion rising in her throat, Beatrice bent to peer closer.

There was the drowning woman, her neck stained purple. There the lines tracking Drake and Frobisher's voyages. There a sea monster, its cerulean tail undulating out of the water, ominous and heavy as a raised harbour chain, forcing you to stay out, battling storms. And there, gliding into view as the globe shifted once more, was the image Walter had insisted was following him. Writhing in the seas off the Norwegian coast, the bear wrapped in the cockatrice's emerald tail.

The bear. *Ursa.* Ursula, their little bear cub, tangled in green skirts and trapped as the cockatrice breathed scarlet flames.

Horrified, Beatrice sank to her knees. There it was: her daughter's fate foretold. And she hadn't seen it.

What else had she missed? *You deserve all that is coming* – was there more? Could the other creatures and cartouches warn her – give her a chance to prevent further suffering? Would the symbols clearly refer to people, like the dark-haired woman lying in the water, or would there be more oblique omens? Were there any small dark-haired boys in danger? Or might there be some play on Walter's name? It meant *powerful warrior* – were there any boys wielding swords against threats? Beatrice scanned the globe, then forced herself to turn it. With a twist of perverse, futile spite, for surely the globe did not, could not care, she chose to turn it backwards, in the opposite direction to its jerking. Touching its surface was like setting her fingertips to rotting fish: her skin recoiled at the prospect, the hairs rising on her arms. It revolted her. But she had to know.

There, on an island in the Aegean sea, was a warrior. But he was fair-haired, and wielding sword and shield against a snake-haired Gorgon: surely that was just Perseus slaying Medusa, rather than any kind of warning that Walter should avoid snakes, or swords, or women. Maybe she shouldn't be looking for warriors at all. They'd named Walter after Sir Walter Raleigh, who'd been granted the royal charter authorising him to explore the New World not long before Walter was born – was there an image near the colony of Roanoke? Only brightly coloured flowers and some turtles in the water, all looking perfectly calm and not about to be devoured by sharks or sea monsters. Raleigh had plagued the Spanish for years – but Spain was only illustrated with pomegranates, which were out of season in any case, so Walter was hardly likely to choke on a seed. But Queen Elizabeth had given Raleigh a nickname mocking his Devonshire accent: Water. Did the water on the globe represent Beatrice's Walter? There were rivers and lakes and oceans depicted, covering more than half the globe – did that mean any image at all could represent a threat to her son?

And what about the rest of her loved ones? Hugh? Florence? Her nieces? William? Or Ridley?

But to depict Ridley, the man in black would have to have known about that moment in the stables, something Beatrice would have thought impossible. Yet someone had entered her grounds to murder Maria. How could Beatrice be certain that was the first time an intruder had entered? What if she and Ridley had been seen after all? What if her adultery were the reason for these punishments?

She shook her head to dispel the notion. It made no sense. The kiss had occurred barely a fortnight before the globe's arrival: Simon had to have begun work on the globe long before then. Besides, surely the only person who'd want to punish her for Ridley was Hugh, and he'd been away. She'd only received the note the day after his return, and the globe had been delivered the next day – too short a time, surely, for Simon to be blackmailed and alter all the illustrations on Hugh's globe. And Hugh had been furious at the changed design. A bluff? No – Hugh was no actor. He'd keep a truth concealed, as Catalina proved, but he wouldn't spin an elaborate artifice to hide a secret.

But just as she'd convinced herself the globe had nothing to do with Ridley, an image caught her eye.

In the middle of the Atlantic ocean, a mermaid rose out of the sea, her blue-scaled tail coiled around her, coral fins flaring like a lady's fan. Circling her brown hair was a silver headdress with a sapphire at her forehead – the same headdress Beatrice always wore with her blue damask gown. And she often wore a coral kirtle beneath.

But that wasn't the most unsettling part. One of the mermaid's hands rested on her hip, thrusting her bared breasts forward boldly, provocatively, while in the other hand, she held a mirror. And reflected in the mirror was not one face, but two: the mermaid's own, and a man's, so close they might almost be kissing.

She'd been wrong. Someone had seen her with Ridley. Someone knew – and had decided to punish her for it. But who?

11

Crouching down, Ridley stared at the globe, frowning as he inspected the image of the mermaid. Beatrice, arms folded, resisted the urge to tap her foot impatiently. Finally, Ridley rocked back on his heels, puffing out his cheeks.

'It's such a tiny image, it's hard to tell. It could be anyone, Beatrice.'

She rolled her eyes. 'It could be – but it's me! Look at her – look at that headdress! You must have seen me wear it a dozen times.'

He looked back at the picture, then up at her, and she shifted, suddenly remembering the mermaid's nakedness. Was Ridley now imagining her disrobed? Did he think she was encouraging him to do so? Blushing, Beatrice brought one arm up, resting her chin on her hand as if in thought, trying to angle her sleeve so it covered as much of her chest as possible.

'Is it such a distinctive piece? I'm no jewellery connoisseur and you're the finest woman I know – but maybe every noblewoman in England has a similar headdress.'

'It can't just be a coincidence! Not after the other two images –'

'Two?'

'Yes – the cockatrice breathing fire on the bear. It's Ursula, don't you see?'

Ridley stood up, brushing a sprig of rosemary off his knee. 'I'll admit there was an uncanny resemblance between the woman on the globe and Maria. But the bear and the cockatrice … Isn't it likely you're seeing things that aren't really there?'

She reeled as if slapped. 'You think I'm mad?'

'I didn't say that.'

'You didn't have to!' she snapped, furious. 'Besides, it wasn't me that saw the connection first – it was Walter!'

'Perhaps the idea had been planted in his mind,' Ridley said, infuriatingly gentle. 'He could have overheard someone discussing the picture of Maria.'

'How? When he followed us to Lambeth, disguised as a pie-seller?' Beatrice shook her head. 'Even if you don't believe me about the cockatrice and the bear, you have to believe me about the mermaid – if only because if there's a chance I'm right, we could both be in danger. You could end up on the pillory – if Hugh doesn't kill you first. As for me …'

She'd never see her children again. Hugh would be legally entitled to exile her from this house, the house she'd been born in. She'd heard of wives being sent to Bedlam for adultery, their children told their mothers were dead. Beatrice couldn't imagine a worse fate.

Ridley's brow was furrowed in thought now. 'But no one else was there. How could we have been seen?'

'I don't know – perhaps we didn't hear a stable boy returning? One of the grooms? Or anyone – the stable has a door, for heaven's sake!'

'Let's think rationally,' he said, and again she bridled at the insinuation.

'I'm not mad, Ridley.'

Except the more times she had to say it, the less convincing it sounded. Even to her own ears.

'No – of course not. But what you've been through, first with Maria and now your daughter … Anyone would be distressed. You mustn't let your grief lead to do something rash.'

'What do you imagine I'm going to do?' She shook her head in frustration. 'I've no intention of screeching from the rooftops that I'm an adulteress, or running through the streets howling that my husband's globe is trying to kill me.'

'But you believe that,' he said softly, and there was such tenderness in his voice that she couldn't bear to look at him. 'And that frightens me more than anything.' He took a step closer. 'Beatrice … you've always been so strong. So courageous, so clever. It's why I …'

'Don't,' she whispered. 'You mustn't say it.'

'Silent or spoken, it is true. And that's why it grieves me so much to see you afraid. You're not being yourself, Beatrice. If you lost your strength, you would be another woman entirely, and it is *this* woman who I admire and respect – and everything else I cannot tell you. But which you know.'

He was so close she could smell the woodsmoke clinging to his doublet: he'd been out with the gardeners burning leaves. He was always close, always had been. Even if he wasn't in the same room as her, even when one of them was away from the house, she'd always been able to rely on Ridley, to trust that he would be there whenever she needed him. That was the difference between Ridley and Hugh. That was why – the *only* reason why – she'd reached out to him in the stables.

Except he'd reached for her. Hadn't he? Or did she just wish that were true? Would it be less her fault that way, if she were not the temptress, or worse, if she had succumbed to temptation?

'Please,' Ridley said. 'Leave this.'

She met his eyes. 'I cannot. If I'm right, then everything I hold dear, everyone I love could be in danger.'

His sigh seemed to rumble inside his entire body, like gunpowder exploding far below the ground. 'Very well. Then I will help you.'

'You believe me?'

He gave a wry smile. 'I didn't say that. But I'm your steward, and it's my duty to protect you, not to judge you. If my help can keep you safe, you have it. You will always have it.'

She didn't know whether to be delighted or disappointed: she'd wanted his support, but did she still want it if he thought she was mad? 'Thank you, Ridley.'

'But can we take a rational approach?' He tried to smile again: still wry, but less sad. 'This image is painted on Hugh's globe – if someone knows about us, why would they wish to reveal it to Hugh?'

Beatrice shook her head. 'I don't know. To blackmail me, perhaps, with the threat of doing so?'

'It would make sense. You're a rich woman, after all.' Ridley hesitated. 'Or perhaps whoever is behind this has another motive. A less mercenary one.'

'What do you mean?'

'What if they have a vested interest in telling Hugh, not because of venal concerns, but out of affection? Familial affection, even?'

Beatrice stared. 'But William always sails with Hugh. He couldn't have seen us.'

'William isn't Hugh's only relative.'

It had always been so easy to overlook Nicholas. Not merely overlook, but even forget. When she remembered to think about Nicholas at all, Beatrice would wonder if Nicholas himself knew this, for really, how could he not? Growing up beside Hugh, golden, strong, daring Hugh, how could Nicholas have been anything other than aware of his own inadequacy? Slight, mousy-haired, quiet: if Hugh were the portrait in oils, Nicholas was the sketch, faint, flawed and limpid. Knowing all this, Nicholas had decided simply not to compete. He couldn't ride a horse as fast as Hugh, or shoot arrows so accurately, but he could translate Greek, Latin, Hebrew, Italian and French as fast and true as anyone in Christendom. He might never have ventured to the New World, but he'd explored Utopia in Thomas More's words, and discovered the stars in the works of John Dee and Tycho Brahe. He'd never led men into battle in the Irish Pale, but he could defeat anyone at chess in fewer than twenty moves. While Hugh had been performing heroics on land and sea, Nicholas had been forging quiet progress of his own, sometimes among the hushed cloisters of the College of Arms, sometimes in the Radclyffe house in Blackfriars that Hugh, after marrying Beatrice, had no use for. Yet no one really noticed Nicholas's achievements. And someone who had gone unnoticed all their life could turn that to their advantage. Especially if they themselves grew adept at noticing others.

She couldn't leave Chelsea to speak to Nicholas: what if Ursula awoke and Beatrice were halfway across London? Instead, she had to think of a ruse to draw Nicholas to her that didn't involve yet another dinner invitation that would never be reciprocated. If she couldn't appeal to

Nicholas's stomach, then it had to be his mind. Some query to do with the gardens? A herb she couldn't identify – a newfound curiosity about the myth behind a certain statue? Or, better yet, a request that combined scholarly insight with a plea for an uncle's guidance. So she'd sent a note begging his advice on whether Walter should study Hebrew, or Italian, or something else entirely: sure enough, Nicholas couldn't resist.

'Thank you for coming,' Beatrice said, gesturing for Nicholas to take a seat. She'd ordered honey cakes and spiced cider to be served in the gallery: if Nicholas had anything to do with the globe's images, she wanted to see him in its presence, to scour his face for guilt – or, worse, triumph. So far, however, he'd only had eyes for the refreshments. 'I hope I did not summon you away from anything vital.'

Nicholas had already taken a bite of honey cake, and tried to swallow and talk at the same time: crumbs peppered his gingery beard. 'Vital, yes, but not urgent. I'm translating Tycho Brahe's newest treatise in order to prepare my own riposte. His ideas about astronomical instruments are decidedly flawed.'

Instruments such as globes? Or was this just an academic dispute about trigonometry?

'Well,' Beatrice said, 'perhaps we should advise Hugh to avoid any instruments made to Brahe's designs. We don't want him using flawed armillary spheres and astrolabes to navigate the Atlantic!'

'Oh, Hugh has long known my opinion on Brahe,' Nicholas said with a scholarly condescension that Beatrice guessed he wouldn't have dared use with his brother. Hugh's wife, on the other hand, was apparently a distinctly less intellectual conversant. 'The Tychonic system is vastly inferior to the Copernican. Why, Brahe claims that –'

'Do you often advise Hugh on his astronomical instruments?' Beatrice broke in before Nicholas could expound further.

Nicholas beamed proudly. 'Why, yes! I may not have used them myself, of course, or at least not for the same purpose. Mapping the stars and calculating their movements isn't the same as using the stars to plot a course across turbulent waves, but I flatter myself that Hugh always values my opinion on the instruments he commissions for the *Silver Swan*.'

'Such as this globe, for instance?' Beatrice indicated the thing with a gesture that contrived to be casual, still holding the honey cake. But she was painfully conscious of her voice: was it too high, too strained, like the wrong note eked out of a viola for too long? Had she wavered on the word 'globe'? 'Did you advise Hugh on this?'

'Of course.' Nicholas spoke eagerly, spraying himself with more crumbs: was he determined to devour every honey cake in case she took them away? 'I heard Master Molyneux was designing them last year, and I have always thought his instruments the most scientifically accurate, and Hugh finds them very robust at sea, so I was delighted to recommend Hugh acquire one. And I think he has been most satisfied – so I believe I may claim a little credit for his happiness!'

'Not entirely satisfied,' Beatrice said with cool politeness. 'Did Hugh not tell you? The illustrations on his globe are not what was promised.'

Nicholas laughed. 'As long as the measurements are accurate and the route maps faithful, what do doodled monsters matter? I suppose they make the globe prettier, more ornamental perhaps, if the owner merely wished to display it. But my brother's a sailor. I'm sure he appreciates that the globe is still immensely valuable.'

'Have you looked closely at the images?'

'Me? Not really. I confess I was more interested in this land of Corea – it's never been marked on a globe before, you know. Why, is the penmanship poor? Or smudged?'

'No,' Beatrice said slowly, 'nothing like that.'

Could Nicholas really be so innocent? His babbling didn't appear any more nervous than usual: Nicholas always grew garrulous when a topic actually interested him, and when it didn't, he'd find fascination in a fork or spiderweb rather than make any effort to converse about things he found dull, like other people for instance. Maybe he was gabbling to cover up his guilt, but Beatrice didn't think so: his eyes were wholly guileless. Besides, how would Nicholas bribe anyone, still less hire a murderer? Both acts would involve talking to people about subjects not related to science – and money. Nicholas was a younger son who spent what little he had on astrolabes and books: more than once he'd considered a finely illustrated volume of philosophy far more worth his coin than food, and he'd twice dined off a bean pottage for a week before Beatrice realised he was almost faint with hunger.

More to the point, she realised, she'd lay good coin on Nicholas not being able to recognise a kiss if he saw one. If he'd seen her with Ridley in the stables, he'd probably have assumed they were intently studying the impact of light on a person's irises, and ambled off thinking about geoheliocentric systems and stellar parallax.

Or about how to foretell the future.

'The children were talking recently about fortune telling,' Beatrice said, careful to keep her voice airy. 'Tell me, have you ever heard of images that could predict one's future?'

'Well now.' Nicholas rocked back in his chair, the honey cake in his hand momentarily forgotten and shedding crumbs into his ruff. 'All manner of forms of divination have been used over the centuries. One young Walter might particularly relish knowing about is anthropomancy, or haruspicy – in Etruria and Ancient Rome, they would use the entrails of a sacrifice to make predictions.'

'Perhaps not one to tell him about over dinner,' Beatrice said faintly. 'Or in his sister's presence.'

'There are less gruesome methods, of course,' Nicholas continued. 'Patterns in melting wax, shapes in the clouds, cartomancy, bibliomancy … I suppose all of those contain images of one kind or another.'

'But is it not …' Beatrice wanted to say *dangerous*, and settled for 'heretical?'

Nicholas grimaced. 'That rather depends on the country and the year in which a fortune teller dwells – what one monarch might encourage, another might deem blasphemous. Although I do believe every English monarch in living memory has had their horoscope foretold at least once – why, Queen Elizabeth regularly commands Doctor Dee to cast hers. Though for anyone to do so without royal decree would be treason, which raises an interesting philosophical conundrum – at what point does the act become malevolent? Can fortune telling itself ever be malign, or is it merely the consequences, the actions taken by those witnessing the prediction, or –'

'Could a painting tell the future?'

Nicholas squirmed, either at being interrupted mid-musing, or at the directness of her question. 'As much as any other form of fortune telling, I imagine. One could choose to see portents in anything. I've heard of people making predictions by asking parrots to choose cards, though I rather suspect such practitioners tend to be charlatans. But then, of course, cartomancy has its own ancient heritage. And the cards do contain images, so if those images can be interpreted to have meaning, at what point was the future decided? When the artist painted them? When the artist imagined them? Or when the parrot, or person, drew that particular card? Is it the object that tells the fortune, or the fortune that shapes the creation of the object?'

She could barely keep pace with his questions. Was it possible that the events predicted by the globe would have happened even without it existing? Or, had the globe never come into their house, but been somehow wedged into Hugh's cabin on the Swan, would Maria still have been murdered, Ursula still injured? Was it knowing about the globe that rendered it powerful, or did its force exist without her fear? And then her rational mind demanded to understand why she was even entertaining the possibility of wood and paper and glue having any kind of power over her, divination be damned.

'Beatrice?'

Nicholas was looking at her, grey eyes wide, less with concern, more with amiable befuddlement. 'I asked whether you'd reached a conclusion about young Walter's studies?'

'Oh – no.' For a moment, she couldn't even remember the problem she'd invented. 'Well – he already studies Greek, Latin and French, of course. But I wondered whether you thought another language might be useful, and if so, should we choose Hebrew or Italian?'

'Italian is more useful to speak, I believe,' Nicholas said earnestly. 'Though Hebrew opens up so many opportunities for reading widely. But really, my dear, it all depends on what future you want for your son.'

'In what sense?'

'Well …' Nicholas spread his hands, conveniently swooping up another honey cake. 'Languages are excellent branches to study for their own sakes. But when one is a grown man, knowing three is perfectly adequate. More is really only necessary for scholars. Unless, of course one wishes to trade with Venice or Genoa without intermediaries. And then of course, there are certain men who ultimately need only ever speak English, for everyone they meet will always defer to them. So you see, it all depends on whether you wish Walter to grow up to be like me, or his uncle Robert, or his father.'

Beatrice stared at her brother-in-law, struck by his words.

Walter would say Hugh. Until now, whatever his flaws, wouldn't she have said Hugh too?

But as Nicholas swallowed the last honey cake, Beatrice realised that she was no longer certain she wanted her son to become his father.

12

Each ring of her shoes on the tiles as she hurried back to the sickroom seemed a rapped reproof. She'd been away from Ursula for too long: already she was racked with guilt. What if her daughter had awoken? If her first question was about where Beatrice had been, 'having honey cakes with your uncle Nicholas' seemed a woefully inadequate excuse.

She forced herself to slow down as she reached Ursula's chamber: even an anxious guilt-ridden mother couldn't charge into a sickroom. Instead, she opened the door as softly and quietly as her urgency would allow, and slipped inside.

Where something had changed. Normally the only sounds were the sighs of herbs sifting, the fire crackling, perhaps a tisane coming to the boil, a distant heron crying on the other side of drawn curtains and closed glass. But today, the window was open, and someone was singing.

Catalina sat by Ursula's bedside, sewing, white thread and lace falling from her dark hands like spun spiderwebs. She was singing so softly Beatrice couldn't make out the words, only their gentle lullaby melody. It ought to have been calming – indeed, Ursula slept silently, her brows free of tension – and yet Beatrice was anything but calmed.

'What are you doing here?'

Catalina dipped her needle in another three stitches before replying. 'Captain Radclyffe asked me to watch over her. So I am watching.'

Beatrice floundered. There was only one chair at Ursula's bedside, and Catalina was already in it: she could hardly ask a pregnant woman to drag a heavy oak chair across the room, and yet why should Beatrice, Ursula's mother, have to do so?

'It's not your duty to watch her.'

'You haven't given me any duties,' Catalina pointed out. 'All I have to do at present is sew and grow fatter. I can do that as well here as anywhere. Besides, Captain Radclyffe and I thought you might be glad of the respite.'

So they'd been talking about her behind her back? Was this the first time, or had Hugh been meeting Catalina for secret conversations and more ever since she arrived?

'Did you indeed? And did you also decide together to ignore the physician's advice about keeping the windows closed?'

'Oh yes,' Catalina said, as if this were perfectly acceptable. 'Fresh air often helps the sick – on board a ship, if one is heaved about below-decks, it worsens any nausea or headache. And the smells are much more bearable this way.'

Now that she mentioned it, the cloying reek of lavender was far less overpowering with the scents of the gardens coming in. Oh, it was still there: Beatrice would never be able to ignore it, but when it mingled with the smell of recent rain on grass, of rosemary and sage, of the nearby river's vast haul of salt and silt, crayfish and clay, she could breathe deeply without panicking. Without being forced to remember.

Catalina was watching her. With the daylight at her back, her brown eyes were deep, inscrutable. 'Why lavender?'

'I …' Beatrice hesitated. No one had ever asked her that before. Perhaps it hadn't occurred to anyone else that her aversion was anything more than a silly womanly whim. And suddenly she found herself glad to have been asked – to have been noticed. Even if it came with the tone of a challenge and from a woman she had every right to despise. 'It reminds me of someone. A person who hurt me. Who would have continued to hurt me if …'

But that was too much. More than she'd ever uttered and already more than was safe to confess.

Catalina nodded. 'I understand. For me, it is ginger. I cannot smell it without my stomach heaving.'

'I thought ginger stopped sickness.'

'As I thought lavender induced calmness.' Catalina dipped her needle again. 'They gave me ginger on board the *Swan*. To help with my nausea. But it was far from fresh, and by that time ...'

Her needle stopped. Light splintered against it, sharp and blinding. Beatrice moved, coming to sit on the foot of the bed, careful not to put any weight on Ursula's mattress, or disrupt Catalina's recollection.

'Like you,' Catalina said eventually, 'the smell reminds me of a time when I was hurt. The worst hurt ever inflicted on me.'

Beatrice wet her lips. Tentatively, she said, 'Do you mean something that happened on board the *Swan*?'

Catalina stared at the jagged light as if forcing herself to look at it without flinching. 'It didn't start there. But on board the ship was when it was worst.'

'Do you mean ...' She could barely utter the words. 'Did the sailors ... violate you?'

Catalina shook her head. 'Oh no. Captain Radclyffe had made it very plain that no man was to touch me again. He said I was under his protection. That I was his woman now. Of course, his command came too late.' Her hand drifted to her belly, her face twisting in a strange mixture of apology and resentment and love. 'You may think that rape is the worst thing that can happen to a woman. I thought so too. But then, afterwards ... I had not realised there was worse to come.'

'What could be worse?'

Catalina gazed at Ursula, still and pale and tiny in her bed. 'You, of all people, must be able to imagine.'

Horror winded Beatrice. 'You mean you had another child? One who – who died?'

'I had another child once,' Catalina said quietly. 'Now, I do not.'

'How – forgive me, but how did your child die?'

Catalina slid her needle into her sewing and rose. 'She died because the men of your country did not think her worth saving. Needless to say, they were wrong. She was far better than any Englishman I have ever met.' She rose, cradling the growing swell of her belly as if her baby were wrought of delicate crystal, both beautiful and breakable. 'I shall leave you alone with your daughter now.'

She moved to the door, leaving Beatrice alone with the horrible real-isation that she had judged Catalina unfairly. Could she have misjudged Hugh as well?

Rain simmered against the glass, concealing the gardens behind quick-ening grey. Winter had well and truly set in: the glow of autumn had yielded to swollen damp and seeping mist and bitter winds. In past years, Beatrice had looked forward to winter, for the cold meant that Hugh would be unable to sail away. Sometimes the Thames even froze solid, locking the *Silver Swan* in icy fetters. A few years ago, they'd gone to the frost fair above Tower Bridge with Walter and Ursula; the river had glittered like spun sugar, and they had glided about on thin bone skates, Ursula's small hands tight on Beatrice and Hugh's as she tottered between them, eyes round as chestnuts as they passed fire eaters and puppet plays, and even horse races, their hooves wrapped in sacking. She'd talked about it for days afterwards.

If the Thames froze again this winter, would Ursula be well enough to visit the frost fair? Would she be well enough to walk by then – or ever again? Beatrice wrapped her arms tight around her ribs, trying to warm herself. She'd had to close the windows against the rain, but she didn't want to draw the curtains yet: here, by the glass, she could hover on the edge of the lavender's reach, but she could feel it pawing at her spine, her neck, her jaw, like a great grey cat toying with a creature it could easily snap in two.

The physician had been again after Catalina left. He'd said the scar-ring alone would be severe, perhaps bad enough to limit Ursula's movements. But until she had healed more, it would be impossible to say how much muscle had been damaged, or whether tendons had fused to bone or been destroyed entirely. The prospect was too awful to contemplate: her lively, lovely daughter, still at the age where she moved with pure joy and enthusiastic abandon, rather than the controlled grace women were schooled into. Ursula had so loved her dancing lessons, had been so proud of learning the steps of a galliard. If Ursula couldn't dance again she'd be heartbroken – and every time Ursula's heart broke, Beatrice's shattered in tandem.

She turned away from the window: there was Ursula, her upper body disappearing into the wooden frame, as if she were trapped in some brutal instrument of torture. For all that she knew the frame made Ursula more comfortable, for all her gratitude to Ridley, the sight of it jolted Beatrice every time. It was so rigid, so angular, so unlike her daughter's soft body, forcibly reminding Beatrice that she could not simply gather Ursula up in her arms and rock her to sleep.

But at least, Beatrice thought, resuming her seat and taking Ursula's hand, she had a daughter left to touch, and hope for, and love. Catalina did not even have that comfort.

What had she meant when she'd said that Englishmen had let her child die? Did she mean the crew of the *Silver Swan*? Did she mean *Hugh*? But she'd spoken of Hugh as if he'd helped her: surely she wouldn't have done that if Hugh were in some way to blame for her daughter's death?

Had the child died before Catalina boarded the *Swan*? And when had that been? The Azores? Virginia? The Caribbean? Or somewhere in the middle of the Atlantic: had she been taken up from another vessel?

Just who was Catalina, truly? Where had she come from? And why had Hugh felt such a duty to protect her?

A sudden draught snaked through the chamber. She started – and there was Hugh, entering Ursula's chamber as if Beatrice's thoughts had summoned him there. His hair curled with damp; his breeches and the front of his doublet glistened, as if he'd neglected to pull his cloak around himself properly. He crossed to stand at the foot of the bed, gazing down on his daughter. 'Has she improved at all?'

'She hasn't awoken,' Beatrice said. 'Though the physician says that may be a blessing. The pain she will be suffering, the horror of the memory ...'

'Minds heal slower than bodies,' Hugh said grimly. 'Did he say anything else?'

Beatrice could barely utter it. 'Hugh, he fears she may never fully recover. That she may not be able to dance again. Perhaps not even walk ...'

'Christ's wounds.' Hugh's hands curled into loose fists and Beatrice wondered if he was imagining beating the physician bloody for his cruel diagnosis, or if he, like her, was simply aching to wrap Ursula in his arms and hold her so tight the world could never hurt her again. 'What can we do? Should we consult another physician?'

'We have to wait,' Beatrice said. 'That's all.'

'The one thing I cannot abide.' Hugh shook his head bitterly.

'You haven't had the practice I have.'

Waiting was women's work: while Hugh sailed the world or strode and rode about London, Beatrice was used to waiting, to filling the time with small bits of daily life. She waited for Hugh to return for months almost every year; she'd spent months waiting for their children to be born; she'd waited for Hugh to give the reins of the household back to her when he put to sea again. If he were Odysseus, she was Penelope: while he garnered accolades for his heroism, she sewed, organised gardeners and kitchens and stables, made pomander beads, ordered clothes and shoes for growing children, made sure their tutors were competent and her children obedient, ticking off tasks and days until Hugh returned to them. But a Penelope would not cavil at her lot, not when her husband had been to war, fought a Cyclops, defied the Sirens' call, dared the underworld. Penelopes were patient and welcoming, gentle and obliging. They did not rage, or resent, or seek revenge. Most of all, they did not judge their husbands for straying, still less reprove them. A Penelope would not interrogate Odysseus about Circe or Calypso, would never be tempted by a suitor of her own. And there Beatrice had failed.

'I spoke to Catalina today.'

'Oh?' Was Hugh's nonchalance feigned? Did guilt simmer beneath that apparent indifference?

'She told me about her first child.' Beatrice paused, letting her words hang in the air: if Hugh took them to mean that Beatrice knew more than she truly did, might he then reveal more than he would otherwise have wanted to?

'Damned sad business,' Hugh grunted. 'The girl should never have been allowed to get so sick, especially not on board a ship, when disease spreads swifter than fire.'

'Allowed? You can't mean you blame Catalina for her daughter's death!'

'Christ, no!' Hugh stared at her, aghast. 'I know you've been angry with me of late, Beatrice, but surely you cannot think me such a monster as that?'

'Then what happened to the child?'

'What often happens to frail children at sea. Our voyages are harsh enough for grown men, let alone tiny girls.' Hugh gnawed at the inside of his cheek, regret furrowing his brow. 'But even so, the child should have been better cared for. Catalina asked for medicine and her message went astray. By the time her child received any treatment, it was too late. We had to bury her at sea.'

Beatrice knew bodies could not be kept aboard ship: as Hugh said, disease spread fast in such close confines. Even captains, even knighted heroes would be sewn up in sailcloth and slid into the sea. But how cruel for Catalina, to not even have the comfort of a grave to visit, only unmarked saltwater, knowing that somewhere below, in a vast, icy darkness, her daughter's body lay on the seabed, where shadowy fish with cold unblinking eyes scoured her bones.

'How awful,' Beatrice murmured, disgusted at the inadequacy of her words.

'If only that were all Catalina had had to endure.'

She stared at him, shocked by the anger in his voice. 'What do you mean?'

Hugh looked at her in surprise. 'A woman carrying a child comes to you seeking refuge – did you imagine her path here was an easy one?'

'No ...' Beatrice hesitated: Catalina had dropped hints, and it seemed prurient to delve for more, but how else to allay her suspicions? 'She said she'd been raped. That you'd made it plain no man was to touch her again. That ... it had happened before she came aboard the *Swan*.'

'All true.' Hugh's eyes darkened at the memories.

'Then why ...' *Why are you so angry at something your men have no doubt done dozens of times before? Something I imagine not a few of them have been doing since they arrived back on English soil.* Men didn't get angered by rape, in Beatrice's experience. Especially not men who'd led soldiers into battle in Ireland and captained ships on long voyages that took them away from women's bodies. Such anger was a woman's lot, as were any and all consequences of such assaults. And not even all women: for her part, Beatrice could think of few crimes more monstrous, and yet she remembered hearing Florence's mother and her friends talk with disgust about maids they'd had to dismiss because the grooms had got them with child, blaming the girls every time. So what was different here? Beatrice couldn't think which explanation was worse: that Hugh was the father of Catalina's baby, or that he actually cared about Catalina herself.

Hugh was still silent, as if weighing up how much to tell her; the sight not only infuriated but frightened her – how many other explanations of his reluctance to explain could there be?

'It happened before she came aboard,' Hugh said eventually. 'The first time, that is. The occasions after that … one of my men disobeyed me.'

'Then I hope he was whipped for his crimes. And will not be sailing with you again.'

Hugh shook his head. 'It's not that simple, I'm afraid.'

'What? How can you have such a man aboard? A vile rapist, and insubordinate and deceitful into the bargain – such a man's presence aboard our ship is both offensive and sets a terrible example to others. What are you thinking, Hugh?'

'What I always am,' Hugh said sharply. 'That everything that happens aboard a ship is the captain's responsibility.'

'You cannot blame yourself for this!'

Hugh shook his head. 'You don't understand. If you knew …'

'Then tell me, Hugh! For God's sake, tell me!'

He took a deep breath. His lips parted.

But whatever he had been about to say was silenced by a small voice croaking from the depths of the bed, 'Mama?'

'Ursula!' Beatrice flew to her daughter, practically crawling onto the bed in order to kiss Ursula's cheek and cradle her little stirring body.

'Oh, my darling, I –' But she didn't say what she'd feared. Instead, she sobbed, 'I am so glad to hear your voice again!'

Ursula blinked at Beatrice, then at Hugh, leaning over from the other side to kiss her too. 'Don't fight,' she said crossly. 'I don't like it.'

'Of course we won't,' Hugh said. 'We were just discussing grown up things loudly, not fighting. No need to fret, my little bear cub.'

As Ursula smiled and nuzzled into her father's embrace, Beatrice knew she should be feeling nothing but gladness and relief. But she couldn't crush the tiny flicker of jealousy: if only she could be so easily convinced by Hugh's excuses.

13

Durham House gleamed out of the darkness ahead of them like some vast black creature crouched on the riverbank, with dozens of flickering golden eyes, its many mouths breathing smoke against a star-pocked sky. As their barge approached, Beatrice could hear viols and lutes seeping out of the Raleighs' home, followed by laughter: sounds that should have been beautiful, and yet she felt them like cold water slithering down her neck.

She hadn't wished to come. She wouldn't have come at all if Ursula had still been unconscious though her daughter was hardly fully recovered, which Beatrice saw as a perfectly valid reason to remain at home. However, where Sir Walter Raleigh was concerned, Hugh's sense of reason evaporated entirely. So here Beatrice found herself, out on the river in late November, the black tide hauling her up to Durham House.

Candles hung from the bare branches of pear and mulberry trees, creating an avenue of wavering white fingers, beckoning guests from river to door. It was beautiful, in an eerie way, but Beatrice couldn't help thinking of courtiers' hands, pale as wax, fluttering to lips to cover the words they were hissing, though not the fact they were whispering about you.

Beside her, Hugh seemed impervious as ever, sauntering between lights as if the candles meant no more to him than mere convenience. He barely glanced at them: his eyes were only for the house ahead of them.

'Remember, Beatrice,' he muttered, 'this is a celebration.'

While Beatrice had been burying her maid and nursing her daughter, Raleigh had been made a member of parliament as reward for his exploits against the Spanish, repelling a third Armada and capturing a retreating ship. After Raleigh and Essex's failure in the Azores, Beatrice wondered if Raleigh had been secretly relieved when the Armada hoved into view: a chance at redemption which he'd eagerly seized. Tonight, they'd all been asked to dress in gold and crimson: 'like fireworks', the messenger bringing the invitation had said. 'Like piracy,' Beatrice had observed when the boy had gone. 'Plunder and bloodshed.'

'Like profit,' Hugh had retorted. 'Coins and rubies, plate and wine.'

But there was a difference between trade and privateering. A ruthless bargain didn't leave men bleeding on a gunpowder-blackened deck.

'It might leave them starving and destitute though,' Hugh had pointed out the first time she'd challenged him on this, years ago, when Walter was still in leading strings. 'Just because you aren't there to see it or smell it doesn't mean it doesn't happen. I'm no more cruel or immoral than your father.'

If only Hugh had known what a pitiful endorsement that was.

Now, as they entered Durham House, Beatrice had to admit Lady Raleigh's edict made for a splendid spectacle. Cloth of gold sparkled in firelight; crimson damask shone like rich malmsey. Rubies, garnets and carnelians glittered against throats and wrists; gilt-embroidered sleeves and gold belt buckles gleamed as guests danced and drank. The sarabande being performed did indeed look like fireworks' circles and spirals coalescing across the marble, forming new patterns with every beat. Beatrice glimpsed Penelope Rich twirling in Charles Mountjoy's arms, both resplendent in gold sarcenet, his sleeves slashed with scarlet silk to match her scarlet kirtle. Rumour had it the child Penelope had borne in spring had been Mountjoy's, not her husband's, and Lord Rich had chosen to turn the blindest of blind eyes. Perhaps women could be forgiven such disloyalty when they were earls' daughters and descended from kings' bastards. When they were merchants' daughters cuckolding knighted heroes, no doubt it would be a wholly different matter. Glancing down at her own honey damask gown and the strings of coral at her throat and wrists, Beatrice needed no further reminder of the gulf between herself and the courtiers Hugh wished to belong with.

'Percy!' Hugh called. 'I hear you nearly blew your stables to splinters with your experiments – have you any eyebrows left?'

The Earl of Northumberland laughed sheepishly as Hugh joined him by the fireplace. 'None at all, but fortunately I still have all my horses. Though the poor beasts are terrified of any noise now – dropped horseshoes, closing doors …'

'Do you dare ride them again yet? Or must you win their forgiveness with every sugar lump in London?'

Beatrice, knowing herself forgotten, turned away. Were all men so cavalier, or just those in the Essex circle and anyone aspiring to join it? What did Percy care for his horses when alchemy lured him? What did Hugh care for her feelings when there was an opportunity to win more glory?

She was being unfair, she admitted to herself as she accepted a cup of burgundy from a passing page, noting that the golden goblet and even the liquid within were both far richer hues than those she wore. Hugh did care: he loved their children, he was an attentive husband by night and a generous provider by day. But honour had driven him to shelter Catalina, pride had led him to purchase that globe, and the pursuit of glory led him across the seas every year. And it was hard not to suspect that Hugh's reputation would always come first, ahead of wife and children.

'Lady Radclyffe, how splendidly you gleam tonight!'

Suddenly bowing over her was the last man she'd expected to pay her any compliments: Robert Devereux, the Earl of Essex himself. His moustache nibbled at her skin as he kissed her hand; even as he rose back to his full height, he didn't release her.

'Thank you,' she managed, searching for a response that was witty enough, respectful enough. He was clad head-to-toe in crimson velvet, his sleeves and breeches slashed to reveal golden silk, as if he might bleed wealth and splendour if you got close enough to cut him. 'I could never hope to outshine an earl, of course.'

'What are we without hope?' Essex retorted, his voice light, his grip on her hand anything but. He wore a ring on each finger, each one studded with enormous gems or heavy with coats of arms, dwarfing the single gold twist on her hand; it was as if she'd been caught by an otherworldly creature with four joints in its clawed hands. 'Hope is what makes us human, I believe.'

'Well. That, and our lack of fur and feathers.'

He let out a loud guffaw; a few people nearby twisted at the sound, and on recognising the man laughing, eagerly broke into obliging grins, as if they might pretend to be part of his jest. But Essex, bewilderingly, remained entirely focused on Beatrice. 'Tell me, Lady Radclyffe, what do you hope for?'

Was it merely wine-loosened nonsense, noise for the sake of noise? Or could she detect something else beneath his words, a strangely jovial menace?

'At present, my lord, for my daughter to be well again soon, and that we may make it through the winter without our windows freezing from the inside.'

'I shall add your hopes to my prayers.' Essex tilted his head. 'I would have thought your hopes had altered of late though – given what was brought back from your husband's latest voyage.'

He couldn't mean Catalina. Was the woman's presence in Beatrice's home the subject of gossip all the way from Chelsea to Whitehall?

'Since until that moment I'd been hoping for his safe return, perhaps you may have a point.'

'Oh, I always do,' he said, with a wink, and the innuendo seemed less for her and more that he simply couldn't help finding lewd silliness in everything. 'We all brought back our own burdens from our voyages this summer, of course. Damaged reputations and hollowed coffers not least among them. Somehow, though, Raleigh seems to have dredged his reputation out of the gutter. And now in the public mind, by which I mean the royal mind, the failure in the Azores is no longer ours, but mine alone.'

He was still gripping her hand: one of his rings was grinding against her thumb and she tried not to wince. 'Surely you will be able to win the queen's favour again. We all know you are her favourite.'

'A position arguably more of an imposition than a privilege,' Essex groused. 'The stakes rise higher as a man's rank increases, for the price of glory is the risk of disaster. But you and your husband must know that all too well.'

Everyone relying on ships for their livelihood knew that. Why was he telling her this?

'You'll mention this to Hugh, won't you? That glory has a price, and its costs can be shared as much as its spoils.'

She stared at him, confused: Hugh was mere yards away, conversing with Mountjoy and Northumberland, the lover and husband of Essex's sisters. 'Can you not tell him yourself, my lord?'

Essex winked again. 'I could – but we all tell our wives things we would never tell our friends. And vice versa, of course, but I shouldn't reveal that to another man's wife!' He grinned, and bent lower, so that his lips almost brushed her hair. 'I know the value of what he brought back, Lady Radclyffe. I'd like to discuss it further.'

Before she could ask what he meant, he had kissed her hand and disappeared into the throng of red and gold bodies.

Was he referring to the cargo Hugh had carried back from the New World? Unless Essex had a particular passion for orange potatoes, she couldn't fathom why the *Silver Swan*'s holds should so fascinate him. Surely he couldn't be talking about Catalina: what on earth could she have to do with Essex?

Without Essex shielding her, the hall was stifling: fires burned in every hearth and hundreds of candles lined mantles and tables, while dozens of whirling bodies heated the hall with their exertions. Tambours and lutes, laughter and teasing all tangled in the close air, coiling tight and low over Beatrice's head like smoke. The smells of dried rose petals and melting wax and the dozens of scents on skin writhed close behind the noise: sandalwood, nutmeg, bergamot, ambergris, jasmine, and somewhere, unmistakeably, the smell of lavender. It smelled of shadows and clammy skin, of crushed breath and wordless fear. It smelled of dying, slowly, painfully, and inexorably.

She had to get out. She felt carved wood beneath her fingertips: the ornate panels of the wall, a door frame – and then empty air as she stumbled into an antechamber.

It was quiet, and cool, and the candlelight was soft: only a few glowed in sconces, calm as clean parchment after the frenetic flare and glower of the hall. Beatrice drew in a slow, steadying breath, counting as her lungs and mind cleared.

And then she saw the globe.

It stood in the alcove before the window, its varnished surface pale against a backdrop of blue velvet curtains. For a moment, Beatrice wanted to flee – and then she realised that, in fact, she did not wish, or need to do so at all. There was no sense of discomfort crawling down her spine, no hairs on her forearms lifting with unease. This globe was perfectly still. She felt nothing at the sight of it save a vague admiration, no different to seeing a well-executed portrait, or an attractively carved lintel or an elegant fountain.

Why was Raleigh's globe so different? Was it just the images? Or was the difference all in Beatrice's mind?

She didn't let herself think of Bedlam, nor of her mother. Instead, she stepped closer to the globe and studied its surface. There was Drake's voyage marked out; there was Guiana, there Virginia, there the Azores. She recognised some of the images – white-sailed ships, the elaborate compass, the giant orange-scaled fish with an eye like a whirlpool. But there was no black-haired woman drowning, no bear in a cockatrice's grip, and the mermaid's mirror held only one face.

What else was different? Cautiously, she set her fingers to the globe: it felt cool and smooth, and when Beatrice turned it, there was no rattling or lurching, no sense that it might suddenly speed up or reverse of its own volition. Only a soft whir as her hand guided it round.

'Do you admire it?'

Beatrice spun around, almost spilling her wine in shock. Behind her stood her hostess, Bess Raleigh. Her fair hair seemed pinioned beneath a pearl-studded headdress, her forehead pulled taut by the hairpins. In a golden brocade gown with a turquoise kirtle, she looked like a weary mermaid, cast out of the sea onto dry sands, growing more exhausted and isolated by the day. Beatrice would never have claimed to know Bess intimately, but she'd never seen Raleigh's wife look so tired before. In her mind, the women of the Essex circle never ceased to be glamourous and elegant, their conversation sparkling as brightly as their jewels. It hadn't occurred to her that they might not be wholly content with their lot either.

'It is a masterful piece of craftsmanship,' Beatrice said neutrally.

'Masterful,' Bess echoed, crossing the small chamber to stand beside Beatrice. 'It would have to be, of course. For a master of the sea.'

She caught the bitterness in Bess's voice and recognised it as her own. 'When does he sail again?'

'Not until spring, thank heavens.' Bess eyed the blue ink of the sea with resentment. 'Though even when he is in England, he is so rarely at my side. Do you know, it almost makes me remember our time in the Tower fondly. At least then I knew he and I were always under the same roof. I sometimes think I would dare Elizabeth's displeasure again if it meant I could have a month or two – or even just a week – of my husband by my side. Do you not feel the same?'

Beatrice had imagined incarceration in the Tower before: what person entering a royal palace hadn't? Cold stone enclosing you like a fist, every sound echoing with its own misery, and the shadows writhing with centuries of ghosts. It was too similar a vision to her mother's fate. 'I do my best to appreciate my independence when Hugh's away.'

Bess gave a hum that was part acknowledgement, part disagreement. 'Independence is all very well – but coming home to an empty house, rolling over in an empty bed: those take away all my enjoyment of solitude. Every room in this house has a Walter-shaped void, and no amount of singing or sewing or reading can fill it.'

Beatrice felt a twist of envy: strange, when Bess was unveiling her sadness. But her sheer love for her husband was astonishing – and forced Beatrice to wonder whether her own affection for Hugh were anywhere near as strong. Did enjoying independence make her a less devoted wife?

'I often think,' she offered hesitantly, 'that it would be nice to be welcomed home, rather than having to organise the welcome.'

'Perhaps,' Bess said. 'But I think I would prefer us to return home together – and if we must leave, then to depart hand in hand.' She extended one forefinger and pushed the globe into a slow revolve. 'That way, we might have shared stories. Guiana might mean something more to me than black ink on a map. The fruit from the Azores would not have an aftertaste of sawdust or cedar from the packing crates – I could have seen it piled high in the marketplace, or better yet, have plucked it fresh from the tree myself. I might have heard the dolphins' chatter and splash as they gambolled in our ship's wake, rather than listening to Walter's clicking impression.' She let out a tiny, mirthless laugh. 'I cannot even truly picture a dolphin, can you? They are as playful as puppies, Walter says, but leap like horses, yet have no fur, so I can only imagine a legless horse with grey leather skin, gibbering as it chases me – which is a terrifying image, far removed from the delightful frolicking creatures Walter describes.'

She'd found a picture of a dolphin on the globe and tapped it as if her fingernail might flick it into life. Beatrice couldn't help agreeing with her: the strange long-nosed thing was no more than brushstrokes. She couldn't envisage it brought to life, sleek and muscular yet childishly delighted by the water in which it spent its whole life.

'There are some wherrymen who swear they've seen dolphins in the Thames,' she said. 'Though I wonder whether an eel might resemble a dolphin after a certain amount of ale.'

Bess smiled. 'Yes – the same wherrymen who'll swear blind they had Anne Boleyn or Cardinal Wolsey in their boats once, even though both are sixty years dead and the wherrymen lacking a single grey hair.'

Beatrice laughed, and their shared mirth gave her the boldness to ask, 'I wonder … has anything strange happened in your house since the globe arrived?'

'Strange?'

'Violent,' Beatrice amended, embarrassed by her voice lowering itself and her eyes flickering away, as if she feared the globe overhearing her.

Bess frowned. 'I heard about your daughter and your maid. You have my sympathies and my prayers. But I cannot see how those incidents were related to this contraption.' She gave the globe a disdainful push. 'Though I understand why you might wish to connect them. When my son Damerai died, I blamed everything – the curtain that had let a shaft of sunlight stab his eyes, the porridge he'd barely touched, the rosemary bush used to dry his blanket. They were cursed, they were poisoned – they were things I felt I could have changed. When the awful truth was that nothing I, or anyone, could have done that would have saved my little boy.'

Beatrice knew she meant to be kind, knew she ought to thank Bess for sharing her grief and her advice. But she couldn't stop herself ploughing on. 'So your globe – it does not frighten you?'

'Frighten me?' Bess shook her head in surprised bewilderment. 'No. It only …' She sighed, staring at the globe. 'It makes me sad. This whole globe – all this is Walter's world, and I can never share it all. And what man would be satisfied with a wife and children and a home, when he could have the entire world?'

'What man indeed,' Beatrice concurred quietly.

Bess gave a small smile. 'I must return to my guests. To hear more tales of that vast world they wish to return to.'

But not even the world would satisfy men like Walter Raleigh and Hugh Radclyffe. They would never be able to hold it all, never be able to bring back the sounds and smells and tastes of all they had seen and done. And so they had to wrestle the world into paper gores over a wooden sphere, and place it in a fine chamber so they could proclaim themselves its conqueror.

Perhaps the conquest had been successful for Raleigh. But the globe Hugh had brought was out of his control.

She knew what was different about Raleigh's globe – she'd felt it as Bess set it rotating, or rather, *hadn't* felt it. It was simply a picture pasted on wood. So why was Hugh's globe so strange, so malevolent? It couldn't just be the different images Simon had painted. There had to be something more. Something *wrong*.

14

A mist had crept up the Thames while the Raleighs' guests caroused and danced, so thick Beatrice could scarcely see the south bank. She could feel the damp curling her hair at her temples and the nape of her neck, like cold fingerprints taking grip of her skull. The barge's canopy glistened silver, beads trembling with every oar stroke, every rippling wave. Some quivered violently enough to fall: a small puddle had formed just beyond the cushions where she and Hugh sat, and she could see the mist reflected in the water, like a white stain on their deck.

Perhaps it was the mist that kept them quiet: cloying and clinging, it made every sound echo coldly, from the metallic plash of oars on water, to the thin bells and calls of watchmen in distant streets. It felt as if anything they said would be overheard, and not just by the oarsmen. There could have been a dozen boats, even an entire armada at their backs, and Beatrice would never have known until the first cannon fired.

Or perhaps it was because she and Hugh were currently incapable of holding a conversation without dissolving into quarrelling. They'd argued about coming to Durham House at all, they'd argued at Ursula's bedside about what had happened on board the *Silver Swan* … when had they last concluded a conversation with a kiss, or at least an amicable parting? There had been a time when every conversation had ended in an embrace, or with Beatrice falling asleep in Hugh's arms, or with fingers lingering on fingertips as they hauled themselves away to duties. When had that stopped? Had it been before Ursula and Walter were born? Or later, after the lost girl, after Hugh returned from the north?

Or after Hugh had brought Catalina and the globe into their home? Beatrice couldn't tell. All she knew was that their love seemed like the city on the other side of the mist: she knew it was there, but a chill surrounded it, and once-familiar sounds rang like echoes, growing stranger and thinner every moment.

Beside her, Hugh cleared his throat as if about to speak – and then nothing. Did he share her discomfort? He'd been garrulous enough all evening, laughing and jesting with Mountjoy and Percy, asking Raleigh a dozen questions about every story his rival told. Was this simply what a marriage became after twelve years? Two people who'd run out of things to talk about, who forgot to speak to one another for the same reason one didn't strike up conversation with a favourite chair: you knew its shape, its position, and you merely relied on it for comfort, not stimulation. In any case, what could Beatrice have to say that could possibly rival tales of soldiers, alchemists and explorers? Her life was small; it was a grain of salt next to the pearls and coral and gold of Hugh's.

A torch glowed up ahead: faint yellow at first, like a drop of lemon juice worming through the mist. If she hadn't been watching for it, she might never have noticed it. But as they drew closer, the torch grew brighter, lemon giving way to amber and copper, and as the light swayed, she knew Ridley would be drawing his arm from left to right to guide them home. She'd barely had a chance to speak with him since he'd vowed to help her: always Hugh or Catalina or one of the children and their tutors and nurses had been nearby, silencing anything that wasn't the price of beef or the state of the eaves.

As they approached the landing stage, the mist grew thinner, like unwinding layers of lace to reveal the body beneath. Vague shadows became wooden steps, the bare mulberry trees, the tall figure of Ridley waiting for them.

'Finally,' Hugh grunted. 'I've never been so cold on the Thames.'

Beatrice looked at him in surprise. 'But you don't feel the cold.'

Hugh shook his head, grimacing. 'I force myself to feel it. Some winters are more painful than others, but I have to feel them.'

The ropes were flying from barge to bank: in a moment he'd leap away from her onto the shore. 'I don't understand. Why?'

The barge was tied up. Hugh rose to disembark. His eyes were dark. 'As penance.'

The stone swans loomed out of the mist, their long necks hooked like silent questions, their carved eyes as disapproving as ever. Beatrice wanted to ask more, but the barge was tied up and Hugh was rising, extending his hand, and with Ridley and the disembarking oarsmen so close now, there was no chance of getting anything further out of him.

'I trust you had a pleasant evening,' Ridley said as Hugh handed Beatrice over the side. For a moment, each man held one of her hands, and she didn't know which to drop first. Underfoot, the wooden wharf was slick with damp and her satin slippers skidded, forcing her to clutch tighter at both hands.

'Let's hope Walter inherits my sea legs,' Hugh said lightly, stepping ashore without the slightest loss of balance. She remembered Nicholas's question: whether she wanted her son to be more like his father or his uncle. But her reservations had nothing to do with sea legs. It was this unsettling ability of Hugh's to switch so swiftly from seriousness to levity, from grim darkness to good-humoured jesting. You could no more rely on his mood these days than you could trust the sea to remain smooth rippling blue: within moments it might rear up into jagged grey beasts, charging and crashing around you, over you, through you.

'You'll be pleased to hear your daughter has passed an easy evening,' Ridley said, lifting his torch to illuminate the path back to the house, sending bronze snakes writhing across the grass and gravel. 'Mistress Catalina sat up with her until she fell asleep – far earlier, I imagine, than if Master William had had his way.'

Beneath Beatrice's fingers, she felt Hugh's arm stiffen. 'William? What did he want?'

Either Ridley didn't hear the odd tension in Hugh's voice, or he decided it wasn't his place to question. 'He didn't say. To entertain young Ursula, I imagine, but Mistress Catalina insisted she needed to sleep. She also said Master William shouldn't be around sick children.'

'True enough,' Hugh said, and there was that sudden switch again: he was all jovial wryness. 'William would probably try to swing Ursula around by her ankles, forgetting her injuries.'

Exactly what Beatrice had been thinking: William was a good cousin when rough and tumble games were wanted, but he was hardly a peaceful sickbed companion. When Walter had toothache, William had offered to distract him by going riding, and had merely laughed in baffled scorn when Beatrice had pointed out that thudding hooves would hardly help Walter's predicament. As for Ursula, William only really noticed her when Walter wasn't there. Which was frustrating and might be thoroughly unpleasant if Ursula ever realised this was the case, but hardly a reason to keep William away from the girl. So why Hugh's alarm?

There was a sudden creak overhead. Then a cracking, groaning, rushing sound. Beatrice could barely look up before Hugh shoved her roughly.

'Get back!'

She saw sharp branches falling, toppling, like the closing jaws of a great whale. Then the torchlight leapt, flared, and Hugh lunged at Beatrice, thrusting her back. She stumbled, crashing to her knees – just as the tree hit the ground with a huge, splintering, crunching thud, pinning Hugh beneath its branches.

'Hugh!' She scrabbled in the earth, twisting. Something was anchoring her; as she rolled onto her back, she saw a branch had fallen across the train of her gown. The damask tore as she wrenched it free, and she didn't care. 'Hugh, say something!'

He lay face down, crumpled, one arm outstretched. The arm that had thrust her to safety. Branches formed a cage of splinters around him, black bark and white sapwood pinioning his cloak. A dark stain was spreading across his left thigh and Beatrice gaped in horror.

'Ridley, he's hurt!'

On the other side of the tree, she saw the torchlight rise, heard gravel crunch as Ridley got to his feet. He was unhurt then – and as she realised this, she also realised that she'd forgotten about Ridley entirely in her concern for Hugh.

'We can't get to him!' Ridley called. 'The branches are too many. We have to get axes. Are you hurt, Beatrice?'

She could see the silhouettes of the oarsmen now flocking to Ridley, but didn't have the will to care that they'd heard Ridley address her so informally. What did that matter when Hugh was hurt?

'I'm fine,' she called back. 'I'll stay with him until you return.'

Even as she said it, she realised she had no choice: Hugh had thrust her into a grassy corner. Behind her was a six-foot yew hedge; to her left more hedge, until the tree trunk broke through; in front of her, the branches. There was a small gap where the trunk lay wedged atop the hedge before the branches formed an impenetrable web – but it was too small, and besides, she didn't dare attempt to crawl beneath the trunk: what if the hedge gave way? What were brittle yew twigs compared to the bulk of a centuries-old beech?

So how had it fallen?

Even as the thought occurred to her, she thrust it aside: what sort of wife asked such questions while her husband lay trapped and bleeding? Guilt- and panic-stricken, she flung herself flat on her belly and crawled forward, trying to contort her arm through the branches to reach Hugh. Twigs raked at her wrists, drawing blood, tearing the lace on her sleeves. She stretched again and the twigs scraped her necks, her cheeks, and she jerked back as one jabbed at her eye. She couldn't reach him. She couldn't touch him to see if he was bleeding, breathing, and she let out a cry of frustration.

'Hugh! Hugh, can you hear me? Say something!'

But he didn't respond. He lay face down, golden hair trailing in the mud, his hat knocked off, the scarlet feather crumpled beneath a broken branch. Another branch lay across Hugh's shoulders, another over his left leg. But the smaller branches had fallen first, halting the larger, so that the full weight of the tree was almost propped up. Or so it seemed in the darkness. So Beatrice told herself.

A branch gave way beneath her straining weight. Splinters and shreds of bark clawed at her skin, needled beneath her sleeves and bodice, but she didn't care. Her fingertips could just touch Hugh's splayed arm, the soft elbow of his velvet doublet, and she gripped it tight between two fingers as if the rasping cloth were a rope.

'Hugh,' she whispered again, blood mingling with tears on her cheeks. 'Hugh, don't leave me alone.'

Torchlight flared. She looked up, through the thicket of branches, to see Ridley leading several men, their axe blades flaring bronze as they rose and fell, hacking a way through to Hugh.

'Mistress Beatrice,' Ridley called. 'Is he breathing?'

'I can't tell!' she shouted, and saying it aloud made the terror sear colder. 'I can't reach him!'

'Are you hurt?'

'Only scratches.'

They were through to Hugh now, carefully sliding him onto a stretcher made of a horse blanket lashed to oars.

'We're all needed to carry him,' Ridley grunted as he and the men heaved Hugh up. 'The physician's been summoned – will you be alright until we can get him inside?'

She nodded a lie. 'Go. Go!'

And they left, hurrying stiffly, awkwardly as they tried to avoid jolting Hugh, and Beatrice was alone in the darkness.

Slowly, she extricated herself from the fallen tree, wincing as more twigs scratched her. Only as she pushed herself up to stand did she register the sodden weight of her muddied gown, the itch of bark crawling beneath her clothes, her dishevelled hair slumping out of its pins.

What now? Wait, she supposed. Wait for rescue. Wait for news, all the while agonising over whether she wished to hear it or not.

Behind her, a rush of wind rattled the yew branches and she started away. But they were only stirring, jostling, not falling. Though if one tree could fall, did that mean others could follow? Perhaps the autumn rains had loosened the earth's grip on the tree. Frost-cracked ground might have exposed more roots; hibernating animals could have dug their claws too deep.

Beatrice shivered. With cold or fear? She couldn't tell anymore, only wrap her torn, wet cloak right around herself.

Another gust of wind, snarling at her spine. The mists trembled, frayed, white tendrils unravelling and separating like the splaying fingers of some vast ghost.

She couldn't stay out here. She had to move. If they'd only left her an axe, she could have hacked her own way free. But she hadn't been thinking logically, and they, if they had been, would have inevitably arrived at the logical conclusion that a woman, especially a cold and frightened one, couldn't possibly wield an axe. In any case, trying to get the axe to her with the fallen beech in the way would probably have caused more problems than it solved. Beatrice looked around helplessly. A gap in the hedge? She could wriggle into the woodland and then go round to the front gates. But there was nothing even Walter could have squirmed through, let alone a grown woman. She couldn't go under the fallen trunk. But perhaps she could go over it. She'd been a good climber once, when she'd gone onto the family ships with her father: she used to slip away while he inspected cargo to scramble up the rigging with the cabin boys. Over twenty years later, surely she could manage to climb over the tree trunk?

She approached the trunk gingerly, set a palm to its bark. Would it take her weight, precarious as its balance on the small branches was? Or would it crash down as soon as she climbed on, tossing her into the chaos of branches to be impaled? Beatrice shook her head brusquely: no point fretting now. She gripped a branch, rucked her bedraggled skirts up as best she could, and found a foothold. Her satin slippers might be useless for keeping her feet dry, but they were thin enough that her toes could get a decent grip: the only advantage she had, as her cumbersome skirts hindered her progress, and her wet cloak kept flapping over her arms as she tried to reach another handhold. But slowly, awkwardly, she made her way onto the trunk and peered around, seeking the safest way down.

Silver glinted.

Beatrice frowned. Trying to ignore the creaking wood she inched her way along the trunk towards the hedge. She leaned forward. And stared.

There, lodged in the severed tree stump, was an axe.

The tree hadn't fallen. It had been *felled*. Someone had waited to strike the final blows until she and Hugh were passing – and then left the axe for any survivors to discover. But how could they have known Hugh and Beatrice would be walking through the garden tonight at all? It was late November, the weather grim. The only people who could have known were those who knew them. Which meant either those who lived with them, or those who had been at Durham House. She remembered Essex's strange words, more threat than friendship, and the laughter of Raleigh, Mountjoy, Northumberland: what really was their relationship with Hugh?

Someone close to them had tried to kill Hugh. Or Beatrice. Or both. She had no way of knowing who their target had been.

Or if the axeman were still here.

She stared wildly around. Shadows twisted, rearing up and slinking close. The river whispered against the reeds; the wind nudged the mist towards her.

A sudden shriek pierced the night. She jerked around – and a dark shape launched itself at her. Beatrice screamed, just as its full weight caught her in the chest, sending her flying, tumbling into the mud.

Dark clouds loomed overhead, smoke-black and swollen. She wasn't dead. Only winded, only bruised. Leathery fingers scraped her cheek, and a wizened face peered close.

It was the monkey! The blasted monkey Hugh had brought back years ago and which had been roaming half-feral in the gardens ever since. Beatrice made a limp sound, half-laugh, half-sob, not sure whether to be relieved or still afraid. The monkey tilted its head, frowning, chuntering to itself. Then it gave a sharp yell and leapt away, disappearing into the night.

For a moment Beatrice couldn't move. And then torchlight glared, someone called her name, and she knew. Whatever, whoever was prowling her grounds, she had to get to Hugh's side before it was too late.

15

With every step she heard her mud-stiff gown rasping against the floor, dragging a swath of filth behind her. The torch she'd seized from the oarsman who'd come for her crackled, her haste bending the flames backwards like broken fingers. Blood pounded in her ears, throbbing a plea. *Let him be well. Let him be well.*

She didn't dare think *let him live.*

A key turned somewhere and a door creaked open.

'Beatrice?'

Catalina was peering out of Ursula's room. Beatrice halted, torn between rushing to Hugh and checking on her daughter.

'Is Ursula well? Has she woken?'

Catalina shook her head. 'I gave her a calming draught earlier tonight – she's still in a lot of pain. But – what's happened? I heard shouting …'

'It's Hugh,' Beatrice said, already shifting to leave. 'There was an accident – a tree fell.'

'Is he –'

'I don't know!'

Catalina glanced up and down the corridor. 'Where's Master William? Have you seen him?'

'William?' Beatrice shook her head impatiently. 'If he's not in a tavern, someone else can alert him – or not, for he'll be no use. I must go – will you stay with Ursula a little longer?'

Catalina nodded. 'Of course. If I can help at all …'

'What's happening? I heard what sounded like a Spanish invasion!' William was striding along the corridor towards them, doublet loose, shirt rumpled. As if he'd dozed off at a gaming table: the closer he got, the stronger the reek of ale. Beatrice swallowed her irritation.

'Hugh's been hurt. I must go to him.'

William looked horrified. Small wonder, Beatrice thought spitefully: the boy wasn't capable of dealing with any crisis more serious than a poor hand of cards.

'I'll come with you,' William said. 'Let me take the torch, aunt.'

He'd taken it and was marching onwards before she could object to his presumption.

It was only as they reached the end of the corridor that Beatrice fully registered the sound she'd heard while William was approaching: the key to Ursula's room turning in its lock again.

Her bedchamber was chaos. The physician had arrived just before Beatrice and William, and the oarsmen were still milling about as he began to examine Hugh, their makeshift stretcher bundled up awkwardly, like a defeated army's banner. Ridley broke off his account to the physician as Beatrice entered, and stared at her.

'By rights you shouldn't be walking,' he said stiffly, gripping the bedpost tight, as if he were holding himself back from rushing to gather her in his arms. How could he be thinking so self-ishly at such a time? 'That tree should have killed you both. If not for Hugh …'

Hugh. She approached their bed as if it were an altar and her husband the sacrifice. He looked so pale – Hugh, her handsome sun-browned husband, his face grey and slack. And the blood – fleck-ing his lips, staining a wad of linen pressed against his thigh. She wanted to be sick.

Behind her, William was talking – too loud, too lightly. 'Hugh's dodged falling masts in storms before now – a mere beech couldn't stop him, not when ninety feet of finest English pine failed!'

As if this were a tale to regale fellow sailors with in a tavern. The valiant Sir Hugh Radclyffe, brave explorer, dashing hero. Except he was none of these things now. He was bloodied flesh and broken bone; he was still and silent.

She wanted them gone. All of them gone, even the physician, so that she could pretend there was no need for him, only her husband sleeping soundly, and as soon as she lay down beside him he would draw her close and kiss her hair, and she would close her eyes for a dreamless sleep.

Then something struck her. Frowning, she turned to William.

'How did you know it was a beech tree?'

William grinned – so broadly, so idiotically inappropriate. 'Was it? A fine guess, I suppose –'

Beatrice cut him off. 'The tree was felled deliberately. The culprit left their axe – a sign of stupidity perhaps. Or maybe they wanted us to know it was done on purpose to frighten us.'

'Beatrice,' Ridley began, 'this isn't the time –'

'So I ask again,' Beatrice snapped, '*how did you know?*'

William stared at her, grin limp but still hovering, as if he wanted to laugh at her ludicrous suggestion. 'You cannot think I had anything to do with it! Hugh's my uncle – you've both done so much for me!'

'Yet never enough,' Beatrice said coldly. 'For instance, Hugh has never let you take command of the *Silver Swan*. Has never entirely given the navigational responsibilities of any voyage over to you.'

'Which is frustrating, I freely admit!' William retorted. 'But if you think I would seek vengeance for it, seek to harm Hugh, perhaps we ought to send you to Bedlam!'

Beatrice froze. He couldn't know. The only way William could know was if Hugh had told him, and he'd sworn, he'd *sworn* –

'Please, I beg of you,' the physician broke in. 'I cannot have such noise around my patient. If you cannot be peaceable, I must ask you to leave.'

Beatrice bridled. 'I will not be commanded in my own home! This is *my* bedchamber –'

'With all due respect,' the physician said, 'this is the chamber of a man with a broken femur, significant lacerations and possible damage to his internal organs. He will need calm and rest if he is to heal.'

She only heard that one word. 'If? You cannot mean …'

His look was of kindly pity. 'It is impossible to be certain yet.'

'No,' she whispered. 'No, he cannot die, he cannot.'

'Beatrice.' Ridley was at her side, a hand hovering above her shoulder, as if he feared his touch might shatter her, or him. 'Your own wounds need tending. Let us leave the physician to his work and I'll have a guest bedchamber made ready for you.'

She wanted to protest. But so many words were throbbing in her head, blood-fast, and if she added any more, she would break.

Bedlam. Damage. If.

If.

The cuts on her face stung as she dabbed at them, and she winced at her own reflection. Hard to believe the woman in the mirror had been rubbing shoulders with earls and countesses mere hours ago. The last time she'd looked into the glass, she'd seen a delicately painted face, lips and cheeks tinged pink, hair curled and piled and pinned, coral swaying in her ears and nestling between her collarbones. She'd felt embarrassed by her relative tawdriness in the Raleighs' home; now she wished she'd been proud.

What would Lady Penelope Rich say if she could see Beatrice now? Or would she not deign to use words? Her narrowing eyes, her arching brows and curving lips would say everything she wished.

But it was stupid to be thinking of Lady Penelope when Hugh lay desperately wounded. When Beatrice had been exiled to a guest bedchamber: with William at home and Catalina ensconced in the first guest bedchamber, Beatrice had been forced to come here. To the chamber that would always – no matter how hard they swept it, how wide the windows were flung, how much rosemary was hung or rose petals strewn – always smell of lavender. For it had not always been a guest bedchamber. Before, it had been her father's.

Something rustled. Something struck wood. Beatrice jerked round, searching, expecting – but nothing was there. Her chest clenched with not-wholly subsided fear, and she bent to retrieve the comb she must have elbowed off the table. Just an accident, just a table whose size had been chosen for a man in breeches, not a woman in a farthingale and Spanish sleeves. She turned back to the mirror, trying to quash the thought that had leapt into her mind – that she'd heard her father's footsteps stalking across the room.

But the woman in the glass looked drawn and fearful, and Beatrice dropped her gaze. She dipped the linen in the basin and watched blood and dirt worm out of the white and become a reddish-brown mist. Specks of bark and scraps of grass rose above her blood, pocking the surface like smallpox scars.

She missed Maria. Since before her marriage, Maria had been there to soothe her hurts. Hers had been the hands mixing willow bark tisanes every month, bringing ginger tea when Beatrice was pregnant, massaging Beatrice's back as the labour pangs gripped her. And of course, it had been Maria's fingers working salve into Beatrice's blood-ied hands on that night, so many years ago. Now Beatrice was alone, and Maria's murder still unavenged.

Beatrice lifted the linen and her eyes again, and sponged blood off her chin. Could the same person have been responsible for Maria's murder and the attack on Hugh and Beatrice? Both had taken place in Beatrice's grounds. Both had occurred on nights when Hugh and Beatrice had gone out on the barge. Whoever lay behind them must have known they would be away, in Maria's case, or returning, for tonight's assault.

William would have known about both occasions. Could he have been behind the attacks? He'd been on the barge with them the night Maria was murdered, but the boy had no household or wife or children to spend his money on: easy enough for him to hire a mysterious man in black to do his dirty work. Or to disguise himself in dark cloak and hat and alter his voice. But why would he? Resentment of Hugh? Was William so petty? He'd inherit something in Hugh's will, true, but nearly everything would pass to Walter, with Beatrice as custodian of the estate. Unless he'd intended for Beatrice to be killed tonight too.

It couldn't be William. He couldn't be so ruthless, not to them. They'd taken him In when Hugh's sister Catherine died, just six months after their marriage. A boy of ten, William had been taught by Hugh how to ride and swim and use a sword. Beatrice had read him tales of Theseus and Icarus, Jason and Odysseus, had listened to him reciting the poems and Latin declensions his tutors had set him, had played hide and seek in the garden with him. And Maria – Maria had smuggled sugared almonds into William's growing hands, had pressed poultices onto scraped knees and teased him whenever he experimented with novel moustaches. How could their boy have turned on them?

But he'd known about the beech tree. He'd been behaving strangely – Ridley had described his odd behaviour towards Ursula. And he knew the globemaker – he'd accompanied Hugh to buy navigation instruments dozens of times. Had he been the one to order the strange pictures on Hugh's globe?

And as if her thoughts had conjured it, she heard it then. Through the door she'd left ajar, floated a rattle like thrown knucklebones. Then a whirring sound, like a gathering wind.

The globe was turning again.

She met her own eyes in the glass. To warn herself not to go? Or to see her own fear and feel the urge to pretend it away?

She rose. The water barely sighed as the linen fell, or as it unfurled beneath the rusty surface like a bloodstained lily. Out in the corridor, her bare feet were near-soundless on the marble, and cold air wound about her ankles beneath her nightgown. The noise was growing louder now, and beneath the whir and rattle, a steady beat. Weight shifting inside the globe, she told herself. And yet, for all the thought's rationality, it sounded like nothing so much as a heartbeat.

At the door to the gallery, she reached for a torch, then hesitated. It could be the monkey again. Or one of the kitchen cats. Or it could be the same person who had left the axe embedded in the tree stump, invading her house as well as her grounds.

Until she opened the door, it could be any of these things, or none. Hugh had once said that known fears were far less daunting than those unknown, that when you knew a shadow in the water was a shark, you could confront that single problem, rather than torturing yourself with endless febrile imaginings.

But she knew what this was. It was the globe, untouched by living hand, and the certainty was more terrifying than all the imagined alternatives.

She could retreat to her father's old bedchamber now. Light a fire and all the candles, wrap herself in blankets and send for a hot caudle. However uneasy that chamber made her feel, it was nothing to the globe. She could summon Ridley to her side; she could go and sit with Catalina at Ursula's bedside; she could keep vigil over Hugh. But that would be running away. And when your home was your entire world, there could be no escape. Besides, Beatrice was damned if she'd let anyone make her flee inside her own house; even scurrying to Ridley for support would feel like surrendering – though to what, she couldn't say. She set her hand to the door, and stepped inside the gallery.

There was no moonlight tonight. The curtains were drawn, the shadows thick. Her torchlight couldn't reach the globe. But she could hear it. Rattle. Whir. Beat. Rattle. Whir. Beat. A drum and a dancer at once, luring her into its measure, commanding her to step, step, and step closer again.

There it was. Her torchlight crept towards the spinning images, bronzing blurred cartouche after blurred cartouche. She was close enough to touch it now, her fingers hovering over the surface, the scarlet and blue veins and arteries of meridians, voyages, rivers pulsing across the map.

Then a thought struck her. Why was it turning now? It had turned after Maria's death; it had turned again the night before Ursula's accident. Now it was turning after Hugh had been injured. Why after, if not to mock? But why before, if not to threaten? Unless it had been mocking her each time, and she hadn't understood. Because if disaster followed disaster, what did before and after even mean? Each time could be after something – perhaps a disaster she hadn't even felt the full impact of yet.

Or perhaps each time was a threat. And she had failed to understand them.

She had to start understanding the globe's messages now. Three of the people she loved most had already been attacked. She couldn't afford to fail again.

Swallowing her revulsion, Beatrice laid a hand on the globe, forcing it to a halt. Her palm stung, pain shooting up her wrist, and she almost leapt back in horror. But the movement had pulled at the raw scrapes on her palm and set her barely healed scald twinging as the bandage came loose. The globe hadn't burned her. How could it have? Shaking herself, Beatrice peered closer.

What should she have seen? She'd searched for water last time, fearing Walter was the target, and she'd been distracted by the mermaid holding a mirror before she could scrutinise the globe further. Had the falling tree, Hugh's injuries been foretold all along? There were few trees depicted: the landmarks were mainly mountains and rivers, with the odd forest dotted over France and the Russias. There had been a bear representing Ursula: was there some sort of wordplay depicting Hugh? A yew tree? Hugh meant mind, or spirit, but how on earth would those appear in a cartouche? A ghostly figure tumbling off a ship? Maybe a crumbling cliff for a felled Radclyffe? Or a red cliff for Radclyffe – a red clef: were there any musical notations, or red keys on it?

Her eyes ached from squinting in the torchlight. She was so tired – and so tired of being frightened. Of being toyed with – if someone wanted to blackmail her, couldn't they just send a note and be done with it? None of this tortuous mocking. But if their intent was to hurt her, they were succeeding. If Beatrice had been confronted with an assailant, chased through the streets, or forced onto a ducking stool, she'd have borne that more stoically, more pragmatically than this persecution. Which they'd known. And acted upon. They'd told her why too: *Your secrets are known. You deserve all that is coming.*

The bear captured by the cockatrice lay before her. Ursula in the flames. But Ursula didn't deserve that. Maria hadn't either. Hugh might have his own sins to atone for, but they certainly didn't merit being punished like that. Beatrice was the one with a sin to atone for.

She had to stop this before anyone else was hurt – or worse. But how?

And then she noticed something that made ice creep over her skin.

The cockatrice's wings were not the leathery pinions of a dragon, nor the bright feathers of a great bird, as she'd seen prowling through books and maps before. They were blue veined with delicate silver, and translucent; she could see the beast's green scales through them. Like a wasp's wings. Like a bee's.

Beatrice.

It had been a nickname once. Her mother had teased Beatrice about her quick temper: *gentle now, my bee-in-a-trice. Stinging others so swiftly will only hurt you too in the end.* And then, just like every other jest in her childhood, it had changed to cold mockery on her father's lips, deriding her for an attempt to comment on a trade deal. *Foolish bee-in-a-trice. Quick to sting is fast to fall, and what's a tiny red welt to your opponent when you've fatally injured yourself?* He'd even mentioned a cockatrice once. When she'd attempted to challenge him about what he'd done to her mother. *What – does the bee-in-a-trice think herself a cockatrice? Addlepated girl. All your snarling is but an irksome buzz – flutter back to embroidering flowers or you'll regret it.*

And the bear? A gold medallion hung around its neck, just visible between the cockatrice's crushing forelegs, and if the light were better, if the candles flickered less, she was certain it would bear the stamp of the merchant adventurers guild. Not her daughter at all. Not Ursa, but Artos. Not Ursula, but *Arthur*.

Beatrice stepped back in horror.

They knew. They knew what she'd done to her father.

16

She cannot breathe. She struggles, with every ounce of strength she possesses, her muscles screaming what her lungs cannot, because his hands are so strong, unnaturally strong. There's blood on his hands — on hers — and she can no longer tell whose is whose: nails torn ragged, skin scraped and slit. The pillow muffles any screams, and all she can hear is a desperate, animal keening. But it's as if the creature is underwater and it's already too late. Death is in the room. She's choking on it, and it smells like lavender. Dear God, she had not thought it would hurt this much. Or last this long.

And then the voice comes, so faint she does not know if it is spoken by the living or the dead.

Beatrice.

It's so dark. The candles have gone out. There is only blackness, and pain, and the press of a pillow against flesh. She tastes blood, and surely, surely she doesn't have long left.

'Beatrice!'

And then there are hands on hers, gentle, familiar hands, their calluses a map she knows lead to safe harbour.

'Maria,' she gasps. 'Help me.'

Maria takes her hands away. Her grip has left puckers and gouges in the pillow; feathers jut like splintered spars. Wreckage, she thinks, and if this is the wreckage, what jetsam can be salvaged? What is she? The wrecker, or the drowned?

'It's done,' Maria says, her voice no louder than a guttering flame. 'You're safe now. He's gone.'

And now she cannot avoid it any longer, not now 'he' has been spoken aloud. Beatrice reaches forward and takes the pillow away. There's a sudden

stench, foul and animal, and wrapped up in a smothering shroud of laven-
der. She fights the urge to vomit.

His eyes are open. Staring at nothing, she knows – and yet he is also
staring straight at her, with her own eyes. Brown as a new ship's hull, brown
as spices, they had glowed with stories once, had danced as her mother
laughed, had smiled steady, silent approval as Beatrice correctly balanced
their accounts. But they had also judged. Concealed. Glared, threatened,
silenced. In the end, they had pleaded.

Now, though, Arthur Gardiner's eyes are blank. And his daughter is
responsible.

Beatrice looks up at Maria, begging for something. Forgiveness.
Absolution. Maria has given her so much, so reliably, so gently. Can she
grant Beatrice this?

'I had to do it,' she says hoarsely. 'You know – you understand why I had
to do it?'

Maria touches her cheek. 'Those scratches need salve.'

'Maria …'

Maria looks her in the eye, and there is savage fury in her voice as she
says, 'It was far kinder than what he did to your mother.'

Unseasonal brightness needled through the windows, striking the
pillows behind Hugh's head. A healthy man would have stirred,
blinked, and smiled at the prospect of such a rare day. Hugh should
have been bounding to the window and declaring grand plans to ride
out to Richmond, to gallop through frost-silvered fields as the low
winter sun glowed white behind black trees, cresting the hills as the
tawny owls and foxes began to call.

Instead, he lay silent and still. She'd never seen Hugh so still. Even
in sleep he normally flung his limbs wide, feet fidgeting in and out of
the blankets, forever seeking the perfect degree of cool or warmth, face
a constant story of his dreams: frowns and clenched jaws chased by wry
smiles and quiet chuckles, for Hugh's dreams would always end in
humour, no matter what bleak grey had begun them.

The physician had been again that morning. He'd had nothing new
to say, no answers about whether Hugh's leg was healing, or whether

there was any internal damage after all. 'It will take time,' he'd said, trying to be kind and gentle, but she'd only been able to see patronising attempts to keep her quiet.

Time. It was what she couldn't bear to spend at another bedside. It meant doing nothing. Praying. Hoping. Waiting. She'd thought herself expert at waiting – God knew she'd had enough practice. But Beatrice was only good at waiting when she could keep busy. When she could take control – if not of her husband's unseen, unknown voyaging, then of the spice cargo newly arrived on the *Starling*, of her children's tutors, of her household. She could only wait well when she distracted herself from fear. And she could no longer pretend to be unafraid.

Someone was attacking her. Repeatedly, cruelly, and with no care for who else was harmed, as long as their attacks succeeded in hurting Beatrice. Her friend, her daughter, her husband – this attacker believed Beatrice deserved to suffer, and therefore those she loved must suffer too. She had to stop them, before someone else was hurt.

But how could she when she didn't know who they were? When they'd made no demands? As if they weren't blackmailing her, not torturing her with the intent of gaining either gold or information – only punishing her. And somehow it was all tied up with her father's death.

No. Her father's *murder*. She had to name it, if only to herself. She'd killed her own father. Never mind that she'd had her reasons, or that in the end she'd had no choice. She'd killed him, and her suffering was justice for her crime.

Except no one knew she'd killed him. No one except Maria – and Maria couldn't possibly be behind this, for Maria had been the first victim. Had she been killed to keep her silent? But the only person who'd have that motive for murdering Maria was Beatrice herself.

None of this made sense. And if it was nonsensical, if it wasn't blackmail or revenge, then the only other explanation was that Beatrice truly was becoming what she'd always feared. That she was going mad.

Frustrated, she sank her head into her hands. Between her elbows, she could see every thread of the damask covers, warp, weft, turquoise, sapphire. Bedclothes were her new horizons nowadays: you could have presented her with squares of damask, red for Ursula's, blue for Beatrice and Hugh's, and she'd have been able to state categorically exactly which part of the bedcovers they'd been cut from.

A knock at the door was followed by a polite cough, and Ridley entered. He came one step in, and then halted. 'Has there been any change, madam?'

She shook her head. 'His leg needs time to heal. Time to see if an infection sets in. As for the damage to his insides … time will tell. Again.'

'Time he still has,' Ridley pointed out. His gaze shifted to the prone figure in the bed. 'How he escaped death, I cannot fathom.'

'His sailors always say he has the luck of the devil,' Beatrice said. 'The mist that so often concealed their approach from the Spanish. Winds that would change, as if at Hugh's command. Once, on the voyage to Novaya Zemlya, a great whale swam up to the *Silver Swan* and hit the keel with its fluke, so hard planks split and the ship tilted, almost into the icy sea. Everyone else thought they were doomed as the whale rolled, seemingly to strike again. But Hugh just ordered carpenters and buckets below, then leaned over the side and said, "You'll find better hunting to the west, my beautiful lady. Catch a silver shoal for me." And the whale gave one long, deep call, sprayed a vast jet of water that knocked William's hat clean off, and swam away. West. As if at Hugh's bidding.'

'I heard of that tale,' Ridley said. 'It happened two days before … the events. One of the sailors speculated that the whale was an omen – even that it had cursed the voyage because Hugh sent it away.'

'Sailors are a superstitious breed.' Beatrice stared at Hugh's slack face. The whale story had been one of the few Hugh and William had shared from that aborted voyage. One of their only positive memories, one of the small handful of stories suitable for sharing with children. But Ridley's words made the tale seem tainted. For every piece of good luck, someone else must have bad. For every augur, there was an auspicious reading and an ominous one.

'It was tavern gossip,' Ridley said. 'Perhaps the sailors preferred to blame the whale rather than anyone else. Especially if it meant speaking ill of the dead.'

She didn't want to hear that word, not in here. It felt too much like tempting fate. 'Was there some business you needed to discuss?'

Ridley nodded. 'The agent is here, madam. And …'

Beatrice had half-risen with a grimace; now, her frown deepened. 'And?'

'Master Robert is with him.'

Outside the study, Beatrice paused. She couldn't be a frightened woman in there. She couldn't be distracted, or dishevelled, or anything less than immaculate. It was hard enough doing business with London's merchants when her only worries were trivial – new shoes for Walter, a shortage of sugar requiring a different pudding. But when she and her loved ones were in danger, the prospect was painful.

Beatrice smoothed her hair, adjusted her garnet-studded hood and pinched her cheeks. Bad enough that she'd had no sleep; she couldn't look as if she hadn't too. She gritted her teeth, and entered.

Holbrook was standing by the window, his leather roll tucked beneath one arm. The light was behind him, so it was hard to be sure, but she was almost certain he wore an apologetic frown. Because of Hugh? Or because Robert was sat in her chair? Not the one behind the desk, true; that would have been unconscionably presumptuous. But the chair before the fire, the comfortable one, not the one with beautifully carved armrests and headboard that looked and were expensive, but were so uncomfortable they always helped Beatrice gain the upper hand in any negotiation, as her counterpart struggled to avoid a kneaded skull or bruised elbows. The chair with hollows shaped by her body and cushions embroidered by her mother's hands.

'Beatrice!' Robert greeted her effusively, rising from the chair but not stepping away from it. 'Florence and I were devastated, truly devastated to hear of Hugh's accident. You have our sincerest condolences, indeed you do.'

'Thank you, Robert. Would you like to have some refreshment in the gallery while I speak with Holbrook?'

'Very kind, very kind,' Robert said. 'But Holbrook and I came here together.'

Beatrice shot a glance at Holbrook, whose face was creased in a polite rictus.

'Master Bristow and I met on the road,' Holbrook said. 'He reminded me of the dangers inherent in riding alone and was kind enough to accompany me.'

'How considerate,' Beatrice said, thinking that any footpad in their right mind would take one look at wiry, wary Holbrook and immediately alight upon the soft-jowled, velvet-cloaked Robert as the easier target. 'All the same, if you would allow me to –'

'Ah, but we have a business proposition for you!' Robert interrupted.

'Indeed?'

'Indeed,' Robert beamed, and Beatrice, for the hundredth time, wished her sister hadn't married a man so closely resembling a parrot. 'I should like to offer you my assistance in your trading ventures.'

Beatrice let her eyebrows drift minutely upwards. It was a signal any of the merchants she'd dealt with over the years would have read instantly: it meant *your offer isn't even worth me expending words on rejection*. But Robert was not one of those merchants.

Silently, she glided to the chair behind the desk, every breath steadying the rage building inside.

'Whilst Hugh is incapacitated,' Robert continued, 'and poor little Ursula continues to recuperate, Florence and I thought we ought to help you. I shall assume the running of your business on your behalf, allowing you to spend time with your family. There's no need to discuss payment at present, of course – we can revisit such details at a more opportune moment.'

'Opportune indeed,' Beatrice said coolly. She turned to Holbrook. 'I know you too well to make the mistake of assuming you had aught to do with this scheme. However, I must ask you to bring the key matters to me tomorrow morning. Unless there is anything urgent?'

Holbrook bowed. 'Perhaps a decision regarding who to sell the saffron to. Reynolds has offered a price I would deem inadequate. Twelve percent below our usual rate.'

'Quite inadequate.' Beatrice tapped her forefinger thoughtfully. 'Offer to Marston. His last delivery was spoiled by storms – he's in far greater need. Try him at fifteen percent above normal – I'd expect him to come back with five, so we'll agree on ten, nine if he's obstinate, eleven if you can manage it. If Reynolds will match, I would prefer to deal with him out of loyalty, of course, but make it clear Marston will bite and that I will not allow Reynolds to rob me.'

'Of course, madam.'

'Thank you, Holbrook. Good day to you.'

He bowed again. 'My best wishes to Sir Hugh and your daughter. Good day.'

As the door closed behind him, Beatrice let her gaze fall on Robert. She did not speak.

Robert cleared his throat. 'That was skilfully handled, sister. But I fear too many dealings at this time will only distress you and keep you from tending to your husband and daughter. Allow me to reiterate my offer –'

Beatrice gave a small laugh. 'Yes, you do like to reiterate, don't you, brother?' She tapped her forefinger again: another sign her associates would have recognised as a warning. 'I used to think you reminded me of a parrot. But I do believe I chose the wrong bird. You are a vulture.'

'Beatrice!' His eyes widened in shock that might have been genuine, if he were truly an idiot. But Beatrice doubted that: a true idiot would have been bankrupted by Florence's tastes in silks long ago. 'I know you are understandably distraught, but please believe that I am here to help! This would be the best for everyone –'

'Everyone?' Beatrice raised an eyebrow. 'Tell me, Robert, did that ship of yours ever arrive, or is it confirmed sunk?'

He stiffened. 'I have heard nothing. She might still return.'

'I think we both know she will not. A sizeable loss, I imagine. And you saw an opportunity to recoup some of your losses, no?' Beatrice leaned back, letting her rage flare now. 'Not even a day has passed since Hugh was hurt, and already you caper up to my door, seeking to profit from our suffering! I wish I could say I were surprised. But you have been a parasite on my back ever since you married my sister – I could have filled ten cargo holds with the dinners I've given you, and not a single invitation in return! And now you look to exploit Hugh and

Ursula's injuries? I will not tolerate this, Robert. I will not.' She shook her head in disgust. 'And to think – I was ready to offer you a loan while you rebuilt your business after your ship's loss. Why on earth should I throw good money after bad? You are a poor businessman, Robert, always have been. I wouldn't put my affairs in your charge if you were the last merchant left in London!'

She'd expected him to cower, weak and pathetic man that he was. But Robert drew himself up, stiff with rage and humiliation. 'You are distraught, sister. I will forgive your insults. But I would ask you to reconsider.'

'Why? Have you suddenly learned how to broker a good deal?'

'Because your sister deserves better. Your nieces deserve better.' Robert swallowed, and she saw how much effort it cost him to admit it. 'I know I am failing to provide enough for them. Five dowries – oh, Cecily may be only eight, but every time I turn around, the girls have all grown. None of them lisps any more, not even little Elizabeth, and there isn't a single leading string left in the house.' He gave a sad smile. 'I know the days when they believe their father to be a hero are numbered, and that number will dwindle long before Ursula ceases to idolise Hugh. You're right, Beatrice. I'm not a great merchant. I'm not a great man. But I would like to be a great father. And my first duty is to provide for my wife and daughters. Which I cannot do without your help.' He spread his hands: apology and appeal. 'Please. Help me delay the day when my girls realise I am no hero.'

When had she realised her own father Arthur was no hero? Was it after he sent her mother to Bedlam? After he brought Florence's mother into her home? Every time he mocked her, scorned her – or later, when she and Maria uncovered the truth? 'All little girls must realise that one day,' she said quietly.

'Too true. In a few years, I know I'll catch Cecily looking at me, and in her eyes there will be no admiration for her blunder-prone father. Only disappointment. If I'm lucky, perhaps a little fond pity. I know it's inevitable. And yet, I fancy it will take Ursula longer than my daughters.'

Beatrice heard the jealousy tightening his voice, and she shook her head with the pity he didn't want from her. 'Of course Ursula believes her father to be a hero. He's never here. What she loves, what she worships – it's a dream. The real Hugh lies upstairs, as breakable as any man. His skin isn't golden armour, he can't grin away every injury. His blood is as red as anyone's, and it spills just as easily. He's not perfect, Robert. He's human, and he's hurt. And he can hurt others too.'

'You and I know that,' Robert concurred bitterly. 'But we'll let our children keep dreaming as long as possible. Let their world glitter, perfect with possibility, and may the day never come when they realise there's far more coal and dirt in it than diamonds and pearls.'

A day that came for every child. And every marriage. But didn't that mean she should value the pearls all the more, no matter how much coal dust she had to scrub away in order to see them?

Beatrice met Robert's eyes. 'I will still give you a loan, as I intended. But I will retain control over my business dealings.'

She could see how much effort it cost Robert not to collapse. 'Thank you, Beatrice. I'll pay you back as soon as I can.'

After he'd gone, Beatrice remained in her chair, gazing at the window. There must be a strong wind outside: the winter sunlight glared and vanished, glared and vanished, so that the glass was suddenly diamond, and just as swiftly dulled, over and over again.

She'd given Robert money to hold his head up high, to meet his own reflection with dignity. To keep his wife and daughters' love as long as he could. If her money could do that, why couldn't it protect her family anymore? Why couldn't it restore Hugh, heal Ursula, and rid her of the troubles the globe had brought?

Gold couldn't buy her a golden life. Only the illusion.

17

How was it that the house seemed so unnaturally quiet? Hugh usually spent eight or nine months each year away from England: his silence was something they had grown their lives around. And yet, as Beatrice traversed silent corridors and echoing stairs, a house with Hugh in but with none of Hugh's noise seemed oddly hamstrung. As if Hugh's heroism, his strength and glory were a castle wall arrayed between her family and the world. Now the ramparts were crumbling, the gate breached, and nothing stood between Beatrice and her enemies. Whoever and wherever they might be.

With her mind clamped around the thought of enemies, a sudden movement on the corridor connecting the bedchambers made her jump. Someone lurked in an alcove, half-concealed by heavy curtains. Then they moved again: a pale, freckled face peered out, dark eyes reaching for hers.

'Walter? What are you doing here? Shouldn't you be at your lessons?'

Walter twisted the tassels awkwardly. 'Master Aldwin left. He said he didn't think it was appropriate to be teaching me Latin while Papa is injured.'

Master Aldwin, Beatrice thought, could share his opinions with the stone swans on the wharf, for all the edification they provided. 'Well, he and I shall discuss his decision tomorrow. Your papa cares very much about your education, and he will want to hear about your prowess with Virgil when he awakes.'

'But …' Walter swallowed, fretting at the rope again. 'What if he …'

His fingernails were ragged. His lips were raw. The sight crashed through Beatrice's gut like a battering ram. That her little boy had been gnawing himself bloody through worry, and her arms had been anywhere other than around him – it broke her.

Beatrice dropped to her knees, grabbing her son's shoulders. How long before he towered over her? Already his head was too high to tuck under her chin like this; if she scooped him onto her lap, his legs would protrude awkwardly along the floor. But she would never lose the urge to hold him. 'He won't,' she insisted. 'He will recover. Ursula is getting better every day, isn't she? It will be the same with your papa.'

He ducked his head, trying to hide his glistening eyes with his hair. 'Do you promise?'

Beatrice kissed his forehead, telling herself it wasn't to avoid looking into his eyes. 'I promise your father and I will always protect you.'

Let it not prove a lie, she prayed.

Walter stirred in her arms: he was looking out of the window. 'Aunt Florence is here.'

Beatrice gaped, then shot up to stare out of the window. Sure enough, there was Florence, shepherding her five daughters out of the carriage – a carriage that Beatrice's loan would pay to maintain? She gritted her teeth. Was Florence here to apologise for her husband, or echo his pleas?

'Come along then,' Beatrice sighed. 'Best go and greet them.'

As they descended the stairs, Walter slipped his hand into hers. 'Mama, do I have to play with the girls?'

Beatrice rubbed her thumb gently over his bitten nails. 'Not if you don't wish to. But I thought you liked playing with Cecily and Dorothy at least, if not the little ones.'

'I do. But … it wouldn't be right. Would it? While Papa … and when Ursula …'

'Walter.' She stopped. They were in the entrance hall; she could hear her nieces giggling and bickering and Florence delivering stern ultimatums. 'You do not have to feel guilty about playing. Ever. You do not have to worry. That's my burden, and if you try to carry it for me, then that both makes me love you even more, and adds another weight for me to bear. Play with your cousins. Run, jump, laugh – and never once feel that doing those things could possibly make your father and I anything less than delighted. That is the most helpful thing you could do. Can you manage that for me?'

Walter smiled, finally brushing his hair out of his eyes. 'Yes, Mama.'

The door crashed open. In skipped Cecily and in twirled Dorothy. Thomasin and Judith stumbled sideways, tugging each other's hair ribbons. Little Elizabeth marched proudly, still pleased at her lack of leading strings. And behind them came Florence, ushering her brood with fond exasperation.

'Afternoon, sister,' she said. 'I bring you a great gift: distraction.'

Of course, Beatrice reflected, there were two meanings to distraction. And while her sister had undeniably fulfilled one meaning by lifting Walter's spirits, Florence had a unique talent for driving Beatrice to the other.

The children's laughter was almost drowned out by the axes: high abandon buried by dull thuds and the groan of splintering wood. Beatrice had ordered the gardeners to chop the beech up. 'Plenty of firewood,' one of them had said kindly, as if he thought it might cheer her up to burn the tree that had injured her husband. Perhaps it might. But every time Beatrice looked at the fallen tree, her first thought was that she knew a cabinet maker who would pay a fine price for that much good beech. And then reality would charge her down: this wasn't a business opportunity. This was attempted murder. And since that attempt had failed, when, and how – and who – would they strike next?

'You're frowning,' Florence said, jabbing her elbow into Beatrice's ribs.

'Are you surprised?'

'Of course not.' Florence's arm was suddenly no longer jabbing, but wrapping around Beatrice's waist in a surreptitious squeeze. 'That this should happen here, in our childhood home … We almost have to expect disaster when our men are at sea, as if assuming all will be well would be to curse them somehow. But when they're here … it's horrifying. I understand that.' Florence nodded towards their children. 'But for heaven's sake, don't let Walter and Ursula see you so vexed.'

Beatrice followed Florence's gaze to where Walter and Cecily were leading Florence's four younger daughters in some sort of game that involved jumping over the artemisia hedges, running around the fountain and then retrieving sticks, and what she was fairly certain were pieces of coral from the curiosity cabinet, surreptitiously pilfered and now being alternately brandished in triumph and used to menace a fleeing cousin. A treasure hunt, perhaps, with some logic only comprehensible to those under ten. She ought to remonstrate with Walter: those curios weren't toys. And yet he was playing, and she needed him to be playing, rather than agonising about his father's injuries.

Or his sister's. Her eyes drifted to Ursula, sat on a bench beside Catalina. Ursula's legs were stretched flat on the bench between thick blankets, and she was leaning back on Catalina, who had one arm loosely draped around Ursula's shoulders while the other hand tapped a gentle rhythm on her growing belly as she hummed.

It should have been Beatrice sat there, helping her daughter feel less left out. The knowledge hooked in her belly like the talons of some great bird. Guilt warred with jealousy: she wanted to take Catalina's place, knew she ought to – and feared Ursula might not want her to.

'Quite the maternal image,' Florence observed. 'She seems to have taken a shine to Ursula. And vice versa.'

'Catalina's been a great help,' Beatrice said stiffly. She still hadn't thanked Catalina, wasn't sure how to: if it might seem like dismissal, or more like ingratitude, or like a mistress to a servant. When the truth was that she couldn't have said precisely what Catalina's position in the household was. She'd made no attempt to attach herself to Hugh, had in fact avoided all the men in the house, and understandably. She wasn't a servant, nor a nursemaid, nor a companion to wait on Beatrice. Instead, Catalina seemed to have appointed herself an honorary aunt: a gentle, unthreatening position, and yet one that still allowed her to keep some distance, retain some privacy. And at some point in the weeks since her arrival, Beatrice had ceased to be able to imagine her home without Catalina in it. She wasn't even sure she wanted Catalina gone anymore.

'I'm sure she has,' Florence said dryly. 'Still, I suppose she needs the practice. Do you know how long she has left?'

Beatrice shrugged. 'Perhaps three months.'

'And then what? Are you to raise her mulatto here?'

'Perhaps. Why not?'

Florence gave her an exasperated look. 'Honestly, Beatrice, do you have to be so obliging?'

'I'm nothing of the sort!'

'Yes, you are.' Florence shook her head. 'Oh, not when it comes to business, the whole of London knows what a canny head you have for bargains, and how doggedly you'll stick to your prices. But with everything else? You let everyone take advantage of you!'

Beatrice laughed in shock. 'And none more so than you!'

'I admit it freely,' Florence retorted. 'You like to give me things, and I like to receive them. If it helps assuage your desire for domestic martyrdom, I'll happily drink your wine and borrow your jewels – and yes, I do keep them longer than is polite, sometimes permanently, because I like their sparkle, and you like feeling superior and useful!'

'Enough, Florence!'

'It isn't though, is it?' Florence fixed her with a steely glare. 'For either of us. You cannot give me enough, and I cannot take enough, because we both know our father's will robbed me.'

Beatrice flinched. Now, of all times, she didn't want to be reminded of Arthur. Of the cockatrice and the bear. 'It was more complicated than that.'

'So you've said. Dozens of times. And yet you never deign to explain.'

She couldn't. Couldn't hurt Florence with the truth, couldn't damn herself by admitting it all aloud. Lamely, she said, 'It's complex.'

'And I too simple to understand.' Florence nodded bitterly. 'If I am, it isn't my fault. It's yours.'

'What?'

'Well, isn't it?' Florence stared across the gardens at her capering daughters. 'My mother treated me like a doll. Always dressing me up, telling me I was beautiful. I don't remember her saying anything else to me. I was only four when she died, and all my memories are of her fingers tying bows in my hair and holding lace up against my little gowns. And then you and our father continued to give me dress after dress and tell me I was pretty and graceful and charming. Never once did any of you tell me I was clever. And now ... Now I'm not much good for anything other than looking beautiful. I cannot do what you do – I can't help Robert by doing wonders with numbers and prices, or raise a loan for a new ship by speaking to a passing earl. All I can do is make myself prettier with gowns that pretend we are better off than we truly are. And I can no longer afford the lie.'

Beatrice stared at her half-sister. She'd never heard Florence speak so openly. So vulnerably. She cast her mind back, pulling on the threads of memory: yes, there were dozens of gowns, she remembered all too well how often Blanche had presented Florence with scarlet damask, ivory brocade patterned with lilies, plum velvet adorned with golden brochures. Arthur had controlled the purse strings then, and Beatrice couldn't understand why he allowed his younger daughter to be draped in finery she'd soon outgrow, while his older daughter wore the same dresses for years. At twelve, she'd eyed her four-year-old half-sister with resentment and envy. At thirteen, after Blanche's death, pity for this other motherless girl had less softened her jealousy, and more made her feel guilty for resenting Florence. Then, later, she'd understood why Arthur had dressed Florence up as a glittering prize, and why he hadn't needed to do so with Beatrice. Glass needed to look more like diamonds than diamonds themselves, in order to trick buyers. But how could she explain this to Florence now? She'd swallowed the truth for so long, to endeavour to hook it out of her throat now would choke her.

'Florence,' she said haltingly, 'if I could tell you, I would. But ...'

Florence's glare was hotter than forged steel. 'If you dare tell me it's too complicated one more time, I swear I will uproot this dead rose and force it down your throat, every last thorn!'

Too late even to try. She'd known that for years. 'I'll give you a loan,' Beatrice said weakly. 'I've agreed it with Robert.'

'Of course you have,' Florence said bitterly. 'And what form will the interest take, I wonder? Shall I offer you drops of blood? An eye? My tongue?'

'Gladly, if it will silence you,' Beatrice shot back.

'Ah, but I already am silenced,' Florence retorted.

Beatrice couldn't suppress a snort of astonished outrage. 'You, quiet? The ravens in the Tower caw less than you!'

'And everyone pays them far more heed.' Florence shook her head. 'Perhaps I talk and talk precisely because no one will listen. I could scream here, now, and all I would get from you, my children, your children, and that Moorish whore are looks of polite scorn. That's Florence demanding more new baubles, you'd think, and if I'm lucky, you might toss me a pretty pair of earrings. But you will never consider why I might want them so badly.'

'Then tell me why,' Beatrice snapped, exasperated.

Florence smiled ruefully. 'I already did. And, as I predicted, you did not listen.'

She did not have time for Florence's grievances. Beatrice knew it was selfish to admit such a thing, but her sister's hurt was two decades old, and unjustified, even if she couldn't fully explain why. Besides, however much Florence felt herself ill-used, her bones were unlikely to break under its weight, nor would jealousy make her bleed. It certainly would not kill her. Whereas Hugh ...

His breathing was ragged. His skin clammy, his face grey, his eyelids trembling feverishly. The physician had avoided giving her a straight answer, insisting it was impossible to be certain about any internal damage, but for all his equivocation, Beatrice was convinced there was more wrong with Hugh than a broken femur.

Beatrice dashed her sleeve across her eyes: the fumes from the yarrow she was steeping in wine were stinging. Blaming the tincture was easier than admitting how frightened she was. Brewing tinctures that needed to stew for a month was hardly logical, unless she were expecting Hugh to lie sick for weeks.

Or she expected someone else to be injured before long.

She didn't want to think about it. So she did what she always did when she was avoiding thought: she brewed one of her mother's recipes. She'd mislaid this one a few months back, but no matter: Beatrice had made it dozens of times. Every time she or Florence had been expecting a child, so they might be saved from fatal blood loss in labour. Every time she'd imagined Walter falling down the stairs and splitting his scalp; every time her father had complained of a toothache or piles. She'd gone to the stillroom, where dried yarrow hung from hooks, its clustered white flowers turning towards her like ghostly faces, and when she'd plucked a handful, green and white dust whispered over her wrist like a vow. Perhaps to Maria, whose body she had washed beneath those hanging herbs. Then she'd retrieved a flask of white wine and her copper pan and climbed the stairs to her bedchamber, and for a moment she'd felt as though her mother were climbing them too, just at her shoulder, inches out of sight.

This was what Jane had done. Small difference between this stock-piling of tinctures and the building of high ramparts and arrow slits: the woman's way and the man's way of protecting their loved ones. If only this time her way would work.

'The mast.'

She almost knocked the pan into the fire as she whipped around.

'Hugh!' Beatrice dashed to his bedside, clutching at his hand. 'Hugh, my love, thank God –'

'The mast fell. I couldn't stop it.' His eyelids flickered. Was he delirious, or could he possibly be recovering?

'It wasn't a mast, Hugh,' Beatrice said gently. 'It was one of the beeches in the grounds.'

'The mast fell,' Hugh repeated, insistent, urgent. 'And the boy died.'

Novaya Zemlya. Beatrice kissed his hand. 'I know. But it wasn't your fault. Just like you said – you couldn't stop it.'

'His screams. I thought the icebergs would shatter with their sound. The storm couldn't drown them out.'

'Oh, Hugh.' Beatrice pushed his damp hair out of his eyes. 'You had no choice, you told me that. And remember how many lives you saved – the rest of your crew, that boy who fell into the rapids at Tower Bridge –'

'Not enough.' Hugh's eyes finally cracked open: dark and fevered, they gaped with guilt and pain. 'Never enough. No number of boys pulled from the water will make up for what I did.'

'But you couldn't have done otherwise,' Beatrice reminded him. She could still hear him now, hoarse and wide-eyed, confessing in her arms the night he came home from that failed voyage. How tightly he'd gripped her hipbones in bed, how he'd buried his face in her shoulder, his still-ragged beard chafing her skin raw. 'You told me the mast came down in the storm and the rigging became lodged in an iceberg. The ship was bucking and tilting so violently you had to cut the mast loose, or the ship would have foundered in icy water, and you would all have drowned. Of course you would have saved the boy if you could – but it was impossible.'

'You don't understand,' Hugh whispered, and his words were no longer merely, if they had ever been, the raving of a sick man. 'I let him die. I chose which life to save. And it wasn't Ben's.'

Beatrice stared. 'What do you mean?'

'We were lost.' Hugh's voice was rasping: the effort of speaking was exhausting him. And yet he had to confess, she could see that. Why, she dared not contemplate. 'We'd been lost for days – first the mist, then the compasses lost overboard. When the storms struck, we were already desperate. So when the mast fell and the two crew who'd been in the rigging were trapped, I knew who I had to choose.' He grimaced, hauled in breath to speak again. 'I ordered the men to take axes to the mast. Sever it before it dragged us all down. I watched them struggling, tangling in the ropes. I made my decision. The axes were almost through the mast: the wood was shrieking as it strained. I grabbed a rope, bound one end around my waist. Threw the other to William. He caught it – leapt free almost immediately. I hauled him up out of the icy water – thrust him into the mate's care.' His voice became a croak, but he jerked away from the cup she offered. 'Then I looked back. I saw Ben's face. Saw him scream "Please!" And I – I turned away. Moments later, the mast split. The waves thrust us away from the wreckage. From the child I had left to die.'

She'd heard the story before. He'd told her when he returned from the aborted voyage, cheeks still blistered red, staring into every fire as if he couldn't quite believe it existed. That the mast had broken and they'd had to abandon both the expedition and the boy. But he had never before mentioned the choice.

'I chose my navigator,' Hugh continued, eyes fixed on the shadowed canopy as if he were watching his memories play out. As if the boy's terrified, receding face hovered above him. 'Or so I told myself. With the compasses lost, we needed a man who could navigate by stars.'

'And your nephew,' Beatrice pointed out. 'Almost as good as a son. No one could fault you for saving him –'

'But William could swim,' Hugh said dully. 'He was sixteen – almost a grown man – I'd taught him to swim. If I'd thrown the rope to the boy, perhaps William would have leapt into the water, swam to the *Swan* …'

'In a storm? In freezing water?' Beatrice pointed out. 'Without your rope, he'd have drowned.'

Hugh shook his head, wincing as the movement jarred his wounds. 'Not William. Throw him onto an ice floe, he'd teach the polar bears to dance. He's got the devil's luck. Same luck they used to say I had. Doubt they'll be saying that again.'

'Have you not considered that *you* are William's luck?' Beatrice pressed his hand imploringly. 'He would be dead without you. Dear God, Hugh, you saved a man's life – you shouldn't be feeling guilty at all!'

His eyes flew to her. 'Don't you understand? I let a child die. A *child*. What greater sin could anyone commit?'

Murder. Deliberate, determined murder. It took every sinew in Beatrice's body to hold her voice and face steady.

'And this,' Hugh continued, 'this is vengeance. Deserved vengeance.'

Beatrice stiffened. 'What do you mean?'

'I heard you,' Hugh said. 'Talking about the axe that felled the tree. A fallen tree – a fallen mast.'

'Hugh …' She hesitated. 'Do you mean you know who did this?'

'The cabin boy – Ben – he had a brother. Anthony Kitson. He was ship's carpenter until a year ago. Disappeared between voyages. Simply didn't turn up when we set sail. We thought plague must have taken him, or a better offer from another ship. But perhaps he was here in London all this time. Planning his revenge.'

She had a name. Finally she had a name for the shadows that had been circling. *Anthony Kitson*. Was he the man in black who'd given her the threatening note? Who'd frightened Maria – perhaps even killed her? Beatrice leaned closer, hungry for clues.

'Anthony Kitson. Where can I find him?'

'*No*,' Hugh hissed. 'Beatrice, you must not seek him out. He's too dangerous.'

'Too dangerous for me *not* to seek him out,' Beatrice countered. 'I will not let him harm us any further. Tell me where I can find him.'

Hugh's eyelids were drooping, his lips slackening. Too exhausted to argue, he breathed, 'Lambeth. He used to live in Lambeth.'

And he was gone, slipping back into unconsciousness.

It couldn't be merely a coincidence. The globe had come from Lambeth. Maria's family lived in Lambeth. And now it seemed their assailant had come from Lambeth too.

She knew what she was looking for now. Beatrice stood before the globe, spine straight, head high. No need to crouch before the thing, scrabbling at its blurring surface, searching for nothing, anything. Now she could look down on the northernmost part of the globe and impale Novaya Zemlya with her forefinger.

There it was. As she had known it would be. Surrounded by ice floes, a silver-grey ship tilted between jagged waves, its main mast broken and pinioned between two bergs. And on the ice, crushed by the mast, not a forsaken cabin boy, but a man in a turquoise velvet hat. *Hugh*.

She could have scoured the globe again, could have found answers to the questions she did not yet know to ask. But there was a simpler way to find out the truth, and to find Anthony Kitson.

She heard Ridley enter behind her, recognising his soft, swift tread: purposeful but not intrusive.

'Ridley,' she said, 'send for Master Molyneux's apprentice. Bring Simon to me.'

18

The apprentice twisted his cap between his fingers; his rain-damp fingers, their nails clogged with paint, left smears of ochre and verdigris on the blue velvet, like the trails of poisoned snails. Spotting them, Simon rubbed frantically at the marks, but to no avail. His face, when he looked up at Beatrice in helpless, anxious appeal was so childlike she almost blurted out 'There, there.' But the apprentice craftsman was no childish innocent. He was a conspirator.

'Tell me,' Beatrice said, 'everything.'

Simon's eyes flickered over her shoulder, as if he were contemplating leaping through the study window. 'I don't know what …'

'You do. You must. You painted the images on the globes – one set of images for those specimens intended for the queen, for Raleigh and the Oxford colleges and so on. And an entirely different set for my husband's globe. Why?'

'Because I was paid to,' Simon mumbled. 'And I – I needed the money. My mother's sick. She can't work, hasn't been able to since the last baby died, four years ago.'

'How touching,' Beatrice began, forcing her voice to clamp down like a vice, even as empathy hooked into her belly. But Simon was still speaking, words spilling like ink.

'I've still got two years of my apprenticeship to work and until I finish I can't afford the woman who sits with her unless I take on other commissions on the side. And she keeps raising her rates and not tell-ing me, just refusing to work until I give her more money, so the first I know of it is when my mother's found wandering in the marshes, or one of her neighbours comes to tell me she's heard her weeping for three days in a row. So I have to paint whatever I'm asked to, even if I'm doing it for hours after the other apprentices have gone to bed.' He took a deep, shuddering breath. 'I'm sorry if what I painted distressed you. Or offended you. But I can't afford not to paint what I'm asked to.'

Beatrice caught herself staring and pinched her lips shut. She'd been thinking of another woman who'd wept and wandered – and who'd died in Bedlam. There were those who'd say Simon's mother belonged in the hospital, just like they'd said it about Jane. But Beatrice would never say it. Nor think it. Not after what she'd seen.

'I didn't call you here to reprimand you,' she said haltingly, painfully aware that her whole demeanour thus far must have indicated otherwise. 'I summoned you to ask for information. There are cartouches on my globe that are identical to those on Sir Walter Raleigh's globe – and there are those which are unique. I want you to provide me with a list. An exhaustive list, detailing all those images included in the original design, and all those you added. Can you do that for me?'

He nodded, his beardless face slackening in relief. If he'd been a puppy, he'd have been wagging his tail and sidling up to her legs, needy with new loyalty now the fear of a boot to the ribs had passed. 'I'll write it all down for you. Tomorrow. Today!'

'That will suit,' she said, trying to bat him back with a business-like tone: she was conducting a transaction, not adopting a stray waif. 'And one more thing. Does the name Anthony Kitson mean anything to you?'

'Kitson?' Simon stiffened: that cowering look darted back into his eyes. 'I don't – I never have anything to do with him. No one does, unless they can help it.'

'What do you mean?'

Simon swallowed. His eyes jerked to the window again, as if he expected Kitson was about to leap through the glass, cutlass between his teeth. 'Everyone in Lambeth knows Kitson. When he used to work away on ship, everyone breathed a little easier. You could drink in a tavern without fearing a brawl was about to break out. He's forever in fights. He might not always start them, but he always finishes them. One of the other apprentices lost an eye when Kitson slashed his face

– just for bumping into his table. Master Molyneux terminated his apprenticeship – said a half-blind artist was no good to him. They say Kitson's killed three men, but he always dumps the bodies in the river so they're never found.'

Like Maria. Beatrice inched forwards, her heart thrumming: had she finally discovered Maria's killer? 'Could Kitson have been the man in black who commissioned you?'

Simon shook his head. 'Not Kitson.'

Her sigh hurt, the disappointment was so visceral. 'You're certain?'

'Positive. The customer was a head shorter and much slighter – Kitson's arms are twice as thick as theirs.'

'I see.' Beatrice slumped back in her chair. 'Then thank you for your time.'

'He smelled odd,' Simon volunteered. 'I remember the smell on account of not seeing his face clearly. Frankincense. And cardamom. Costly scents, I thought. Kitson wouldn't be able to afford such things. Or not honestly, anyway.'

'That's very helpful,' Beatrice said, not sure she spoke truthfully. 'You must have a great deal of work to catch up on – you may return to Lambeth.'

After he'd gone, she let her head drop into her hands. Frankincense and cardamom. Was she supposed to sniff out Maria's murderer like a hound seeking a fox? Should she sniff every man in London? Besides, half the men Beatrice knew were spice merchants. They all smelled like frankincense and cardamom – and cedarwood, and cypress, and saffron, because she'd sold the spices to them.

She'd been so certain. And now she was back to the beginning, no closer to finding Maria's killer than before.

Just as she was sinking lower in her seat, she heard footsteps hammering towards her. And then the door crashed open.

They arrived in state, with all the pomp an earl descended from royalty felt he was owed. The Essex arms snapped against the pale sky, their azure and crimson and gold reducing the already grey November sky to sodden ashy abasement. Sixteen quarters emblazoned on Robert

Devereux's shield, surrounded by the Order of the Garter motto: lions rampant, fleur-de-lys, crosses and cinquefoils and chiefs, symbols brandishing the bloodlines of kings and queens, dukes and earls, magnates and potentates, all of which had produced the dazzling creatures that were the Devereux siblings.

Beatrice couldn't help gaping in awe and bewilderment as the Essex barge swept up to her wharf. Far grander than hers, even more coats of arms glittered in its house's glass windows, and gold chased gold along railings, among the whales – and yet the most splendid things aboard the vessel were still Robert Devereux, Earl of Essex, and his sister, Lady Penelope Rich. Clad in black and gold and ivory velvets, damasks and silks, their chestnut hair gleaming beneath one pearl-studded hood and one black hat adorned with vast, swooping black feathers, they looked like twin flintlocks primed to fire. And Beatrice was right in their sights.

'Why are they here, Mama?' Walter, who had dashed to Beatrice's study to tell her of the approaching barge, now sidled closer, tucking himself behind her russet brocade skirts.

Queen Elizabeth's favourite and his sister, her Majesty's lady-in-waiting? Beatrice shook her head. 'I've no idea.'

The Essex barge docked, and the earl was first to spring ashore, doffing his hat to the stone swans. His sister, raising her skirts and eyebrows as she alighted, gave an elaborate sigh. 'Hardly an appropriate occasion for your nonsense, Robert.'

'Hugh would wish it,' Essex retorted. 'Besides, it must be ill luck not to greet Hugin and Munin here.'

Helen and Clytemnestra, Beatrice wanted to correct him. That was what she'd called them as a child, naming the swans after twin Spartan sisters, both imperious, both bold. As a girl she'd dreamed of being a Helen: hadn't they all? But she was more of a Clytemnestra: abandoned, embittered, and enraged by any assault on her children. Though that would make Hugh Agamemnon, and everyone knew what Clytemnestra did to him when he returned from his long voyage.

But even if she'd had the temerity to correct the earl, she wouldn't have had the chance: Walter poked his head out from behind her and piped up, 'Those are ravens' names, not swan names.'

'Is that so, young man?' Essex gave Walter a lazy smile. 'I bow to your superior knowledge. How should I address your stone guardians?'

'Sophia and Solomon,' Walter said, pointing to each in turn. 'My sister named the girl and I named the boy.'

Beatrice had started at the name Solomon, and she was uncomfortably aware that Lady Rich had noticed: the woman was eyeing her thoughtfully. Being held in that grey gaze was like being ducked in cold water until you were too numb to know which way the surface had been.

'A cob and a pen!' Essex's laughter rang like applause. 'And of course the pen is named for wisdom. One should never tell pens they are anything less than wise, eh, Pen?'

At last Lady Rich's eyes left Beatrice in order to roll at her brother's teasing. 'Naming the cob for peace, however, is rather wishful thinking. I dream of a calm brother who ruffles no feathers.'

'You do not,' Essex said affably, 'not for one moment. Peace is dull, and you like lustre.'

Lady Rich ignored him, drawing up a smile like a veil. 'But we are being unforgivably remiss in our manners. Lady Radclyffe, pardon our rudeness, especially in arriving unannounced. We wished to pay our respects to you, and to Sir Hugh.'

'Might I see him?' Essex glittered his teeth at Beatrice. It was no more a request than a wolf asking a sheep if she preferred to be gnawed or gulped.

'He needs rest.' Beatrice offered a token protest.

'He'll need cheering up,' Essex countered. 'Who better to provide mirth than an old comrade? I've always said laughter is a far better physician than the quacks charging outrageous sums for poultices full of mulch.'

As if his deigning to grace Hugh with his noble presence could mend broken bones and dispel infection. But the blithe arrogance sounded familiar: it was Raleigh's, it was Hugh's. The cheerful conviction that the world would do as it was bid because it almost always had, and even disasters like Hugh's Novaya Zemlya expedition and Essex's Azores campaign would not dare hold them back.

Except Hugh's might have done.

'This little chap can lead the way,' Essex declared, taking Beatrice's stunned silence as acquiescence. He clapped a hand on Walter's shoulder, reaching across Beatrice as if she were a curtain obstructing his view. 'Onwards, valiant soldier!'

As Walter trotted obediently away with Essex, Beatrice had to allow that, however irksome Essex's presumptuous entitlement might be, he had achieved the impossible: he'd made her son smile.

'Well then,' Lady Rich drawled, 'while the men share their *highly* embellished war stories, perhaps you and I might take a cup of something together. Do you have spiced cider?'

'Indeed,' Beatrice said tartly, turning back towards her house, 'and we even have cups from which to drink it.'

Cider with Lady Penelope Rich: Beatrice couldn't decide which of them was most displeased to find themselves here. But watching Lady Rich perch on her chair as if forcing herself onto a ducking stool, Beatrice had the strange suspicion that the other woman was unsettled by something. As if she were steeling herself for an ordeal, and not merely the social sullying that meant she was associating with a merchant's daughter. What could Lady Rich be afraid of? And how could Beatrice have any impact on that fear?

Then Beatrice glanced past Lady Rich, down the gallery, to the globe. It was still, dormant. Like a swollen beast sunk into hibernation. Or like those tales of mountain ranges that were really dragons or trolls turned to stone: at any moment they might bellow their rocky shackles away, wrestling themselves up for vengeance. Could Lady Rich feel it too?

For a moment she almost wished the globe would start into life again. Any witness to its terrifying spinning might be reassuring, but to have someone as seemingly indomitable as Lady Rich see the globe revolving untouched … well, it might help Beatrice believe she wasn't going mad.

Eventually, Lady Rich said, 'You have some interesting paintings displayed here.'

'Indeed.' Beatrice offered limp agreement: what was she supposed to say? With a guest as revered and lofty as Lady Penelope Rich everything she said ought to dazzle – but the noblewoman almost seemed to expect an inventory of Beatrice's art. Would she start listing the contents of the cabinet of curiosities next? 'I am fond of landscapes. And of course Hugh appreciates paintings of the sea. Ships. Islands. That sort of thing.'

'Understandable.' Lady Rich nodded, tapping her cup and then rubbing forefinger and thumb together, as if to rid herself of any speck of common dust. 'London can feel so hemmed in, especially in winter. One longs for distant horizons. To be away from the smell of other people's excrement.'

Beatrice laughed, half-shocked, half-pleased that a woman allegedly descended from King Henry VIII circled back to the same conversational topics as her nine-year-old son. 'All the more so when you're married to an explorer.'

'And when you lack a country estate, of course.' The tone was sweetly sympathetic, but the smile anything but. 'Though I suppose Chelsea is fairly distant from the more vibrant parts of London.'

Perhaps not distant enough, Beatrice thought darkly.

'Or maybe there's another reason for your preference,' Lady Rich continued. 'Maybe you have so few portraits because you dislike the feeling of being watched.'

Beatrice stared at her. The carved parrots on the back of her chair pecked at her spine: she'd stiffened without realising. Unwilling to betray her discomfort by shifting, Beatrice replied, 'I imagine few people truly enjoy that sensation.'

'The conduct at court would prove you wrong,' Lady Rich countered. 'I believe our beloved sovereign has over two thousand gowns, and her fondness of peacocking is embraced by her courtiers.'

'Perhaps it would be truer to say they enjoy their clothes being watched,' Beatrice pointed out, 'and not they themselves.'

'Which is rather the whole point of silken clothes,' Lady Rich said archly. 'So no one pays enough attention to what your hands, or face, or words might be doing.'

'Rather a flawed tactic,' Beatrice said drily. 'I'd have thought silken clothes make people pay you too much attention.'

'Touché.' Lady Rich eyed Beatrice's skirts. 'By your reasoning then, with a gown like yours, it's unlikely you'll be paid any. A misfortune, or a blessing?'

It might well be ten years old and unfashionable, but the russet brocade was hardly sackcloth. 'Did you come all this way merely to criticise my wardrobe, Lady Rich? Have you really nothing better to occupy your time?'

Lady Rich's eyes glittered. 'Oh, I fill my days, Lady Radclyffe, with matters both trivial and weighty. Do not presume my comments on clothing are mere frivolity. I wish to know why you, heiress to a great fortune, owner of a grand house, inconvenient location notwithstanding, wife to a revered knight, refuse to dress the part.'

There was something almost savage in her voice, a feline hiss. But not just a predatory aggression: Lady Rich seemed to be striking before she was struck. But why? What did she have to fear from Beatrice?

Beatrice sipped her cider slowly before replying: provocative, and a chance to steady her nerves. 'My fortune would not be so impressive, nor my house so grand if I spent all my coin on cloth of gold. Besides, it will take the queen over five years to wear those two thousand gowns. My merchant forebears would turn in their graves if they thought I were frittering coin on clothes I might wear twice at most.'

'You deliberately miss the point,' Lady Rich said coldly. 'We all know how ludicrous this game is. Yet still we play, for there is no other choice. If no one sees your worth, you have no worth. That is how our world works, madam. But you … you hide away here in Chelsea. And I want to know why. To uncover what you are really hiding.'

Beatrice schooled her face into a mirror of Lady Rich's own: haughty, outraged, disdainful. 'This is a poor return for my hospitality, Lady Rich. You are not your illustrious ancestors, however much you may wish it. A sovereign might arrive uninvited at a subject's house and fling insults and accusations, all while a man lies severely injured merely one storey away. But you are no queen, and I am certainly not your subject.'

'And I certainly haven't even begun insulting you,' Lady Rich retorted. 'Not by my standards, that is – I can tell they are very different to yours.'

'Then deliver your insults!' Beatrice snapped. 'Unvarnished, unhidden – if you wish to accuse me of something, for God's sake, get on with it, for I have a thousand things I would rather be doing than squabbling with you!'

Lady Rich leaned back, lifting her head; the golden necklace winding about her throat and the glittering jet studding her black lace ruff made her look like a cobra, elated to have found the right moment to pounce. 'Very well. Lady Radclyffe, this house is a harbour of spies.'

Beatrice almost spilled her cider. Whatever she had been expecting, it certainly was not that.

'Spies,' she repeated, stalling for time. 'Is that so?'

'Indeed.' Lady Rich leaned closer, her tongue flicking across her teeth as she savoured her words. Beatrice wouldn't have been surprised if it were forked. 'So I ask you, Lady Radclyffe, are they spying for you? In which case, what have you ordered from them, and what have you discovered? Or are they spying on you? In which case, what have you been doing that would render you either a traitor, or a threat, or both?'

Beatrice tossed a laugh into the air, all too aware it must sound hollow. 'You'll have to be more specific, Lady Rich. To which of the spies we harbour here do you refer in particular?'

Lady Rich smiled: a glittering, predatory smile. She knew Beatrice was stalling, prevaricating. 'Oh, you poor innocent bumpkin. Don't tell me you know nothing of the Velasquez history.'

Velasquez? Beatrice stared in consternation, completely at a loss. Who did Lady Rich mean?

'I see.' Lady Rich sighed. 'Ignorance suits few faces, but least of all those who think themselves at no risk of it. I have seen lampreys ready to go in a pie with less gaping mouths than yours. Unless you are an astonishingly gifted actress, I must assume you are not the one pulling the spies' strings.'

'Then …' Beatrice struggled to marshal her thoughts. 'Am I being watched? But why? And by whom?'

Lady Rich gave the dregs of her cider a cursory swirl, and set the cup down on the silver tray. 'Perhaps when you know the answers to all those questions, you might wish to share them with me.'

'Why would I share anything with you? We cannot even share a cup of cider without quarrelling.'

Lady Rich gave her a pitying look. 'Because, of all the women in London, there are few who know more about being watched than I do. And even fewer who understand how to deploy watchers of their own. You may not like me, nor I you, Lady Radclyffe. But we can, I hope, prove useful to one another.'

She rose, flowing to her feet in a ripple of shadow and gold, a snake charmed by its own tune. 'Perhaps you might start by asking your husband to tell you the truth about the Azores.'

She watched Lady Rich glide through the gardens, the black-clad woman and her shadow twin blots on Beatrice's grounds. The Essex barge waited, silhouetted against sky and river, where lavender bled into coral above and coral bled into lavender below.

She'd expected rudeness. Disrespect, hostility, mockery – all this she could have borne. But it was as if Lady Rich had boarded the vessel of Beatrice's home and taken an axe to the hull, severing the anchor rope and tossing the cannon over the railings for good measure.

There was a spy in Beatrice's house. But why? And could this spy be the same person behind the attacks on Maria and Hugh? Could they even be behind the globe? She shifted her right shoulder, thoughts racing through her head, blocking the globe from sight. If only she could put it out of mind so easily. Every rustle, every creak, every breath was the globe about to turn.

And then she saw something that almost made her forget it.

Essex had emerged from the house, following his sister back to their barge. But he wasn't alone. At his side, her rounded belly cupped in the arm that wasn't hooked into the crook of Essex's elbow, was the unmistakeable figure of Catalina.

What was Catalina doing with the Earl of Essex? As she watched, the two figures halted by the fountain, their dark reflections jostling with purple ripples. A sudden mist obscured them: Beatrice had leaned so close to the window her breath had fogged the glass. As she scrubbed it away with her sleeve, making it worse, she squinted at what Catalina and Essex were doing. Had Catalina tried to pull away – or was she holding on to Essex, pulling him back? His free hand went to her face – her cheek? Her throat? – and then to her belly. Gestures of tenderness, or threat?

The glass was clear. Essex was striding away towards the wharf; Catalina was hurrying back to the house. As the distance between the figures grew, Beatrice tried to recognise what she'd seen. Queen Elizabeth's favourite, and the strange woman Hugh had brought into their home: what could the connection between them possibly be? And how had it become so clearly intimate?

Essex's words at Durham House suddenly came back to her: *I know the value of what your husband brought back, Lady Radclyffe.* Had he meant Catalina? If so, what value did she hold for the earl?

Beatrice rested her forehead on the glass. This time, when her breath fogged the glass, she let it, the Essex barge disappearing behind white.

Whatever the connection was, she had a horrible suspicion it was linked to the name Velasquez. Which, if Lady Rich were to be trusted, meant Catalina was either spying on Beatrice – or was herself in great danger.

And then it happened. The sound she'd dreaded, and expected, and even wildly almost hoped would come when Lady Rich was here. A whirr. A click. A whirr and a click.

Beatrice turned. Her legs trembled with the effort of neither collapsing nor moving, her toes curled inside her fleece-lined slippers as if trying to get a purchase on the carpet, as if the gallery had become a tidal river, hauling her inexorably towards the globe. She couldn't bear to approach it. She couldn't bear not to. Not curiosity so much as dread. The globe was a festering canker in the flesh of her home: she couldn't just pretend it away. She had to see how deep the rot had set in.

The last light guttered on the globe's polished surface, coral leeching away, leaving only muddied browns. As though stagnant waters had heaved themselves out of their stone and soil shackles, swelling, bulging, glutinous, and now hovering among the flies. She was close enough to touch it now. Her skin rippled with revulsion; her hands crept beneath her sleeves, clenching so tight around the brocade cuffs she could feel every ridge reddening her palms.

Still it turned. Slowly, deliberately. As if it were mocking her, challenging her. *Can't you see? Look harder.* The cartouches paraded past her. A sneering fish, its fins rising into fiery spokes, lazily pursuing a mermaid. Pale ships sailed away from land, always leaving, never arriving, their destinations spinning out of reach. And then the images that only stained Hugh's globe. A kiss watched. A felled man. The cockatrice strangling the bear. Secrets that were no longer secret, sins that had gone unpunished. They'd been hiding in plain sight, emblazoned on the globe. And now it was about to brandish another image. Whose secret would be revealed? Whose danger would be promised?

Now the globe spun faster, the lines blurring, chasing each other so rapidly they clashed, blurred, black smeared red. The cartouches contorted, bloated and grotesque, place names became jagged trails, as if the hand scribing them had fallen away, quill tumbling.

'Stop,' Beatrice breathed, and she didn't know if she were addressing the globe itself, or the person behind the threatening pictures. 'Please, stop.'

With a low rattle, the globe slowed, and halted. Almost as if it had heard her.

They hadn't yet lit the candles. Moonlight crept in from the east, smoky fingers inching along the globe's surface, hunting, seeking, finding.

She'd known where they would alight. A group of islands scattered in the midst of the Atlantic, like shards of broken pottery, some jagged, some round, outlined in pale pink and yellow, or discarded scraps of fruit. Terceira. Faial. Pico. Vila de Orta, Sao Miguel, Flores, Santa Maria, Graciosa. The Azores islands. And between Flores and Faial, a ship with a swan figurehead. She did not need to peer closely to know that on its decks would be a golden-haired captain and a brown-skinned woman.

She didn't want the globe's version of the truth. She wanted Catalina's. She wanted Hugh's. And she'd be damned if she let either of them hide it any longer.

19

Florence would never have stood for this.

As she strode out of the gallery, Beatrice couldn't help thinking of her half-sister. If their positions had been reversed, Florence would have had the truth out of Robert before he could remove his boots, and any woman attempting to seek shelter under Florence's roof would have been sent fleeing from the house under a hailstorm of hurled gravel and rotting apples. Florence had tried to incite Beatrice into bold defiance, unable to bear the sight of her older sister being so meek. But Beatrice had accepted Catalina – not without question, true enough, but without any concerted attempts to have her questions answered.

She'd always let people take advantage of her. Lady Rich thought Beatrice's outdated garb hid secrets, and she was right: Beatrice had never been able to justify spending money on her own appearance because she'd never believed she deserved her good fortune.

Except that good fortune had run out. Had been ebbing away, treasure by treasure, since Hugh and Catalina stepped ashore almost two months ago.

There were too many secrets under her roof. Seeping through the stonework like river water, finding cracks in walls, eroding foundations, breathing dark clouds of mould across ceilings: once the water was inside, windows and doors and rooves were useless. The structure was unsound, and it would collapse unless Beatrice took action.

She reached the top of the stairs just as Catalina came in from the gardens. Both women halted. Their eyes met. Silver skeins of moonlight trailed behind Catalina as if a net were unreeling from her skirts, as if she were sweeping up a haul in her wake, catching fish, flotsam, jetsam wherever she walked. Then, with a stirring of cloud, the silver threats tangled, tightened, and Beatrice suddenly thought, perhaps Catalina was the one caught in the net. But in that case, who was Catalina's captor? Essex? Hugh? Beatrice herself?

Catalina's lips pressed together. For a moment, she looked unspeakably weary. Then she took her scarlet skirts in one hand, cupped her belly in the other, and began ascending the stairs, her eyes never leaving Beatrice's. She came to a halt one step below Beatrice: half a head taller, Catalina's eyes were level with Beatrice's.

'You have questions,' Catalina said quietly. 'But the answers are not all mine to give.'

'I know it,' Beatrice said grimly. 'Enough evasion. You and my husband have some explaining to do.'

Had she ever liked these bed-hangings? Seahorses swam up past dolphins and coral, the repeating diamond patterns disappearing into dark folds, the draped Syrian damask forming caves, trenches, unseen channels. By daylight the damask was a deep, lustrous turquoise, but at night, it became murky, full of brooding shadows that stirred at the corner of your eye. They'd belonged to Beatrice's mother, and when Jane was gone, Maria had insisted Beatrice claim them before anyone else could, as if she'd known what manner of woman Arthur would choose next. And inevitably, Hugh had been delighted by the sea creatures, so there had been no question of changing them, especially when Walter and Ursula began naming their favourite seahorses. So Beatrice had slept beneath sea creatures for over twenty years. Sometimes, during Hugh's lengthy absences, she'd convinced herself she felt comforted by the damask, as if she were seeing what her husband saw, gazing upon the same horizons, gasping as dolphins leapt from dazzling blue waves, their sleek bodies gleaming under a golden sun, the salt spray tingling, alive on her bare skin. But at other times she'd felt as if she were drowning, flailing underwater, her cries for help silenced in the shadowy depths.

Now, facing Catalina across the bed where her husband lay injured, she felt adrift. The moorings of her marriage were collapsed, the anchor chain rusted, its broken links unravelling too fast, about to crash onto unseen rocks that lurked on the seabed.

Catalina was silent. Her dark eyes rested on Hugh. Was she waiting for something? A signal, a cue? But Hugh lay inert, his eyelids flickering, his forehead damp, and Beatrice wondered if he even knew they were there.

'Tell me,' Beatrice began, then halted, her words clattering to a halt like dice dropped beneath the gaming table. She didn't know where to start: with Essex? The baby? No. 'How long have you known my husband?'

Catalina gave a slight smile, not so much amused as wistful. 'For many years now.'

'Then was he ...' Beatrice forced herself to continue. 'Was he the father of your first child? Is he – is the child you're carrying his?'

Catalina looked up at her, pity stirring and ducking down in her eyes like uncertain hands. 'He assured me you would never ask me that. If he had not done so, if he had not been so certain ...' She shook her head. 'I thought perhaps I would not have taken advantage of your hospitality. But I had no choice.'

'Answer the question!' Beatrice hissed. 'Are you carrying Hugh's child or no?'

'I am not. I swear to you, I am not.'

A noise escaped Beatrice: a choke, a cry, a gasp, something fragile and feeble and fluttering in between all three. She hadn't realised how suffocating her suspicions had been. 'But then ... why did he bring you here? If it is not his child, why does he feel responsible for you?'

Catalina eyed Hugh with a strange expression. Gratitude? Fond exasperation? Wistfulness? Beatrice couldn't decipher it. 'I suppose it has become a habit for him.'

'I beg your pardon?'

Catalina sighed. 'I regret that it falls to me to tell you. I wanted him to be the one – when we were washing Maria's body, I suggested that you should speak to him about the truth of his voyages. Perhaps you felt me presumptuous.'

'Perhaps I did not need your advice to speak to my husband!' Beatrice retorted, knowing she sounded petty – especially as she hadn't followed Catalina's suggestion.

'Of course.' Catalina's brief glance was unreadable. 'If Hugh could … if you were to ask him here, now, I am sure he would tell you himself.'

That chafed: that Catalina had presumed to know Hugh's mind. 'Since he remains silent, perhaps you might oblige.'

Catalina nodded. 'The truth is, Hugh and I have known one another for many years.'

'Many?' Beatrice repeated, resenting her own shrillness. 'How many?'

'Ten, perhaps eleven.'

Her entire marriage. For the whole time that she had known Hugh, he had also known Catalina – and kept it from Beatrice. But why? If not for the obvious reason, then why on earth keep such a secret from his wife? Unless Hugh had wished to seduce Catalina and been rebuffed – a possibility that almost seemed worse.

'So long?' she managed. 'But –'

'May we sit?' Catalina asked. She gave Beatrice an apologetic smile. 'My back, my hips – you remember how it is.'

She almost refused. But petty cruelty, even if it might grant her a fleeting sense of power when all seemed to be crumbling beneath her – she couldn't do it. Beatrice gestured weakly towards the armchairs before the fire. She sank into her own, watching Catalina lower herself into Hugh's. The other woman looked suddenly smaller: perhaps it was seeing her in Hugh's chair, seeing several inches of walnut carved with foxgloves and berries rise above Catalina's head where ordinarily Hugh's face would be.

'It is a long story,' Catalina began haltingly. 'And I fear you will judge us both harshly. For my part, I am prepared. But I do not like to speak ill of Hugh. Or not ill, for I do not believe either of us should be ashamed, not when all is weighed together. But what I have to say will change things for you. Your memories. Your feelings for your husband, even. So I must ask: are you certain you wish to hear my tale?'

Beatrice could have snarled with impatience. 'If you do not tell me soon, I will imagine you both to have murdered an archbishop in his sleep and danced on his grave.'

Catalina's mouth stirred in gentle sympathy. 'Very well.' She stared up at the painting of Ariadne on Naxos, where the blue-robed princess gazed out at distant white sails, and it was impossible to tell if the ships were abandoning her or returning. 'Since I came here, nearly everyone has assumed I must have been born elsewhere. Portugal. Guiana. The New World. And yet no one has in fact asked me. Even Maria assumed I was not from here. And that was easier. Safer. For I thought it meant no one remembered me. Until today.'

'You mean ... Essex?' Beatrice stared in astonishment. 'But how?'

'Let me tell you,' Catalina said patiently. 'It begins in a house full of secrets. Where you could hear whispers in the walls and smell incense burning after dark. Where people slipped out late at night and hid letters in barrels and oranges, writing one letter in ink and another message in lemon juice so you could only read the second message when you held it up to candlelight, and in the morning the grates would be full of ashes that had once been paper. This is the house where I was born, where my father was steward to a doctor called Roderigo Velazquez.'

'In Spain?'

'No.' Catalina met her gaze – and suddenly the lilting Spanish accent was gone. 'In Lambeth.'

Lambeth again: Beatrice would happily never have heard the name for the rest of her days.

'Velazquez was a Spaniard,' Catalina continued, the London accent that must have been her own making her words sound plainer, unadorned, 'and a Catholic. And a doctor – which gave everyone three reasons to mistrust him. But despite all this, he had many very wealthy patients – or perhaps because of his foreignness. Queen Elizabeth used to consult a Spanish doctor, I believe, and some people liked the thrill of visiting Velazquez. As if he might either cure them or murder them – I heard some of the ladies giggling about the dangers they were walking into. Of course, they would not have laughed if they had known how close they were to the truth. You see, Velazquez was indeed a Spanish spy. And my father had been placed in his household to spy on Velazquez.'

Whatever she had imagined Catalina's secret to be, it was not this. How did Spanish spies link to Hugh? She struggled to know what to ask first. 'So who did your father report to?'

'Why, Walsingham, of course.' Catalina gave a tight smile. 'The queen's own spymaster. To speak of my father thus, it sounds like a prestigious appointment. As if we might have been invited to Twelfth Night feasts at Whitehall. But it was no such luxury. It was poorly paid, and perilous, and there was no leaving Walsingham's service unless in a coffin. It was like walking back and forth over coals in exchange for a few husks of barley. My father risked his life every day, and for a pittance.' Catalina grimaced, as if the memories were rising up like bile to choke her. 'And then, when I was just six years old, Walsingham recruited me.'

Six. Ursula's age. Beatrice shook her head in appalled disbelief. 'How could he have been so ruthless? And what good would a six-year-old be to him?'

'A great deal, as it turned out.' Catalina sighed. 'Of course, I reported more about the burnt cakes the kitchen maid had given me than about Spanish codes. But I could also tell him what Mistress Velazquez had said to her sister when I was playing in the courtyard, or what messages the doctor had asked me to carry to his neighbours. And in amongst my chattered nonsense, Walsingham found many a gem to hoard for later use.'

'I see.' Beatrice pressed her nails into the palms of her hands to stop them trembling. 'So you have been a spy from girlhood. Are you still?'

Catalina gave her a sad smile. 'One never truly stops being a spy.'

Beatrice narrowed her eyes. 'I think you have been elusive enough, don't you? Time for honesty.'

'If you are sure that is what you wish.' Catalina made it sound as if Beatrice were asking to be flogged. She swallowed before continuing. 'Living in a house of Spaniards was never, as you can imagine, wholly comfortable. Or, as it transpired, safe.'

'What do you mean?'

'Nine years ago,' Catalina said, 'the Spanish Armada tried to invade. As you know, they failed. With your husband's help. But that thwarted invasion stirred up all the ill-feeling towards the Spaniards. One night Doctor Velazquez's house was attacked. I never knew for certain who by. Drunkards, perhaps. Or men riled up by Walsingham's agents. They used clods of mud at first. Then stones. And then flames.' Catalina lifted her eyes to Beatrice's again. 'The house burned. Only three of us escaped alive. One of the stableboys and a kitchen maid had been canoodling in the courtyard and they fled before the rioters lit their torches. And me.'

'Then … your father …' Beatrice couldn't finish.

'Burned to death,' Catalina said, biting off the words with brutal grief. 'Along with the doctor, his wife, and all their servants.'

'How did you escape?'

Catalina rested her hand on her belly. 'Because once upon a time I was slim. And fast. And no one knows better how to escape a house unseen than a child who grew up there. I used a passageway built for visiting priests – it led out into a nearby lane. But as soon as I stepped into the passageway, I heard a great crash of wood behind me, and I knew the way had been blocked for any who might follow, be they my friend, my foe, or my father.'

'I am sorry,' Beatrice offered, hearing the inadequacy of her own words.

'That I suffered, or that I survived?' Catalina gave a wry smile, and Beatrice realised with a confused jolt that the woman was trying to jest with her: perhaps Catalina thought humour preferable to hysteria. 'Afterwards, I had nowhere else to turn. I went to Walsingham.'

'And he helped you?'

'Well. He used me to help himself. I was sixteen by then. There were other uses I could be put to apart from eavesdropping and errand running.' Catalina rubbed her belly again. 'He arranged my marriage. To a man named Antonio Lopez, a Spaniard in Walsingham's employ.'

'Another spy?'

Catalina shrugged. 'It made for a happier marriage than you might expect. Perhaps there were more secrets in our marriage than most, but at least the greatest secret was in the open.'

Beatrice shifted irritably; she didn't want to hear about other couples' domestic bliss, not here, not now. 'I don't see what any of this has to do with Hugh. Or Essex.'

'You will,' Catalina said, and it was far from reassuring. 'When Walsingham died, his spy network passed for a time to his daughter's husband. The Earl of Essex inherited me, and who knows how many others, like a deck of cards along with all the secret pockets containing their marked counterparts.'

'Then you work for Essex? You've been spying on us – on Hugh – for Essex?'

'I worked for Essex,' Catalina corrected. 'But not for long. My husband's work was discovered. We had to leave England. Essex paid our passage to the Azores, gave us enough money to set up home on Vila de Orta in the Spanish settlement. We built a life there. We had a printing press, a house with a garden where a black cat used to bask beneath our orange trees and our daughter learnt to walk all the faster because she was determined to stroke his belly, though he was more determined to elude her. And occasionally, Essex would ask us for information and we would be able to afford a new roof in exchange for letting him know what our friends and neighbours were up to.'

'Then you do work for him.'

'No.' Catalina glanced over at the bed. 'No, Beatrice, I work for Hugh.'

It was as if a vast wave of saltwater had crashed through the bedchamber, hitting her hard enough to bruise, leaving her soaked and shivering.

'What do you mean, you work for Hugh? My husband is a sailor, an explorer – what would he employ you for?'

'I told you,' Catalina said. 'The answers are not all mine to give. The rest must be Hugh's.'

But Hugh did not stir. There was silence, gaping.

And then came the screams.

20

Beatrice hurled herself out of her bedchamber, crashing her shoulder on the doorframe. Pain shot through her bones, but she didn't care. The screams were coming from Ursula's room.

'Mama! Help me!'

Her slippers skidded on the polished floor; she clutched at a painting for support, knocking a mountainous valley askew. Regaining her balance, she rushed on down the corridor, clattering against Ursula's door. The handle rattled: for a moment she thought it locked – someone was inside! – but it was only her haste making her clumsy. Forcing her hand steady, Beatrice opened the door.

Ursula was sat bolt upright, her fair curls damp with sweat and tangling across tearstained cheeks. Her face was screwed up, scarlet, mouth taut with screams.

'The fire! Mama, the fire!'

'I'm here! Darling, don't fret!' Beatrice scrambled onto Ursula's bed, gathering her daughter close. 'There's no fire in here, my love.' Even as she said it, Beatrice wondered how long they'd be able to keep the grate empty over winter nights. She'd been insisting the fire be lit only during the day and extinguished before Ursula entered, but come December, the chamber would be positively cave-like without a fire, and adding furs to Ursula's blankets might weigh too heavy on her still-raw legs.

Ursula burrowed her head into Beatrice's chest. 'I heard the flames crackling.'

'Not in here,' Beatrice assured her. 'Next door, in Walter's room, perhaps. Or someone outside snapping a twig.'

'In the fireplace,' Ursula insisted. 'It *was*.'

'It can't have been. All the servants know not to light this fire over-night.'

'But I heard it.' Ursula's fingers tangled in Beatrice's partlet, clinging to the linen. It was a gesture from her babyhood: every time she'd fallen, or been feverish with teething, she'd gripped onto Beatrice's clothes as if convinced the pain would worsen if her mother put her down for one moment. 'I did, I heard it.'

'You were dreaming,' Beatrice said. 'Just a nightmare.'

Something crackled in the fireplace.

Ursula wailed through lips clamped tight, pressing so close to Beatrice she felt Ursula's cheekbone grind against her collarbone. Beatrice almost tried to extricate herself, but changed her mind: she didn't want to let go of her daughter any more than Ursula wanted to let go of her mother. Instead, she pushed Ursula's blankets away and, careful not to jar her bandaged legs, lifted Ursula onto her hip. Haltingly, Beatrice edged across the chamber. The light from the corridor couldn't reach this far; the copper smoulder of the doused fire was near-smothered by ash. A shiver of wind moaned in the chimney. Ursula keened softly. Beatrice swallowed, peering into the shadows, uncertain what she was looking for, or whether it would be worse to find something, or to find nothing.

Beneath her slippers, something crunched. A sharp jab through her sole. Beatrice knelt down, tucking Ursula further back on her hip to keep her away from whatever it was. Glass? A stone? Her fingers quested across the floor, running gingerly over the edge of the rush mats and onto the wooden boards, searching through the shadows.

There. Small, hard, a curving smoothness on one side, jagged ridges on the other. Warily, she picked it up between forefinger and thumb. Beatrice squinted but to no avail.

Then Ursula said, 'It smells like Twelfth Night.'

Beatrice inhaled. Smoky, dark, sweet. Chestnuts.

She stretched out her hand again: there were more chestnut shards littering the floor. She had no intention of putting her hands in the fireplace: the logs would still be hot even if the fire had been put out.

But she was certain there would be more chestnuts tucked into the crevasses between logs, packed behind knots of wood, concealed under a dusting of ash.

Someone had hidden chestnuts in Ursula's fireplace, knowing they would burst. Knowing the sound would mimic crackling flames, knowing it would terrify her.

Well. There was something else the culprit should know. Beatrice clenched her jaw. If Beatrice got her hands on them, she would take a red-hot poker to their eyes.

'Ridley!'

Her voice echoed, rebounding off stone floors, whitewashed walls: no Italian carpets or oak panelling in this part of the house, no nymphs startled by gods or transformed into laurel trees, no painted ships caught between one oil wave and the next. Down in the servants' quarters, all was plain, simple, serviceable. As a child she'd thought it calming: here tasks were allotted and completed, loaves kneaded, proved, baked; linen soaked, scrubbed, starched. Now, she found the blankness infuriating in its mute pallor.

'Ridley!'

He'd be abed, perhaps, like all the other servants. She'd be waking them from much needed rest before their dawn rising, and she felt herself blushing at her own presumptuousness. But what choice did she have?

He wasn't in the kitchens: two maids stirred, bleary-eyed and bewildered, but Beatrice spun away before they could emerge from their blankets. Nor in the wine cellar, nor the pantry.

'Ridley!'

She pushed open the door to the stillroom – and crashed into Ridley's chest. Solid warmth, leather softened into the shape of his muscles, the scent of cedarwood and horses: she flinched at his nearness and all it reminded her of. He stepped left, she right, then both went the other way, an awkward, clumsy dance. Ducking, Beatrice slipped past him.

'I must speak with you.'

Ridley merely pushed the door closed behind him, and she felt a rush of gratitude for his steadfastness. 'I gathered as much. What's amiss?'

She'd stood too close to the hanging herbs; she batted rosemary away and a brittle sprig broke off in her hand. 'Who put out the fire in Ursula's bedchamber this evening?'

'Alice, I should imagine. Why?'

Beatrice dug in her pocket and thrust the handful of chestnut shards she'd plucked from the floor around Ursula's grate. 'These had been placed among the logs. A deliberate, malicious act, clearly intended to frighten my daughter.'

Ridley frowned. 'And you think Alice might be responsible? I'd be surprised – she's a reliable girl. Besides, I doubt she has the time for pranks, still less the inclination.'

'You think this was done as a *joke*?'

'Well – yes.' Ridley eyed her dubiously. 'Why else?'

'To terrify! To mock, even – as if her injuries, her perfectly natural fears were something deserving ridicule!'

'Is that ...' Ridley paused, then changed tack. 'Forgive me, Beatrice. I do not believe anyone in the household feels anything less than the greatest sympathy for your daughter. Might this not have been an attempt to reintroduce some levity into Ursula's days?'

'How can you say that?' She'd clenched her fist; the chestnut shards jabbed her palm.

'A misguided, rather insensitive attempt, true, but ... does this not seem more likely to be a childish jape gone wrong than a servant seeking to frighten a girl they all view with fondness?'

Beatrice twisted the rosemary sprig in her other hand: the scents of herbs and roasted chestnuts were too strong, too close. 'Are you suggesting Walter did this?'

'To cheer up his sister?' Ridley gave a gentle shrug. 'It will have been well-meant, of course, but I imagine Ursula was far from entertained.'

'She was terrified,' Beatrice snapped. 'She woke up screaming about flames – I thought it another nightmare –'

'Of course. But Walter may not have understood. After all, he's played tricks on his sister before – I remember him laughing for an age when he hid a young frog in her writing desk.'

'But he wouldn't …'

'Consider which is more likely, Beatrice. A boyish prank gone awry, or a servant seeking to – what? Terrify? Convince Ursula she's seeing visions? Convince you that *you're* seeing visions? Why would anyone want you to believe yourself or your daughter delusional?'

Because they know there is nothing that terrifies me more.

Beatrice turned away, fighting to control her face. She seized a bundle of sage, began to retie the cord, pretending busyness. 'Wise counsel, as ever, Ridley. I shall see you in the morning.'

Bedlam. She stared hard at the herbs, forcing her eyes to see grey-green leaves, bound stems, lines and curves, softness and delicacy. Not metal bars. Not bound hands, matted hair. Not her mother's eyes.

She heard the door click shut behind her. What if Ridley's suggestion was correct? He'd offered it up as nonsensical, as madness even. But although madness might be a distant, ephemeral rumour to many, like tales of elephants as tall as houses, dolphins with hides the colour of peonies, great white bears with maws wide enough to crush a man's skull, for Beatrice, madness was a threat close enough to draw blood.

She'd thought no one knew. That Jane's death, or the explanation her father offered the world was accepted – that no one had cared, or been crass enough to question it. But someone knew about how her father had died, how Beatrice had killed him: wasn't the globe proof of that? And if they knew about Arthur's death, might they also know how it connected to Jane's?

But who could possibly know? And even if they did – even if they knew how horrifying the idea of madness was to Beatrice, especially madness passed from mother to daughter – how could they have got into her house, into Ursula's room, to place the chestnuts in the fireplace?

Suddenly Beatrice frowned. She'd shredded the sage without thinking, dropping the torn leaves onto the table. Sixteen fragments, fallen into a cluster in the shape of a shield.

Essex.

He'd been in her house – he'd invited himself in. How easy would it have been for the earl to slip out of Hugh's chamber and along the corridor to plant the chestnuts in Ursula's? What time had the earl and his sister left? About half an hour before Ursula had gone to bed: the fire might still have been burning, or not long extinguished. If Essex had planted the chestnuts then, there would have been time enough for him to be long away before they started exploding. Or even if he hadn't placed them himself, he could easily have bribed someone else – what servant would dare refuse the queen's favourite? Or, though it pained Beatrice to concede it, what nine-year-old boy could have refused the bold, dashing earl?

He'd had the opportunity. But that didn't explain *why*. What possible reason could Essex have for wishing to frighten Ursula – to frighten Beatrice? She thought back to Lady Rich's strange insinuations: that Beatrice was harbouring spies, even commanding a ring of spies. Was this supposed to be a warning? That if she didn't stop spying, Essex would punish her, perhaps even have her committed to Bedlam? Yet she could hardly stop what she had never started. And another thought struck her, one that made her blood run cold: if Essex were willing to go to these lengths to stop her spying, what exactly was the secret he was so determined to conceal?

She'd been afraid before. Afraid of the unseen enemy behind the painted globe, the person who'd commissioned Simon's altered paintings. But to have drawn out the enmity of one of the most powerful men in England? Beatrice was far out of her depth.

21

She couldn't sleep. Every time she closed her eyes in her father's old bedroom, she smelled lavender, heard those horrible, muffled moans. When she did manage to sleep, she awoke to a seethe of pain in her hands, only to discover she'd been picking at the nailbeds, turning them rough and raw. Just as they had been on the night she'd smothered him. But to ask the servants to make up a different bedchamber, a less impressive chamber – she couldn't bear the thought of their looks, their questions. If only Maria were still alive. She was the only person who would have understood.

It was still dark when Beatrice gave up on trying to sleep. But then, she told herself, it was winter; it might still be dark long after cock crow at this time of year. Rather than summon one of the maids who weren't Maria, Beatrice broke the ice in the ewer and splashed her face before wrestling her way into a front-lacing gown.

And then she walked. She walked the corridors outside the bedchambers, telling herself she was inspecting the wooden panels for warping, for woodworm. Not patrolling. Not guarding. She passed the staircase with the damaged swan finial, and realised she'd never remembered to have it mended. She noticed an abandoned piece of coral on the window seat Walter liked best, and changed direction so that she could return it to the cabinet of curiosities.

Except it wasn't a change. She knew it wasn't. She had always been going to walk this way: towards the gallery where Ursula had been injured, and where the globe waited for her.

The gallery door barely made a sound as she entered: well-oiled, well made. Was it merely that the globe was neither of those things? For all

Molyneux's royal favour, for all his self-importance, had he just done a poor job of making Hugh's globe? Were her fears merely the by-product of shoddy craftsmanship?

From the shadows, there came a rustle, and it sounded like quiet laughter. Brass gleamed, like false teeth revealed by a jeer. Of course it wasn't poorly made. Of course not.

Beatrice swallowed as she stepped into the gallery. Her fingers tightened around the coral, its ridges and spines gnawing at her palm. She resisted the urge to hold it high as she crossed the chamber, as if offering the pale fragment up as an excuse for her own presence in her own home. Or as if it were a weapon. A friable, feeble weapon.

She edged around the globe, kicking at the train of her gown to keep it from brushing the frame, and awkwardly opened the curiosity cabinet door to replace the coral. Next to the salamander skeleton, it looked like the bones of another creature, pale and deformed, and in the shifting shadows, for a moment she thought both shifted, about to crawl on ticking claws.

Stop it, she told herself angrily. They'd had the salamander for years, and the coral was more often purloined for games than displayed in the cabinet. There was only one sinister object in the gallery, and it was the one creaking derisively a mere hand's breadth from her spine.

Beatrice turned fast, scolding herself even as she did: this wasn't one of Ursula's games, where she had to freeze before Walter spun round to catch her moving. But the globe was still, and she couldn't help feeling the stillness was the globe playing along, humouring her. The way she'd seen bears feign distraction in the pit, only to lure the hounds close enough to pounce. And there was the painted bear, struggling in the cockatrice's grip, and she remembered the pain in her fingers, her bloodied skin, the frantic lash of limbs, and how she'd been terrified Arthur would suddenly throw her onto her back, press the pillow over her mouth until she couldn't breathe. Was she a hound being lured in? Was she about to be seized between clamping jaws and then tossed aside, her neck broken? If only she could read the globe, turn its cartouches into words the way Nicholas translated ancient Greek, the characters dancing for him like puppets.

But what would she read there if she did? Threats? Warnings? Or mockery? Did that sea monster mean something lurking in the water outside her home, or that she was unable to *see* the monsters hidden beneath some other surface – or was it just a giant green creature paddling the Atlantic, just malachite mixed with egg and daubed onto a paper gore? Were all the cartouches sinister? Could any possibly be benign? And how could she discover which was which before someone else was hurt?

'Beatrice? Is that you?'

She started, jerking away from the globe and jolting against the curiosity cabinet. Frantically, she twisted, stilling tutting shells, straightening jutting corals, grasping at the Roman siliquas before they could slip between her fingers. Behind her, the globe rustled – or was it footsteps? Because now she recognised the voice: Nicholas was cautiously venturing into the gallery.

'I hadn't thought –' He paused, awkward. 'I suppose you are having trouble sleeping too?'

Beatrice set the final coin back in the cabinet and tried to smooth her skirts without being seen to smooth her skirts. 'Yes. A little.'

Nicholas gave a wry chuckle. 'In much the same way as Cassandra had a little trouble with having her prophecies doubted, I suppose.'

Beatrice twitched at the mention of prophecies. She tried for lightness: 'I ought to be on my guard for wooden horses on the horizon then.'

But her words hung like smoke on the air, and the globe creaked, reminding her the wooden horse had already been welcomed through the door.

'Speaking of prophecies …'

Beatrice's head whipped up. 'What?'

Nicholas spread his hands as he came closer, that half-shy, half-apologetic way of his. 'I wondered if you might permit me – that is, I wished to cast a horoscope.'

Beatrice blinked. 'A – why?'

'There is method in it, I promise! Doctor Dee is a great proponent of the science, and the Earl of Northumberland too – they see astrology as a tool to harness the power of the heavens. I know there are some who are dubious – and of course the misuse of the horoscope by the queen's enemies hardly helps the cause –'

'Misuse?' Her throat was dry; her spine cold.

'Yes – I believe I mentioned it before – it is of course treason to cast the queen's horoscope, although she often asks Doctor Dee to do her the honour, and she had hers cast at birth, like all royal children –'

She cut him off before he could digress further. 'Nicholas, what are you asking me?'

'Sorry.' He was beside the globe now, and his fingers hovered above its surface: marvelling, curious – or as unsettled by its presence as she was? 'I wanted … I cannot bear the thought of my brother, you see, of him lying … I wanted to cast Hugh's horoscope. But I did not wish for you to get wind of my drawing up charts and … well, and think ill of me.'

Beatrice eyed him across the globe. At the bottom of her vision, the cartouches seemed to throb like veins. 'You speak of fortune telling – speak as if it were true.'

'Why not? Every great civilisation has thought about how to foretell their fates, whether through oracles, or haruspicy, or cartomancy – or astrology. Who are we to decry the wisdom of the ancients?'

'You believe the stars a better indicator of my husband's health than the physicians?' Again her attempt at sarcasm hovered, its failure mocking her instead. She tried hard not to look directly at the globe – but the effort made her gaze on Nicholas too intent, near-frenetic.

Nicholas set his hand to the globe; it was all she could do not to shout a warning. Slowly, he walked his fingers across the cartouches, almost caressing them. Which ones was he touching? The mermaid with a kiss reflected in her mirror? The woman in the red dress? Would he recognise what he was seeing?

'Sometimes,' Nicholas said softly, 'it is not the images themselves that hold the power, but the power we allow the images to hold over us.'

Beatrice stared. Was it possible her brother-in-law might believe her? Should she voice her suspicions?

But there was something in his gaze as he beheld the globe – somewhere between fear and fascination. The way she'd seen other men watch the bear pits: horrified, but clinging to hope that their wager might hold, and unable to resist the temptation to look closer at the gore spilling open before them. And she couldn't ask him.

'Will you allow me, sister?' Nicholas lifted his eyes to hers. 'If only that we might be prepared lest anything else regrettable occur.'

'I – do you not need to wait? Daybreak is barely past – we could not be further away from the stars.'

'The stars are always there, even if we cannot see them. I find that comforting, don't you?'

No, she wanted to say, *for it seems too much like being watched*. 'How long will it take you?'

'It is not a process that can be rushed.' He gave a weak smile. 'I confess, sister, I am much in need of a project to distract me. May I proceed?'

How could she say no? Why did she want to say no? This was Nicholas – a more harmless man she could not imagine!

'Why not?' she said feebly, and she tried to ignore all the voices in her head crying out the reasons why.

'Wonderful!' Nicholas beamed. 'And if you do not object – might I go and sit with my brother? I have missed him, you know.'

'Of course.' Beatrice plastered on a smile, and she even managed to keep it in place until Nicholas had trotted from the gallery. She kept it steady as she edged around the globe, kept it steady as she did not hurry away; even kept it steady as she heard the globe sigh behind her.

Kept it steady until something struck her: *regrettable*, Nicholas had said. Which meant something terrible, of course. But it also meant that someone had cause for regret. What could Nicholas possibly have done that would make him feel remorseful?

The tree was gone: branches lopped, trunk split and hewed, the wood gathered and stacked and taken away to dry. Ridley said he'd spoken with several craftsmen interested in buying some of the wood: a cabinet-maker, a spear-maker, and a carpenter who built gallows. Beatrice felt slightly sickened by each prospect: she wasn't sure which was most repulsive – that the branches which had broken her husband's bones might become a platform that gave way beneath a convicted felon's feet, or a hurled weapon piercing another man's flesh, or a piece of furniture in which aldermen's wives would place their finest ornaments, all oblivious to what the wood had once done.

Beatrice pulled her cloak tighter around herself, willing her feet to move. She'd come outside this morning with such good intentions: that she'd walk until the headache brought on by her unsettling exchange with Nicholas had cleared; that she might venture downriver to call on Holbrook at the warehouse; that she might inspect the progress of the repairs to the malthouse roof. Instead, she'd got no further than this: the great gouge in the grass, churned soil littered with splinters. A ragged gap plunged through the hedge, as if some vast jaws had torn a chunk away, leaving snapped twigs, some hanging limp as dislocated limbs. And where Hugh had lain, the rain had pooled in hollows: one for each limb, one for his torso, one for his head. A wisp of turquoise floated on that last pool: a fragment of feather from his hat, dyed drab and murky by the muddy water. How often had she seen that feather declare itself against the sky, or sweeping broad arcs as Hugh doffed it in a bow, or hastily tossed aside in their bedchamber as Hugh drew her close for a kiss? And now? Now she couldn't let herself think further, or she would be wholly undone.

'You ought to plant something there.'

Beatrice looked up to see William sauntering across the grass, his coltish limbs loose and indolent with what could no longer reasonably be called last night's drinking: she'd wager he'd only left the gaming tables an hour or two ago. Had any members of her family managed a full night's sleep?

'Ought I indeed? You have work to do if you fancy yourself a gardener as well as a navigator – it's the wrong time of year to be planting.'

'Is it?' William rolled to a halt beside her, rubbing a palm over his unshaven jaw in surprise. 'Well, I wouldn't know, I suppose. I've not seen an English garden in bloom for, what, seven years?'

Nor had Hugh then. The realisation jabbed at Beatrice like a blow beneath her ribs. The *Silver Swan* always sailed before the snowdrops had given way to daffodils, before green buds had unfurled into leaves. And when they returned, the trees were shedding damp brown scraps and the roses were long gone: only thin black twigs and thorns remained.

But she wouldn't let William see how his words had unbalanced her. 'I hope you're not fishing for my pity. I imagine the flora and fauna of the Azores provide ample compensation.'

'Do you?' William half-heartedly grappled with a yawn and let it win; she caught a whiff of ale as his jaw stretched wide. 'Maybe you're right. But I sometimes catch myself in a maudlin humour, all bereft for the things I never see grow.' He gestured vaguely at the gardens. 'Flowers, shrubs, hedges. They're just *there*. Either blossoming or not, wilted or not. I don't stay long enough to know when they do, or how, or indeed if. They say some plants in the Azores and the New World never cease to produce fruit.'

'They also said there were giants with two heads in Patagonia, and a city made of gold in El Dorado.'

'Sailors talk all manner of nonsense,' William agreed, so easy and affable that Beatrice felt awkward with guilt: how could she have suspected this good-humoured boy of anything so vile as plotting an attack on his uncle? 'Why, only last night – or this morning, truth be told – I heard talk of a globe that can foretell the future!'

Beatrice froze. Her tongue seemed to sweel against her teeth; she almost choked. 'What – what nonsense.'

'Quite.' William stifled another yawn. 'I tell you what though, such a contraption could be mighty useful aboard ship. Imagine – instead of shivering in a downpour and squinting through gales atop a crow's nest, we could simply glance at a globe and say, "Aha, we shall reach port today", or "Tomorrow we'll encounter Spaniards, so let's sharpen our swords". Only consider how many more hours sleep a fellow might gain.'

'Assuming, of course,' Beatrice said cautiously, 'that one could understand its predictions in time enough to benefit from them.'

'Ah, that's simple,' William said, infuriatingly offhand. 'It'd be no different from using an astrolabe, or a compass – most of the deckhands wouldn't know which end was which, but with a little learning and a smidge of cunning, I reckon I'd master it faster than I did the clove hitch.'

'Maybe you should practise then,' Beatrice said, striving for lightness. 'Have a look at Hugh's globe and see what our future holds.'

'Easy,' William shrugged. 'We'll encounter mermaids and cockatrices and enormous robins – I'll be sure to stockpile cannonballs to fight them all off.'

She wanted so desperately to laugh about the images as readily as her nephew did. To dismiss it all as superstitious nonsense, as wild sailors' tales, of no more credence than stories of dragons swooping over jungles and beaches made of pearls. But how could she dismiss the evidence of her own eyes? Maria's murder, Ursula's injuries, Hugh's accident – the globe had *known*. No. Whoever had ordered the altered images had known. When would Simon bring her the list in full? She both dreaded and ached for his return.

And then something William had said snagged in her mind.

'Of course Raleigh thought it a great jest,' William was saying. 'Said his globe wouldn't be allowed out of his wife's sight if she believed it could tell the twists and turns of his voyage. Then Percy said he didn't know if that was better or worse than what his countess would do, for she'd not give it even a cursory glance –'

'What did you say?'

William blinked at her, eyes starting to turn bleary with fatigue. 'About Percy's wife? They can't stand each other.'

'No – before. About the images on Hugh's globe. There are robins?'

'Oh, yes.' William's face broke into an easy grin. 'Of course, you won't have noticed them. Unless you ever happen to lie on the gallery floor to stop the world spinning and then spin the wooden world?' He wrinkled his nose. 'Which was a very fine bit of wordplay when I was sloshing with brandy, but on reflection needs honing.'

'The robins,' Beatrice prompted.

'They're on the underside,' William said. 'A pair of them, bloody-breasted, talons like scimitars – makes you think, if garden birds really were over thrice the size of swans, we might never come out of our houses.'

'Swans?' Beatrice stared at him, realisation seeping over her skin.

'Aye – they're pursuing a silver swan. Some sort of jest, though damned if I can fathom Uncle Hugh's sense of humour. Maybe the robins are meant to be wounded Spaniards. Or something about small folk attacking the large – could be one's young Walter and the other's Ursula.'

'Maybe.' Beatrice forced a tight smile.

'Anyway.' William yawned widely. 'I'm for bed. Wake me if Uncle Hugh – you know. Awakes.' He turned his 'or' into another yawn, and his saunter towards the house had the grace to be slightly sheepish.

Beatrice watched him leave, unable to prevent her eyes being hauled up, past lintels and creeping ivy, to the gallery window, and the pale shape rising behind the glass, like a moon that refused to set. The globe that she now knew contained another allegory. A silver swan: that was obvious. But the two robins were naught to do with Spain, of that she was certain.

Sweetrobin. Queen Elizabeth had used the nickname twice. Once for her late favourite, Robert Dudley, the Earl of Leicester. And again for his stepson. Robert Devereux, the Earl of Essex. But then what of the second robin? Robert Rich, Lady Penelope's husband, dispatched by his wife? Or might it represent the robin's sibling joining in the attack: Essex's closest ally, his sister, Lady Penelope?

She knew Lady Rich despised her. Had known it for years. But what had Hugh done that could have provoked the enmity of the most powerful noble in England?

Grey cracks of light inched between the curtains and the oak panels of Beatrice and Hugh's bedchamber. Somehow they made the room seem even gloomier than if it had been pitch black.

How much of her life had she spent in a sickroom that wasn't her own? Beatrice had always been blessed with health: a robust child, with apple cheeks and sturdy legs that could make the virginals rattle when she stamped really hard, so she'd sometimes feigned tantrums just to hear the instruments twang discordantly at her whim. She'd been fortunate in her childbeds: both Walter and Ursula had been as straightforward as any birth could ever be, and even her lost child hadn't left her feverish or weak from blood loss. Was it penance then, for her own good health, that meant those around her were felled over and over again?

There'd been her mother first. The portrait of Jane hanging by the window was vibrant with colour – an apricot gown, a springtime garden backdrop, yellow roses in her hand, a peacock flaring its tail just behind her – in stark contrast to the sickroom of Beatrice's memory. Those grey days when everything seemed shrouded in cobwebs and dust: forced into stillness, quietness, and with the sense that something unnameable and wrong was coming. Maria had ushered Beatrice away at first, but when she'd realised nearness to Jane was far more comforting to Beatrice than being forced away, she'd let Beatrice play on the hearthrug, or taught her new embroidery stitches at the foot of Jane's bed. She'd made her first pomander beads in her mother's sickroom, using Jane's recipe and Maria's guidance, stirring and scooping and moulding as quietly as she could, eyes darting guiltily towards the bed with every plash of oil or chink of spoon, until a small amber gem had glowed in her palm, its sweet jasmine scent enough to eke a wan smile out of Jane's drawn face.

After Jane, Blanche. Florence's mother had been an irritable patient, all tossing and turning, plaintive sighs and spurious demands. She'd enjoyed summoning Beatrice to bring her trifles – marigold nosegays, marchpane butterflies – or round up her honey-coloured lapdogs, who despised everyone's laps, but especially their mistress's, with her bony fingers that made every fondle a pinch, every caress a jab. Until her final sickbed, when the dogs had crawled onto the coverlets that hid the bloodstains and nudged at Blanche's limp hands, letting her fingers curl around their tufted ears one last time, either as apology for their frequent rejections, or self-sacrifice, giving their mistress all they could as her breathing ebbed away.

And then, of course, Arthur. Those dark, lavender-cloyed nights, the sneers and demands. Beatrice rubbed her hands awkwardly, not needing to glance down to where the scars silvered her knuckles.

How could Essex know about her father? No one knew about her father, not even Hugh.

The painted peacock caught her gaze again, its tail curling against Jane's apricot skirts. Sapphire and jade and onyx eyes stared out, never blinking, following Beatrice's every movement.

If anyone had eyes everywhere, it would be the earl. Catalina had told her he'd inherited Walsingham's network of spies not long after marrying the old spymaster's daughter. When had that been? The wedding had raised a scandal; but then, any marriage concerning one of the queen's favourites did, for they were never permitted before the fact, and only grudgingly accepted afterwards, following screaming and threats, exile for the new bride, and urgent promises from the groom. Raleigh's marriage had been the same; she suspected Hugh had been vaguely disappointed that their wedding hadn't occasioned anything like such a stir. But there was a vast difference between a favourite and the merely favoured.

Walsingham's death: that was a more memorable point in time. After the Armada, after Walter and Ursula were born. But before her lost baby. 1591, six years ago. Yet that was four years after Arthur had died. Even if Essex had placed a spy in Beatrice's house, how could they have discovered her secret over four years later? Only Maria could possibly have revealed the truth, and Maria would have …

Beatrice swallowed bile. Maria *had* died. And there was no way of knowing whether she'd been forced to give up her secrets before her murderer's hands closed around her throat.

Had they been Essex's hands? The ring with its strange pattern of curved lines – were they among Essex's numerous heraldic symbols?

'Beatrice?'

Hugh's voice stirred so weakly, like dust slumping from a sill, and Beatrice tasted bitterness yet again. He should have been commanding sails be hoisted, ropes coiled, cowing the wind with his vigour.

'I'm here.'

'Always,' he murmured fondly. 'No one ever had a more faithful wife.'

Dear God. If only he knew. But how would it help either of them to reveal that she'd once kissed Ridley now? And yet. He thought her a Penelope, but she'd been more of a Clytemnestra in his absence.

'Is it day?'

Beatrice glanced back at the grey fissures of light. 'Nearly noon. But some November days never brighten.'

Hugh's dry lips flinched with an almost-smile. 'I have seen days at sea so bright we were almost blinded. Faces scarlet, eyes streaming, heads searing. We dreamed of dreary English Novembers. But we always wish for what is out of reach. Raleigh's golden city. My north-east passage. A new world that was truly new, not tainted by whatever we dragged onto its shores.'

'Tainted?'

'Aye.' His lips parted weakly; she leaned forward to drip water into his mouth. Even swallowing was an effort. 'They say the Indians have started dying of smallpox. That they call it a white man's plague. And that's without considering the Pandora's box we break open every time we land, merely by being the men we are.'

'Hugh, no.' She heard the word drop, weak as a bubble falling into a waterfall. 'You're a good man. A good father –'

'I am not.' He forced his eyes open. 'Beatrice. Beloved. I have been lying to you. For years, I have lied to you. And I would have you see me for who I am, not who you dream me to be, before …'

'Don't,' she whispered, and she didn't utter the words *don't say it*, because they were not enough, not when what she really meant, really needed, was *don't die.*

'You have to know,' Hugh rasped, insistence stiffening the tendons in his neck as he tried to lift his head. 'About me. And … and about Catalina.'

Had some other words shivered in that gap? Some other name?

'She told me she worked for you.' Beatrice tried to keep any accusation, any resentment from her voice; it proved impossible. 'But nothing else – no details.'

Hugh gave a laugh so dry, so desiccated it was little more than a sigh. 'Of course not. She's too adept for that. Reticence serves people well in her trade.' He met her eyes again. 'In our trade.'

'What do you mean?'

'I mean that I am not the man you believe me to be. That the world believes me to be.' Hugh's eyes were dark with pain and guilt. 'Sir Hugh Radclyffe, the intrepid explorer, the bold hero of the Armada, bringing back treasure from the New World. That is not me. Oh, there was a time when I seemed stood fair to become that golden figure. But that was before my failure.'

'Novaya Zemlya?' Beatrice shook her head. 'But that was years ago.' *Have you been lying to me for four years?* She wanted to scream it, but somehow didn't dare. As if Hugh's story were an ice sculpture, glittering forms emerging slowly from the white, and her words torches, bludgeoning and burning wherever she swung them.

Hugh grunted assent. 'When we returned ... the queen sent for me. I was broken, body and soul. We'd lost Ben, failed to reach any destination, let alone the one we set out for. And then I came home to find you'd lost ...' He swallowed. 'Lost our baby. Before I ever knew there had been a child to lose. It was as if the life I'd dreamed of had been ripped away without my knowledge, and I was left, bruised and desolate in a barren field. That was before Queen Elizabeth turned on me.'

Beatrice rarely let herself think of those days. They were too raw, too ruinous: she flinched away from them as if refusing to touch a scar for fear it would break open and agony would wrench her apart. But as little as she'd let herself think of it, she'd considered Hugh's response even less. In her mind, it hadn't happened to him. He hadn't been there. Hadn't felt the baby quicken, tapped a rhythm on her belly to echo the kicks. Hadn't seen the blood, or the grey-blue eyelids, or the limp, curled fingers that would not grip her own. It had been her loss, not Hugh's, and she hadn't realised what a wound the baby's absence had left on its father.

'I ...' She didn't know what to say. 'Hugh, I wish ...'

'I know.' He lifted a finger to brush the back of her hand: a more eloquent gesture than anything either of them could voice. 'So you see,

I was in no state to vie with the queen. Not that any man can withstand her onslaughts when she turns the full force of that Tudor rage on us. Had I not been her target, I would have called her magnificent. A forty-cannon galleon bristling with armed soldiers would be nothing to the silver-gowned Elizabeth bearing down on me. She berated and harangued, raged and roared, calling me all manner of insults, and I cowered before her. And then … then she offered me a way to redemption.'

'How?'

'Piracy.' Hugh gave a weak smile. 'Or privateering, I believe was the term she used.'

'But …' Beatrice hesitated. 'I thought you all – Drake, Raleigh, you – I thought it an open secret. That you would challenge any Spanish vessel you saw en route to the New World, and would plunder them if you could. That it was all … part of the game.'

'It was. It is.' Hugh's smile turned bitter. 'But that was not my role. Beatrice … these past four years, I have not set foot in the New World. The *Silver Swan* has departed and returned in the same seasons as if we had been voyaging to Virginia or the Canaries. But the truth is, we have been no further than –'

'The Azores.'

'Yes.' Hugh stared up at the canopy, where dolphins dived in and out of shadows and seahorses coiled into dark knots. 'We would put into port at Vila de Orta or Faial. Discover which Spanish and Portuguese ships were expected to dock, or had just set sail. And then we would attack them.'

Beatrice swallowed. It was far from admirable. But hadn't she always half-suspected Hugh of dabbling in piracy? He'd been a soldier; he'd fought in Ireland and against the Armada alongside Charles Mountjoy and Walter Raleigh and Essex. He had killed men; she'd known that when she met him, had married him with eyes and mind open. 'If you imagine I would judge you for this –'

'That isn't all.' Hugh paused: was he fatigued, or weighing up, once again, how much to tell her? 'When there was no news of the Spanish treasure fleet, there were raids. On Spanish settlements. Villages. With women and children. We'd attack. Steal. And sometimes set them aflame. Then we'd simply sail away with our holds full of olives and peaches, pigs and chickens, with the villagers' screams echoing in our wake, and if we only looked at the horizon, we could almost convince ourselves they were no more than squabbling gulls.' He sighed. 'I am not proud of this. I was not then, nor am I now. I did it because the alternative was the Tower. Because I am a coward.'

'Hugh –'

'No. I make no excuses for myself. Please, don't make them for me. I don't deserve them.' He gripped her hand, suddenly almost strong again. 'I am ashamed of what I did, Beatrice. But nothing is more shameful than what happened – what I allowed to happen to Catalina.'

Horror crept over her. She didn't want to hear this: she almost willed Hugh to fall silent, so she didn't have to hear what he had to say.

But Catalina had *lived* it. And Beatrice had judged her, and suspected Hugh without knowing the truth. The least she could do was listen. And afterwards, later, there would be time to atone.

'I met Catalina eleven years ago,' Hugh said, and was it exhaustion or something even more draining that dragged at his voice: guilt? Regret? Shame? 'Before I met you.'

'But …' Beatrice shook her head. 'I don't understand – that was long before Novaya Zemlya. How – why?'

'Walsingham.'

'You … spied for Walsingham. Before Novaya Zemlya?'

Hugh snorted wanly. 'Show me an ambitious man without an earldom, and I'll show you a man who dealt with Walsingham. He paid me for information. About my army days. About Mountjoy, Essex, Raleigh …'

'About your friends.'

'Aye.'

She didn't know what to say. Had Hugh's insatiable need to inveigle his way into the Essex circle been less about social climbing, and more about espionage? How had he kept this secret from her all these years?

But of course he'd only had to keep it for a handful of months at a time. Far easier to dupe a wife who couldn't see you.

'After Walsingham died … Essex took over some of his spy rings. Or so he thought.'

'What do you mean?'

'You know Essex. He's never been one for subtlety. He wants what other men have, and he wants it loudly: not exactly desirable qualities in a spymaster. But there is a man who has those qualities in abundance. The queen's Secretary. Robert Cecil.'

Her head felt heavy, fogged with lies and the stale air of the sickroom. 'What has this to do with Catalina?'

'We all serve someone. Cecil serves the queen. I serve Cecil. Catalina serves me. And all of us have been watching Essex.'

'In the Azores?'

Hugh nodded. 'What do you know of the campaign this summer?'

Beatrice spread her hands: she'd paid it little heed. Men she didn't care for showing off and embarrassing themselves: it hadn't touched her. The Azores were islands Hugh paused at to refill the *Silver Swan* with fresh water, a name that glittered azure and gold like the flag on a distant barge: pretty, but blurred, and always out of her reach. 'I heard it was a failure. That they couldn't capture the Spanish treasure fleet. But it ended in August – a month before I'd expected you to be there. So I didn't seek out any news, or dwell long on what I heard. Yet now … were you there all along?'

'Or thereabouts.' Hugh had the grace to look sheepish. 'I know those islands better than my own children's faces. The coves where you can hide a ship. Where the full moon exposes, where the shadows might conceal us, which groves of fire trees might veil our hunters. Which tides and currents might hasten a retreat, where the winds gather apace, and where you might be sheltered. We watched the Spanish ships and the English ships as they chased each other, as they fired cannons and boarded and clashed. And we gathered information.'

'But … why?'

'Because the queen does not trust her admirals.' Hugh sighed. 'Essex has royal blood. Too much. Enough that some say he fancies himself Elizabeth's heir – or that he plans to lead a coup and establish himself as a crone's regent, leaving Cecil ruined or imprisoned, and relegating

Elizabeth herself to an old woman growing greyer and greyer in the shadows. She and Cecil suspected that if Essex captured any Spanish ships, he might well keep it a secret.'

'Essex, keep quiet about something that would paint him as a glorious hero? Surely not!'

'Keep quiet about enough gold to buy an army?' Hugh lifted an eyebrow. 'Enough gold to keep King James at bay, to bribe any supporters of Lady Arbella Stuart? With enough gold, Essex could conquer Elizabeth's kingdom.'

'But the treasure fleet sank, didn't it?' Beatrice stared at Hugh. 'Didn't it?'

'Not all of it.' Hugh tried to shift, pain arching his neck. She reached to adjust his pillows, but he shook his head. 'We know that at least one of the ships was plundered before it was scuttled. And we know this because Catalina told us.'

'How did she know?'

'Because Essex asked her husband where the treasure could be hidden. And a day later, Essex's men slit his throat.'

Beatrice bit back a gasp. She thought of Essex and Catalina in the garden: had his grip on her arm been a threat, or an apology? Had Catalina feared the earl had come to kill her?

Had the earl *tried?* Maria's murder – could Catalina have been the target?

'Then – she fled to you?'

Hugh nodded. 'We had to get her out of there. Her – and Maria.'

'Maria?' The name fell against her like new rain: a cold shock, yes – but she wanted to close her eyes and lift her face up to it, let it wash her cheeks like tears.

'Her daughter. She was four. And Catalina was with child – I couldn't leave them there. I thought …' Hugh's eyes were wet and dark. 'I thought I was saving them. Protecting them. But I failed.'

'Catalina said her daughter had a fever …' She offered the information as if it might absolve Hugh. But it was like trying to heal a severed hand with a tisane: wholly inadequate.

'A fever I gave her. A fever she should have survived – after all, I did.'

'But you're a grown man …'

'I was well-treated. Well-fed. Given medicine and fresh air. Catalina and her daughter were not.'

'You cannot blame yourself for what happened while you were unwell!'

'I can. I do. The *Silver Swan* is under my command. Everything that happened on her decks was my responsibility. Catalina was raped. Her daughter died. And all because of me. While I was lying sick, I put the wrong man in charge, a man unable to control the crew.'

'Then isn't he to blame?'

'If he is … then once again the blame falls on me.'

She knew. She knew before he could speak again. She knew who had done nothing to prevent a woman's rape, who had allowed a tiny child to die.

William. William, who had spent last night, and most of the nights since the *Swan*'s return, carousing and gambling and Christ knew what else besides. Beatrice shook her head in frustration.

'Hugh, you are his uncle, not his keeper! He is a grown man – at some point the blame for his misdeeds must fall on him!'

Hugh's eyebrows furrowed: it was the most vehement expression he could manage after the exertion of confession. 'I raised him … I showed him how to be a man. And my example was far from adequate.'

'That isn't true!' Beatrice seized his hand. 'Everything you do – everything you have ever done has been in order to look after others. Your crew, your children – me.'

'Even lying?'

She hesitated. Did she truly believe what she was telling him?

'*Yes*. Sometimes the greatest deceptions are woven with the best of intentions.' *Like mine.*

'But … I'm a fraud.'

Beatrice kissed his fingers, laced through her own. 'I did not fall in love with a knight who sailed out of Avalon with an enchanted sword and promises of Camelot. I fell in love with a man who was brave, who always wanted to be good, and true, and kind, even if he sometimes fell short of his own aim. A man who dived into the Tower Bridge rapids to save a stranger's child, a man whose first instinct will always be to care, to help. The example you set to our son is far from tarnished. It shines, Hugh. It shines. For Walter, for Ursula. And for me.' She kissed his fingers again. 'Always, my love, for me.'

He lifted his forefinger to brush the freckles on her cheek. 'If either of us shines, it is you, Bea. My guiding star. My lodestone.' He sighed weakly. 'Thank you for forgiving me.'

It was on the tip of her tongue then, to tell him everything. Simon's paintings. Arthur. Ridley. But he had already slipped into sleep.

22

The river glinted black and gold: late winter sunlight ebbing between ripples like cold sack. Shadows reached downwards, the upturned reflections of leafless beech trees trailing like ragged hair. Nothing moved across the surface: no gliding swans, no stalking herons, nor scavenging gulls. The Thames was empty. Almost as if it were warning Beatrice to stay away.

This was foolhardy. She glanced back at the house, its upper storey still candle-bright, its lower floors shrouded in dusk. Ursula and Walter had been reading together when she'd left, bickering contentedly over who would be best at taming dragons, while Catalina sewed nearby. She could go back now – could join in the squabbles, suggesting what tricks they might teach their dragons, debate whether they would be best cajoled with rabbit scraps like their hounds, or peaches, the only thing that had ever persuaded Hugh's monkey into a semblance of obedience.

But if she turned back, who would be hurt next?

Beatrice gritted her teeth, gathered her skirts, and stepped onto her barge.

She did not sit down as the oarsmen pushed the barge away from the wharf, refusing to let herself sink onto velvet cushions beneath the canopy's soft shadows. This was no pleasure cruise. There would be no lutes echoing on the gilded water, no wine-softened laughter. Only confrontation, and, if her nerve held, resolution. So instead she stood at the prow, hands laid firmly on the railing either side of the figurehead: it was a firebird, not a dragon, but nevertheless Beatrice tried to conjure some of Walter and Ursula's giddy bravado and imagine she had harnessed a wild creature, and was riding it into battle.

Before her, the river split around the prow, fraying gold, as if she were ripping a tapestry in two, tearing her way past the myths and glamour to the chamber concealed behind them. And there they were, lounging behind vast gardens, indolent, languorous, haughty, like gods of stone and glass, reclining at one of Bacchus's feasts. The mansion houses of the greatest families in England. Somerset. Arundel. Leicester. Durham. And Essex.

The oarsmen drew up alongside Essex's wharf, and Beatrice at last pulled her hands away from the railing. Even in the bitter November air, her palms had left sweaty prints on the wood, and she quashed the impulse to scrub them away before anyone noticed. Instead, she focused her gaze on the steps, where there was a chipped stone, a green bloom of damp just above the watermark, exactly as there was on her own steps: it was somehow bolstering to see that earls and countesses had the same repairs demanding their attention and their coin.

As she stepped off the barge, Beatrice kept looking out for more flaws. That guard asking her name had some loose threads on his livery. There was moss growing on the lawn by the rose bushes. As for the lintel above the door, the earl had left it too late to replace the peeling wood: it would be far too cold and wet until spring.

Inside, however, it was harder to find such comforts. A page led her across elegantly painted floors, past vast, ornate fireplaces and austere busts sneering from marble pedestals. She followed the page alongside walls painted with Grecian friezes, hung with Turkey carpets, panelled with elaborately carved oak brandishing the Essex coat of arms. There were dozens of doors, all closed; from somewhere behind one came a woman's throaty laugh, and from behind another the slow, mocking strum of a harp. She almost stumbled, and then again at the sight of Lady Rich: the earl's sister eyed her coolly from a golden frame, a painted fan poised to swat irritating intruders out of her presence.

But it wasn't Lady Rich she had come to see. Nor would she be so easily dismissed.

The page halted before a door inlaid with gold. He glanced back at her, as if to say *Are you sure?* Beatrice pressed her lips together and lifted her head: assent and command. She would see this through. She would face the earl – she would face him down. She would not leave until the earl had agreed to her demands.

The page knocked.

'Enter.'

The door opened. Beatrice stepped through. And the smell of lavender swarmed around her. Her throat closed up. Her fingers flexed, desperate to shake off ghostly hands. She couldn't breathe – couldn't see –

'Why, Lady Radclyffe. What a pleasant surprise.'

His voice was jovial, light – but she could sense the power behind it, almost smell the menace. Or was she imagining it? Was it just the smell of lavender, vile death-scented lavender? She forced herself to think, to make the room swim into focus.

Essex was seated at a mahogany desk, his feet crossed atop a pile of papers, twirling a quill between his slender fingers. A half-written letter lay atop the leather-bound book propped on his lap, and she suddenly hated him, hated his lazy, feckless posture, the ease and strength of his long legs, the casual flourishing of power. And most of all, she hated him for what he had done to Hugh.

'I have not come here for pleasure, my lord.'

'No? A shame.' Another twirl of the quill, a white flash of teeth: how many times had his lazy charm extinguished someone's smouldering rage? Did his tricks work on Queen Elizabeth? Or did she, like Beatrice, find them utterly infuriating?

'A shame, perhaps, but surely you cannot truly be surprised by my visit.' Beatrice took another step forwards, trying to take up more of his sight, his territory. 'No doubt you have been expecting it.'

Essex laughed. 'Do you think me a clairvoyant, Lady Radclyffe? I fear you've got the wrong earl – it's my sister Dorothy's husband you're after. You'll find Percy in his laboratory, hunting for captured angels and magic elixirs. My powers are entirely earthbound.'

She felt a shiver flit up her spine, invisible footsteps cold on her bones. She didn't want to think about any other kind of power. 'I'm not here to accuse you of dabbling in alchemy, my lord. I am here to demand that you leave my family alone.'

Essex tilted his head quizzically. 'An unusual request. I'm well-accustomed to pleas for patronage, to people begging me to drop a word in the royal ear. But …' He let out another laugh. 'Lady Radclyffe, have you really come all this way, entered my house for the first time, to demand that I *not* pay you any attention?'

She would not falter. Squaring her shoulders, Beatrice said, 'I want you to stop attacking us.'

'Attacking?' Essex's lips quirked, on the edge of another barely repressed laugh. 'Since when did visiting a sick friend constitute an act of violence?'

'Stop playing games,' Beatrice said softly. 'You and I both know to what I am referring.'

Essex sighed. 'I wish I did. Come, treat me like a forgetful nine-year-old miscreant. Like that young son of yours – Walter, yes? Assume I have forgotten, amidst all the distractions of my wooden swords and rumbling stomach. What exactly do you mean?'

'I mean your attempt to kill my husband!'

For a moment, they both froze. The air was sharp, echoing. Her words fell between them like shattered, priceless porcelain. There was no unsaying them, no unbreaking of the shards.

Slowly, deliberately, without taking his gaze from Beatrice, Essex uncrossed his ankles and swung his legs to the floor. He leaned forward, resting his bearded chin on clasped hands; his gold rings glinted like watchful eyes. 'Say that again, Lady Radclyffe. Plainly, clearly, bluntly – so that there may be no misunderstandings between us.'

Beatrice tried to swallow without his seeing; her throat seemed shrunken, her lips painfully dry. 'You did not come to his bedside to wish him well. You came to see how much damage you had done.'

'A pity there is no mirror in this chamber,' Essex drawled. 'I know myself to be taller than nearly all my acquaintance, but I didn't realise I'd transformed into a tree capable of crushing a man.'

'You have hands more than capable of wielding an axe,' Beatrice retorted. 'A voice more than capable of ordering one of your lackeys to do the deed.'

'And why would I wish to have done this particular deed?' On his mocking lips, her words were spat up like gristle, fit only for tossing to the hounds. 'Please, continue to state your case.'

'Because ...' She couldn't marshal her thoughts fast enough, horribly aware her hesitation was undermining her cause. 'He knew what you'd been doing in the Azores.'

Essex smiled. 'I believe my so-called failure in the Azores was widely reported. Do you see me dropping tree trunks on every scandal-monger in the kingdom?'

'Perhaps not,' Beatrice said, trying to disguise her need to swallow. 'But you did murder Catalina's husband.'

'A traitorous double agent working for the Spanish.' Essex shrugged dismissively. 'A shame Catalina had to be widowed in the process of dispatching Lopez, but as fond as I am of her, England's interests must take precedence. I was relieved to see Hugh had granted her safe haven.'

She was blundering. He was so much better at this game than she was – his counter-moves so much nimbler. Could he be telling the truth?

No. It had to be him. Who else could have wanted Hugh dead?

'Relieved – or threatened? You knew she'd have told Hugh everything, and you wanted to silence him before he reported to the queen. You sent the globe as a warning – you ordered Molyneux's apprentice to change the cartouches –'

'I did *what?*'

She stared at him. Could a man really perform bewilderment so – so unattractively? Essex's eyebrows had shot up, carving lines into his forehead; his mouth had dropped open, his eyes widened, all in vacant, flummoxed roundness. 'The globe,' she said again, hearing her echo falter. 'The fallen mast, the ship carrying Hugh and Catalina, the robins attacking the swan ...'

'What have those globes to do with – with any of this nonsense?' Essex flapped a hand impatiently, and she suddenly realised he was pointing – indicating the far corner of the room behind her. She'd barely turned around before Essex had bounded out of his seat, seized her arm and marched her over to the globe, his grip so tight she thought the bones of her elbow would snap. Essex swatted the globe with his free hand, sending it into a juddering spin. 'This globe spins, Lady Radclyffe. It spins, it shows us the routes of Drake and Hawkins, it lets us know Corea is a very long way away and there is no blasted El Dorado anywhere outside Raleigh's imagination – and that is all! What it does not do, what it cannot do, is implicate a man in an attempt on his friend's life! His *friend*, damn you! I might well jump on my barge and sail upriver to tell him his wife's gone mad!'

She wrenched herself away from him, away from that word. 'But you knew – you'd discovered what Hugh had been doing –'

'You mean spying?' Essex snorted, giving the globe another shove of disgust. 'Everyone's a spy, woman! You think Raleigh doesn't tattle my secrets to Elizabeth? You think I don't tattle his? The only person I trust not to gossip behind my back is Pen! And even she has her own network of informers and intrigues. We're all at it, you fool. Elizabeth's court is riven with spies. I don't begrudge men for it – I certainly don't chop down trees to stop them doing it! If I did, there wouldn't be a forest left standing in England, and then where would I go hunting?'

Her lips moved unbidden. She couldn't tell if it was a tremor or an attempt at words – an excuse, a grovelling apology, another accusation.

Essex huffed out a sigh – and abruptly turned it into a barked laugh. Was there nothing the man couldn't find amusing? 'Look,' he said, suddenly gentle, 'I understand. It can't be easy, having a husband badly wounded. I held my Frances's hand as Philip Sidney died, and it was neither swift nor poetic. It was agony and stench, and when the end came, we were almost glad – and contrary to some tittle tattle, my relief had naught to do with my desire to marry Philip's widow.' He patted her elbow, the same one he'd near-crushed, a gesture whose awkwardness might have been endearing if Beatrice hadn't been burning with shame. 'What I'm saying is that grief drives us all a little bit mad. But running around London flinging accusations, especially at earls, isn't going to heal Hugh's wounds. Or win you any friends.' His patting paused, and was that the slightest curving of finger and thumb against her bones? 'You want to be careful, Lady Radclyffe. Women ranting and raving … we've all heard stories of where they end up.'

And then his hand was patting again, and she couldn't tell whether she'd imagined that pressure. Beatrice wanted to run – but why would a sane woman run from a man who was comforting her?

'But … if it wasn't you, then …'

'Accidents happen. Sometimes so many, so hard on each other's heels that it may well feel like a curse – but that's nonsense. There are no curses.' Essex winked. 'Don't tell my brother-in-law though. He'd be so disappointed.'

He was being so affable, so offhand. How could he be? She'd been unforgivably rude – she'd accused him of attempted murder – and yet here he was jesting with her, offering her consolation. She'd never felt so small.

Unless his kindness was no kindness at all. Even a dagger sheathed in silk could slit a throat.

'Go back to your husband,' Essex said gently. 'Tell him he was sorely missed at the Accession Day jousts, and I look forward to unhorsing him next year.'

'Yes,' she said numbly, turning away. 'I'm sorry, my lord.'

And she staggered out of Essex House, dizzy with embarrassment and confusion. Somehow she found herself back on her barge, not standing proud at the railing this time, no; she collapsed on the cushions, burying her face in the rasping velvet.

What had she done? She hadn't thought at all – she who was renowned among merchants for her shrewdness, her measured judgement. She'd blundered into an earl's home and slandered him. People had been arrested for less. If she hadn't already been persona non grata among the noble ladies of London, she'd guaranteed her exile from fashionable circles now.

She'd behaved like a madwoman. The one thing she'd sworn she'd never do. What if she'd been seen? Essex might have been sympathetic – or feigned sympathy – but would Lady Rich deign to be merciful? Would Essex's countess? His servants? Her own oarsmen?

There were eyes everywhere. Dangers everywhere. And if the danger that had been looming over Beatrice's household since that cursed globe's arrival hadn't come from Essex House, then where had it come from?

Dusk had fallen. They'd nearly reached home: she could see the swans, gilded bronze in the torchlight from the barge.

And then the bronze rippled.

There was another torch. Its light flared, jerked, flickered: someone was running with it. Beatrice rose, squinting to make them out. As the barge was tied up, Ridley burst onto the wharf.

'Mistress – it's Sir Hugh!'

Her heart clenched. She froze, one foot hovering above the stone step. And then the torchlight caught Ridley's face, and she saw the grim set of his jaw.

'I'm so sorry, Beatrice. He's dead.'

23

Somewhere in the darkness, an owl was calling out, its unseen cries faintly mocking: *Hugh-Hugh. Hugh-Hugh.* She had screamed it. Many times. Had not long ago ceased to scream. Her jaw ached; her throat stung, raw with howls; her lips were dry. A half-remembered recipe echoed at the distant edge of her mind: *for a sore throat, mix horehound with honey,* but a syrup or an infusion? And how could she possibly care? It was as though her brain was attempting to protect her with distractions, each digression luring her away from the horrifying truth – that her husband was dead.

He lay beside her, in the bed they'd shared. The bed he'd loved her in, the bed he'd died in. She'd have to order the maids to launder the sheets, change the blankets – and again, how could she be thinking of practicalities? What kind of a wife was she?

She wasn't. No longer a wife of any kind, but a widow – and not so much an explorer's widow, as it turned out, but the widow of a spy. Did that matter? How could it? She was *Hugh's* widow, because *Hugh* had died, and not only would she have to live her life without him, but at some point she would have to tell her children that their father was dead. Perhaps they'd already guessed: she'd screamed so loudly. She couldn't decide which would be worse: breaking the news to them, or seeing in their small white faces that they already knew, and they'd been waiting for her to tell them it wasn't true.

But she couldn't bear to. Not yet. She wanted to stay here a moment – a lifetime – longer, because until she left the room, it would not be over. Her last time with her husband would not be over.

'Oh Hugh,' she whispered. 'How could you leave me?'

He'd always left her. Year after year, he'd sailed down the Thames and out to sea – but he had always, always come back. That was their covenant. And now it was broken.

Beneath her cheek, the pillow had grown damp again; she'd thought her tears had dried up, but it appeared they were drawn from a tide, not a pool, and they were rising again, only to fall. She pressed her forehead against Hugh's shoulder, wishing she could believe its hardness was just muscle, its coldness merely a lack of blankets. That at any moment he would lift his arm and draw her close, his hand wandering from her back, perhaps up to her neck, the softness behind her ear, or tracing a route from her waist to hip. He couldn't stay still. He was Hugh. Sir Hugh Radclyffe never stayed still. He hated it. So this still body couldn't possibly be Hugh's.

But it still smelled like him. She nuzzled closer, pressing her nose, her lips against his neck, feeling his beard rustle against her skin, breathing in that salt and sawdust captain's smell, the cedarwood and bergamot of his hair, the *Hugh*ness of him.

'I should have been here, my love,' she murmured, her confession hot between their skin: it was almost as if the warmth were emanating from him. 'I should never have left you.'

Had he called out for her? Had he known his last moments were his last? Or had he slipped away into silence as he slept? She hadn't asked – hadn't asked Ridley anything, except to tell her it wasn't true, and he couldn't give her the answer she wanted, so she'd slammed the bedchamber door in his face.

'I never told you,' Beatrice whispered, 'what I did – what Ridley and I did. You confessed all your secrets, and I only buried mine deeper. You deserved better. A better wife.' One who didn't abandon him to harangue earls about tampering with globes. Or spend their last few weeks together suspecting him of adultery – when it was Beatrice, not Hugh, who had been the traitor within their marriage.

'I'm sorry,' Beatrice breathed, reaching for his hand and lifting it to her lips. It was heavy, heavier than it ought to have been, and she clasped it in both of hers so she wouldn't have to think about its new heaviness, only press her lips against the scar-silvered knuckles she knew so well, those long fingers –

Beatrice stiffened. Were those shadows? Or … Frowning, she peered closer, lifting Hugh's hand so the torch above the bed cast a golden glow over his skin.

She'd been right. There were scratches on his hands. Old ones, brown and scabbed, from the night the tree had fallen. And other ones, still pink, raw, fresh.

On their own, the new scratches might have been proof enough. But there was something else, something she'd seen before, years ago in a room that reeked of lavender.

Beneath Hugh's fingernails, there were crescents of blood. Just as there had been beneath Arthur's, when he'd torn at Beatrice's flesh as she pressed the pillow lower.

Hugh hadn't died of his wounds. He'd been murdered.

How could this be happening all over again? Maria's murder still remained unsolved, and now Beatrice's beloved husband had been killed. And there was heartbreak, of course there was the utter gaping, gnawing agony at her very core, but that didn't mean she wasn't also horrified. Because both murders had happened inside her home. They'd happened while Beatrice sailed downriver on the barge, giving the assassin ample opportunity to sneak in.

Think logically, Beatrice urged herself, but her mind shook as much as her hands, knees, belly, and she gripped the windowsill to steady herself. She'd staggered over to the window to let in more light, as if peering at Hugh's hands anew by moonlight might have helped her, proved her wrong. But there was no light. Only a sooty smother of clouds and an inky mass where she knew the river slithered away.

They could have come by river. Easy enough: she'd never employed guards, and with the oarsmen out rowing, no one would be near the wharf to challenge an intruder. Someone could have hidden a craft behind the eyot, or crouched in the reeds upriver, or watched from a Battersea window on the far bank. She'd always seen the river as the edge of her world, the moat protecting her castle from attack, as an absence of neighbours. But it wasn't a defence. It was fluid, unsteady, not a barrier but a breach, and anyone could come creeping in. What had kept them away before? Only human decency, and the assumption that men simply wouldn't dare trespass in someone else's garden. But if you were plotting murder, why on earth would you be troubled by trampling a forbidden lawn?

She wasn't safe here. None of them were safe here. And without Hugh to protect them, what hope did Beatrice have of keeping her children from being harmed?

The knock ricocheted against her ribs and she whirled around, empty hands rising as if she could scratch an enemy into submission.

'Who's there?'

'Beatrice?' A soft, patient voice. Not pitying, but kind. 'Ridley told me about your husband. May I come in?'

Catalina. Of all people. And yet, it was not so surprising, for hadn't she known Hugh? Known and seemingly admired, even liked him. She could not think *loved*. Now wasn't the time to dredge up that foolish suspicion.

'Come in.' Her voice startled her: it was too clear, too normal. She might have been addressing a tradesman or greeting a fellow ship owner on the docks.

The door opened. She should have locked it. Did she need to bolt it against Catalina? Or someone else?

Catalina entered, a woollen robe over her nightgown. Beatrice kept forgetting how late it was. The other woman's face was slack with – what? Grief? Horror? Pity? Before she could measure it, Catalina had crossed the chamber and embraced Beatrice. Her hands were still raised: between that, her shock, and Catalina's swollen belly, it made for an awkward clash of bodies. And yet neither woman broke it.

'I am so sorry,' Catalina whispered against Beatrice's forehead. 'He was a good man. He was far too young to die.'

Beatrice's eyes blurred. She could barely see Catalina's black curls now, only smell the almond oil on them, and she wanted to scream, because of course Hugh was too young. Too strong, too beautiful, too loved. Too *needed*.

'He was murdered.' The words came out as a croak, and she said it again, 'He was murdered,' and if she said it a third time, she thought it would cast a spell, binding them to bloodshed and to death and no way to break it.

Catalina stiffened. Drawing back slightly, she frowned at Beatrice. 'You do not mean the accident? You mean … since then. Today?'

Beatrice nodded: once, jerkily, not taking her eyes away from Catalina in case she might read something in the other woman's eyes. Fear, or doubt; incredulity even. But Catalina's thoughts were inscrutable.

Slowly, Catalina turned towards the bed, and Hugh's body. Beatrice followed her gaze, stupidly half-expecting Hugh to have moved, risen, rolled his shoulders and sauntered to the window, tousled and yawning. Never again.

'How?' Catalina asked quietly.

'He was smothered. While … while I was gone.'

'You're certain?'

'I know the signs.'

Catalina's hand drifted to her belly protectively. 'Then it was done while I was with the children. While we were only a flight of stairs away. Sweet Jesu, if we'd stepped onto the corridor at the wrong moment …'

'Then …' Beatrice hesitated. 'You believe me?'

Catalina rubbed her belly again. 'What choice do I have?' She looked back at Beatrice. 'However horrifying it may be to imagine a murderer stalking this house, I would far rather believe the worst and be prepared than cosset myself with denials. On Vila de Orta, we used to say that if we left our gunpowder to go damp simply because we enjoyed seeing the horizon was clear, it would not stop the raiders coming.'

Beatrice felt something shift in her belly; it took a moment to recognise it as relief. After the Justice of the Peace – and Hugh, and William, even Ridley – had dismissed her concerns about Maria, she'd expected scepticism. 'I take it you know how to fire a pistol then. That might be a useful skill.'

Catalina's lips pinched. 'Pulling the trigger is easy enough. It's aiming that requires true skill. Do you have any notion of who your target might be?'

A man who smelt of frankincense and cardamom. Not Essex. Not Anthony Kitson. Unless Simon had been lying to her, to throw her off the scent? He'd been so frightened of Kitson; why wouldn't he seek to dissuade her from pursuing Kitson if it meant he could then tell Kitson how helpful he'd been? And Simon hadn't returned: he'd promised to bring her a list of changed images, and never appeared. Perhaps he'd never intended to. Perhaps he and Kitson were working together.

Catalina must have seen her thoughts roiling, because she said, 'We can talk of this more another time. For now … there are people downstairs. Waiting for you.'

'People?' She was still thinking of Kitson: she imagined an assembly of men in black, bristling with threats and blades and blackmail.

'Your family.' Catalina glanced at the door and lowered her voice. 'Beatrice … I think it would be wiser not to share your concerns with them.'

'Why?' Beatrice's eyes narrowed. 'You suspect one of my kin?'

Catalina shook her head. 'I didn't say that. I only meant that they will not listen. Not now. A grieving woman's words are never heard as anything other than weeping and wailing. They will not believe you tonight. Trust me.'

Trust Catalina? The spy who, until recently, she'd suspected of being Hugh's paramour? A woman who'd admitted she'd dealt in secrets all her life? A few weeks ago, Beatrice couldn't have imagined herself even entertaining the possibility of trusting Catalina.

But that was before the globe came into her life. Before Ursula's injuries. Before Maria. Before Hugh.

Slowly Beatrice nodded. 'Very well. I won't reveal my suspicions yet.' She looked back at the bed, then at the door.

When she walked through it, she would be leaving Hugh. She would no longer be a wife, only a widow. And the world would stare at her with new, dark judgement.

She would not hide away. She had to face the world sooner or later. Squaring her shoulders, Beatrice left the chamber she would never again share with her husband.

*   *   *

The men were in the gallery, gathered near the windows, and the first thing that struck Beatrice was how out of place they looked. Four dark-garbed men with empty hands, doing nothing but looming, like a ring of stones on a hilltop, sombre and faintly obstructive. The second thing that struck her was that they had gathered beside the globe: as if it were the tumulus around which they lurked.

They'd fallen silent as she and Catalina entered, and as the women crossed the room, Beatrice could see them rearrange their faces. Ridley solemn, William guarded, Robert overly sympathetic, Nicholas struggling to conceal his distress. And something else, in all of them, something she couldn't quite read.

'Thank you for coming, brothers,' Beatrice said, offering a hand first to Robert, whose avuncular squeeze ground her knuckles together, then to Nicholas, whose fingers trembled as he clung to hers, unwilling to let go. 'I only wish it could have been in happier circumstances.'

'He was a great man,' William said. 'Irreplaceable.'

'We will all feel his loss gravely,' Robert said. 'Though naturally you most of all, dear sister.'

There was a slight pause. Barely a breath, but enough for glances to flicker, shoulders to brace – and then Nicholas said, 'I cannot think how you will manage without him.'

Another pause. As if they were waiting for her. Had she so forgotten social cues? Usually it was Robert bumbling and Nicholas oblivious, while Beatrice tried not to sigh, and she wondered abstractedly if this was what people meant when they said grief struck everyone differently.

Robert cleared his throat. 'And the children. They are so young. To lose their father …'

'It is a terrible thing,' William said. 'When my father died, my mother nearly collapsed under the weight of her grief. Without my uncles' kindness I do not know what might have become of me.'

'But we were happy to help,' Nicholas said stiffly. 'Out of duty, of course. And … and out of love.'

Then his eyes darted up to Beatrice's, and she saw a shadow of guilt even as he gave her a mute, plaintive appeal. And suddenly it became clear to her that she was not part of a conversation at all. No: she was the audience to a wooden, poorly rehearsed performance.

'What is this?' Beatrice breathed, fury crackling in her belly: if she so much as raised her voice above a whisper, she'd be unable to stop herself howling, bellowing, roaring. 'Tell me you haven't planned this!'

Robert gave an awkward laugh – but when was his laughter anything but? 'My dear, there is hardly a conspiracy afoot here! We are merely here to offer our support.'

'Our help,' William said, and if it hadn't been so dark in the candle-lit gallery, she would have sworn she saw him kick his uncle's ankle.

'Our guidance,' Nicholas said sadly.

'You don't need to worry about anything apart from Walter and Ursula,' William said soothingly.

She could have boxed his ears. Only seven winters ago, a fever had had him asleep with his head in her lap, his hot fingers clutching hers, his still-soft cheeks flushed and stained with tears only her singing had calmed. And now he thought to give her advice?

'Are you men?' Beatrice hissed. 'Or wolves? Hugh is barely cold, and already you come snapping for scraps of power, as if you might tear away his strength and devour it like strips of flesh!' She shook her head in disgust. 'God knows he was the best among you. But even I had not realised quite how far you had sunk beneath him.'

She'd expected them to be cowed. To look abashed – last time Robert had come trying to wrest control from her, the man had wept when she upbraided him. But now ... They didn't look down at their feet, nor shift awkwardly. Instead, they glanced at one another, as if in confirmation – but of what?

'This is sickening!' she snapped. 'How dare you come here, feigning sympathy, pretending you're only here to comfort me in my grief, when all the while you seek to exile me to the nursery while you ratchet through my accounts?'

'But aunt,' William said slowly, 'none of us have mentioned money. I didn't expect you to be so quick to think of coin so soon after my uncle passed away.'

'Do you think me a fool?' Beatrice gave an exasperated laugh. 'I know what you're doing, and I find it wholly reprehensible! Christ's wounds, I don't have time for this! My husband has been murdered!'

There was silence. Enough for her to hear Catalina catch her breath: was that a sigh of disappointment? Or horror? She glanced back to see Catalina frowning – but not at Beatrice. Catalina's eyes were narrowed at the men, and when Beatrice followed her gaze, she saw that they were all looking at Ridley.

He was standing slightly back, almost behind the globe. And only now did she realise that, at no point since she'd entered the gallery, had Ridley met her eyes.

'Is this what you meant?' Robert asked.

'Come now,' Nicholas blurted out, so flustered he was plucking at his broken nails, 'this can't be necessary. It's grief, that's all, perfectly natural grief –'

'Raving,' William stated flatly, but with no sense of triumph, only bleak resignation. 'Just like when she accused me of felling the tree. Grief, perhaps, but this goes beyond grief.'

'But –'

William cut him off again. 'And this isn't the first time. Is it, Ridley?'

Beatrice stared at her steward. His dark eyes were lowered – out of respect, or reluctance? He shifted under her gaze, rocking slightly on his heels. His doublet brushed against the globe, and there was a snicker of wood and brass as it stirred.

'It is not the first time,' Ridley confirmed, his voice wincing low, the words eked out of him like splinters. 'She – we – went to Lambeth to see the craftsman who had made this globe.'

'Because?' William prompted, and Beatrice realised in horror that this was not the first time Ridley had told William about their visit to Molyneux's workshop. And now they were repeating, performing their conversation – but for who? Robert? Nicholas? Catalina? Or for Beatrice herself, forcing her to confront her own actions?

'Because she thought the globe had …' Ridley's jaw worked, awkward with words he did not wish to utter again. 'Had foretold Maria's death.'

'But in itself that is not evidence!' Nicholas burst out. 'The science of fortune-telling is inexact, I grant you, but Doctor Dee and Nils Hemmingsen, Tycho Brahe – these gentlemen are most learned and –'

'Evidence of what?' Beatrice interrupted. She looked from her steward to her brothers-in-law to her nephew. 'Of what, damn you?'

They shared a glance again, and she knew. She knew what they were insinuating, and the idea of it reared up like a black snake she'd thought was merely a shadow, washed up seaweed, but now uncoiled, jaws bared, venom seething in its fangs.

'No,' Beatrice hissed. 'This is not – I am not –'

'Beatrice,' Robert said, cajoling, smiling fixedly, 'we are merely thinking of your welfare, and that of your children. Allow us to –'

'I will allow nothing,' Beatrice snapped. 'This is my house, and I will not be insulted.'

'You must see how it looks,' William said, and the lordly condescension stung: he was a boy, a stripling with delusions of grandeur and maturity. 'Even now you're practically raving –'

'Because I am furious!' Beatrice retorted. 'And justly so! Besides, Catalina believes me!'

Behind her, Catalina made a small noise, half-sigh, half-moan.

'Well, naturally she says as much,' Robert said. 'What else could she say, given the circumstances?'

'Given that I speak the truth, you mean?'

Robert spread his hands apologetically. 'Given that her protector has sadly passed away and she is now not only in a delicate condition but also entirely dependent on you for shelter and succour. It would hardly be a logical act for the lady to scorn your claims as the madness they truly are.'

He'd said it. The syllables lashed her cheeks, left, right, searing like hot oil. She reeled away, both recoiling and seeking Catalina's eyes.

'Tell him,' Beatrice said hoarsely. 'Tell him you believe me.'

Catalina was cradling her belly with one hand, kneading her back with the other. She looked drawn, exhausted, as if she wanted nothing more than to sink into her bed. 'Beatrice,' she said, and the soft caution in her voice was damnation enough. 'Perhaps we ought to continue this conversation another time. After we have all rested. And grieved. Let us not forget what has happened this night.'

'Did you know they were planning this?' Beatrice demanded, ignoring Catalina's plea for clemency, for a delay. 'Did you pretend to believe me just to lure me into their trap?'

'You see?' Robert said, before Catalina could answer. 'The vitriol, the refusal to listen to reason – these are all signs, as clear as the cartouches on the globe. I fear our choice has been determined.'

'What choice?' Beatrice tried to fix him with a glare, the one she'd cowed him with before. But neither Robert, nor any of the others would meet her eyes.

'It is for the best,' Robert said, nodding to William, patting Nicholas's shoulder. 'We shall assume control of all business arrangements. My wife will take up residence tomorrow to ensure the household runs smoothly and the children are well looked after. And Beatrice will have some time to compose herself and grieve for her loss.'

She'd never heard Robert so – so *canny*. He'd always been buffoonish, clumsy. But now he was measured, his every syllable steady with good sense.

What had he said about the cartouches? Why had he brought them up? Surely not as a warning?

'Then …' Nicholas hesitated. 'That other step we discussed – it will not be necessary? She can remain here?'

Bedlam. Beatrice felt as if she'd fallen through ice. They didn't just think her mad, they thought her mad beyond all saving. They believed she ought to be locked away.

'We cannot rule it out,' Robert said sorrowfully. 'But nor will we be overly hasty.'

'Overly hasty?' Beatrice echoed, terror and rage making her voice shrill. 'My husband died mere hours ago and you believe yourselves to be acting with respectful slowness? You sanctimonious imbeciles!'

'Sister, please –'

'Do not speak!' Beatrice hurled her words down on him like a thunderbolt. 'I have heard enough from you – from all of you! I have never been so insulted or so disgusted in all my days.' She shook her head angrily, as if she could shake herself into pure fury, expelling all fear. 'Robert, Nicholas, leave my house. At once. William, whichever tavern you stumbled out of at dawn this morning, I suggest you skulk back to it. Follow the stench of your own vomit, perhaps. Master Ridley –' she flung the words at him as if she had never touched his skin, never felt the slightest tenderness towards him '– return to the servants' quarters. I shall deal with you in the morning. And as for you,' she turned to Catalina, 'if you imagine I would turn any woman onto the streets alone and in the darkness, you have grossly misjudged me. If I am known for anything in this family, it is for allowing people to take too much advantage of my hospitality. Go and sleep anywhere beneath my roof, as long as I can neither see nor hear you.' She gave them all a look of unadulterated scorn. 'All of you, get out of my sight.'

And they obeyed. As men had many times, when she'd dismissed them at the end of an unsatisfactory meeting, when she'd berated Holbrook for poor bookkeeping, when she'd upbraided Robert last time he'd come sniffing for scraps. There had been satisfaction then, relief. Now, it was like watching a flood recede, leaving detritus in its wake: broken pottery, bent blades, sodden carcasses of unrecognisable animals, all giving rise to a miasma of rot and putrefaction, and the grim knowledge that she would somehow have to deal with them. The glances, the muttered confirmation and warnings between the men – they would be back. They would not give up. Maybe they would give her a chance to grieve; maybe they would strike again with no regard for decency. Beatrice glared at their backs as they left, at the wrongness of each set of spines and shoulders: Ridley too wiry, Robert too bulky, Nicholas too slight, William so nearly identical to Hugh that it gouged at her heart.

Catalina was moving away too, heavy, slow, pausing to seek Beatrice's eyes. She wouldn't meet them: her own were stinging now, and she couldn't bear the thought of Catalina's pity.

'Beatrice …'

'You have said quite enough.' Beatrice turned away, her voice grating with the effort of not crying. 'No doubt you are in need of rest.'

There was a pause. Then Catalina said, 'I am not alone in that, I think.'

Footsteps; the rustle of skirts; at last, a closing door.

Beatrice let out a gasp: ragged, fast, a keen of anguish that sounded too much like *Hugh*. And then another, another, and she couldn't stop them, and they *hurt*, raking her throat, jolting her ribs and lungs as they collapsed from her mouth, out of rhythm with her breath. She pressed a palm to her chest, her side, as if she could reach her own pain, mould it smooth and small like a pomander bead. But it was too vast, too jagged, and with every gasp something was shredding inside her, and perhaps it was her mind, perhaps they were right, and there was nothing to stop her going mad, because without Hugh, she was unanchored, adrift. Or perhaps she had been the anchor all along, wedged in sand and silt, and drowning without knowing it, and now that the chain had been severed, the cool shadow of the ship above had vanished and there was nothing to haul her back to the surface: she would flail down in the darkness forever.

She couldn't breathe. She staggered forward, bending, straining, and then she was on her knees, coughs hacking her throat, and the globe, the blasted, cursed, stupid globe was in front of her. The cartouches, lurid as plague sores. Lines cavorting across the surface, dancing away towards a new world, an old world, towards another symbol that she hadn't understood meant pain.

Her first blow landed before she'd realised she would strike it. Feeble, like a leaf blown against stone. And then she hit it again. Harder. Faster. Blow after blow, thundering against the swollen surface, pain shooting up her wrist, flaring on her knuckles, as if she were plunging her fist into a wasps' nest, but still she struck. And now her gasps were words, barely recognisable, but she knew her own intent, she was certain of her own mind.

'What do you want from me? What do you *want*?'

A shudder, a creaking. Then something half-groan, half-gasp, and the globe split. It caved in: a hole the size of her hand, and then a crack scissored upwards and another section swung loose, hanging disjointedly like a broken shutter.

Beatrice rocked back, startled that she had actually broken it – that she *could* have broken it at all. It had seemed so powerful, hulking with menace and foreknowledge. And now it gaped, like a face ravaged by leprosy, the dark cavity fringed with torn paper and splinters.

Then it stirred. Tilted, and spun. Not all the way round, only a shifting, like the stumble of a stabbed man, clutching his innards. As it moved, the loose section swayed, billowed. And Beatrice saw what lay inside the globe.

24

She didn't move at first. Didn't dare, didn't know if she could. She caught herself wondering whether the men had been right after all and she was deluded with grief. And perhaps because that grief was still too raw, too fragile, Beatrice leaned closer to the globe.

On the reverse of the loose section was writing. Crabbed, slanting to the left rather than the right, the tails of each *y* and *g* curling backwards then suddenly jerking up like fishhooks: she knew that hand. When she'd first opened the accounts ledgers, she'd seen columns of figures and baffling abbreviations that she'd since come to use as instinctively as the alphabet. When she'd had to copy the style faithfully in the days when they were still pretending he was capable of writing. And she'd seen it again when the lawyer had broken the seal and unfurled the will, revealing Beatrice to be the sole heir.

It was her father's handwriting.

Her breath caught in her throat, and for a moment she smelled dried lavender, sickly grey dust – and then she coughed, blinked, swallowed, and it was gone.

How could her father's handwriting be inside the globe? He was ten years dead. Beatrice forced herself to think, remembering Molyneux's workshops, the long gores hung up to dry, rustling like whispers. The hemispheres were made of layers of paper, stiffened with glue and resin. Could Molyneux have simply used any old paper for this globe? Had her father ever corresponded with him, ever purchased a sextant or astrolabe from the Lambeth workshop – and had Molyneux kept the letters for over a decade? It was too great a coincidence. Arthur's writing had been deliberately used to make Hugh's globe. But why?

Her hand was throbbing. Glancing down, she saw blood on her knuckles, and felt sick: her blood must be on the globe, or the globe must be on her, its inks seeping beneath her skin, black and green serpents writhing up her veins.

She clamped her left hand over her right wrist, as if she might suffocate such thoughts with her fingers. Just as she'd suffocated Arthur. No. Another thought thrashing loose, yanking her off balance, and she needed balance, needed steadiness, needed the anchor that had been stolen from her.

Stop. Think. You are Lady Beatrice Radclyffe, renowned for your level-headedness, your common sense, your rational mind. You must think.

Beatrice tightened her grip on her right hand, pressing her fingers into her own skin in turn, counting off thoughts. If Arthur's letters had been used to make the globe, then someone had put them there. To frighten her? Well, that goal had certainly been achieved – but that had been before she'd known what lay beneath the map. Or something else – something more powerful than fear? Could Arthur's letters – Arthur's spirit – be behind the globe's menace?

She did not understand such things. Nicholas knew all about the language of angels, the power of astrology; Beatrice knew the price of a bale of indigo, which merchants might try to cheat you. She knew that Arthur – if it were Arthur's ghost, if ghosts could rise – could not have done this alone. Someone had harnessed his spirit, someone had passed his letters to Molyneux's craftsmen. Who? Robert, manoeuvring to take control of her finances? William, who'd made no secret of his desire to take the Swan's helm? Nicholas, with his knowledge of the arcane: he had been the only one to express reluctance when Bedlam was alluded to, but was that a feint? Had his absent-mindedness always been a ruse?

Be rational, Beatrice. No use speculating. In order to find out who, surely the best thing would be to inspect the letters.

And in order to do that, she would have to reach inside the globe.

Years ago, Arthur had taken her to see the menagerie at the Tower, some sort of misguided attempt to distract her from the absence of her mother. She'd expected to see animals capering, frolicking – the only animals she'd known were eager hounds and affable horses, gluttonous hens and playful kittens. But the animals caged in the Tower were furious. Some sullen, like the jackal with the matted hide; some coldly imperious, like the hooded-eyed eagles; some belligerent, like the yammering gibbons. And some, like the lions, prowling the bars with menace, eyes narrowed with hatred, low snarls baring curved, blood-flecked yellow teeth, everything about them saying *I can kill you. Any of you. All of you. I only have to open my jaws, and your throat will gush crimson.* But the keeper had been bragging about how tame they were. How he'd once placed his arm so far inside the biggest lion's maw he could tickle its tonsils. And in the middle of his boast, the lion had swung its great head, eyed him scornfully and then opened its jaws wide, as if to say *I dare you.* The crowd had cheered – *go on, go on!* – and the keeper had let out a nervous trill of laughter, then hesitated before edging one step closer and reaching towards the creature.

The lion's jaws had snapped shut. The keeper had jerked away, just in time, and tried to laugh again, but Beatrice had seen sweat beading his brow, even as the lion grunted and stalked away. A bloodless victory, but she'd still had nightmares about long teeth sinking into flesh, ripping muscle from bone, tearing arteries as easily as embroidery threads.

Now, reaching into the globe felt exactly like reaching into the lion's maw. Her breath came too loud, too shrill, like the keeper's laugh. She felt searing heat, like the animal's breath, something festering and rotten lodged deep in its jaws, could almost smell the rancid meatiness. *It's the glue*, she told herself, *they boil animal hides for glue.* And yet.

She had to put her whole arm in to reach the bottom of the globe, and the fragments fallen there. The globe pressed against her hip, her ribs, her armpit, bulbous and swollen, its wooden frame digging into her waist like a pulled knife. She contorted her neck, refusing to let her cheek touch the varnished surface, or come too close to the gap. Out of the corner of her eye, the bear strained in the grip of the cockatrice with bee's wings.

Her scrabbling fingers closed around the fragments, and she pulled them up as fast as she could, shooting backwards before the jaws could close.

She held three fragments, one vaguely triangular, one a sort of diamond, one a crescent. Or scythe, if she let herself see it. On the back of the triangle, a few phrases – *delayed shipment, quantity of cinnamon, spoiled saffron*. On the diamond: *frequent bouts of, the only solution remaining, permanent*. And a capital *B*. A small *e*. It might have been her own name. Or Bedlam. Was that where the letters had come from? One of the physicians, clearing out old correspondence? But the letter about the spices – that was merchants' business. She turned over the crescent – and almost dropped it in surprise.

It wasn't Arthur's handwriting. But it was a hand she knew just as well.

Take a spoonful of ambergris and one of rosewater.

It was her mother's pomander bead recipe.

Beatrice cradled the fragment, half-marvelling, half-horrified. She'd thought it lost, this fragile memento of her mother, and to have it back in her grasp was like recalling a memory near-forgotten, a scent that had only been tendrils now suffusing the air. But – she had to shake her head, forcing herself away from nostalgia – but for her mother's recipes to have found their way into the globe was impossible. They had been in this house. In Beatrice's study. The only way for Molyneux to obtain them was if someone in her household had stolen them.

Or someone who visited her house regularly. Who was *invited*. Nicholas, Robert, William any one of them could have done it.

There was a thief in her house. A thief, a traitor, a murderer.

Slowly, hardly daring to breathe, Beatrice edged away from the globe, pushing herself back against the velvet curtains, like a spaniel cowering against its master's legs. Behind the globe, the cabinet of curiosities hunched against the wall, all murky shadows and sly glints of glass and inlaid gilt. The antlers forked like lightning made bone, and she could almost believe she heard it crackle.

No. Not a crackling sound. A rattle. A rustle. And once again, the globe began to turn.

Beatrice bit back a scream as the hulking thing moved. It was like seeing a mangled corpse lurch to its feet: halting, ungainly, and bent on its ungodly purpose. Slowly the globe turned, until the gaping wound was before her, grotesque as a broken-toothed leer, blind and black as a skull's socket.

It wanted her. It had taken Hugh, taken Maria, wounded Ursula. And now it would devour her.

She had to get out. But she'd backed herself into the alcove, and the only way out was past the globe. Her breath came in ragged gasps, jarring against the globe's rattle, rasp, rattle. Beatrice edged crabwise along the wall, pressing her back against the panels, so hard she could feel the oak rake her shoulder blades, her wrists scraping against the skirting board. Her throat felt too exposed; her skirts chafed too loudly against the carpet. And as she inched further into the room, the globe turned. Watching her every move, a stalking predator. Again she caught that rancid, animal stench, as if the jaws had widened in readiness. The torn edges convulsed.

And then she was out of the alcove, scrambling on all fours, diving away. Her skirts tangled around her ankles, miring her in brocade. She kicked, flailed – and somehow she was on her feet, hurling herself across the gallery. She fumbled with the door, clumsy with panic, snapping a fingernail in haste. Yanking it open, Beatrice flung herself into the corridor, and slammed the door behind her. Panting, she collapsed against the oak.

Rattle. Rasp. Rattle.

It was still turning in there. She could almost see it, swinging itself around like a huge head. Searching? Or rocking itself as if with cold, mocking laughter?

It turned when disaster was imminent. Something was coming.

She'd thought the worst had already happened. Christ's wounds, she was barely a widow. What more could the globe want from her?

Her mind. Her freedom. And far more terrifying: her children.

25

There was no map for this. No bold explorers had set down on paper a chart for navigating your own grief, let along for guiding your children through theirs. There were no stars to plot a course by, no neatly labelled straits and channels, nothing to tell you which rocks to avoid, or which currents would drag you down, or if there would ever be a safe haven again, let alone where to find one.

She'd let her children sleep as long as possible. Putting off telling them, letting them have a father just a few hours longer – and Beatrice had been in no fit state to tell them after her experiences in the gallery. Convinced she wouldn't be able to sleep, she'd dragged a chair from the second-best bedchamber – trying not to think of it as Arthur's bedchamber – and placed it on the corridor where she could see both Ursula and Walter's doors, as if she could guard against whatever was coming next. Her eyes had stung with exhaustion and apprehension and tears, both shed too often and still unshed, so much her head throbbed. And yet, somehow, she had slept. Had jerked awake in guilt and fear – and disappointment, for it was the first day she'd awoken to that Hugh would never see. And there would be countless other new dawns to come. The first week Hugh had never been part of. The first month, first year, first Twelfth Night, Lady Day, Easter. The first autumn when he did not return from a voyage and they would all have to acknowledge that this absence was not one he could sail out of, turquoise feathers jaunty on his velvet hat. But the hardest of all these firsts was breaking the news to her children.

She'd woken Walter first, and simply asked him to come to Ursula's room. Still crumpled and babyish with sleep, he'd padded alongside her obediently; only when she'd guided him to sit on Ursula's bed, had he blinked, realisation gathering in his eyes. Then she'd gently woken Ursula, and once she'd helped her daughter to sit up, Beatrice had taken their hands and broken the news, and it would have been less awful to thrust her own hands through glass. There was no blood, no bruises, nothing broken. But inside everything had been wrenched askew, every bone hollowed, every organ punctured, each drop of blood tainted by gall, and all the more bitter because Beatrice knew she had wrought this invisible damage on her children too.

And then? What did you do with the rest of the day after you'd learned your father was dead? She had a vague memory of the day Florence's mother died, ushering Florence out into the garden in the hope that she would play as normal, that the little girl might skip, dance, hide. But Florence had merely stood in the middle of the laven-der hedges, stiff in her peach brocade, hands limp, as if Beatrice had abandoned her on a desert island. Then what? Surely she hadn't left Florence there for long. Had they read a story? Gone for a ride? She couldn't recall. Perhaps it had simply been something so mundane as to be forgettable. And so Beatrice flung herself into the mundane.

There were clothes to don. Faces to scrub, breakfasts to eat. Yes, the bodies coaxed into kirtles and doublets were shaking with sobs, the faces shining with salt, the breakfasts listlessly picked at. But what was the alternative? Collapse? Madness? Beatrice shivered at the thought. They wanted to believe her mad; she couldn't give them any excuse.

They were still at the table in the hall, Walter quietly picking at pastry flakes, Ursula staring numbly at her buttered roll, when Catalina came in. Dressed in a soft woollen robe the colour of pomegranate seeds, her black curls loosely bound with a sapphire-blue ribbon, she looked too bright, offensively warm. And after Catalina's deception last night, Beatrice wanted to hurl the butter dish in her face.

'What are you doing here?'

Catalina came slowly to the table and squeezed Walter's shoulder, a gesture that would have seemed cursory, brusque, from anyone else, but from Catalina it was gentle reassurance and heartfelt compassion. Then she lowered herself into the seat beside Ursula and slipped an arm around her shoulders. Immediately, Ursula flung herself into Catalina's embrace, burying her face against the pink wool.

'I'm here for breakfast,' Catalina said, 'and to comfort the children.'

Was there a challenge in her voice? Or simple honesty? Beatrice had never been able to read Catalina, and didn't have the heart to try now.

'I am not just here for the children,' Catalina continued, stroking Ursula's fair hair. 'Remember, I too know what it is to lose a husband.'

Beatrice glanced away, fixing her gaze on the manchet loaf she was picking at. White crumbs littered her plate, sifting like maggots.

'And I also know,' Catalina said quietly, 'what it is to be doubted by men.'

Beatrice jerked up in surprise. Was Catalina saying what Beatrice thought she was?

'It is so much easier,' Catalina said, 'for them to accuse us of lying. To say our grief has unsettled our minds. But for those who have never been threatened, the concept of danger can seem so outlandish as to be wholly fantastical. They would rather we be mad than that their world be influenced by things they cannot control.'

Beatrice glanced at Walter, not wanting him to hear this discussion, to realise what his uncles were accusing his mother of, lest he start to believe it. 'Are you saying you … you do believe me?'

Catalina toyed with a lark pasty. 'They say the stars can tell our future. That elaborate charts full of distant moons and constellations and planets can foretell our entire lives.'

Beatrice shivered, remembering Nicholas speaking of various forms of divination. How *had* he learned of such things? His naturally voracious curiosity – or something darker?

'I do not know if that is true,' Catalina continued. 'But supposedly wise men believe it. Why should that be any more plausible than a painted globe warning you of danger?'

Warning. Something nagged at Beatrice's mind, and her hand strayed to the crescent fragment tucked into her pocket. But before she could think further, there came a knock at the door, and Ridley entered.

If she'd been angry at Catalina's entrance, now she was furious. After everything she'd confided in Ridley – after she'd *kissed* him – that he should not only doubt her, but confess his doubts to her kinsmen was an unforgivable treachery.

'You dare show your face here, Master Ridley? I thought you bold; I did not realise you were also foolish.'

Ridley merely bowed, implacable. Was what she'd taken for calmness actually insolence? His composure, calculation? 'Forgive the intrusion, madam – and that I have not attended you sooner. I've sent messengers to the coroner, and to the verger at All Saints, as well as to certain among Sir Hugh's friends.'

'You had no right –'

'I thought it would help, madam.' He met her eyes, and his were molten with silent apologies and restrained tenderness. 'I genuinely – everything I have done has been in the hope of helping you. But …'

'But what?' She kept her voice civil, loath to frighten her children. 'You thought slandering me might somehow be to my benefit? That a ruined reputation would comfort me? That gossiping behind my back could dry my tears?'

'No,' Ridley said quietly, sounding almost lost. 'I only … I was only going to say that Lady Rich is here.'

Striding down the corridor, Beatrice tried to think of anyone she would wish to greet less than Lady Rich. Plague victims. Cannibals. Her nephew and brother-in-law. But even if she had not been mourning her husband, the Earl of Essex's haughty sister would never be eagerly welcomed. Especially after Beatrice's embarrassing visit to Essex House.

Ridley had ushered Lady Rich into the gallery, and Beatrice felt sick at the thought of returning there. Had Ridley seen the damage she'd inflicted on the globe? Had Lady Rich? But when she entered the gallery and her eyes shot straight to the globe, the hole was hidden from view. As if the thing had turned its face away, to slumber, perhaps, or scheme. Or as if to hide any evidence that might be used to prove Beatrice mad. Yet that would be a kindness, surely, and why would the globe be kind?

She was still staring at the globe when Lady Rich spoke, her cool, clipped voice like cut diamonds.

'Forgive the intrusion, Lady Radclyffe. I understand you will be in no humour for entertaining guests. But I –'

'Understand?' Blinking, Beatrice turned to see Lady Rich standing by the fireplace. Garbed in dark green, she looked like a growth of ivy that had twined its way inside, gleaming and sinuous and warping all she touched. 'Your husband I believe to be hale and hearty. Unless lightning struck Essex House last night, or Baron Rich's horse threw him into a gutter, or he finally challenged your lover to a duel and took Mountjoy's bullet through his heart, I do not think you can claim to understand what it is to lose your husband to senseless violence.'

Lady Rich glanced down, toying with her rings. 'In law, I grant you, I am no widow. But it's no secret that I have never loved my husband. Or that the man I did love was lost to, as you term it, senseless violence.' She stepped closer to Beatrice, lips curving bitterly. 'Eleven years, one month and thirteen days ago, Philip Sidney died of his wounds at Zutphen. And I was not there. His wife was, of course – the rather forgettable Frances, who somehow became my brother's wife four years later. But I had no chance to say goodbye to Philip, to hold his hand or kiss his lips, or even share a smile knowing it was the final time. So yes, Lady Radclyffe, I do understand. I, more than any other woman, know what loss and grief and rage are wracking you now. And you may not believe me, but since I know the vileness of such feelings, I do offer you my sincerest condolences.' She took Beatrice's hands in hers; the long white fingers were less like the marble she'd expected, and more like rosewater bathing her skin. 'Sir Hugh was a good man. He will be greatly missed.'

'I ...' Beatrice swallowed, trying to summon up some infuriation to stop the tears threatening to spill. 'Thank you, Lady Rich.'

Lady Rich pressed her hands gently. 'I must ask, though ... did he happen to mention the gold before he died?'

'The – what?' Beatrice shook her head, any fears of weeping vanished. 'Gold?'

'Precisely. The gold.' Lady Rich's smile was strained, like a lace veil pulled taut. 'Specifically, its location.'

Beatrice stared at her, exasperation warring with bewilderment. 'Have you lost your wits?'

'Quite the opposite, I assure you.' The fingers tightened; the smile quivered. 'Robert says Sir Hugh made it quite plain that only you would know where he had hidden it. If Robert had realised it would be his last opportunity to ask –'

'Well, I do not,' Beatrice snapped. 'Still less do I care!' She wrenched her hands out of Lady Rich's grip. 'Don't expect me to believe that the Essex fortunes are so imminently imperilled that you think I must provide you with some sort of treasure trove! That you couldn't wait even one day to come treasure hunting, like some deluded jackdaw!'

'You don't understand!' Lady Rich hissed. 'It isn't the coin so much as what King James and Queen Elizabeth believe about the gold! My fool of a brother has promised it to both of them, and your husband has hidden it somewhere, and if the secret died with him we are all not only ruined, but bound for the Tower – and I pray God not the block!' She clutched at Beatrice's sleeve, her desperate grimace cracking the fine white powder on her forehead. 'So please, Lady Radclyffe, tell me your husband wasn't lying! Tell me you know where he hid the Spanish gold!'

'I –'

Beatrice couldn't think clearly; the woman seethed with lavender laced with bergamot: stifling, sharp, stinging. This was impossible – terrifying and impossible. A conspiracy involving both the Queen of England and the King of Scotland – how could Hugh have become entangled with something so hazardous? How could he not have told her? He'd confessed so much – one more secret ought not to have stuck in his throat. Yet this was not just one man's guilt – it was potentially treason. And when a man was labelled a traitor, his entire family was attainted along with him. His titles, lands, goods – all became forfeit to the Crown. Surely Hugh wouldn't have done that to her – or to Walter and Ursula.

'Lady Rich, I –'

The woman's nails pinched, and Beatrice glanced down in pain and irritation.

And then something caught her eye. Lady Rich's ring. Not the diamonds surrounded by tiny sapphires, or the amethysts set in scrolled gold, or the ruby nestled in the cluster of pearls, but the least jewelled of them all. A signet ring, embossed with a coat of arms: a shield with three circles above a broad bar. *Torteaux*, she thought distantly, *and a fess*. Like three suns hovering above a horizon, a pattern she'd seen once sketched in ink, and once imprinted on the bruised flesh of a murdered woman.

Maria's killer had worn this ring. The person who'd commanded Simon to paint different cartouches on Hugh's globe had worn this ring. She'd assumed it had to be a man, but now, feeling Lady Rich's fingers tighten on her flesh, Beatrice was no longer so certain.

Striving to keep her voice level, Beatrice said, 'That ring – those arms. What are they?'

'What?' Lady Rich glanced down impatiently. 'They're the Devereux arms, our family crest. But –'

'Who else has one?'

Lady Rich's grip tightened, and she looked about to shake Beatrice in rage. 'Any Devereux of course! My brother, my sister Dorothy, any long-lost cousins from Normandy in the Conqueror's reign for all I know! What does it matter?'

Beatrice stared at Lady Rich's hand. Long, slender white fingers lacing around Beatrice's arm like tightening stays. Nails smooth half-moons, the wrist bones delicate as porcelain. Tendons rose like eel backs beneath blue-veined white, sinuous, rippling. Could these hands have closed around Maria's neck, choked the life out of her? Could they close around Beatrice's? Lavender surged against her nostrils, her throat. It would be on Lady Rich's wrists, that delicate blue, the scent bleeding onto Beatrice's clothes.

'I want you to leave,' she heard herself say. 'Leave now.'

'Don't be so hasty.' Lady Rich's voice dropped, low and dangerous. 'You cannot hope to keep secrets from me. And you are a fool if you think you can hide the gold from a queen and a king.'

'And you are a fool if you think I have the slightest idea of – or interest in – what you are talking about.' The retort clattered like thrown dice: decisive, victorious. Hiding how close she was to losing the game. Beatrice wrenched her arm away with a defiance she could not convince herself she felt. 'Show some dignity, Lady Rich, and go home.'

Lady Rich's eyes narrowed. Contemptuously, she released Beatrice's arm, as if discarding a soiled handkerchief. 'Forgive me if I do not choose to be advised on dignity by a woman of such low breeding.' Despite her words, she took a step back: retreating, or recoiling? 'You will change your mind, Lady Radclyffe. And when you do, you will come to me. Or else, when treason becomes the word whispered in every alley, every tavern, every shadow, I will know where to send the hunters.'

'Knowledge I share,' Beatrice countered.

Lady Rich's smile curved like a scythe. 'Dead men cannot testify in their own defence. As for their widows … few will flock to their side if those of royal blood are arrayed on the other. An earl, or a merchant's daughter? We both know who would be believed.' She held Beatrice's gaze a moment longer. 'My goodness, Lady Radclyffe, the venom in your eyes would out-glare a cockatrice!'

Beatrice froze. A coincidence? Or a warning? That she knew what was on the globe – and *why* it was on the globe. And if she knew that, then … How easy would it have been for Lady Rich to acquire her father's letters? Essex and his sister probably kept an informer in every house in London – Essex had said himself that there were spies every-where, and one of his former employees was currently dwelling in Beatrice's house, helping to care for her children. Surely Catalina wasn't still working for the Essex circle?

Or was she leaping to conclusions? *Bee-in-a-trice, quick to sting, quick to fall.*

'Naturally, I understand that you are not in the right frame of mind to consider my proposition with anything resembling appropriate rationality,' Lady Rich said silkily. 'Nevertheless, the offer remains. My deepest condolences, Lady Radclyffe.' Then, with a curl of her lip and a billow of bergamot and lavender, she was gone.

Beatrice didn't move. Didn't turn. Didn't let herself look at the globe she knew would be turning, creaking like a gibbet in the wind, the rattle and rustle the voices of bones beneath a shroud.

26

The river had frozen. Overnight, while she'd huddled in a chair on the corridor, eyes burning from trying to spy threats through shadows and tears? Or perhaps during the day, ice creeping in the wake of Lady Penelope's barge as if the stern itself were the source of the cold? But no – Beatrice shook herself irritably – Lady Rich couldn't have come by barge, nor was someone so self-important likely to have donned bone skates to swoop down on Chelsea. She would have ridden. Which was further, and less stately – both of which made Lady Rich's fears more frightening, and her threats more threatening. There had been an urgency in the noblewoman's voice and eyes that Beatrice recognised, might even have pitied: the desperation to be believed. To not be dismissed as mad.

And perhaps the easiest way to deflect accusations of madness was to turn them on someone else. Someone less noble, less powerful. Someone like Beatrice.

She was not mad. She could not be. But that could only mean the world had gone mad. Noblewomen spouting conspiracies and accusations, globes foretelling dire prophecies, her kin plotting to throw her in Bedlam, and maddest of all, Hugh lying dead, the mark of a murderer on his skin.

She hadn't left the gallery, wasn't certain how long she'd stood here, gazing out at her frost-rimed garden, the artemisia whitening to mist, the fountain glistening as if a thousand pearl necklaces had shattered across its stone. Beyond, the river, halted in ice, reeds clenched in frozen fists, caught ripples splayed across the surface like a drowned woman's hair. How far did the ice go? It had never occurred to her to wonder before, still less to follow the glittering white road all the way to its end – and what would that be? Ice crunching against the stanchions of Tower Bridge, the rapids pummelling it into white fragments like punched teeth. A slow thinning, shadows blooming underfoot, eels mouthing against your footsteps, the river's glassy skin trembling between you – and then a sudden gape into which you'd plunge, too fast to scream. Or else a frayed edge, white tattering above the dark water like the broken wings of a swan. And then water, ebbing, flowing, turning and rising, falling and returning, blue and silver and ink and dusk, until somewhere in the far north it became ice again and great white bears prowled the jagged landscape in search of slick-skinned seals, and perhaps somewhere in that distant cold lay the pale bones of a boy, flesh long torn away by ravenous jaws. Only the brown threads of English wool, tangled about his shinbones, the scraps of yellowed kersey about his ribcage revealing to the vast and silent sky that here had died a boy who should have lived. Or had Ben's body slipped from the ice floe, dislodged by storm-barged waves, into salt-water, sinking down to the seabed where fish who had never known daylight nibbled his bones bare, and his skull stared blindly up at a black gulf?

Beatrice caught her own reflection in the window: was it the glass rendering her so gaunt, or her maudlin thoughts? Or grief? Maria had had to cajole her to eat after her mother's death, and the gowns she'd just grown into had become too loose for even the tightest lacing to pull them against her ribs. But that had been weeks. Not days. In any case, what did it matter if her skin shrank below her bones? Hugh was dead and no one would ever again whisper against her neck that she was beautiful.

'Lady Radclyffe?'

She started, clattering her forehead against the latticed window. Wincing, irritable with embarrassment, she turned with a sharp dismissal on her tongue – and stopped.

'Simon! Why, I'd –' *Almost forgotten*, she thought, not wanting to probe her absent-mindedness too closely. Let it be due to distraction, and not to anything worse. 'I'd not expected you to come unannounced.'

The apprentice was twisting his blue hat in both hands as if he could wring out his shyness like water. 'I'm sorry, madam. I didn't know – I didn't realise you were – your husband was – that is, my master wouldn't let me out of his sight until today. It's my half-day and the river's froze, so I had to walk, and the ice was so slippery and I wasn't sure I could trust it, it being so new, so I only inched along –'

'You walked here on the ice? All the way from Lambeth?'

Simon shook his head, and his unruly hair flailed against his ears and eyebrows. 'Only across.'

'But … why not wait until it had melted? Or go east to cross the bridge?'

'Maybe I should have done.' He swallowed. 'But I didn't want to be … Besides I wanted to give you this as soon as I could.' He dug in his cloak pocket, almost dropping his hat in the process, and thrust out a piece of parchment towards her, realised she couldn't reach it, and scurried forwards. On another day, in another life, Beatrice might have laughed. Florence would have, Lady Rich too, probably. But she was stripped bare of mirth.

Before she unfolded the parchment, Beatrice frowned. 'Why the urgency, Simon? I know why I needed this soon, but not why you felt the need to risk new ice to bring it.'

Simon glanced over his shoulder as if someone might have followed him and be stalking through the gardens even now. 'Kitson's back in London. I've seen him. Master Molyneux sent me to the Royal Exchange to get more indigo, and I saw him there, talking with – with the person who made me paint your globe different.' His eyes darted to the globe, then away, then back, as if its hulking body might be concealing Kitson and his employer.

'I thought you said you never saw his face? And that his only distinguishing feature was that he smelled of frankincense. How would you discern that at the spice stalls?'

'It was the way they stood – the way they moved. I didn't realise how much I'd noticed – Master Molyneux schools us to watch people's stances, how they lift their arms and tilt their heads. But I had noticed, and when I saw them together at the Exchange, I realised – and I should have known it all along, except ...'

'Except what?' Beatrice shook her head impatiently. 'Tell me!'

'It wasn't a man who paid me,' Simon whispered. 'It was a lady.'

Lady Rich.

Something rustled – not the globe, for once, but the paper in her hand. She was shaking, Beatrice observed, frightened at how detached her own body seemed from her thoughts, from any chance she might control it. Forcing her other hand to seize the paper, Beatrice unfolded it, willing her hands to pull it taut, so taut it almost ripped in her two. The words swam, black eels whipping after black minnows.

The drowned woman, gowned in crimson.

The mermaid and her harlot reflection.

The abandoned boy.

The cockatrice strangling a bear.

The captain and his Moor.

The robins capturing a swan.

The abandoned boy.

'You've put this twice,' Beatrice said, irritability a relief after the real-isation that Lady Rich was behind all this, had truly been plotting against her, that Beatrice wasn't mad. 'Did you mean to put something else? Is there another image I should know about?'

'No.' Simon shook his head. 'There are two. She said there had to be two. One on the ice, and one –' He broke off, his eyes widening in horror.

'What?'

And then she heard it. The rustling she'd thought was her own trem-bling hands was growing louder, faster. In its wake, the whirr, click. Whirr, click.

'What's happening? What's making it move?'

'You tell me!' Beatrice snapped. 'You made the damned thing – you put my father and mother's writing into it. Does Molyneux teach you necromancy along with painting?'

'I never – I didn't!' Simon clutched at her sleeve, his ink-stained fingers scrabbling, like elongated maggots. 'I didn't know they were your parents' words! She just told me those were the papers I had to use!'

'And what else?' Beatrice demanded. 'You put all kinds of papers in your globes, no doubt – the deeds to a bakehouse wouldn't turn the globe into a loaf of bread! What else did you do to mine?'

Simon tried to seize her hand; she wrenched it away. 'You have to forgive me! I've never done it before – I'll never do it again! I'm sorry, I'm so sorry –'

'For what? You damned fool, what have you done?'

'*Blood.*' Simon's voice cracked. 'She bade me mix the ink with blood.'

Beatrice recoiled. 'Who – whose blood?'

'I didn't know! I just thought it would be pigs' blood – something from the shambles – I didn't think it could be –'

Black magic.

Using blood in divination – what had Nicholas called it? Haruspicy, anthropomancy – he'd told her about a variety of fortune telling methods. She knew Nicholas read endlessly, about all manner of things – but what if his reading had a purpose beyond eclectic fascination? She'd wondered how Lady Rich could possibly have got hold of her father's letters, her mother's recipes – could Hugh's mild-mannered, scholarly brother have been conspiring with Lady Rich? And when he'd protested that the science of divination was advocated by Brahe and Hemmingsen, had that been his scholarly pride, offended that doubt had been cast on his methods?

Simon's hands dropped, trembling too much to grip her, and Beatrice backed away in horror, as if she could get away from his confession – from her suspicions.

'You laid a curse,' Beatrice breathed. 'You laid a curse on my house – you and her –'

'No!' Simon shook his head frantically. 'I just painted the pictures I was told to –'

Whirr. Click.

Silence.

The globe had stopped. But Simon's look of horror hadn't vanished; if anything, he'd gone whiter, his eyes more frenzied. Beatrice turned to see the gaping hole she'd torn in the globe, yawning wide like a dark mouth. There was a stench like mould, like rotten meat. A low groan: it might have been wood creaking, or jaws stretching.

'What have you done?' Simon gasped. 'You – you've butchered it!'

'Did you expect me to treasure it?' Beatrice snapped. 'If I hadn't broken it, I'd never have realised what you hid behind your blood paintings!'

'But it's not dead,' Simon whispered. 'Only wounded.'

'It's not a beast –' Beatrice stopped.

Because it was. Of course it was. Not a bull-gored hound, or a goaded bear, nor even something fantastical, a thrice-beheaded hydra, a Minotaur bleeding from Theseus's sword blows – but something that frightened Beatrice far more. Someone who had locked a woman away to die, who had always lashed out hardest when provoked. Who had laughed at his daughter's defiance.

And whose spirit would have every reason to wish Beatrice ill.

Creak.

'It's moving again,' Simon breathed, but there was no need for words. Beatrice could see, even as she wished she couldn't, wished she could deny the evidence of her own eyes. But there it was: the globe, tilting, left, back, right, back. Rocking from side to side, each creak like barked scorn. Like the mocking laughter of a large man.

Arthur.

'May God forgive me!' Simon blurted out. He turned to run, and it was Beatrice's turn to seize him.

'Wait! You said there were two abandoned boys. One on the ice – but what of the other?'

'I'm sorry.' Simon shook himself free. 'He's in the water.'

Water?

Walter.

Beatrice stared at him, aghast. Then she fell to her knees before the globe and pressed her palms to it, trying to still its rocking so she could search. Behind her, she heard stumbling footsteps: Simon fleeing. She'd wanted to ask him so much more – but the questions all dropped from her mind like discarded bones. There was only one thing that mattered now.

She'd looked for water before, had scowled at a world half-covered in seas. But she knew exactly what she was looking for now.

There. In England, in London, an image so tiny it must have been painted by a boy with young eyes squinting through a magnifying glass, so tiny it could only be found by a desperate mother so close to the globe her breath was hot and damp against its curved flesh.

There was a boy in the River Thames.

27

'Walter!'

Beatrice raced through the corridor, hurling herself at the stairs, her brocade skirts hideously cumbersome, slapping at her knees and feet as if about to trip her. Where was her son? She'd last seen him at the table, uncharacteristically uninterested in his breakfast, but how many hours ago was that? Beyond the windows, dusk was pressing down, shadows lowering like hands pushing you underwater: between Lady Rich and Simon's visits, to say nothing of the hours lost to grief and worrying, the day had dwindled away. How long did she have left to find her son before he went into the frozen Thames?

She burst through door after door, her cries echoing in empty rooms. He wasn't in the schoolroom. What nine-year-old boy would be, the day after his father's death? Nor in the deserted hall. Had he sought solace in the kitchens? Warmth, food: you could briefly convince yourself those were enough to fill the gaping hole inside you, that happiness tasted like a piecrust oozing gravy, that licking sugar from your fingertips would smooth the edges of your grief.

But the kitchen was empty, cold cuts laid out beneath muslin on the table, and she couldn't fathom why for a moment. Had they all gone to church? Had Walter gone too, to pray for his father's soul? Surely not: Walter spent church services jostling his sister and covering up certain letters in the hymn book with his fingers to form rude words and make Ursula get scolded for sniggering during the sermon.

He'd be in his room. He had to be. Solitude, blankets, his pewter knights – if there was any comfort to be had when his mother had abandoned him to talk to unwelcome guests, he might have found it in recreating Thermopylae beneath his tented bedcovers. She clattered up the stairs, retracing her steps along the corridor, her home a labyrinth she could no longer navigate.

'Walter!' She'd barely turned the handle before barging the door open: it stuck, jolted, and then she staggered through into her son's bedchamber.

His Robin Hood puppet lay on the pillow, limbs askew, as if Walter had flung him there. She rounded the bed: perhaps he'd hidden behind it like he'd used to do when he first slept in his own room, giggling so loudly he revealed his hiding place. There were his toy boats on the windowsill, each one capsized; the walrus tusk Hugh had given him lying in the midst of the toppled boats, as if they'd all been hulled by a white sea monster. Toys, books, kicked off shoes, a silent lute, the hobby horse he'd long outgrown, his favourite bits of coral pilfered from the curiosity cabinet: all Walter's things, but no Walter himself. Could he be in Ursula's room? She spun to leave – and realised that the room wasn't empty at all.

Ridley sat in the chair before the fireplace, one ankle crossed over his knee. The way Hugh had sat in that very chair to read Walter tales of Odysseus, Walter in his nightshirt, bare toes wiggling on Hugh's leg, cackling if he got them stuck in Hugh's slashed breeches. Now, seeing Ridley there, Beatrice wanted to shove him out of the chair, out of the way of her memory.

'What are you doing here? Where's Walter?'

'You won't find him here.'

Ridley smiled: a slow, barely curved smile that was almost a sneer. Those same lips that had once touched her: all tenderness was gone now. Her own mouth tingled as if pocked with nettle stings, and Beatrice felt suddenly cold.

'Where is he?'

'By now? Surrounded by ice, and perhaps even rimed with it himself, I imagine.'

Ridley was dangling his keys from one finger; he gave them a slow swing and brass tolled against iron. Beatrice abruptly realised the empty silence at her waist: her own chatelaine wasn't there. She must have left it in her bedchamber. And suddenly the idea that Ridley was the only one with the keys to her house no longer seemed reassuring, but utterly terrifying.

'Or else beneath it.' Again Ridley swung the keys mockingly. 'But either way, even more poetic than I could have imagined.'

'I haven't time for riddles,' Beatrice snapped. 'Where is my son?'

How often had she asked Ridley that question, trusting the answer would be that he'd allowed Walter to help groom the horses, or play with the hounds? Now she dreaded what Ridley would reveal.

'Where do you think?' Ridley leaned forward. 'He's on the eyot. Abandoned in the ice – just as your husband abandoned my brother.'

'Your brother?' Beatrice shook her head, confused. 'No – Ben was Kitson's brother.'

Ridley's lip curled in disgust. 'You rich folk truly do care nothing for those who serve you. Minions, slaves – that's all we are. You knew nothing about Maria, for all you claim to have adored her, and you know nothing of me.'

He was right, she realised. She knew he loved horses. Smelled of cedarwood. That he was always there when she needed him. But she'd had no idea such malice festered beneath his dark eyes.

'Nor did the great Sir Hugh Radclyffe know anything of the boy he left to die.' Ridley rose, stalking towards her. A wooden knight snapped under his boot, and she was horribly aware that he was now between her and the door. 'Ben Kitson was my half-brother. He was everything Anthony isn't – kind, generous, affectionate, clever.' He bit off each word as if he wanted to tear chunks out of her flesh. 'Of course, Anthony lacking those qualities has its benefits. Tell him where and when to strike his axe, and if there's enough coin for ale and whores in it, he'll topple any beech you like.'

Bile rose in her throat. 'It was you. You killed Hugh – you tried to kill me –'

'And you know how greatly I dislike leaving tasks unfinished.'

He swung the keys again, and she realised just how much damage so much metal in the fist of an angry man could do to a woman's skull.

She had to keep him talking. Keep him distracted, and then edge towards the door.

'How long have you despised us? Have you been nursing this grudge in secret for four years?'

He laughed coldly. How had she ever imagined his laughter to be gentle? This was raven-coarse, bitter as gall. 'Words only a rich woman could utter. You may think yourself a fine and generous mistress, admired, respected, even liked by your servants. But trust me, they all bear grudges towards you. Every curt command, every time you count pennies into their hands with fingers that gleam with jewels; every time they wash your sweat and grime out of linen so fine they'd never touch it otherwise; every time they serve you syllabubs and marchpane and saffron-dusted meat before they have to scrape the end of a stew onto stale trenches, to say nothing of your pathetic obsession with lavender – every time they curse your name.' His eyes narrowed. 'I hated you when I worked in your stables. I hated you when your husband employed my half-brothers without realising we were kin. Even though I'd recommended them in the first place, he forgot everything about them other than what knots they could tie and how fast they could climb the rigging. I hated you when you appointed me your steward and expected me to be grateful. I have always despised you, and when your husband turned out to be a murderer as well as a popinjay, I discovered I could loathe you even more.'

Beatrice inched sideways as he spoke, her feet barely moving beneath her farthingale, keeping her eyes on Ridley's. 'Since you'll be in need of new employment before sunset, perhaps you'd consider a career on the stage. To kiss a woman you loathe requires immense skills of deception.'

He sneered, and it was like seeing a favoured hound turn rabid: that trusted softness, those loyal eyes, now impossible to discern beyond the foaming jaws and slavering tongue. 'Oh, Beatrice. Did you think I loved you? That I'd worshipped you from afar, treasuring every moment I was permitted to slide your little foot into a stirrup, each time our hands brushed as you handed me keys and coins? That was exactly what she said you'd believe.'

'She?' Beatrice almost tripped over her own ankles. Carefully, she resumed her incremental glide. Was he about to confess Lady Rich's involvement?

'Wrack her with guilt, she said,' Ridley continued, relishing each revelation as if he was slicing it into her skin. 'She's so pathetically lonely she'll clutch at any affection, but you'll never win her away from her husband. You can just ruin their last days together. And then, when she wants you to confess – deny it all.'

'I thought you didn't want to hurt Hugh,' Beatrice said weakly, horrified at this harsh reflection of herself.

'Now you know I wanted nothing more than to hurt him,' Ridley retorted. 'Which is why I whispered the truth into his ear as I smothered him.'

Oh, Hugh. She couldn't bear to picture it. 'You utter bastard.'

'I've been called worse.' He stepped closer, cutting off her escape. 'You'll call me worse before she and I are done with you. But the beauty of her scheme is that no one will believe you.'

'What? I don't –'

'You do. You're no fool – which is why what happens next will hurt you so deeply. Deeply, but not fatally. She wants you to suffer. I thought your husband despising you for a harlot until his last breath would suffice – but no. There's another punishment she deems more fitting for you.'

Bedlam. How had Lady Rich found out? Had Ridley somehow discovered her secret? Had he, or his brother Kitson – the revelation still sickened her – beaten it out of Maria before murdering her?

'I told her she'd be disappointed,' Ridley continued, toying with the keys as if imagining each one unlocking her skin from her bones. 'That you might be a selfish, mercenary bitch, but you were nothing if not level-headed. But she insisted. Madness is in your blood. And whether she's right or not, you've made it so easy for us to prove you out of your wits. Railing about haunted globes and conspiracies and paintings that foretell disaster ... why, I could almost believe it myself.'

'Then perhaps yours are the wits in doubt,' Beatrice hissed. Some part of herself was astonished that she could still scratch – but they were the swipes of a cat cornered by hounds, running out of room to swing. He'd backed her up against the windowsill now; she heard the curtains whisper against her skirts, felt the wooden sill jab her spine.

'Perhaps we won't even need to tell the world about our little tryst,' Ridley mused, running one key along her jawline; its teeth bit her chin. 'The plan was always for me to deny it. One more outlandish claim, further evidence of your delusions … But if your gaolers and nurse-maids don't know, perhaps they'll let me visit you in your cell. The devoted servant – it's a role I play well, you must admit. I can remind you every month – or fortnight – or week, how easily duped you were. How you willingly opened your doors, and your lips, to your own undoing. Maybe even your legs will open for me in Bedlam. After all, you'll be starved of love, of information about your children's wellbeing, if indeed they remain well – you might long for my visits. My touch.'

'You repulsive braggart,' Beatrice spat. 'Do you think I enjoyed your touch? Do you imagine for one moment that anything you do to any woman, let alone me, could ever have compared to Hugh? You were a mistake. A moment of madness – my only one. There was no desire in that encounter in the stables. Only loneliness. And I would rather never feel a man's touch again than endure yours for even a single breath.'

Ridley's face twisted in rage. 'What you would rather, I'm afraid, is wholly irrelevant.' He suddenly leaned forward, jerking his hand up to scrape the smallest, sharpest key's teeth down her neck, across her collarbone. She felt skin rip, the sting of blood beading. 'She said I couldn't kill you. But she never ruled out carving my brother's name into your flesh a hundred times. I'll enjoy that infinitely more than forcing myself to kiss your desiccated lips again.' He eyed her throat, her shoulders, then pressed the key against her breastbone. 'I'll start here, I think. Above your shrivelled heart.'

The key gouged deeper. And then a deafening crack split the air.

For a moment she thought her ribcage had split. Then Ridley grunted. His face clenched in confusion, pain, thwarted fury – and he slumped to the floor, a black-scorched hole in his back. Behind him stood Catalina, a pistol in each hand, one cocked and smoking, the other held firm across her pregnant belly, as if reassuring the baby, who would no doubt be vigorously kicking at the noise.

'Catalina,' Beatrice gasped, trying to fathom this latest shock, her guest appearing as half-Madonna, half-pirate. In her bewilderment, she asked the least constructive question. 'Where did you learn how to fire a pistol?'

Catalina arched an eyebrow, as if the answer were obvious. 'Hugh taught me. I might not have been able to shoot my own rapist in the gut, but damned if I'll let any man do that to any woman again. Least of all Hugh's widow.'

'Thank you,' Beatrice whispered. And then the horrible truth came surging back. 'He took Walter – he's left him stranded on the eyot! I have to rescue him!'

Catalina nodded, unflappable. 'Then you'd best take this.' She stepped over Ridley's corpse and handed Beatrice her other pistol. 'I'll reload this one and stand guard over Ursula – she'll have been frightened by the retort.'

Guilt wracked Beatrice. 'I should –'

'I'll take care of her.' Catalina pressed her free hand to Beatrice's cheek. 'No one will harm your daughter while I have shot and powder. After your husband's teaching, I could hit a gull in the crow's nest, never mind a brute coming through the door. Trust me.'

Beatrice hadn't thought she could ever say those words again. But here, now, there seemed nothing more natural than to say, 'I trust you.'

'Aim for the guts,' Catalina said. 'You're less likely to miss, and they'll die slowly. Now go and save your son.'

28

The pistol hung from her shaking hand, awkward as a broken bone as Beatrice edged out into the garden. She didn't know how to hold it, whether to brandish or cradle it, for her grip to be firm or ginger, which was more likely to set it off accidentally. As for firing it … But she thought of Walter and her resolve tightened. Anyone who stood between her and her son would be easier to shoot than a stag at arm's length.

She felt moisture prick against the broken skin at her neck, tried to convince herself the cold was steeling her, not cowing her. Ahead, a rising white tide of mist seeped through the garden. The blueberry shrubs were shadowed grey humps and hooks, like the sloughed skin of enormous serpents. She picked her way through them, her footsteps crunching the gravel like eggshells, too loud. There were too many shadows looming behind the mist, and now, despite having trod these gardens every day of her life, she couldn't remember where everything was, or should be. That hulk: a fountain, or an intruder, a rose bush or Kitson?

The ground suddenly dropped away and she stumbled, almost dropping the pistol. Her heart pounded her ribcage; her stomach lurched. But it was just the edge of the parterre, the steps down onto the lawn. Something gleamed to her right, and she'd raised the pistol before recognising a croquet hoop, moisture pearling on the iron, a mallet abandoned beside it. Walter must have set up the game – or Ridley had helped him, for a nine-year-old boy would have struggled to hammer anything into frost-stiffened earth. Helped him, comforted him with distractions, then betrayed him, luring him out onto the eyot. He'd be cold now, so cold, and so frightened, and the thought wrenched at her.

She didn't dare hurry – there'd be other hoops lurking in the grass, and she was certain that somewhere in her grounds, Kitson was waiting for her. He'd be in the boathouse if he had any brains – no better place to hide. Or else the orchard. Or waiting on the eyot with Walter, a gun to his temple.

Or behind her, matching his every step to hers.

Suddenly an arm snaked around her neck, squeezing tight. One hand clamped over her mouth; she smelled sweat and stale beer and meat, and she couldn't retch, couldn't breathe, and even as the thought repulsed her, she bit hard.

'Bitch!'

Choking, spitting blood, Beatrice tried to turn. But one hand was on her forehead, the other on her chin: he was going to snap her neck. She fumbled, thrust the pistol behind her – and fired.

A grunt. A bubbling sound. The hands scrabbled at her face, suddenly weak, and she flung herself forward, away. Her wrist flared with pain, as if a horse had kicked her, and she dropped the pistol, gasping, cradling her arm against her belly.

Behind her, a large man had slumped to his knees, one hand clutching at the blood oozing from his belly, the other trying to draw the blade at his hip. His black hat tumbled to the ground; his black mask had slipped down, revealing a bearded face that was a swarthier version of Ridley's. Kitson.

'A woman,' Kitson coughed in disgust – and fear. Not a highwayman, not a mercenary, not even a pickpocket: this hardened man had been slain by a mere woman.

Beatrice took two steps forward and kicked hard at his wrist, driving it back so she could snatch the blade from his belt. 'Not just any woman,' she snapped, thrusting the blade tip against his eye socket. 'Maria's friend. May you rot in hell for what you did to her.'

Kitson collapsed backwards, partly to get away from his own dagger, more because the blood was now gouting thick and scarlet between his fingers. 'For Ben,' he rasped. 'For my brother.'

'Liar.' Beatrice shook her head. 'If it was for him, you'd have challenged my husband in broad daylight. But murdering Maria, attacking me, threatening my children? That was for you. For coin. For swelling your pride.' She kicked him again, this time in the groin, and he groaned, curling around his bleeding belly. 'Now you'll die with neither.'

She left him whimpering in the dirt, and the mist sealed up behind her. She hurried now, desperate to find Walter, to wrap him in her arms and bring him safe ashore. Somewhere beyond the mist, bells rang out, once, twice, thrice, four times. It would be dark soon, not that it would make much difference to visibility in this mist. But dark brought deeper cold, and Walter would already be half-frozen, and she was running out of time.

The ground sloped away beneath her feet, and she half-slid, half-scrambled onto the wharf. The stone was dark and slick with ice, and she stepped gingerly across it until she'd reached the edge. Ahead, ice stretched away, pale as insects' wings. Was it any more substantial? It was barely a day old; she'd never let the children venture out onto ice until it had had several days to harden.

But her own son was stranded on the other side of the ice. She had no choice.

She could just about see the eyot, a bruise-dark swelling against the pallor of mist and ice. You could swim it easily in summer if the current wasn't too strong, row it in no time at all. But inching towards it across ice was another prospect entirely.

Was he even there? The thought suddenly struck her: was this merely a ruse on Ridley's part? Had he and Lady Rich schemed to lure her out to the eyot in the hope that she'd fall through the ice and drown, and they could dismiss her death as the tragic demise of a grief-maddened woman, and deny her burial in sanctified ground? She wouldn't put it past either of them.

'Walter?' she called out, tentative, half-hoping, half-fearing to get a response. Her voice echoed against the ice, her words coins dropped into a deep well.

Nothing. Silence.

And then, a cry so plaintive she might have mistaken it for a lost lamb, bleating hopelessly. A voice weak from cold and terror and weeping. 'Mama!'

'I'm coming, Walter!' Urgency surged through her, and she stepped down onto the frozen river.

Almost immediately her left foot skidded out from under her and she clutched at the wharf just before her knees could slam into the ice. She should have stopped to don her boots: embroidered slippers were beyond inadequate. But there was no time to run back inside. There was only Walter and the need to save him.

Her breath was ragged, tattering; she pushed it out, long, slow, trying to convince herself she was calm, or at least competent. With each drawn-out breath, she glided a foot forward, not putting her weight down until she'd reached a solid white patch, avoiding any areas still mottled grey. Once she glanced back, thinking she'd heard something, and the twisting almost made her lose her balance: she had to fling her arms wide, beating at the air to catch herself before she fell. Then it was onwards again: breathe, glide, breathe, glide.

And suddenly there was the eyot: reeds blanched with frost, scrub rimed white, abandoned nests looking pale as tangled cobwebs. Beatrice fell forwards onto her knees, grateful for solid ground, grabbing cold roots and reeds to pull herself up with hands blistered red.

'Mama!'

'Walter!'

He was hunched beneath the willow, tearstained and shivering. Ropes bound his hands to the tree, and rage flared: Ridley hadn't even allowed him the chance to chafe his own limbs. She scrambled across to Walter, gathering him against her body, trying to warm his half-frozen limbs with her own numb ones, rubbing his arms, his shoulders at the same time as clutching him close.

'Mama,' Walter choked out, 'he left me! Ridley left me!'

'I know, poppet,' she murmured. 'He won't do it again, I promise.'

'He said we were playing a game. I'd be King Arthur on Avalon, and he'd be Sir Bedivere, and he took the skates and tied me up, but he said he'd come back!' Walter rubbed his face against her neck, his tears the only heat on either of them. 'I waited and waited, but he didn't come!'

'It's all right,' she whispered. 'I've got you, my darling, I've got you now. Let's go home.' She fumbled at the ropes, her fingers stiff and blunt with cold, then cursed herself for a fool: Kitson's dagger was in her pocket. She sawed urgently at Walter's bonds, terrified of catching the delicate, red-blistered skin between gloves and cuff. Three strands left – two – one – and he was free and she could haul him to his feet. But he was weak, sluggish and clumsy from cowering in the bitter cold for hours, and he stumbled against her. She'd have to half-carry him across the ice, and she didn't dare either think about or ignore what their combined weights might do to the ice. Yet what alternative was there? Walter wouldn't survive out here much longer, and neither would she, in her embroidered slippers, with no gloves.

'Come, Walter,' Beatrice coaxed. 'This way.' She helped him to the edge, then stepped down gingerly onto the ice. Did it creak, or was that the low groan of trees shifting in the wind? She drew a smile across her face to encourage Walter down. 'Hold my hand. That's it. And the other foot.'

He obeyed, mute and docile with exhaustion. Almost as soon as his right foot hit the ice, it skidded out from under him, and Walter screamed, Beatrice screamed. His fall jerked them both to their knees and she braced herself to plunge through the ice. But it held. It held.

'It's all right,' Beatrice forced herself to say, her voice thinned by false cheer. 'We're all right. Come on.'

She rose awkwardly, Walter clinging to her arm. Together they set off, stepping, gliding, Beatrice striving to keep her steps out of rhythm with Walter's in case the simultaneous blow cracked the ice.

How much further? Her shoulders and knees throbbed from tensing. The mist swirled before her and she thought of William and Ben, stranded on the ice floe, praying for a rope. Had they known only one of them would survive? Had they both condemned the other in their thoughts? Or had one of them managed to consider self-sacrifice? She doubted it. William had been little more than a boy himself, and only a mother would gladly send her child to safety while she remained stranded.

Behind the mist, lilac-grey shadows, darkening as she inched closer. The low ridge of the wharf. And waiting for them, the swoop of wide skirts, the glitter of a ruff, a jewelled hat.

Lady Rich, come to finish what her mercenaries could not. Beatrice's hand flew to Kitson's knife.

But it wasn't there. She bit back a moan of frustration and fear: she'd left it on the eyot.

Then the woman stepped forward. And it wasn't Lady Rich.

It was Florence. Relief surged up like fresh water. Robert had said she'd come today – to help with the household; if only Beatrice had known how much help she'd turn out to need.

'Thank God!' Beatrice exclaimed. 'Help me – Walter's frozen –'

Florence didn't move. A slow smile flickered at the corners of her mouth. 'I think not,' she said softly, letting her words tilt, poise, and drop, like the quiet pour of poisoned wine.

Beatrice swallowed. 'Florence,' she said carefully, 'let me take my son inside. Or at least onto the wharf. It isn't safe.'

Florence laughed. It echoed, rising like ravens startled from their nests. 'Oh, Beatrice. That's precisely the point.'

She didn't want to hear this. Didn't want to consider the possibility of this being true. It was Florence. Her Florence, the little sister she'd adorned with ribbons and trinkets.

'Whatever grievance you have with me,' Beatrice implored, 'let Walter go. He's done nothing. He's a boy.'

'Let him go?' Florence echoed. 'The late Sir Hugh Radclyffe's heir, the heir to our father's fortune? No. That would not do at all.'

Wind hissed, rattling the reeds like chattering teeth. Beatrice couldn't feel her toes anymore, couldn't feel the ice beneath her feet. She tried to shift, frightened to stand too long on one patch. Beside her, Walter moaned, beyond words now, beyond understanding, and she was angry now, angry on his behalf more than her own.

'Florence, for God's sake, help us up! Let's discuss this like civilised adults in a warm chamber with a solid floor.'

'We'll discuss it now,' Florence said, toying with something she'd drawn from her cloak pocket, twirling, spinning, tilting.

'No – the ice could crack at any moment!'

'I do hope so,' Florence said. 'It would save me having to reload.'

The object in her hand glimmered as she raised it. A pistol.

The ice creaked. Walter moaned again, and it sounded like 'Mama', but he was slumping against her, all his weight bearing down on her. Beatrice was almost glad he couldn't know what his aunt was saying, doing. What she must have done.

Another seethe of wind, and this time it flicked a scent across the bitter air. Sweet, woody, with a hint of citrus: a scent she'd grown so used to over the years that she'd ceased to notice it at all. The smell of frankincense.

'You commissioned the cartouches on Hugh's globe,' Beatrice breathed. Her accusation writhed white between them. 'You sent Kitson to kill Maria.'

'She'd seen me,' Florence retorted, tossing her head in dismissive defiance. 'I knew she was suspicious about my trips to Lambeth after she found me buying men's clothes that were too small for Robert. And then she saw me leaving Molyneux's workshop, and I had no choice. She should have taken the image of her drowning as a warning, but she was either too foolish, or too pathetically loyal to you.'

'There was nothing pathetic about Maria!' Beatrice hissed. 'She was a good woman – she helped raise you!'

'She was an interfering, self-important slattern!' Florence snapped. 'I was almost glad she gave me an excuse to get rid of her! She always hated me – scolding me every chance she got –'

'Scolding a child isn't an act of hate.' Beatrice shook her head in exasperation. 'What's wrong with you?'

Florence was suddenly cold again. 'Oh no, Beatrice. What's wrong with *you*? That's what everyone will ask when word spreads. Of you flinging accusations at the Earl of Essex and his sister – what a treasure that ring he dropped in the Exchange proved to be! And I shall tell them all. With a tremor in my voice, dabbing away a tear. "She's gone mad. Just like her mother. Quite incurable, I fear."'

Beatrice stared at her sister, appalled. 'It would have hurt less if you'd fired that pistol at me. This – this warped campaign of yours – how could you hurt my family – *your* family – like this? How could you betray me so?'

Florence's face twisted. 'You accuse *me* of betrayal? You? You murdered our father and stole my inheritance, and ever since, you've acted as if giving me and my children the odd meal is great charity!'

The whisper in the lavender-edged dark. *Beatrice.* She'd assumed it was Maria, but had she been wrong? Had a young girl cowered out of sight, then fled in terror, believing her sister, her soon-to-be guardian a cold-blooded killer?

'You saw,' Beatrice breathed numbly. 'You saw me ... But – oh, Florence. You didn't see what you thought. I wasn't ...'

'You smothered him!' Florence cried. 'You waited until he was weak with illness, and you murdered him so you could inherit everything!'

'No,' Beatrice whispered. 'Florence, he begged me to do it.'

Florence stared. Her hand wavered; the gleam of the pistol faltered silver, steel, silver. 'You're lying.'

'I swear it.' Beatrice wanted to close her eyes, as if darkness could obliterate the memory. But it never had. She remembered the damp shrapnel old poultices left on her fingers, the wet tremble of throat and lungs, sheets streaked with ochre, brown, rust. The stench of stale lavender. 'He wanted me to end his suffering. He knew how his illness would progress – he'd seen our grandfather and our great-grandfather succumb. First the tremors, then the fits. He knew his speech would go next, and that thereafter it would be brutal. Undignified, demeaning, and an agony that he soon wouldn't be able to ask me to help with. So yes, Florence, I killed him. I pressed a pillow to our father's face and I smothered him. And even though ...' She swallowed, hesitant. She'd never voiced this, not to Maria, not to Hugh: it had festered inside her belly, rot and bile contorting, corrupting. 'Even though he asked me to put him out of his misery, I have never stopped feeling guilty.'

'You! Don't pretend you regretted it! You hated him – you were glad to see him dead so you could lay claim to everything!'

'Yes, I hated him!' She wanted to clap her hands over Walter's ears to stop him hearing what a monster she was. But he was sagging, reeling, his eyelids closed, near-delirious, and she had to finish this, somehow, somehow. 'He was a vile beast. I didn't feel guilty for killing him – that was a kindness. I felt guilty because I was glad I'd done it.'

'Exactly!' Florence howled. 'You murdered him and stole my inheritance!'

'No – oh, Florence, I couldn't tell you – I didn't want to hurt you –'

'Then you failed! How could you ever imagine robbing me wouldn't hurt me?'

Beatrice gritted her teeth, striving for gentleness, because even a Florence aiming a pistol at her was still her little sister. 'Florence, you would never have inherited anything, no matter what I did. You couldn't have.'

'Why? Because it was your mother's money originally? She gave it all to our father by marrying him – and anyway, she was dead!'

'She wasn't.'

'What?'

'My mother wasn't dead.' Beatrice held Florence's wild stare, as if she could convince her sister with her eyes as well as her words. 'She outlived our father by six years. She died only four years ago, in Bedlam.'

'But …' Florence's eyes widened in horror. 'Then …'

Beatrice nodded. 'He was never married to your mother. I don't think she ever realised what he'd done – how he'd deceived her. But an illegitimate daughter could never inherit equally. If you'd been born a boy, it might have been a different story … But he had no choice.'

'That's nonsense.' Florence's retort rang hollow: did she even believe her own protests anymore? 'Why, Queen Elizabeth herself was a bastard most of her life.'

'Our father was no King Henry,' Beatrice countered. 'Law courts and churches would never have bowed to his whims – especially since his first wife, his only true wife, was still alive.'

Florence hesitated. Was she going to let Beatrice and Walter go? Beatrice slid her right foot forward surreptitiously, hoping …

'None of that matters.' Florence's head and hand snapped up. She cocked the pistol. 'Both your parents are dead now. You could have given me an equal share.'

'I didn't want to shame you!' Beatrice protested. 'I'd have had to tell Hugh – and then others would have found out. William, Nicholas – *Robert*. How would your husband have felt? How would your daughters have felt? Florence, I have given you and your family so much – I have helped you all these years – I've done everything I could, short of signing over an inheritance that is rightfully Walter's, and a dowry that belongs to Ursula!'

Florence's lip curled in scorn. 'That's why your son must die.'

Beatrice instinctively turned, trying to shield Walter's lax body as best she could. Beneath their feet, the ice moaned, and Walter whimpered: fear or weakness? 'Florence, please – let him go. Christ's wounds, you helped bring him into the world! You were the first to hold him –'

'I should have broken his neck there and then,' Florence said coldly. 'Still. Better late than never.'

She swung the pistol towards Walter. 'Kiss him farewell, sister dear.'

Beatrice moved. Thrusting Walter towards the wharf, she lunged for Florence, for the pattens lifting her skirts above the frost. Her ribcage jarred against the stone and she gasped, even as her hand seized Florence's foot, and yanked.

Florence screamed. The pistol fired. Walter cried out and Beatrice howled. But then came another crack, just as loud and harsh as the gun. But no flash of powder, no sear of smoke: the bullet had hit the ice.

Beatrice had no time to think. She grabbed Walter, heaving him up onto the wharf, then tried to swing herself up. But her feet tangled in her skirts – she slipped back, flinging up a hand, reaching, grabbing, pulling herself up. Or trying. Her flailing hand had caught Florence's skirts, and her staggering sister screamed again as she fell to her knees.

And then she toppled onto the ice.

'Florence!'

The ice split. White shards sheared wide like opening jaws. Dark water gaped – and Florence vanished.

'No!'

Beatrice flailed for an oar – a branch – anything. But the wharf was empty: nothing for Florence to cling to. She gave Walter another shove, further onto solid stone. Then Beatrice slid back onto the ice.

There was a mooring ring at her shoulder: she wrapped her right wrist through it and gripped the metal, her fingers so numb she could barely close them, couldn't feel the iron on her skin. Then she plunged her left arm into the river. The water seared her flesh, like thrusting her hand against a thousand blades. Her stinging fingers quested blindly, desperately.

There! Something blundered against her hand – rough, yielding. Almost immediately it tore, and a fragment of Florence's sodden ruff came away. Beatrice couldn't shake it off: it clung like weeds and she could only lunge again.

This time she caught flesh. Florence's arm. She hauled, hauled – and finally her sister's head broke the surface. Limp, lolling – she caught a glimpse of closed eyes, parted lips glistening and blue. She tried to pull again, but she was so cold and so tired, and she had no strength left in her body. Only her voice, and even though Ridley had sent all the servants away and there was no one left to hear, Beatrice screamed.

'Help! Somebody help us! Please, help!'

There was silence. The ice creaked again, and it sounded like the globe, turning, crowing. Her arm sockets burned. Above her, Walter lay still. Florence's body dragged at Beatrice: she couldn't hold on much longer. She couldn't pull herself up either. Any moment she would slip, fall, disappear into the blackness along with her sister.

'Help!' she tried again, hoarse, sobbing. 'Please!'

Her muscles screamed. Her grip on Florence wavered.

And then out of the mist came the bronze light of torches, and a golden-haired man ran towards her. For a moment she thought it was Hugh – Hugh's ghost. But then she remembered, and knew, and she was neither dying nor mad, because here was William, with Nicholas and Robert not far behind, and she was safe, Walter was safe, and pray God it was all over and her punishment was at an end, and not just beginning.

Epilogue

Gulls beckon in the blue sky; as if in response, the *Silver Swan*'s sails ripple in their ropes, eager to loose and swell. On her decks, the bright-haired captain claps a hand to the helmsman's shoulder, giving commands, then a smile that is camaraderie and a silent, respectful acknowledgement of skill. It is a smile he both observed and was eager to receive; it is his uncle's smile, and despite the tears plucking at her lashes, Beatrice knows it is right to see Hugh's legacy continue on the ship he so loved.

The docks heave: spring tides and fair winds of late have brought many vessels in ahead of time, and still more are venturing forth, eager for the horizon. Trade is prosperous: the merchants' cheeks are plump, their purses plumper. All signs point to a good year. God knows, for the Radclyffes it cannot be worse than the end of the last. Yet even so, Beatrice is hopeful.

Seated on her chestnut mare, she can see, over the heads of oyster-sellers and officials, the mudlarkers with their trays of broken pottery they claim belonged to Boadicea, to Brutus of Troy. She's tempted to buy some for Walter and Ursula: yes, she recognises sales patter when she hears it, and the shards are as like to be a carpenter's chamber pot as an Iceni queen's dagger hilt. But there is value in a story, in a dream, and so she smiles as she hands a coin to her new steward.

While she waits for Saunders to return, she watches the river. The Thames is a dozen blues today: unspooled bolts of indigo velvet and cornflower silk and hyacinth damask. Its ripples murmur: *taste me, touch me. Let me take you to faraway lands with spiced breezes and sweet fruits, where scarlet birds call you to the shade of exotic trees.* It is a voice she is happy to listen to, without needing to follow: you can enjoy a song without feeling the compulsion to leap up and seize the lute yourself.

A cheer rises: the *Swan* is away. Six small boats row her out into the current, pulling her east. As the gap between wharf and stern widens, the golden-haired captain turns, and the sight is so familiar it aches – but this is William, not Hugh. William, taking on the captaincy he so yearned for. Oh, he is young yet, but he has most of the men's respect, and is capable of earning the others', and they have given the love for Hugh over to his nephew: they sail in his honour. And for Beatrice's part, there comes a time when you must trust the children you raised to assume the responsibility you have always shouldered for them. If William was gullible, she could have broadened the horizons of his mind; if he was quick to judge, so was she. After he'd realised how Florence and Ridley had tricked them all, there was no one more penitent than William. She'd had reservations, as had Catalina, given how painfully William had once let her down. But while there are some mistakes that embitter a man and some that he will carelessly make again and again, there are others that force a man to recognise their gravity, and how vital it is that he never fail in that way again. Perhaps it is less about the mistakes themselves, and more about the man who makes them – and about the man who raised him to learn from his mistakes. And so Beatrice nods: farewell, and a blessing, and maybe even forgiveness.

William will sail the *Swan* past Greenwich, Richmond, Deptford, out of London, all the way to Gravesend, where she will change direction. South, around Kent, then west, west, west, until she reaches the Azores. And in the Azores? He has a mission to accomplish, and the thought kindles warmth in Beatrice's belly.

The *Swan* is now the size of her namesake in the distance, and Saunders returns with what might actually be a dagger hilt rather than a door handle, and some ornate bone hairpins which she rather suspects did not belong to the daughter of Emperor Claudius. Saunders swings back onto his black mare with ease and efficiency, and she is pleased again with her new appointment; Bess Raleigh recommended him, and when the *Starling* returns Beatrice will send her some of the saffron as a token of thanks. Together, she and Saunders ride out of the throng and through the streets to the far side of Tower Bridge, where the barge awaits. Saunders helps her dismount and returns the horses to the waiting groom. They will hire these again: he has as good an eye for horses as Ridley, though hopefully fewer secrets and grudges.

Beatrice boards her barge and sits beneath the canopy. The sunlight blooms against the embossed damask, gilding the entwined *H* and *B*. She rests her black-gloved fingertips against the emblem, aware that she has again sat on the left-hand side, and the cushions to her right remain plump and undisturbed. Perhaps one day she will sit in the middle; perhaps one day she will stop expecting Hugh to fold up his long legs and recline beside her, a cup of spiced cider in one hand, the other threading the stars together as he spins glittering tales of new worlds.

They are sailing past the great riverside mansions: Arundel, Somerset, Durham. Essex. Another barge is putting off: gleaming gold and black as jousting armour, the sixteen blazons on its flag chafing against each other as the wind rumples it this way and that. Striding the deck impatiently is Essex himself, a frown creasing his handsome brow. Trouble with the queen again, no doubt, or about to be, and Beatrice feels a surprising twist of pity for the Devereux siblings and their lofty ambitions. Essex, after all, is a hard man to dislike face to face, unlike his sister. Now, as their barges pass, he doffs his hat to Beatrice, and she raises a hand in greeting, and they both sail on by.

She has spoken to him once since Hugh died, at Hugh's funeral. Essex wore an obscenely large black plume in his hat, and she had stared at it for half their conversation, wondering what kind of monstrous bird could have shed such a feather.

'I must apologise for my sister's conduct,' he'd said, after expressing the usual condolences, and Beatrice had frowned, wondering if Lady Rich were about to storm the churchyard. 'For her visit, shall we call it, on the morning after Hugh's passing. She is furious that I am apologising on her behalf, of course – "A Devereux should not stoop," she says. But stooping is the only way one can see the earth beneath one's feet, and so here I am, and I do not find it remotely demeaning after all.'

'How very revelatory for you.'

He'd had the grace to laugh. 'Life is full of revelations. The world turns on and so do we. Not every turn can be to Pen's liking, but there we are – sometimes the robins out-peck the swan, just as our globes have it. My little jest. Molyneux appreciated it, though Pen rather less so. Perhaps she disliked the idea of me allying with her husband.'

She'd almost laughed in realisation – the first time she'd felt like laughing in connection with the globe, though there have been plenty such occasions since. Sweet Robin Devereux, and Lord Robert Rich, both pecking at a pen – the name for a female swan. Nothing to do with the *Silver Swan* at all.

'All that being said …' Essex had cleared his throat. 'I don't suppose you've thought about where Hugh put that gold?'

Was he so straitened? She suspected he hadn't even realised he'd lost his signet ring in the Royal Exchange, the one Florence had ordered Kitson to don when he murdered Maria, taking care to break her tender skin with it. All so Beatrice would accuse Essex – all to bolster the accusations of madness.

'No, my lord,' Beatrice said gently. 'I find myself somewhat preoccupied of late.'

'That will teach me to place all my trust in one man,' Essex sighed. 'But giving Hugh the gold to hide seemed such a delightfully noble gesture at the time.'

'I'd question whether stealing gold is ever noble,' Beatrice said dryly, adding a somewhat cursory 'My lord.'

He coughed, mildly abashed. 'Ah, well. I'll think of something. Elizabeth and James will scowl and storm, but I flatter myself that I know how to sweeten the old woman, and the Scot will yield to my charms before long.'

'You sound very certain.'

'Everyone does, in the end.' He'd flashed a grin. 'Just you wait, Lady Radclyffe. The Essex star will rise again.'

Perhaps he is right. Perhaps he is wrong. But, Beatrice thinks, as the gap between their barges widens, the Spanish gold will have nothing to do with it. She has plans for the treasure, and they do not involve royal politics.

For that is where William is sailing: to the hidden gold. Not to bring home in triumph; oh no. Instead, it will be given to the towns ransacked by Essex and Raleigh's men – and by Hugh's. She cannot pretend the crew of the *Silver Swan*, or its former captain, were wholly innocent. But the past cannot be changed; only the future. So Beatrice has plans for her own money too: not lintels, or tiles, or panels, but gifted to certain causes: a portion for Maria's brother Solomon, another for Simon, to help care for his mother – and a portion for another woman of Lambeth. Dorcas, her name is, a twice-widowed laundress, who has now lost all three of her sons, two to gunshots and one to the northern ice, and is soon like to lose her sight as well.

But she also, for once, plans to spend gold on something for herself. She wants to plant a palm tree in her garden, and she expects the acquisition, and transport, and care for such a tree will not be easy; the struggling blueberry shrubs have warned her of that. She thought first of planting it where the beech fell, but the children have claimed that area for re-enacting battles with toy soldiers: the divots in the earth make good defences for miniature Romans. Instead, Beatrice is going to plant the palm tree in sight of the river, so that, if it flourishes, she will be able to sit beneath its broad leaves and watch boats come and go around the bend, and kingfishers will dart among the reeds, and every time she will think of the palm trees she never saw.

'There is a place,' Hugh had told her one night, his tanned hands sketching the scene against their bed-hangings, like falcon's wings against a deep blue sky, 'high on Faial, beside a waterfall. You can only reach it after a long climb, but it's worth it. There, you can sit beside the falls, eating fresh-caught fish and newly ripened peaches, and gaze out at the sea. Come sunset, a wind-bowed palm tree seems to curve around the setting sun, like a hand cradling a glowing candle. I think of you there, cupping the candle flame as you look in on our sleeping children, as you soothe them back to sleep, as you check all is well in our home, as you finally go to your own rest. And every time I raise my hand, just so, and it is as though I am shielding the same flame, and we keep it burning together.'

She knows. She realised when she was singing Walter to sleep, the first night after his ordeal on the ice, when she'd cupped the candle flame, and she'd understood immediately why Hugh had told Essex that Beatrice was the only one who knew where the gold was hidden. And she'd also known what she would do with the Spanish gold. She hadn't thought it possible – what captain could she trust? But then William had come to her, begging forgiveness. He'd come to a realisation of his own: a letter had arrived the same day Ridley took Walter to the eyot, from one of the keepers at Bedlam, asking when they might expect his aunt, for there was a place available if he and the lady's sister would like to inspect it. He'd realised then that Florence had been scheming something – and later that Ridley had been posing as William himself when they visited Bedlam to make preliminary arrangements. William had gone to Florence's house, where he'd found Robert and Nicholas fretting about Beatrice – and all three had realised they were worrying about the wrong sister. 'We were so wrong,' William had said. 'And it isn't the first mistake I've made, nor can it be the last. But I will strive to make amends however I can, I swear it.' She believed him then, and she believes in him now. He is not Hugh: they both know he can never live up to the golden shadow cast by his uncle. But he can sail out of it, and find his own way to shine.

They have reached Chelsea now. As the barge moors, Beatrice casts a glance over at the eyot: the carpenters are making good progress. They are building a sort of tower, one which an imaginative child can easily transform into a castle, a mountain, a jungle, and which will also have plenty of comfortable benches, where mothers and children who think themselves too old for games can sip warm lambswool, until they are all lured into the games too. She will not let the eyot become a haunted isle, a place of fear.

Beatrice steps ashore, thanking the oarsmen. She mentions the orchard walls to Saunders, who nods and immediately leaves to assess them, and Beatrice ascends the slope alone.

The garden bubbles with laughter. On the benches, Ursula and Cecily are playing cats' cradle while Thomasin rests her chin on Cecily's shoulder, insisting it's her turn next. Walter is letting Elizabeth and Judith chase him, leaping over the artemisia hedges. His heels clip the newly planted lavender, startling its heady scent into the air. Beatrice doesn't flinch as she passes; lavender has a new association for her now. She smells it again as she reaches the blanket laid out on the parterre, where Catalina is feeding little Isabella: the baby's linens are always folded with lavender, and it is her mother's favourite hair oil, and so the scent means life now, life to be lived and relished.

'A fair sailing?' Catalina asks, detaching Isabella and letting Dorothy hold the baby as she rearranges her clothes.

'Most auspicious,' Beatrice says. 'Is all well here?'

'Aside from the odd mutiny over finishing Latin exercises. I also had to avert a minor crisis when there were only enough cinnamon jumbles for two each.' Catalina gives Dorothy a teething ring for Isabella, the same coral one Walter and Ursula cut their baby teeth on. 'Otherwise, all is well.'

'Thank you,' Beatrice says, and Catalina scoffs.

'None of that. I told you, I'm not your servant. As soon as Isabella's weaned, I'll be the one gallivanting off downriver and you can watch our dozen children, or however many we have now.'

Beatrice laughs, but she and Catalina share a glance of understanding. They are more than friends now, more loyal to one another than sisters – especially in Beatrice's experience. They have saved one another in more ways than they can count; it was Beatrice who staunched Catalina's bleeding after Isabella's difficult birth, using one of her mother's recipes to bring her back to health. She would never have expected to feel this way six months ago, but now Beatrice sees Catalina as the woman she trusts more than anyone else in the world, and she senses that Catalina views her in a similar way.

'I mean it,' Beatrice says. 'Friends can thank each other too.'

'Ah, well.' Catalina grins. 'You might not say that when you realise I ate the last lemon cake.'

Beatrice laughs, and heads inside. There is one more member of her family to check on.

The gallery is still and drowsy with sunlight; the carpet sighs as Beatrice's skirts nudge its vines. In one of the window alcoves sits a woman. Despite the spring warmth, a blanket knitted by Beatrice's mother covers her knees, jaunty with turquoise and yellow, contrasting starkly with Florence's pale face. She does not stir as Beatrice approaches, only continues to pick at the flesh around her nails, which is already red and raw. Beatrice doesn't try to stop her now, only keeps Florence's nails short, and rubs beeswax balm into her sore flesh every evening. Her sister has not spoken since the night on the ice; it's why her daughters live with Beatrice now, Robert being even more flummoxed by their femaleness without the crutch of his wife's leadership. That, and Beatrice's guilt, because she doesn't know how to stop feeling guilty.

Beatrice kisses her sister's hairline, where the white laces the red. Shock and her immersion in the frozen Thames have hastened Florence's ageing, and the difference between their ages may soon be imperceptible. But for all Florence's vanity, Beatrice doubts this is the reason why her sister has not spoken since that day.

No one would have been surprised if Beatrice had dispatched Florence to Bedlam. Robert even wondered, through great gulping sobs, if it might not be the best thing for her, and Catalina had gently queried whether it might be the best thing for Walter. But he doesn't seem to recall Florence's part in his ordeal, and he treats his aunt with the fleeting kindness of a boy who would rather be riding at a quintain. And besides, Beatrice will not leave her sister to a cell. For all that Florence would have done the same to her, Beatrice will not. This is both her penance and her pleasure. She takes care of people; it's what she's always done.

She squeezes Florence's shoulder, and moves to the centre of the alcove. She hasn't just come to check on Florence. There's another entity she harbours, and watches.

The globe rests in the light. Round and smooth, and whole once more. She had Simon repair it, this time using gores made from her mother's other recipes, for she'd known them all by heart for years anyway, and so, if a spirit does still haunt the globe, it will be a beloved, benevolent one. There are new images now, none of them painted with blood-tainted inks, and not all done with Simon's skill. He supervised Walter and Ursula's efforts with a slightly pained horror as Ursula gave a mermaid purple hair. There are five mermaids and three pink dolphins gambolling around a silver ship helmed by a golden-haired captain. And there is an island, with a palm tree framing a sunset. But there is also a red brick house on a riverbank, with mulberry trees in its orchard and eight children playing among the lavender, and two swans guarding the wharf.

You do not have to leave the old world to find a new one. You build a new world by changing your old one for the better, one act of love at a time, seeding new memories among the old, so that both can bloom together.

Beatrice rests her palm upon her globe. It is smooth and warm. It does not turn unless she spins it. It is quiet, restful, like a mother watching you drift off to sleep.

Of course, there is no one so fierce as a mother. And as for two mothers? There are inks and brushes in the house; there is a pencil sketch kept in Beatrice's writing desk of a golden-haired captain and a cockatrice with the wings of a bee, poised to sting. It is just pencil and paper, for now, but who knows what it may become, should she and Catalina decide it needs to. Thoughtfully, Beatrice walks her fingers across the varnished sea, tracing William's route to the Azores. Blood, she muses, is easy enough to come by.

Beneath her touch the globe stirs into a murmur. The whirrs and rustles seem to ask *now? Yes?*

Softly, Beatrice clucks her tongue: *not yet*. She gazes out of the window at her family, and the ribboning blue Thames beyond, and she smiles.

Here, on the riverbank, she and Catalina will make a new world of their own.

Acknowledgements

Copy to follow ...

About the Author

NAOMI KELSEY is the author of *The Burnings*, and the winner of two Northern Writers' Awards and of the HWA Dorothy Dunnett Competition 2021. Her fiction has been published in *Mslexia* magazine and shortlisted for several further awards including the Bridport Prize and the Bristol Prize. By day she is an English teacher in Newcastle, where she lives with her husband and their two children.

For more unmissable reads,
sign up to the HarperNorth newsletter at
www.harpernorth.co.uk

or find us on Twitter at
@HarperNorthUK

**Harper
North**